WITCH'S MOONSTONE LOCKET

WITCH'S MOONSTONE LOCKET

A Coon Hollow Coven Tale

by

Marsha A. Moore

***

Witch's Moonstone Locket
A Coon Hollow Coven Tale
By Marsha A. Moore

Cover design © 2015 by Marsha A. Moore
Editing by Megan Patricia Orsini

Chapter One:
Great Aunt Starla's Cornbread

WARM RAIN MIXED with Jancie's tears, and she rose to stand beside her mother's grave. She bent at the waist and her fingers followed the arc of her mother's name—Faye Sadler—in the headstone. From numerous visits, she knew the unyielding shape well. The word goodbye stuck in her throat. She'd said it aloud many times since her mother died six months ago, only to have the cemetery's vast silence swallow her farewells. Rain beaded on the polished granite. Her hand, bearing her mother's silver ring, slid down the stone and fell to her side.

If only she could've said goodbye to her mother before she died. After years of caring for her mom while she suffered with cancer, Jancie had missed the final parting moment while getting a quick bite of dinner. The pain still cut like a knife in her gut.

On foot, she retraced the too-familiar path toward her work at the Federal Bank. Although she'd landed a job as manager at the largest of the three banks in the small town of Bentbone, the position was a dead end. Within the first six months, she'd mastered all the necessary skills. Now, after a year, only the paycheck kept her there.

Jancie turned onto Maple Street. As usual, wind swept up the corridor, between old shade trees protecting houses, and met her at the top of the tall hill. September rain pelted her face and battled the Indian summer noontime temperatures. She zipped the rain parka to keep her dress dry, pulled on the strings of the hood, and corralled strands of ginger-colored hair that whipped into her eyes. She gazed farther into the valley, where the view spanned almost a mile out to the edge of town. Usually, farmers moved tractors across the road or boys raced skateboards and bikes down Maple Street's long slope.

Today, on the deserted acreage just east of Bentbone, people moving in and out through a gate of the tall wooden fence breathed life into the rundown carnival. Surprised, Jancie crossed the street for a better view. She'd lost track of life around her since Mom passed. The coming Labor Day weekend in Bentbone meant the valley coven's yearly carnival. She and her girlfriends always looked forward to the cute guys, fair food, and amazing magical rides and decorations, even if her father didn't approve of witches or magic. The residents of the sleepy town awoke to welcome a host of tourists wanting to see the spectacle created by the witches of Coon Hollow Coven.

Somehow, Jancie had forgotten the big event this year. Last year, she didn't go since Mom was so sick and couldn't be left. Jancie sighed and turned onto the main street toward the bank. She'd lost so much since her mother passed. Really, since the diagnosis of cancer.

At that time, four years ago, Jancie withdrew as a sophomore from Hanover College, a select, private school in southern Indiana near the Kentucky border—too far away. Instead, she returned to stay with her mother and commuted to Indiana University. Balancing hours with the home health care nurse, Jancie had few choices of career paths. Not that it mattered, since her remarried father expected her to find a job in Bentbone and continue taking care of her mother. Despite the sacrifices, Jancie loved her mother, who'd always managed money for a few special things for Jancie—a new bike, birthday parties, prom dresses—even though their income was tight. Mom had paid for her tuition and listened to every new and exciting college experience.

Jancie smiled at the memory of Mom's twinkling brown eyes, that mirrored her own, when she asked about what happened during the day's classes: if Jancie liked the professor; if she'd made new friends.

When she rounded the last corner, she returned to her work day. At the bleak, limestone bank building, reality hit. Jancie pulled against the heavy glass door, and a gust swept her inside. She peeled off the drenched jacket and hung it on the coat rack of her small, plain office.

Through the afternoon's doldrums, punctuated by only a handful of customers, her mind wandered to the carnival. She'd gone dozens of times before and loved it. But since Mom passed, nothing seemed fun anymore, like she couldn't connect with herself and had forgotten how to have a good time. She organized a stack of notes, anything to put the concern out of her mind.

***

After work, Jancie drove her old blue Camry the five miles to the other end of town where she lived in her mother's white frame house, the home where she grew up, now hers. Glad to own her own place, unlike her friends who rented, she'd made a few easy changes. In the living room, a new brown leather couch with a matching chair and ottoman. She replaced the bedroom furniture with a new oak suite for herself in what used to be her mother's room. With pay saved from the bank, Jancie could remodel or build on, but she didn't know what she wanted yet. Her great aunt Starla had told her to just wait and hold onto her money; she'd know soon enough.

Pouring rain soaked the hem of her dress as she darted between the garage shed and back stoop of the small ranch house.

Glad she'd chosen to get her run in this morning before work, she changed into cozy sweats, pulled the long part of her tapered hair into a ponytail, and headed for the kitchen.

Her phone alerted her of a text, and she read the message from her friend Rachelle, always the social director of their group: <u>R we going to the carnival?</u>

Jancie typed a response. <u>I guess. R Lizbeth and Willow going?</u>

<u>Yep whole gang. What day?</u>

<u>Don't know yet. Get back to u.</u> Jancie worried she'd spoil their fun. Even though they'd all been her best friends since high school and would understand her moodiness, she didn't want to ruin one of the best times of the year for them. Since Mom passed, they'd taken her out to movies and shopping in Bloomington, but this was different. Could it ever match up to the fun of all the times before? "I don't know if I'm up to that," she said into open door of the old Kenmore refrigerator while rummaging for leftovers of fried chicken and corn.

The meal satisfied and made her thankful she'd learned how to cook during those years with Mom. Not enough dishes to bother with the dishwasher, one of the modern upgrades to the original kitchen, Jancie washed the dishes by hand and then called Starla. When she answered, Jancie asked, "Can I come over tonight? There's something I'm needing your opinion on."

"Why sure, Jancie. C'mon over," the eighty-five-year-old replied with her usual warm drawl. "Are you wantin' dinner? I made me some soup beans with a big hambone just butchered from Bob's hog. My neighbor Ellie came over and had some. She said they were the best she's eaten."

Jancie glanced at the soggy rain parka and opted for an umbrella instead. "No, I just ate. Be right over." Keys and purse in hand, she hung up and darted for the shed.

Five minutes later, she turned onto the drive of the eldercare apartments and parked under the steel awning where Starla gave her a whole arm wave from her picture window. Jancie made her way to number twelve on the first floor.

The door opened, and Starla engulfed Jancie in a bear hug, pulling her into the pillow of a large, sagging bosom. Starla smelled of her signature scent—rosewater and liniment.

Jancie had loved her great aunt's hugs as long as she could remember. Stress and worry melted away, and she hugged back. Her arm grazed Starla's white curls along the collar of her blue knit top embroidered with white stars—her great aunt's favorite emblem.

"It's so good to see you. Come sit a spell, while I get us some iced tea." Starla pulled away and gestured to the microsuede couch decorated with three crocheted afghans in a rainbow of colors. "I thought we were done with this hot weather, but not quite yet. That rain today's been a gully washer but didn't cool things off much." The large-boned woman scuffed her pink-house-slippered feet toward the kitchen. "Would you rather have pound cake from the IGA or homemade cornbread?"

Jancie laughed and followed her into the kitchen. She wouldn't get through the visit without eating. "You're just fishin' for a compliment. You know your homemade cornbread is better."

Starla arranged plates with thick slices of warm cornbread and big pats of butter on top, while Jancie transferred the refreshments to the aluminum dinette table.

"With your hair pulled back like that, you're a dead ringer for your Ma. So pretty with that same sweetheart-shaped face." Starla folded herself onto a chair beside Jancie. "You look to be getting on well...considering what all you've been through."

"I'm doing okay," Jancie said through a mouthful of the moist cornbread. She washed it down with a swallow of brisk tea that tasted fresh-brewed. "But sometimes, lots of times, I feel lost, like I can't move on." She ran a hand across her forehead. "I didn't get to say goodbye. I spent time with her through all those years, and it shouldn't matter, but it does every time I visit her grave and most every night in my dreams."

"Oh, honey. I know it hurts." Starla smoothed Jancie's ponytail down the middle of her back and spoke with a voice so slow and warm, it felt like a handmade quilt wrapping around her. "You spent all that time and gave so much. Just like when I cared for my husband some twenty years back. I know. I never got the chance to tell Harry goodbye either. Time will heal all hurts."

Jancie looked down at the marbleized tabletop to hide her teary eyes. "I don't think I'm ever going to heal, Aunt Starla. I don't know if I can ever move on."

"There is one thing you can try. I'd have done it, if I'd have known before decades softened my aching heart. Way back, I was desperate like you."

Jancie looked into Starla's blue-gray eyes, set deep inside wrinkled lids.

Her aunt leaned closer. "Not many know about this," she whispered as if someone outside the apartment door might hear. "There's an old story about how a member of the Coon Hollow Coven, one who's recently lost a loved one, is made the teller of the moonstone tale."

Jancie rolled her eyes. "That's just a silly story, one of lots that Mom and Dad told to scare me when I was little, so I'd stay away from the coven. When the moonstone locket opens at the end of the tale, you'll get your wish but also be cursed."

"Oh no." Starla shook her head and pushed away from the table. "Let me get Aunt Maggie's old diary. I got this in a box of old family things when Cousin Dorothy passed." She lumbered to her spare bedroom and returned with a worn, black-leather volume only a little larger than her wide palm. Once seated, she thumbed through the yellowed pages. "Here." She pointed a finger and placed the book between them. "Aunt Maggie lost her husband to a heart attack at a young age, not but two years after they married. She pined for him so bad, cried for months, and eventually turned to the coven's psychics. They tried and tried but couldn't reconnect her with his spirit. One of them felt for the young woman with a baby not even knowing her daddy. The psychic took Maggie to the moonstone story teller. Read here about what happened."

Jancie silently read the flowery cursive with difficulty and slowed at the part about the story teller.

When I dared to gather my courage and tell the widower warlock that I wanted my Marvin to meet our daughter Dorothy, the man's dark eyes softened wide over me and my little one. He held out a locket set with a large moonstone. He said if the locket were to open for me, which it hadn't ever before in his recollection, there'd be a price to pay for the gift I'd get. I didn't care what price. I wanted Marvin to see our baby.

The widower went on and told the sad tale about how the locket came to be, all the while tears leaked from his eyes. Straight away after he finished, the moonstone sparked blue, and the locket opened a crack. In the air above the locket, I saw the face of my Marvin smiling at Dorothy, and she cooed back at him. It was a miracle! But just for an instant. His face faded, and the locket clicked shut.

The warlock smiled, but his eyes looked sadder than before. He told me I was lucky, that most see nothing, or a few see just a flash of light. He bowed his head, hung the locket around his neck, and used the table we sat at to push up straight, like the necklace weighed him down. The psychic witch patted the warlock on the shoulder and walked me to the edge of their village. I don't know if I dare to tell anyone what happened. But it's enough that Dorothy and me saw her daddy.

When Jancie looked up, Starla said, "So there. She got what she wanted and didn't have any problems. Maybe that's worth a try. Could be since you're related to Maggie, you'll be able to see your Ma."

Jancie skimmed the following diary entries for keywords—moonstone, locket, warlock, and coven—but the cursive made it difficult. "Can I take this for a while to read?"

"Sure can." Starla bit into a wedge of cornbread. "I've read the whole thing, and nothing odd came from that visit, near as I can tell. This weekend at the carnival, you could find the coven member who's the moonstone story teller. That way, you don't have to go to their village, if you're worried about that."

"Well. I am, sort of. Dad always seemed strong against those witches. He wouldn't let me go to the carnival for years after all my friends were allowed. It didn't matter how much I begged."

"I remember that now." The old woman took a sip of tea. "I used to try to tell your pa how the carnival's safe for tourists and townies. That's one of the coven's biggest money-makers. They don't aim to hurt people there. That'd only hurt themselves. I never figured out what your pa had against them."

Jancie shrugged. "How will I know who's the story teller?"

"I reckon the witch will be wearing the moonstone locket."

"Have you seen it?"

"Can't say I have, but these old legs haven't been up to walking for hours through a carnival for years." She chuckled and displayed a calf encased in a support stocking, showing the lines of varicose veins through the elastic material. "But if I was young with my life ahead like you, I'd give it a go."

Jancie finished her cornbread. "Thanks for the advice, Aunt Starla. I'm going to head home and read some of this tonight." She tapped a finger on the diary's cover.

"Let me get another piece of cornbread for you to take." Starla moved to the counter, cut a huge wedge, and wrapped it in plastic film.

***

Sunshine streaming into her bedroom window awoke Jancie. She'd fallen asleep early while reading the old diary. Up at six, she took time for a long run, then showered and slipped into one of the boring polyester wrap dresses she wore to work. After applying a scant bit of make-up and enjoying Starla's cornbread with milk and juice for breakfast, she tidied up the kitchen and bedroom.

She gently folded the crazy quilt Mom had made for her before the cancer hit. When Jancie touched the diary sitting on the oak nightstand, a passage she'd read crossed her mind—several days after Maggie's encounter with the story teller, she wrote an entry wondering why the man seemed so burdened. Her description of the sorrow she'd seen in his eyes haunted Jancie while she drove to work.

Luckily, the mental image left her during the busy morning with a couple of farmers who wanted to reorganize loans. It made her feel good to help them get their finances in order so they could afford what they needed to stay in business. Times like these made her job seem worthwhile.

After getting lunch at the café on Main Street, Jancie stopped at the corner florist two doors down and bought a bouquet for the grave, hoping that would give her the sign from her mother she'd been wanting the past six months. She picked out a sunny arrangement of red and pink zinnias and yellow mums. Mom always planted zinnias, and when she couldn't, Jancie had grown them to please her. But not this year. It hurt too much.

She laid the flowers at the gravesite and sat on a bench nearby, watching for anything that might be a sign. After a few minutes, mosquitoes roused by yesterday's rain forced her to leave earlier than usual.

With time to spare before returning to work, she walked down the hill, past her usual turn onto Main Street. The breeze tossed her hair in the warm sunshine. Halfway down, she made out distinct shapes of men and women moving through the carnival's entrance. Her pulse quickened. *Why am I heading toward the carnival? I don't know if I believe in that crazy moonstone tale.* She swallowed hard, remembering her father's strong opposition to anything to do with these people. Still, she kept walking closer. The idea of being able to say goodbye to her mother was too tempting, too important.

She stopped across the road from the entrance. Above the head-high wooden fence with peeling layers of black and barn-red paint, the rusty Ferris wheel creaked back and forth as if someone coaxed it to life. Through the planked gates which stood open, tents of every color lined the central path, some only puddles of fabric on the ground waiting to splash up. Women in shirtwaist dresses moved about draping gold cording around tent support angles. The ladies' bias-cut skirts rippled around their hips and legs with the slightest breeze like the flags atop the tent poles. Men in wide-legged trousers unloaded crates off the back of a vintage 1930 model Ford pickup's wood-paneled bed. With long sleeves rolled above elbows, streaks of sweat lined the backs of their white dress shirts. Foregoing style for practicality, wide-brimmed fedoras were pushed back on their heads.

From time to time, small groups of coven members visited Bentbone for groceries or other supplies in their long sedans with stretched hoods and seductive fenders that reminded Jancie of a woman's rounded hips. But to see so many of their folk together, dressed as they always did in styles from eighty years ago, made Jancie feel like she stood out.

She'd never watched them set up the carnival. The process—an orchestration of both ordinary manual labor and magic—left her entranced. While boys and young men grunted to tote crates, adult men and women levitated tents into position. Jancie wanted to tour the grounds to witness the transformation of the abandoned and dilapidated park. Lured by the magical sights, she crossed the road.

"You lookin' for someone?" the voice of a teenage boy by the pickup startled Jancie.

She whirled sideways as if caught doing something wrong. "Um. I'm needing the teller of the moonstone tale." Her voice cracked proclaiming her reason to be there while still trying to convince herself.

"That'd be Rowe." The youth spit into the gravel at the side of the road. "He'll be here straight away. We're delivering things he needs. Just wait by that gate, miss." He tipped his cap and took a crate off the truck bed.

Jancie stepped closer to the gate. She peeked around the corner and walked into the wide chest of a man wearing a freshly pressed shirt with cuff links at his wrists. "Oh, I'm sorry," she blurted and took a step back.

"No, excuse me. I should have taken more care." The man, who appeared to be in his late twenties, touched her elbow. "Are you all right?" From under a straw fedora angled low over one brow, brown hair grazed his broad shoulders. Unshaven whiskers shadowed his jaw.

"Yes, I'm fine." Jancie uttered, unable to look away from his eyes—brown with glints of gold that seemed to convey sincerity. Or witchcraft? She managed to pull her gaze free. Or not?

"What can I help you with?" His calm voice contrasted with the chaos around them.

A loud bang sounded from behind. His hand at Jancie's elbow grabbed her forearm and pulled her closer to the gate's frame in time to miss collision with two men carrying a crate.

Jancie stared at the wooden box, which jostled from side to side as if something inside moved on its own.

"Dangerous spot." The man released her.

"I guess." From where she hugged the edge of the entry, Jancie uncoiled toward him, and her gaze rested on a thick opalescent pendant hanging against his chest where his shirt hung open. She stared at it in surprise.

He saw her expression and her gaze, fixed on his necklace. "Is something wrong?"

"It's just that...Are you the moonstone story teller? I came to find you."

"Yes, I am. My name is Rowe McCoy. Come outside the gate area where it's quieter...or at least safer." With a chuckle, he led her beside the old pickup and turned to face her, his gaze more serious and intent on hers. "Why are you looking for the moonstone story teller?"

"I've lost someone..."

"I'm very sorry for your loss. Who was that person?"

"My mother, Faye. I'm Jancie Sadler. I cared for her through a long bout with cancer but missed the moment when she passed. It hurts that I didn't get to say goodbye. I need to do that."

He nodded. "I know that feeling well." He removed the moonstone locket from his neck and held it between them. Rose gold filigree secured a gem the size of a half dollar coin and milky white. "Hold out your palm." He placed the locket into her hand and cradled hers with his own. "This locket was made in 1850 by a warlock, Jude Oatley who lost his wife, Charlotte, to tuberculosis. He set the magic of the gem, and it's his tale I tell. Be warned, if the locket opens, you will pay a price for the gift you seek. You understand, the locket does not open on command—in fact, it has not opened in many years. But the magic dictates it may happen if—"

"Look!" Jancie exclaimed as the moonstone flashed a brilliant blue.

Rowe flinched, a look of surprise on his features, and clasped her hand tighter, steadying it with his other hand. "The story begins with the tale of their tremendous love." His voice cracked, and he took a breath before continuing. "Jude placed the essence of that love inside this gem and—"

"Rowe, there you are," a woman's husky voice called. "I'm needing your help, darlin', with manners of the carousel horses. No one else can seem to make them change gaits." A woman slithered over to them, dressed in a fine silk flowered dress that draped around her voluptuous curves. She glanced at the locket in their joined hands and scoffed. "I'm sorry if I interrupted anything important. The moonstone locket. Are you telling this girl the tale? She's too young to have a broken heart, other than from puppy love." Her painted red lips drew into a smirk across her pale face.

"Jancie, this is Adara, our coven leader. Adara, this is Jancie." Rowe collected the locket, his face now drawn and solemn as he looked at Jancie. "I apologize. We have a lot to do before the carnival opens Friday night. It is important for me to tell you the tale. Promise me you'll come by during the carnival. I'll make sure to have time to talk without interruptions."

Adara's sharp laughter trailed off in the blare of a horn from a new off-road Chevy pickup that whipped past kicking up dust and gravel.

Jancie sucked in deep breath. She'd been discovered talking with witches by her resentful ex-boyfriend, Harley Hincks. Her dad would know before sundown.

The wind that blasted them after the truck passed lifted the waterfall of Adara's black wavy hair styled to hang over one eye. A long, jagged scar across the high cheekbone marred her otherwise beautiful face.

The woman's odd reaction and appearance made a chill pass along Jancie's spine. She glanced into Rowe's eyes, wanting to promise she'd return. Instead, she scurried across the road toward the safety of the Federal Bank.

Chapter Two:
Blue Vervain

ADARA SMOOTHED her black shoulder-length hair forward from her side part to cover the exposed scar on her cheek. No matter the girl had seen it. The disfiguring gash proved useful when she wished to look like a wicked witch and frighten troublesome townies away.

Rowe replaced the moonstone locket around his neck, and his gaze followed Jancie ascending the long hill toward Bentbone.

Adara eyed him. "A townie? Really? That twit isn't your type. You need a woman."

"It's none of your business." He arched a thick brow at her.

Making use of his attention, she turned and added a bit of a wiggle into her walk back inside the carnival. She was certain he couldn't resist the swish of silk around her gams. Footsteps behind her confirmed her expectation and brought a grin to her lips. Winding her way through coven folk, she doled out directions and wondered about what she'd seen between Rowe and that girl. The moonstone had given a brilliant flash. With only that much information, there was no way to know whether the locket would open for that townie, but Adara intended to prevent Rowe from finding out.

She stopped at the carousel and turned to face him. "The pink fillies only trot, while the red steeds just gallop. Everything else canters. This ride was your creation, so make it work."

"Not a problem." He waved to a mature male witch working on the ride. "Albert, snazzy paint job." Rowe circled through each row of fearsome wooden animals. Some growled or whimpered through clenched teeth. Others puffed wisps of smoke from reddened nostrils. He stroked the head and neck of each, sometimes stopping long enough to whisper into the perked ear of a horse, or rub a tiger's ears to soothe its irritable pawing, or guide the long neck of a camel closer to receive his communication. After he visited each, he bounded off the lowest level and moved closer to Albert at the control panel. "Give it a go now and work through all the gears. They should behave better now."

Albert muscled his weight against the stiff lever and gave a groan. "First gear, Rowe."

Adara crossed her arms under her full bosom and strolled to where Rowe observed the circling ride.

"Looks a-okay." Rowe lifted his hat and smoothed his hair. "All are at their trot now. Power up."

Albert braced his bum leg against the gear column and pushed his weight into the shifter. "Canter speed."

Rowe gave a thumbs-up and stepped to the control box. He passed a palm over the stiff shift lever and pushed it to the highest notch. Horses, elephants, tigers, sharks, camels, and bears alike stretched their torsos and lengthened their legs or fins into long, elegant strides with a uniform rhythm.

Adara clapped her hands. Few witches achieved that level of animation. She'd admired his intelligence and witchcraft talents for years. Now that he was a widower, she intended to learn whether his other skills would be equally outstanding.

Rowe yanked the lever back through the slower gears to halt the carousel. "The animals are all performing proper gaits, but this shifter is needing more than magic." He faced Albert. "See if Trenton can oil the mechanism."

The older male witch nodded and pushed his sleeves above his skinny arms. "Will do. Should be easy for him. He's been a real carny before. You did the hard part. Thanks, Rowe."

"Not at all." Rowe tipped his fedora.

Adara snaked her arm through Rowe's crooked elbow. "You always impress me," she remarked, beaming into his face. "No one else in the coven can animate like that. I've been thinking. Maybe the time is right for you to become part of my council."

He shook his head and opened his mouth to speak.

"Don't say no yet." She gave a hasty reply and squeezed his firm bicep with her free hand. "I know you've been through rough times losing both your father and your wife. Maybe working for the greater good of the coven will give you the purpose and direction you've been missing. Think about it."

"Do I have a choice?" He glanced at her with a smirk.

"Well, I'd love to have your help with coven leadership. You'd be perfect. We'd make an exceptional team."

Albert returned with Trenton, who carried a tool kit. He tipped his ball cap to Adara and got to work.

Adara pulled on Rowe's arm. "Come walk with me while I check progress on other attractions, and we can discuss our plans for the coven's future."

"I want to stay until Trenton is done, to make sure my adjustments are still in line." Rowe walked with her around the perimeter of the carousel.

Trenton opened the panel and tightened bolts and oiled gears, while Albert served as his assistant.

As Adara and Rowe strolled, she smiled to everyone who passed, hopeful they noticed she and Rowe were a couple.

Several women smiled back at her. The jealously she read in their eyes made her pulse quicken. She needed the other females to know he belonged to her now.

As Rowe and Adara returned to the control panel, Trenton replaced the cover, and Albert pulled the lever. "Should be smooth as silk," the carny said.

Rowe shook off Adara's arm and braced himself against a fence support while eyeing the animals trotting past. "Up one level."

"Shifts like butter and that's as pretty a canter as I've ever seen," Albert sang and turned on the ride's music system.

"That is keen, Rowe!" a girlish voice called from behind. "They all look like rockin' horses. What kid wouldn't want to ride this carousel for hours? I would."

"Lenore!" Rowe turned and took the lissome young woman's hand. "In that case, why don't you and I test the animals' temperaments while carrying riders? I could use some help."

"I'd love to. I'm so glad I was nearby and heard the carousel's calliope music. I was hoping I could help you."

Adara bristled at Lenore's easy, likeable manner. Although in her twenties, the young woman bordered on plain with a freckled complexion and dishwater blond hair past her waist. Her hair-do, if it could be called that, was old-fashioned, hanging in pigtails tied with light blue ribbons that matched her flowered feedsack dress. What did Rowe see in Lenore when he could have herself, an exotic beauty with eyes and hair as black as jet set off by milky skin, high cheekbones, and red lips? Not only that, she filled out a dress in ways that simpleton's flat-as-a-board figure could never do. She seethed as he placed his hands on Lenore's waist, boosted her onto the back of a baby elephant, and took a position next to her on a growling tiger.

Rowe signaled Albert, and the ride started with the animals walking faster with each revolution until they reached a trot.

When they sped to a canter, Lenore's fluty laughter carrying over the top of whimsical calliope notes sent Adara into hiding, taking refuge in the doorway of a nearby tent. She didn't dare let coven members see her while Rowe entertained that girl, not after she'd been so obvious about her intentions for him. How could he take her affections so lightly? Her brow pulled together while considering his resistance to her plans.

"Adara, is there something I can help you with?" the voice of a woman asked from inside the tent. "Something's troublin' you, my dear. I'll be glad to read the future for you again, if you wish." She stepped forward and squinted the already small eyes of her ferret-like face. Her gaze followed in the direction of Adara's stare. "Ah, knowin' the future is not what you want. Be careful or you'll turn green, my friend. Don't you trust the cards I dealt you at Beltane?" The middle-aged witch maneuvered her plump body around a maze of crates toward the tent's door, her peppered hair falling from her bun to the Peter Pan collar of her shirtwaist dress,

Adara glanced at her closest friend. "Sibeal, I know better than to doubt the word of the coven's eldest psychic, and I know you have my best interest at heart. Your reading said that the man I chose wouldn't fall for Lenore's winsome charms." Adara curled her pointed, red nails into a fist. "But that's only because I'll see to it that their friendship ends."

"Adara." Sibeal placed a gentle hand on her shoulder. "You mustn't meddle with fate. The Goddess will play hard against you."

Adara thrust out her chin, shook off the psychic's grip, and marched out of the tent, doling out curt orders as she toured the grounds. Some coven folk sneaked quick glances her way while their hands never left their work. Others scurried down alleyways between tents.

A flutter of a crow's black wings down the carnival's main thoroughfare separated a group of witches arguing about the colors to conjure for the signage of the rides. The bird gave a loud squawk and circled inches above their heads, dodging raised wands and dozens of curse words. The sleek, iridescent crow landed on the corner of a tent next to where Adara surveyed a centripetal swing ride. The chairs wound in and out braiding their chains while a circular motion lifted them into flight.

"Those lights aren't in sync with the ride. Get it right, you there," she barked with a husky voice at Darin, the gangly operator.

"Uppity today." The crow flapped a few times before folding his wings. "Bee in your bonnet, Adara?"

Adara looked around them to make certain no one heard the bird's outspoken comment. "It's Priestess Adara, you loathsome black devil."

"You just wish I was the devil," he retorted. "Word is you're a pill today. Is someone gumming up the works?"

"Dearg, you don't know squat." She eyed him without her usual interest in bantering with the quick-witted bird. "Why don't you blow?"

"Hmm. Must be a troubling matter of power or love. I wonder which?" He clapped his beak with raucous laughter. "Maybe both."

Adara focused her eyes and channeled her gift of transformation onto the metal pole where he perched.

"Yeow!" Dearg lifted one claw, then the other from the hot metal. "You got an axe to grind, or what?" He hovered above her head a moment, then circled the Ferris wheel and set to work helping its male witch operator.

Flustered, Adara shook her head and headed toward her Packard sedan. She grabbed the wheel as if trying to choke any life out of it. *You need to get control. Even that damn crow knows you can't reel in a man as extraordinary as Rowe.* She tilted her head up and looked in the rearview mirror, letting the curtain of hair fall away from her scar. *See that? Don't forget what you're fighting for—a second chance at what you lost.*

***

In the parlor of her rambling brick Victorian house, Adara yanked the drapes closed, their brown velvet worn thin next to the draw cord. She crossed the room to the writing desk. With her weight balanced on one foot to the left of the desk, the single pine floorboard creaked underneath the red Persian rug. With the small stipend awarded to her as the coven's high priestess over the past five years, she'd at least managed to purchase new carpets and accent rugs. The 1915 Tabard family homestead looked much the same as it did when her mother, the former priestess, passed. Adara's home breathed with familiar personalities through its old but fine leather wing chairs, tufted ottomans, and shabby window seats. Scents of her family's long-gone witches permeated leather, fabric, and wallpaper. They taunted her with icy stares from black and white family photographs from where they'd always hung in every room, save the kitchen and her bedroom. Their glares were a constant reminder that she hadn't been the one chosen to own this family home.

Still balancing on one foot, the floorboard finally dropped down a half-inch, and Adara strained to reach the key from the upper right desk drawer as it sprang open. She drew a circle in the air counterclockwise twice around the lock before inserting the key and opening the rolled top. She removed her most valuable possession—the family grimoire. The book had passed from mother to daughter for more generations than she knew. Most often, the eldest daughter was the recipient. Keeping to tradition, her mother had willed the oldest of three daughters, Evelyn, to receive the coveted book.

Father served as High Priest of the coven for decades, and Mother, even more powerful with the Sight, led the coven after his death. She must have known her eldest daughter would die, or at least that's what Adara told herself to hide from what she believed to be the truth.

As a teenager, Adara had made a fateful mistake, all for the love of a young man, her first and only love. While joy-riding one summer evening, they'd drunk too much hooch, and he swerved his fast car into an old model T driven by her only brother Clement with Evelyn along as his passenger. Both were killed. Adara and her boyfriend suffered many cuts and broken bones. Adara healed except for the three-inch long white jagged scar marring her cheek, which served as a daily reminder of not only her siblings' deaths, but also heartache after her boyfriend left her. Whether he was scared of repercussions of her mother's strong witchcraft or fearful of being charged with manslaughter by the law, her boyfriend stayed clear of Adara thereafter. Twenty-four odd years later, her heart still ached for him and her family. She knew loneliness too well.

Adara's mother publicly shunned her, giving her favor and the inheritance of her grimoire to the middle daughter, Fia, who learned about her witchcraft gift only minutes before that grievous accident. Fia inherited Mother's talent in a strange way as Dark Sight, a negative clairvoyance that happened too close to the oncoming events to deter those in harm's path. She saw the hot rod and model T accident unfold without time to stop it from happening. Marked by that black gift, Fia chose a life of solitude, claiming she'd be better off not knowing anyone. Perhaps it was a way to block the gruesome mental awareness. Adara could only guess, since Fia lived as a recluse farther south along the Ohio River and avoided even her family's company. She'd heard word that the Dark Sight turned on Fia and drove her to madness.

Upon Mother's death five years ago, her will left the family house and all possessions to Adara by default as the last in line, including the grimoire she found under her mother's mattress. Assuming the magical book had been repossessed from Fia, Adara knew her mother hadn't wanted to give it to her. To Mother's last breath, she must have blamed Adara.

Adara did her best to cast aside those ill feelings of the past. She rubbed her hand across the black leather cover, worn with age. Thumbing through pages, she took in a host of fragrances worn by witches before her, who'd used the volume. Scents of green wood, sandalwood incense, chili pepper, and ashes wafted past her. She let their strength and conviction enliven her as she selected the needed spell. With the volume clutched to her, she retreated to her favorite room in the house, the large country kitchen. There, without the condemning stares of framed faces of relations, she set to work creating a mixture of dried lavender and vervain flowers that would instill peace. She covered the mixture and placed it on the mudroom bench near the back door. From under the bench, she snatched a small gathering basket and headed outside to the property's far edge where the wood-line met a pond.

At that junction, stood a prized patch of blue vervain she'd planted under Mother's guidance. Their blossoms only three-quarters up the spikes, Adara found plenty for her needs. She clipped a handful of the late summer bloomers and made a mental note to dry the rest soon. Prickles of some Joe Pye Weed grabbed the hem of her silk skirt. Cursing the plant, she bent and freed herself.

Back inside her kitchen, she used a large mortar and pestle to press the juice from the stems over a bowl. She poured the liquid into a small glass and set it alongside the dried flowers on the back bench. In the alcove off the kitchen used as a sewing room, she located some thin gold cord, cut a thirty-inch length, and dropped it next to the other items. Adara locked the grimoire back in the desk and stepped out into the late afternoon sunshine of her garden. In a large market basket from her shed, she gathered half a dozen dried corn stalks, their ears drooped and shrouded in golden husks.

She walked the mile to Lenore Whiting's house where the young woman lived with her elderly mother, Freda. When she arrived at the crumbling frame farmhouse, Adara rapped on the door, and their Terrier mutt barked.

The door opened, and Freda gave a wide, nearly toothless smile. "High Priestess. What honor brings you visit?"

"I'm delivering blessed corn for the coven's doors in preparation to welcome the gods to our homes during the Mabon equinox." Adara opened a pocket knife, slashed three ears off a stalk, and held each for a few seconds. "From this life, life to come." She passed them to the stooped woman. "As we always do, open the husks and tie them to your door."

"Thank you kindly." Freda accepted them into her knotted hands. "I'll do that soon as Lenore gets herself home. Should be anytime now."

Adara gave a polite smile. "If she does arrive soon, will you have her follow the road to my house and help me distribute these offerings to the Smiths and the O'Neills? I'd be ever so grateful. With more than two hundred homes in our coven, I'm always happy for help."

"Be glad to. I'll send her along straight away."

Adara nodded with a grin as she stepped from the cracked cement stoop. The dilapidated looks of the broken down abode frustrated her more that Rowe paid Lenore such undeserved attention. Her own home sprawled across six acres landscaped with several gardens through both lawn and woods, still pastoral if a bit wild and untended. Perhaps Adara's home was not quite on par with Rowe's grand manor house, but the dwelling where Lenore lived marked her well beneath his standing in the coven. Adara clenched the handle of the basket into her fist and took her time retracing the road home.

As expected, before twenty minutes passed, Lenore jogged up. She joined Adara leaving the Harper's log cabin door with her basket now empty. "Mama sent me to help you pass out blessed offerings for Mabon," Lenore said between gasps for breath.

"Thank you for your help." Adara smiled having snared the naïve girl. "I've run out of corn and need to return to my garden for more to deliver to folks farther along this road."

"I'll come with you."

"You're such a good helper, Lenore." Adara led the way and made small talk about the carnival's progress while they walked the quarter-mile.

At the edge of her garden, Adara set the gathering basket down and found two long knives in the shed. She returned, and they cut stalks. "While you're here, I could use your help with another project for the Mabon ceremony."

"Sure. What is it?" Lenore brushed a strand of dark blond hair from her pale face which was flushed in blotches from physical activity.

"During the autumn equinox ceremony, I need a young woman blessed with a female mandrake to honor the earth's fertility stored in her seeds."

The girl's gray eyes grew wide. "But Priestess, I beg you. I'm not wanting children now. I have no husband."

Adara's lips curled. "Perhaps, this will attract one. No one else in the coven is as well suited as you for this tremendous honor." She hoped the young woman's ego desired honor, or her hormones desired a husband. It didn't matter which reason prompted Lenore to accept as long as she did. Adara held her breath.

Lenore straightened. "I'm not ready for no husband, but for the coven, I'll do my best."

"Very good. Let me get what we'll need from my house." With only one step inside her back door, Adara collected the supplies she'd left on the bench. She didn't want to waste time and let Lenore reconsider. "Come here around the side of my house and kneel with me at this planting bed." When the girl joined her, Adara sprinkled the dried flower mixture over a section of mandrakes, their tops withered and brown at the season's end. "This potion will bring peace to the mandrake and block the root from making screams, which can drive the one pulling it up mad. In addition, drink this juice to protect you, in case it manages any harmful noise."

Under Adara's watchful eye, Lenore gulped the liquid without question. "Okay. But if it yells, I'm gonna let go." Lenore took a handful of the papery leaves and twine-like stems. After a breath, she yanked. The gnarled root resisted, only its top shoulder coming out of the soil.

"Try again," Adara said. "There was no verbal complaint from the root. Put your weight into it."

The girl screwed her face and pulled. With more encouragement from Adara, she leaned back and gritted her teeth. Finally, the tan root came loose, and Lenore fell backward onto the grass. The root wiggled in her hand but remained quiet.

"A female mandrake on the first try!" Adara declared. "I knew you were destined for this role in our coven. Keep a hold of it while I tie it up." She secured the writhing root with the gold cord and hung the now compliant mandrake around Lenore's neck. "Wear this day and night until after the ceremony." She smiled and stood. "Let's deliver this corn now."

With the second part of her plan completed, Adara sprang along the half mile trek to four more log and limestone cabin homes tucked along a wooded lane. Smoke twisted from the cabin's chimneys and reminded Adara of her devious, convoluted plan. She smiled to herself and reached home before dinner hour.

***

Home again and too eager to eat, Adara prepared for the evening. Even though Lenore claimed she wasn't ready for a husband, Adara knew better. The temptation of being able to control a man's favor and seduce his desires would prove too great. Only a naïve girl could think otherwise.

Adara showered and anointed her skin with a lotion she'd made of vanilla and patchouli. She inspected every angle in the tall, ebony-framed mirror. Over her forty-three years, her hips had widened into delicious curves. Her stomach remained flat and bosom pert since she'd not borne children. She dressed in a black silk garter belt and rolled sheer nylon stockings over her long legs. Tap panties and a matching brassiere of cool slippery silk, fine Parisian lingerie she'd purchased with Rowe in mind, made her feel like she covered herself with fresh air. Inhibitions flowed off of her skin, a feeling she'd long forgotten. She buckled black patent Mary Jane's with high stacked heels onto her feet to complete the outfit.

From a pink Depression glass tray, she slipped on a marcasite ring she'd worn since being appointed the coven's high priestess. Accepting the family leadership role, she chose the ring, originally owned by her great grandmother, to focus her own power. In the shape of a snake, it coiled around her left ring finger, a constant reminder that her path in life was coven leadership. Dreams of exciting new love belonged to the girl she once was, but the woman she'd become appreciated the advantages of power and control.

In her bedroom, she walked to the black cherry bureau that held a large inlaid jewel case. She opened it and selected onyx drop earrings and threaded their wires into her lobes. Last and most important, she lifted a massive onyx pendant to her throat.

Unlike Adara's mother, whose Sight required no aid, her father had adopted that pendant as his focus amulet when he became high priest. He died while wearing it, and therefore much of his power remained in the gemstone.

While cleaning out the house she'd inherited, Adara worked for a week to find the spell that opened the locked drawer of the roll-top desk. Her reward was that pendant and the energy it contained.

Since then, Adara had taken to wearing it on special occasions, when she needed to borrow his skills. At first, she resisted using it, wishing to lead by her own merit. Over the years, she needed more and more control to validate her purpose, tempting her to wear his amulet often. She still didn't fully submit to her lust for authority and wear it at all times. Tonight, she needed her father's magic to satiate her desires.

Adara slipped her bare arms into a dark trench coat and tied the belt tight at her waist. If her plan failed, she couldn't face being disgraced.

Downstairs, she peered out through windows to make sure the road was clear. A quiet, purple dusk settled over the rolling terrain. She darted through the breezeway to her garage, rounded the side, and pulled open the double barn doors behind her Packard.

She drove to the next coven road, a rough dirt lane extending the length of the hollow as it twisted along Owls Tail Creek. After a meandering mile, she parked in the meeting hall's gravel lot in the front of the two-story box of a brick building. Since she often made use of the coven's office at all hours, the presence of her car wouldn't be questioned.

Adara slunk from beside the car's wide front fender to the tree-lined walking trail that followed the creek behind the meeting hall. Her fancy shoes made the hike difficult, costing her valuable time as she picked her way over roots for a half-mile behind a cluster of three log homes until she reached the back of Rowe's massive acreage. *This better not be a trip for biscuits. This needs to work.*

His manor house, the McCoy family home, loomed an impressive three floors, a pale stone Tudor that rose like a ghost haunting the navy sky. Similar to her own, it retained a shabby art nouveau charm of the early 1900's. High arched windows and gothic towers stood intact despite numerous cracks and discolorations to the walls.

Sheers at the French doors did little to hide the yellow light bathing the interior. She'd not arrived too late. A nervous smile lifted the corners of Adara's mouth.

Rowe and Lenore schmoozed at the corner of the grand dining room table where they shared a bottle of wine.

Against the buttoned bodice of a clean but plain shirtwaist dress, the girl wore the mandrake talisman as Adara hoped. Rowe looked snazzy in a burgundy waistcoat over a French-cuffed white shirt and pleated trousers. With his dark hair sleeked back into a low ponytail, lamp light shone along the strong angle of his jaw.

Fearful of being discovered at her hiding spot behind a trellis, Adara stood stock still, even held her breath shallow.

Rowe leaned across the table and took Lenore's hand. He kissed her fingers and stood, pulling the girl into an embrace.

Adara held her breath, watching the final stages of her spell on Lenore unfold. She moved closer, behind a yew outside the door.

While Rowe favored the girl at least a little, perhaps to ward off his loneliness, the female mandrake enchanted him and transformed his fondness into outright lust. He encircled Lenore's waist and locked his mouth hard on hers.

Adara leaned toward the window.

Lenore pushed him off and gasped for air. "Please, you don't understand." She held up the curvaceous root. "This charm is to make me a suitable wife for a man who needs one, like you."

"Of course, and also a good man's folly." He pulled her closer, groping her thin frame more like an animal than a man.

"No. Not like this." She pushed against his chest, breathless. "I can't do this."

"Why not?" He leaned against the edge of the table. "What's wrong?"

"We have to wait. Adara said I was chosen to present my fertility to the gods first before the man who wishes to be my husband."

"Adara." Rowe shook his head and sighed. "You don't have to do as she says."

"But she's the high priestess." As he moved for her, Lenore took a step backward. "I want to. It's an honor to serve the coven. Mama was impressed." She picked up her pocketbook. "I have to go now."

Adara voiced a silent cheer. The vervain juice did the trick she intended, rendering the girl chaste. For seven years, according to a note in the grimoire made by her great aunt Mildred.

Adara crept around the outside of the house to watch Lenore leave on foot. Adara checked her watch by the flood light hanging at the garage gable and hunkered lower into the bushes to wait. Her pulse thrummed in her ears, louder with each passing minute.

Ten minutes later, she unbuttoned her coat and felt for Father's pendant at her neck. She pressed the onyx gem into her palm, and concentrated, silently repeating the phrase, *Muto schema*. She'd practiced personal transformation with Sibeal's guidance over the summer with some success. Adara's gaze dropped to study herself. She wore a dress identical to Lenore's. Even the run-over brown spectator shoes looked the same. Adara twirled a mousy blond strand of hair before her face. With a confident smile, she wrapped the knocker on one of the paneled double doors.

It opened, and Rowe grinned at her. "You're back, and without that mandrake charm. Good to see that you decided not to follow Adara's demands." He waved her inside and rubbed the back of his neck. "I apologize for my forward behavior earlier. Without that mandrake, I assure you I'll act differently. The charm affected me in a bad—"

Adara wasted no time claiming her hard won prize. She threw herself at him and kissed him with pent up passion. She ran her hands down his chest, unbuttoning both vest and shirt. Touching his bare skin, heat instantly bloomed deep inside her, and her body trembled.

He broke away and gaped at her, speechless.

Standing before him in her true form, her coat gaped half off of her lingerie-caressed curves. Nervous laughter crowded her chest and fluttered at the back of her throat, finally filling the silence between them. She followed his gaze down her voluptuous body, and tugged at the belt at her waist, her lips curling as the coat slipped to the floor. His eyes widened as she swayed toward him to claim her victory.

Chapter Three:
Not So Familiar

ROWE CAUGHT ADARA by the wrist and glared into her smoldering black eyes that promised pleasure but seeped venom from their golden glints.

"You're hurting me." The desire in her gaze extinguished as she writhed and pulled against his grip with her free hand.

"How dare you trick me. I won't let go until you tell me why you cast those spells." His fingers squeezed Adara's soft, pale flesh harder. "Tell me!"

"As high priestess, I don't have to answer to anyone about my magic." She jutted her chin at him.

"You have to answer to me when you hurt my friends."

She sneered. "Friends? Really? You'd run circles around simple-minded Lenore in any conversation."

"What chastening spell did you put on her?" He gritted his teeth, holding back his desire to make her feel pain for her actions.

Adara grinned at him but said nothing.

He twisted her arm behind her back. "What spell?"

She groaned. "What could it matter? The coven will be better off without a simple fool like her procreating."

He pulled Adara's arm until she winced.

"The vervain spell."

Rowe stared down on her with disgust. "That's seven years of chastity." He released Adara with such force that she fell to the floor at his feet. He clenched his hands into fists, his mind raging. Anger clouded his thoughts. Undoing that spell required complex witchcraft. He wanted to slap sense into Adara, but couldn't harm her either physically or magically. As high priestess, coven rules protected her.

"What gives you the right to change someone's life like that?" He spat the words at her.

Rubbing the delicate skin of her injured wrist, she stared up at him with hurt in her eyes.

He felt a pang of empathy but worked to cast it off. Likely another transformational trick.

"Seven years is nothing," she said and pushed herself to standing. "She's only twenty and will have plenty of time left to bear a houseful. Nothing as drastic as what my mother did to me. You don't remember. You were only a toddler then." She took a step closer. "We're the same, you and I. I lost the love of my life. You've lost your wife, Edme. Neither of us have any relations left."

The hairs on the back of Rowe's neck bristled at her mention of Edme. "No, we're not alike."

"We're meant for each other. Your right mind is still confused with grief." She grinned and held out a hand to him. "We could be great together."

"Take that spell off of Lenore."

"I can't." When he failed to accept her hand, she dropped it to her side. "We need a female to pledge her fertility to the gods at the Mabon festival."

"After the ceremony, undo the spell."

"The gods will keep her fertility until Imbolc in February at the earliest. Whether the spell can be undone after that is up to them." Her lips curled. "So you see, you and I have even more in common. With the gods claiming Lenore, you and I are the only folk in the coven who aren't spoken for, unless widow Ester or old maid Tansy appeal to you." She smirked.

Heat rushed into Rowe's face. It was clear to him now, how Adara had calculated this down to the last cold detail. She'd manipulated him into a corner and believed he had no choices but her. He stepped past her and opened the door. "It's time for you to leave."

"Not till I've had my goodnight kiss." She leaned into him and ran a hand along the open placket of his shirt. "You seemed to like the one I gave you earlier."

His back to the door, Rowe took hold of her upper arms and pushed her away. A pewter candleholder hurtled toward them and thumped hard against Adara's lower back. It took Rowe only a moment to comprehend. Apparently the spirit of Uncle Petrus didn't like how she was treating his great grandnephew and took swift action with his favorite reading light.

Adara winced and spun around. She planted the toe of her dress shoe on the top rim as the candleholder rotated to get away.

Glad for the help, Rowe nodded to the wing chair, which contained the magical spirit of his deceased aunt Tilly, another accomplished animator. The only chair that could hold the butterball of a woman, the huge upholstered piece lurched with wide strides on a straight course for the coven leader.

Great Aunt Tanita's favorite fireplace poker for building fires under her cauldron led a battle cry.

Adara froze, her black eyes widened.

Upon Tanita's signal, a host of objects, each animated with the original owner's skills, crawled, flew, or slid toward the trickster. A cavalcade formed: Ernie's silver cigar cutter, Wona's letter opener, and Maxwell's pistol, among many others.

When Bertrand's enormous antique hall tree loomed over Adara, she pleaded to Rowe, "Help me! Make them stop." She glanced his way and received only a glare.

The heavy oak piece grabbed hold of her wrists with its garment hooks and pinned her in place as if facing a firing squad. Writhing, she stared down the objects coming for her. "I should have known the McCoy home would be filled with animators' enchanted toys."

The wing chair pressed its smothering girth against her, and she moaned.

An instant later, the poker gave a shout to release. The furniture backed away, and Adara was not there.

A chill breeze blowing through the open door signaled Rowe to run outside.

The flood lamp on the old carriage house cast dim light over the side of the property. Far to the back, the pale striped face of a badger bared its sharp teeth. The animal hissed at Aunt Edna's white lilac bush that swept low limbs back and forth across the ground like a hockey goalie. The bush snagged the critter's stubby tail. With a vehement growl, the badger pulled free and escaped along the path to Owls Tail Creek. Dark wings fluttered after it, followed by the caw of a single crow.

Rowe walked to the lilac and collected Adara's trench coat. He peered at the now empty path and snickered. *Yeah, it would be an ugly creature she turned into with that wicked heart.*

A series of low hoots came from high in the old willow tree that overhung the creek. Rowe looked up to find his witch's familiar, an adolescent barn owl.

"That was one mad badger," Busby said and flew to a low branch nearer his master.

"Did she keep moving or hide in the thicket?" Rowe asked in a hushed tone.

"Made a beeline down the trail." The owl's white dished face captured the lamp light. "Was that the high priestess?"

"Yes." Rowe nodded and examined the coat.

"Whew, boy. You're in a heap of trouble now." Busby fluttered his wings as if unbalanced, then resettled on his perch.

"Yep, I am." He let out a sigh. "And I'm not sure what to do about it." He turned and strode to the front door, the small owl sailing behind him.

Rowe found his relations' favored belongings waiting for him. With the wave of his hand, he said, "You can all relax. Thank you for coming to my aid." He patted the wing of Tilly's chair. "After Edme died, you all did your best to comfort me. It's good to know you still support me, but I need to fight this battle myself." Rowe accepted his fedora from the top hook of Bertrand's hall tree that extended to meet his hand. He collected his blazer from the dining room, removed keys from his pocket, and said to Busby, "I'm going to the cemetery. I probably should keep you with me. I'll drive slow so you can follow."

"Ready when you are." The owl winged to the gable point overhanging the carriage house Rowe used as a garage.

Rowe hadn't used a witch's familiar until after his wife Edme passed. For years, she'd kept a female barn owl familiar and allowed it to nest while she herself was pregnant with her and Rowe's first child. Edme urged Rowe to take his choice of the five owlets for his own familiar. He'd put up a fuss, preferring to work alone, unlike most witches. He couldn't imagine sharing his magical spirit with an owl, or any creature for that matter. He'd agreed to make Edme happy. Not intending to make use of the gift, he chose the runt of the nest in order to spare it from the hard hunting life of a non-magical owl. Once chosen, Edme fussed over the owlet. She named the runt Busby days before she died birthing their still-born child.

The hapless bird seemed to have adopted Edme's warmth and wit, traits which endeared him to Rowe. But using Busby as a familiar had proved awkward. Now, embroiled with the vengeful high priestess, Rowe needed to have all magical avenues accessible. A familiar could use his magic for him if needed.

Rowe locked his house, in case Tanita or Tilly got an urge to be over-protective and follow in the forms of their preferred household items, but knew no barrier would stop them if they decided to help. He slid open the carriage house doors in front of the hoods of two Studebakers, his father's favorite makes made locally in South Bend. The long cars filled the length of the building. Rowe chose the President convertible coupe and cranked the top down so he could keep an eye on Busby for his first flight following a car. After Rowe's encounters tonight, though, he would have preferred the stealthier black sedan to the light green coupe.

He drove along Owls Tail Creek Road only as long as necessary to reach a connector, afraid the twists and turns might confuse Busby. Although the day had been warm with Indian summer temperatures, the night air blowing past made Rowe shiver. Or was it from fear of how to handle the predicament that faced him? He maintained a speed of fifteen miles-per-hour, and the barn owl kept pace. Together, they traveled to the opposite side of the coven, where the valley's elevation rose.

Bordered by coven farms on three sides and a woodlot on the other, the cemetery stood dark and quiet. Rowe followed the gravel driveway back a hundred yards between fields of golden corn. He parked in a small lot under a wide sugar maple. On the other side of the tree, stood a tall wrought iron gate. Smoldering autumn brush fires at neighboring farms tinged the air with the smell of burnt sap.

Rowe waved his hand in front of the lock and the gates opened. He passed without breaking stride. Although he'd been to the cemetery many times during the past year and a half, his grief had been too fresh to share with Busby.

Without a word said between them, the owl glided at Rowe's shoulder. His footsteps fell with measured rhythm through the maze of boxwood hedge-lined paths, crunching the pea gravel underfoot.

Several statues nodded as he passed, although no voices greeted him. Usually at this hour, mothers sang lullabies. Only the calls of locusts and crickets filled the close night air.

He stopped in front of a graceful female statue, a diminutive likeness of his former wife. Her alabaster face glowed as if lit within by the moonlight. Troubled with the uproarious evening, Rowe's inhibitions fell away. He knelt at Edme's marble feet and hung his head. "Damn, Adara! She tricked me. Why didn't I see through her? She enchanted a young woman, who's just a friend, causing me to become attracted to her. Then Adara used that attraction. She transformed herself into that woman to seduce me. I've been played for a fool."

Cool stone hands caressed his neck and shoulders.

"Your love was so pure, so true. I need you, Edme." Tears welled into the backs of his eyes, but he refused to let them fall. Many times, she'd told him to stop crying over her. "What can I do against Adara? Her position as high priestess protects her." He looked up at his wife's chiseled face, wondering why she remained silent.

Her features contorted into a pained expression, and she opened her arms to embrace him.

Busby circled above them.

Rowe hugged her and tried to fool himself that he felt her heartbeat next to his. "Why don't you speak to me?" Pulling back, he caught a glimpse of the black crow, Dearg, Adara's familiar, winging away from the tree-line across the field. His cawing echoed throughout the woodlot trees like an ominous chant.

"Did Adara curse you?" Rowe asked, studying Edme's ashen face.

She nodded and drew her hands to her mouth.

He stood and shook his hands in the air, letting out an animalistic scream. "Damn that woman! Does she think by taking you completely away from me that I'll need her? Is she insane?" He faced Edme, temples pulsing. "I vow to get your voice back." He gave her cheek a gentle kiss and left to search for clues through the maze of grave markers and statues of all shapes, ages, and sizes.

Those he recognized from when they had lived lowered their heads as he passed. None spoke, and he assumed Adara had enchanted them as well.

Enraged, he walked every path looking for any who could speak to offer advice. With no consequences to pay, words of the dead rang truer than those of the living. But on this night, even the dead paid a price to the evil coven leader. Their silence granted her more power.

Rowe reached the central roundabout marked with stepping stones that paid homage to the four pagan gods. Standing upon the eastern point, he said, " Lords of Air, I summon, stir, and call you up to aid those who lie in this sacred ground." He stepped to the southern stone. "Watchtowers of the south, Lords of Fire, please bring aid to the spirits lying herein." He repeated his appeal to the lords of water and earth at the western and southern positions.

When he stepped off the final stone, the face of the moon peeked from behind a cloud and shone down on the circle. A boy called to him from behind. The voice of his brother Grant.

"Rowe, come here," Grant whispered.

Rowe spun and dashed to where the statue of his brother sat on a bench. He wore knickers like he did when he fell from a tree limb and died.

"Vika was here and cast a shield over me." Grant spoke in a hushed tone. "She tried to protect Edme and the others, but that crow came too soon. Go get Vika."

Rowe nodded and patted Grant's knee. "I'll find her."

Rowe left him and dashed through the maze, sliding on the pea gravel as he rounded turns. When he reached his car, he looked up at Busby fluttering overhead. "I'm going to Vika's. Do you know the way in case we get separated?"

"Nope." He blinked his wide-set eyes at Rowe. "I only met her once at home."

Rowe let out a sigh. "You can ride in the car."

Busby gave a sharp shake of his head. "I'm scared. Would rather fly, if that is okay with my master."

"All right. I'll drive slow. Let's go." Keeping track of a familiar, especially an untrained one, cost Rowe time he didn't want to waste. He hopped into the driver's seat and took the most direct route to the old witch's home. She'd been a family friend for decades, even helped his mother give birth to him. A good soul he always turned to in times of need.

Rowe turned away from the coven's fields and drove through the rugged pasture lands. A herd of dairy feeders stared at his car as he passed. He turned onto a narrow lane into a stretch of woods. He hoped, like the cows, Busby could see the pale green hue of his car since heavy branches darkened the road. Unable to find the owl's white face overhead, he reminded himself that owls had great night vision.

He pulled off onto the gravel tracks leading to Vika's. Under the dense tree canopy of mature oaks and hickories, he strained to see anything other than what his headlights illuminated. The Studebaker's wide tires bumped over a series of potholes, and the tall front gable of the house came into view. As a child, he was always afraid to visit, believing the house belonged to the evil witch who wanted to eat Hansel and Gretel. His mother reassured him there were no witches as evil as that one in the story. After his evening with Adara, he wasn't as sure.

As soon as he parked, sconces lit the porch, and Vika stuck her snowy head through the cracked door. "Rowe, is that you at this hour?" she croaked.

"Yes, Vika. It's me," he called loudly to be certain she heard. In the last few years, her hearing had diminished. He rounded the rear of the car and scanned every tree elbow and knot visible in the darkness for a sign of Busby.

She padded onto the wooden porch in her doeskin slippers and adjusted wire-framed eyeglasses on the bridge of her hooked nose. "What are you searchin' for?"

"I...ah." Not looking where he walked, his toe hit a root to the side of the path. He jerked and replied, "I'm trying to keep a familiar. A young male owl who's the offspring of Edme's bird."

The old lady chuckled. "You? With a familiar? Hard to believe. Is that the owlet I met when I visited you six months after Edme passed? I haven't seen that bird since."

"That's the one," Rowe replied while keeping his gaze to the trees.

"And you still haven't trained him? That was a year ago when I first saw him," she chided him and turned in place, her nightgown wrapping around stumpy calves. The whiteness of the fabric caught the lamp light and shone like a beacon. She took several steps off the porch, and the wind lifted long strands of her wiry hair. Rowe paused at the sight of her. An angelic vision that matched the purity of her heart.

A sharp hoot sounded through the darkness, and Edme's huge barn owl, Maeira, glided on silent wings to the porch rail. Her chest heaved. She rotated her head to look behind.

Moments later, Busby's flat, white face appeared. Flapping as much as soaring, he spread his talons wide and clamped onto the railing beside his mother. Misjudging his speed, momentum thrust him forward, and he dropped to the floor. Tail tucked close, he hopped up beside his mother, who clapped her beak at him.

Maeira faced Vika. "While on my way here from the cemetery, I heard Busby's hoot in the distance." The magnificent owl rotated her head and blinked at Rowe. "Apparently, he failed to turn when you did."

"Mother, Rowe offered for me to ride in his car," Busby volunteered.

The female owl's feathers ruffled, her gaze still fixed on Rowe. "Why is my son not trained to fly the coven?" Her esteemed position in the coven as a familiar imbued with the spirit of their deceased master or mistress required her own character to be restrained. Despite that, displeasure and concern stabbed at him from her black eyes.

Rowe tipped his hat to her. "I apologize, Maeira." Realization that he was responsible for the advancement of her son hit Rowe like a splash of icy water in his face. He'd mourned the death of his own daughter, born without even the chance to enjoy one breath. All the pleasures and lessons she would never experience chased him daily. He now understood, in the same way, Maeira wanted the best for her son and entrusted him to Rowe. Prepared to right his wrong, Rowe stood taller and looked her square in the eye. "I allowed my grief to distract me from my duty to Busby. That isn't fair to him. I will do better from this moment forward."

That seemed to satisfy the great barn owl. She faced Vika. "The reason I came, which is likely Rowe's as well, is that Dearg bewitched the statues. Their voices are lost. I do not wish to see the spirit of my mistress suffer in this way."

Vika spoke up. "When the wind changed direction after nightfall, the tingle of Dearg's shadow lifted the hairs on my arms. I knew what he set to do. So I got a ride from Herta and Tom, in the log cabin down the way, to take me to the cemetery on their trip to Bentbone's K-mart."

"I was just at the cemetery to talk with Edme." Rowe followed Vika onto the porch. "I appealed to the gods, and they fixed your potion so Grant could speak. No others. Is it too late for you to help them?"

She stroked a bony finger along her temple, and the light radiating from her gown dimmed. "Maybe not. There's a simple potion that might work. Haven't made it in eons. I'll need the strength of your spirit to spread the magic 'round to all the graves."

"Not a problem," Rowe replied.

She moved to the door and motioned him to follow. "C'mon inside while I do my cookin'."

He looked back to the two owls on the railing. Unsure whether Busby needed to be exposed to potion-making, something he himself rarely did, he offered, "Would you both like to join us?"

Busby spread his wingtips away from his sides, but remained stock still when his mother snapped, "No, thank you. We have important issues to discuss."

The small owl hunkered down onto his talons.

Rowe felt bad for what seemed like a stern parenting talk the young owl was about to receive when the incident had largely been his fault. He left them to their bonding time and caught up with Vika in her potion-kitchen.

Connected to the main kitchen but much larger, it looked like a room from a colonial farmhouse. Glass-shaded ceiling lamps cast brighter light in the potion room. A fireplace, wide enough to heat a cauldron, lined one outside wall. Across the back corner of the house, a door cut into the other outside wall. A long tavern tables filled the center of the room, crowded with books and jars filled with herbs and extracts Vika had made from her garden. As a young man, Rowe and his father had felled several trees in the backyard that blocked light from her patch. Those trees were milled for lumber to make her tremendous work tables.

Cabinets and shelves lined one wall. Vika hoarded and collected ingredients in case someone in the coven came to her with an unusual need. She often served as their doctor if their own healing salves and herbals failed. They repaid her with food and rights to gather from bushes and flower beds on their properties. Sometimes, townies came to her for cures, their eyes bugged out as they drove through the coven land. Rowe admired how Vika treated them all alike, with care and kindness. Many witches looked down on outsiders, only using them for a source of income.

At the long table, Vika flipped through one of her many grimoires and horticultural guides. After a few seconds of fluttering pages, she said, "There it is!" She grinned, and two large dimples appeared in her peach-blossom cheeks. Her knotted fingers moved with unusual dexterity. In less than a minute, she selected five jars of liquid from the storage wall and plucked a handful of leaves from one of hundreds of dried bunches hanging from the ceiling. Examining one jar, she said, "This one's scarce as hen's teeth. Glad I have some left." She ground and sprinkled ingredients into a porcelain bowl, then looked up at Rowe while she stirred. "What's troublin' you? There's a strong reason you needed to talk with Edme tonight. I can feel it."

"It's nothing. Really." He pretended to study the contents of one jar, not wanting his problems to overshadow what was more important. Honor of the deceased witches needed to be restored.

She peered at him over the frame of her glasses, and her brown eyes narrowed. "Ain't nothin'. I've known you since you were knee high to a grasshopper. Fess up."

"I had a run-in with Adara this evening. Seems she's set herself to possess me as her lover. I don't know why. She and I aren't alike, despite what she claims."

"Land, no! I'm glad you see that much." She paused and stirred the other direction. "Siddie, I see you under that bench. Count out a minute for me." Her familiar, an enormous Maine Coon cat with ears that looked more like antlers, stepped out and stretched her spine and limbs. The cat, like a dog in size but more vicious, went everywhere with Vika, serving as a fearless protector to her aging mistress. More than once, the tabby's teeth and claws had torn into bobcats that ventured too close while Vika did her gathering in the woods. Well-suited to each other, Siddie served Vika for over a decade.

The cat sniffed the air in Rowe's direction, then relaxed the lifted hairs on her spine.

Vika glanced back at Rowe. "Adara is power-hungry. She won't be denied. If you're the prize she wants, you're up the creek without a paddle, boy."

"Don't I know." Rowe took a seat on a bench across the table from her. "Because of her position, I can't fight her with magic. According to coven rules, any claim against the high priestess must to go through the council. But she did harm to someone else to get closer to me, and I am allowed to fight for my friend's welfare. She put Lenore under a seven-year chastity spell."

The old witch nodded. "Vervain juice."

"Time's up, m'lady," Siddie said in a soft, purring voice as though half asleep.

"Thank you, sweet one." Vika poured the potion into a half-gallon amber bottle and capped it tight.

"Adara said the vervain spell could only be undone by the gods. She coupled it—"

"That's cruel! She enhanced the girl's fertility with a mandrake charm, then followed with the vervain." Vika rubbed her hands on a dishtowel for so long Rowe thought she was trying to remove that awful news. "I don't know what I can do to help Lenore. Poor girl. Are you sweet on her?"

He shook his head, picked up the bottle, and met her as she walked to the end of the table. "Only friends. She's a nice young woman. She doesn't pass judgment like most coven folks."

"You got that one right." Vika faced him and patted his shoulder. "Let me study up on it. I might think of something. Regardless, count me as an ally if you need a hand against Adara."

"Thanks, Vika. That means a lot."

"I may pass word along to some in the coven I trust. When we appointed Adara to her mother's position, everyone had high hopes. Since then, we've lost more coven members each year."

He nodded. "I'll talk to my friends, Logan and Keir, as soon as possible too. Logan has connections through his work with the coven's elderly, and Keir's insight as a seer is invaluable."

She picked up the moonstone locket hanging outside of his shirt and studied it, then glanced at him with raised brows. "The energy in this is stirring."

He shrugged. "That magic is so old, it doesn't work in today's world." He often considered the pendant nothing more than a coven brand marking him as someone who grieved, like Hester forced to wear the scarlet letter 'A.' "It's just a tale to tell visitors to lighten their wallets at our attractions. I feel like a hawker. Sometimes I don't even charge, like today." The image of the young woman, Jancie, he'd met today at the carnival flashed into his mind. "It feels wrong." The ideas that he reeled off routinely to himself and now to Vika seemed hollow as they left his lips.

"Rowe McCoy!" Her exclamation startled him from his thoughts. "I'm glad your Daddy's not alive to hear you." She stepped back and glared at him with hands on her hips, white hair billowing up as her energy flared. "That magic is old, indeed. Stronger than anything we work today, you hear me?" She snatched up a shawl from the end of the bench, thrust out her chin, and marched through the door to the kitchen, the mammoth cat on her heels. The front door flung open with such speed that the owls flinched.

Rowe rubbed a hand over his forehead. Somehow he'd managed to upset a lot of women tonight, including his Edme who looked so pained being unable to speak.

Outside, he opened the passenger door of the coupe for Vika, despite her insistence that she preferred to walk. Solid like an oak, the old witch often walked the coven to do her gathering.

Siddie leapt into the storage area behind the seats, filling it completely with her long tail.

Vika clucked her tongue and took a seat.

Once seated on the driver's side, Rowe called to the owls, "Busby, should I go slow or have you learned the way?"

"A-okay, no need to wait for me," his owl called with a quavering voice that sounded like a forced attempt at confidence.

"Familiars need to have keen directional sense," Vika said primly, pulling the shawl around her shoulders. "He'll learn. His mama will see to that now, since you didn't."

As they drove, Vika's silent disappointment allowed time for Rowe's mind to wander. He ran a finger over the pendant.

At the cemetery, all tension melted as they worked together, paying respects to former coven witches. Those who'd achieved stature in their former lives were granted the honor of spirit voices. That ability needed to be restored. Vika sprinkled her potion on each statue, large and small alike, while Rowe repeated his appeals to the four gods of nature like before. His voice rang loud and clear, soon joined by a host of others.

Dearg flapped from a farmhouse roof toward the burial grounds, but Siddie took off at a tear with Maeira and Busby chasing the crow from the sky.

Vika joined Rowe in the center, tears staining her cheeks. "We've given them back their honor. Thank you." She took his hand and led him to Edme. "She has something to tell you."

He knelt at the statue of his former wife and looked up at her blank stone eyes.

"I now know the gift of speech is a treasure that can be lost, so I have something important to tell you," Edme said with a voice more calm than he'd heard since before her death. "Rowe, you've come here to me, again and again. It is time for you to put yourself first, before me. Nothing would make me happier."

Her words rang without meaning in his mind as he stood and kissed her cheek. "I'll try."

At his car, he found a yellow maple leaf in his driver's seat. He looked up at the tree ablaze with yellow in the moonlight, the first color change of this autumn he'd seen. He fingered the leaf, tucked it in his pocket, wondering if it was an omen of change.

Along the drive back to Vika's and later to his own home, Edme's message wove into each of Rowe's thoughts. His hand moved to the moonstone, which now seemed to weigh more than he remembered. At least twice as much. Was he going crazy? How could it change?

Walking up the stairs to his bedroom, Busby sailed past him to the brass perch once used by Maeira. The pendant seemed to drag upon Rowe's chest. He trudged up the half flight past the landing turn. Upon reaching his room, he peeled out of his clothes, yanked the chain of the necklace over of his head, and fell into bed. He tossed the locket on the rumpled blanket beside him. From that distance, the moonstone's magic felt heavy on his eyelids and Edme's words echoed in his dreams.

Chapter Four:
The Fern Café

JANCIE HAD AVOIDED encounters with her father for two days after her visit to the carnival grounds. But her time was about to run out, since she was expected to be present for family dinners on Thursday nights.

Harley would be there for sure. Such a mooch, he never missed a free meal or a way to kiss-up to Jancie's dad, his boss, who wanted her to get back together with Harley. Dad had plans to make Harley the body shop manager, along with a vision of his only daughter marrying Harley in order to keep family involved with his business. Since the couple's break-up more than six months ago, Dad found ways to put Jancie and Harley in the same place, despite the fact she'd made her choice clear. Thoughts of her father's manipulation, along with the idea of marrying Harley, formed a hard pit of anger in her stomach. She'd made a mistake dating him and wanted to put that past her. He was hot to look at, but that had worn off fast. She sighed, and a rush of regret flushed heat into her face. If only it'd been sooner, like after the first date.

Harley oscillated between trying to get revenge on her for leaving him and doing his best to win her back. Most days, Jancie didn't know and didn't care which bothersome tactic he was up to. She just wanted him out of her life.

She let out a heavy sigh. Armed with ammunition of having seen her talking to Rowe, how could Harley resist revenge mode. He'd likely tell Dad. During the past days, she'd wished on her lucky German coin, her rabbit's foot, and favorite rock from her collection that Harley would pick the choice of reconciliation tonight. Tonight, an evening of his sweet-talk would sound like honey to her ears. But that didn't seem likely. With no way out, she accepted meeting the consequences of breaking one of her ironclad father's rules: no talking to witches.

At home after work, Jancie changed into jeans and a t-shirt. She glanced in the full-length mirror on the bedroom door and wrangled out of the bottoms. Her roundish heart-shaped face made her seem younger than her age. Dressing down didn't help. Looking like a teen would only give her father more power.

She searched one side of her closet, then moved the panel door and flipped through older garments crowded together on the other, things from high school that weren't right for much now. Jancie thought of the glamorous coven leader she'd met at the carnival. Her style commanded authority. She had no problem interrupting Rowe from telling the moonstone story. Something about the way the woman spoke to Rowe made Jancie think the two were a couple. Or, maybe, she led the entire coven with a firm hand.

Jancie stared at her choices and settled on a navy short-sleeve blouse she usually wore to work and paired it with trim khaki pants. She picked out leather ballet flats from her limited shoe selection. While brushing her hair, she rechecked the mirror, happy to find she now at least looked her twenty-three years. Still, the new outfit did little to camouflage her long neck. She couldn't wait for cool fall weather, so she could hide it underneath turtlenecks and cowls. Her mother had always said Jancie looked as graceful as a swan with her delicate neck, and thin arms. Somehow Jancie saw a giraffe in the mirror instead.

She peeked into her jewelry box, frowned, and closed it. She needed to get out and do more shopping, something she'd not felt like doing during Mom's long illness and afterward. The last six months seemed like a blur. All Jancie remembered were daily chores and missing Mom. The simple silver hoops she still wore from work would have to do.

She grabbed her purse and keys and made her way to the car. *Why do I worry so much about what Dad thinks anyway? I don't need his approval.* She backed out of her driveway, clamped a hand on the steering wheel, and drove to the subdivision at the town's outskirts.

The houses were new but small, ranch homes all built by the same developer. Her father had bought a place there to please his new wife. She always wanted the newest of everything. Even though Dad could easily keep any car running, Heather insisted on getting a new Honda Rav-4 for herself.

Jancie followed the maze of streets through tan aluminum-sided houses and parked in the drive behind her father's old Dodge Ram pick-up. Harley's Silverado wasn't there. Unsure whether to be relieved or concerned, she walked to the open screen door and called, "Hi Dad, Heather. I'm here." A black and white fox terrier mutt bounded to greet her. She pushed dog and door aside to enter and reached down to pet the barking, jumping pooch.

Heather poked her head around the corner. "Jancie! I didn't know who it was over Gonzo's barking. Come on in." The bleach-blonde woman waved her flabby arm toward the couch. "Dwayne's cookin' steaks tonight. Mmm. Don't know what's the occasion, but it's good with me."

Jancie glanced past the kitchen table to the patio where her dad worked the grill. His back to her, she couldn't see whether he looked tense. She assumed he already knew what she'd done and dreaded his anger, which could be fierce. Did he think steaks and a fancy meal would obligate her to follow his wishes? She glanced at her stepmother. "Can I help in the kitchen?"

"Thanks, hon, but it's all ready for now." Heather plopped her wide bottom, covered in white knit stretch pants onto the couch. She fluffed her shoulder-length hair, then made kissing noises at the dog while slapping a huge thigh. Gonzo bounded up and barely filled her lap. She stroked his ears while he hid his nose up her wide tunic sleeve. "Have you had a good week, Jancie?"

"Yeah, work's been good." She perched on the armrest of an overstuffed tan armchair. "Farmers wanting to refinance loans." Jancie usually hung with her dad during family get-togethers because talking with her stepmother was never easy. "How are things going at the beauty salon?"

Heather chuckled. "Darned good. With so many of the gals taking vacation time, I've made a ton of overtime. I'm thinkin' about buying me some new high-heel leather boots for winter. Hear it's gonna be a bad one."

"That's what the guys at work have been sayin'." Jancie's father walked inside and stood under the archway connecting the dining and living rooms. He'd changed from his usual work uniform into clean jeans and a golf shirt. His clean-shaven hard face, lined from manual labor, seemed sunken with age since he'd left Jancie's mom and remarried eight years ago. In that time, his wavy brown hair had gone stick straight, wiry and gray. He worked his sinewy muscles with weights daily, like a compulsion. Despite looking fit, the doctor had put him on medication for high blood pressure. Dad always complained about money. Jancie thought his second wife's bills caused the pressure. "The coals will be ready in a couple minutes." He eyed his daughter with a gleam in his eye. "You spiffed up for Harley?"

"Heck, no. Why? Is he coming?"

"Do you think that boy'd miss a free meal?" Heather laughed.

Jancie shook her head.

"Give the guy another chance, will you Jancie?" Dad moved beside her and rubbed her shoulder. "You know, you being with him is extra insurance that he won't get out of line with my business once he's manager."

Jancie pushed his hand away. "I've told you that I'm not going back with Harley. And I'm not changing my mind."

Dad moved back and leaned against the archway, his gaze fixed on her. "He said he'd be along a few minutes after six, so at least try to be polite." He turned his face downward. A muscle spasmed in his jaw. That twitch made Jancie wonder why he wanted her back with Harley so badly. If Harley needed to be kept in line, then why make him manager in the first place? Or had Dad learned she'd talked to a witch?

Gonzo jumped off of Heather's lap and ran to the door.

Outside, a car door slammed and moments later, Harley opened the screen wearing a t-shirt stretched tight across his muscled chest. "Hey all." He ran grease-stained fingers through the loose curls of his damp golden hair. "Just got out of the shower. Had to work longer than expected on the MacElroy's old Nash Ambassador. Good thing you started stocking parts for them vintage models, Dwayne. I was afraid the man'd turn me into a frog or something if I had to send away for parts." He laughed and slapped his boss on the shoulder.

Jancie stared at her father. He'd always been opposed to the local witches. Why, now, was he taking in cars from the coven for repairs?

Dad's eyes met hers, and he turned toward the kitchen. "That fire should be ready to put the steaks on. Is everyone hungry?"

"Mmm. Yes." Harley slid an arm around Jancie's waist. "Steak night. Kind of like when we were dating."

"It has been that long since I've had steak." She moved several steps away and forced a smile at her ex, at least relieved to have the honey-sweet Harley tonight.

Dad rummaged in the refrigerator and carried a tray of marinated meat through the patio door.

"Jancie, I could use a bit of help with the table," Heather called over her shoulder on the way to the kitchen.

"Sure thing." Glad for at least a little space from Harley, she grabbed a handful of flatware and set places.

Harley's goo-goo eyes followed her while she worked and about made her gag. She reminded herself that this was the better of his two personalities and shot a grin at him.

By the time she and Heather finished, her father returned with thick, charred New York strip steaks. The savory smell made Jancie's mouth water. She sat at her usual spot, and he filled her plate. "Only the best for my little girl."

Everyone settled into their places and dug in. Jancie cut her first bite, and the pinkish-brown center tempted her taste buds. In her mouth, the salty juice flooded over her tongue.

"Jancie, I hear you've been at the carnival talking to witches," her father said while slicing another bite of meat. "Is that so?" He forked the piece to his mouth and eyed her as he chewed.

Jancie choked on her own saliva and grabbed her glass for a sip of water. Avoiding her father's gaze, she looked across the table at Harley, his face plastered with a too-innocent-to-be-true smile.

"Not just any witches." Harley pointed his fork at her father. "Holding hands with some warlock."

"Jancie, you know how I raised you." Her father's gaze prickled her skin even though she stared at her plate. "Witches hurt people. You know better. There are plenty of nice young men here in Bentbone." He gestured toward Harley.

Never one to stand as Jancie's ally, Heather bent to the floor and feed Gonzo a meat scrap, then excused herself to the kitchen.

Trapped two on one, fight or flight took over. Jancie glared back at her father, and her defense rushed out. "I'm not socializing. I just want to use their magic to contact Mom so I can say goodbye. That man you saw." She glared at Harley. "He can help me."

"What about that woman with black hair over one eye? She looked scary but kinda hot." Harley belched and took a swig from his beer bottle. Jancie wondered what she'd ever seen in him. Looking like a model hadn't been near enough.

Dad gripped the edge of the table and swallowed hard. "That's the coven leader. What trouble have you got yourself up to, girl?"

"Nothing." Jancie forced her voice to sound calm. "Mother never minded me going to the coven's events."

He bristled as if steam was about to burst from his ears. "Your mother isn't here." His gaze locked onto her with a beady-eyed stare. "You follow my rules now. I don't want you at that carnival. Stop fighting me, Jancie."

"I'm not fighting, and I don't have to follow your rules. I don't live with you. I just want to say goodbye to Mom. Why don't you understand? And why are you taking on cars from coven folks now?" She spat the words at him. "Why don't you follow your own rules?"

He lurched toward her, then pulled back. The spasm in his jaw pulsed faster, and a vein throbbed in his forehead. "Times are hard. We need the money. I won't permit you to be around those folk, you hear? People I know got into big trouble with them."

"Like what?" she asked.

"One man had his teenage son turned into a toad after the boy pranked a witch."

Jancie lifted a single brow. "In this small town, I would've heard about that."

"It happened. Honest." Her father took a deep breath and leaned forward. "The man had to pay a thousand dollars to get the spell reversed."

"I promise I won't prank any witches." She shook her head, pushed away from the table, and rose to leave.

"Sit and eat your dinner, hon." Heather returned with a pitcher of ice water. "He's just worried they'll take advantage of his kin now that he's working on them old Packards."

Jancie glanced at her father who sat silent with a blank look on his face. She took a few bites, but her constricted esophagus made swallowing uncomfortable. "I'm sorry, Heather. I've lost my appetite."

"Let me wrap up your leftovers then. It's too good to waste." Heather gave Jancie a concerned smile.

"No, thank you. Give it to Harley. He's better at following Dad's orders." Without a word to Dad or Harley, Jancie held her head high and strode past to the front door.

***

Jancie's phone chimed with a text alert, and she jerked her head off the couch pillow where she'd fallen asleep. *Not Harley again. How does he think that stunt of telling on me will make me like him again? Or maybe he's been calling to apologize. What a dope.* She checked the phone and found a message from her friend Rachelle: Carnival starts tomorrow nite. R we going?

Jancie typed a response. Maybe another nite. Her father's agitation bothered her even though it didn't make sense.

What's wrong?

Jancie sighed. Meet me for lunch tomorrow to talk?

K. At the Fern.

Jancie needed to talk but not yet. Too upset to sort out how to deal with her father, she'd spent her evening downing a pint of rocky road. Talking with Rachelle now, Jancie would end up a mess of tears and not solve anything.

***

Friday at work the three bank tellers buzzed about their plans to attend the carnival.

Jancie ducked into her office to avoid being pulled into their conversation.

Debbie peeked her head around Jancie's door. "Are you going to the carnival with your friends? If not, you can go with us. We're getting a group together."

"Thanks, Debbie. I haven't made plans yet." The lie caused a sour sensation to form at the back of Jancie's throat. "I'll give you a call if I need folks to go with."

Debbie smiled and took her place at the front counter.

Jancie's stomach shook. The whole town would be going. Heck, folks would probably even ask afterward why they hadn't seen her there. She'd always been allowed to go if she went with friends. At least, that'd been okay with Mom. Apparently Dad thought he was in charge now. Jancie twisted a paperclip out of shape until the wire broke. *What right does he have to disapprove of my choices? Does he feel like he has to step up now that Mom's gone? A little late for that.*

Sure, he dislikes witches and has for as long as I can remember, but what's making him so afraid of my involvement with them? Can't he understand I just want their help to contact Mom and say goodbye? Maybe he's against that. He did leave Mom and ask for the divorce. Jancie lined up question after question without any answers.

A phone call from the regional bank manager interrupted Jancie's thoughts and gave her enough work to fill the morning.

Lunchtime came fast, and Jancie looked forward to talking with Rachelle.

"Beautiful weather for the carnival," Debbie said as she stepped out of the bank beside Jancie, the breeze lifting the teller's dark bangs. "It's going to be nice all Labor Day weekend, then turn chilly. I hope you can join us. Want to grab lunch together at the deli?"

"No, but thanks. I'm meeting my friend Rachelle at the Fern Café."

"Oh, Sarah and I almost picked there. They have their meatloaf special today. See you after while."

The two women separated, and Jancie crossed the street to the local hangout, thankful that the tellers wouldn't be there. In a position of authority at work, she didn't want them knowing her family issues. Cars filled all the angled parking spots along the block in front of the Fern. Even a couple of 1930s model roadsters from the coven. Jancie wondered if one of the cars belonged to Rowe. Where the green café curtains parted, she studied the picture windows for his face without any luck. She stepped inside the door, and Rachelle waved from a booth.

Jancie scanned the room as she made her way down the center aisle. The green on green prints of the décor confused her efforts. Trellis and vine patterned vinyl on the booths conflicted with lily pads on the plastic tablecloths. The floor of checkered mint green and black made her eyes cross. Accented with hanging baskets of ferns, she usually thought the place looked quaint, but now it boggled her mind. She slid in across from her friend

"Looking for someone or just trying to avoid Harley like normal?" Rachelle took a sip of her iced tea.

"Harley." Jancie spun around and rechecked the room. Finding neither guy present, she turned back to her friend.

"Hmm. Harley's not on your mind. Who is?" She brushed strands of her shaggy brown hair out of her eyes and fingered her pink feather earrings. "This should be good. What's up?" Her raspy voice rose with a lilt.

Jancie focused on Rachelle and remembered why they seldom did lunch. Jancie looked like a stiff banker in her sedate gray dress. No fun compared to Rachelle in her long, bohemian flowing skirt and armfuls of eclectic bracelets. Working as a graphic artist in the local print shop allowed her friend more freedom with her wardrobe. But this talk couldn't wait until after work. Jancie leaned close and whispered, "I saw two coven cars outside. I only saw one couple in the back. Did any others come in here?"

Rachelle's brows lifted an inch, and she nodded toward the bar. "They can't hear you. Now spill."

"My dad was mad at me last night. Thanks to Harley."

Rachelle rolled her big brown eyes. "Like you needed another reason to hate Harley."

"Hey, gals." Rhonda, a middle-aged waitress, stopped at their table. "What'll you have? Meatloaf's the Friday special in case you can't tell by the way we've packed 'em in today." She pulled one of the plastic flower pens from her lime-colored uniform's breast pocket that jutted out with her ample bosom.

"Oh, the meatloaf plate sounds great! With slaw and green beans." Rachelle replied.

"And I'll have the meatloaf sandwich with fries." Jancie slid the two unopened menus to Rhonda.

"Gods, I hate having lunch with you." Rachelle tossed a wadded straw wrapper at her. "You can eat everything."

"Come run with me sometime." Jancie smiled.

"Get up in the wee hour of five in the morning. No thanks." She reached a hand laden with silver rings toward Jancie and leaned across the table. "I'm dying to know what happened."

"Hey, y'all. What's the occasion?" A slender young woman approached their table. "Our meatloaf?" She wore a wide, pearly smile that seemed out of proportion for her sylph-like features, made even smaller with a hairnet pulling her flyaway white-blonde hair close. She chuckled and sat beside Rachelle.

"Hey, Willow." Rachelle scooted over to make room. "The meatloaf's a bonus. Jancie's about to tell why her dad doesn't want her go to the carnival."

Willow's blue eyes grew round like a doll's. "What right does he have?" She leaned close to the others at the center of the table. "Make this quick. I'm on break from the kitchen."

"At our Thursday night family dinner, Dad accused me of hanging out with the coven's witches."

"Did you?" Rachelle asked in a quiet raspy tone that Jancie strained to hear over the bustle in the café.

"Aunt Starla shared some witch lore with me she read about in one of relations' diaries. There's some magic moonstone locket worn by a member of the coven who's grieving. That witch is expected to share the magic with others who've lost a loved one and want to reconnect with that person."

"What's so bad about that?" Willow adjusted the elastic of her hairnet. "Everyone knows how you missed the moment your mom passed."

Jancie took a sip of ice water. "That's what I thought. But the witch who wears the locket is this insanely gorgeous guy. Harley happened to drive past just as the witch began to share the magic story."

"Bummer." Rachelle twisted a bracelet around her wrist. "So you didn't get to talk to your mom, and got spotted with a hot guy who happened to be a witch. Harley must've enjoyed ruining that much."

"Yep." Jancie stirred the straw through her water. "Harley is just jealous. He must've loved taking that juicy tale back to Dad. Somehow Harley had the smarts to use Dad's prejudice against witches to get revenge on me. Dad's fired up, not wanting me go to the carnival now." She looked from one friend to the other. "What really gets me is that he's now taking in the coven member's cars at his shop. He says he needs the money." She rolled her eyes. "I told him to follow his own rules to stay away from witches and then walked out."

"You go, girl." Rachelle held up her palm for a high five that Jancie returned.

"Oh, Jancie. That's no fun." Willow's voice squeaked, and she wrung her hands.

Rachelle let out a sigh. "I'm glad my dad's far away. I couldn't handle having him around."

"I wish Dad and I got along better. I don't want us to have these disagreements, but I'm tired of him giving me orders when he doesn't like something I do. A chance to talk to Mom and say goodbye is more important. More important than anything." Hot tears stung the backs of Jancie's eyes, and she looked down to hold them off.

"And you're going to have that chance." Rachelle reached across and took hold of Jancie's hand. "We'll help you get to that witch."

"We sure will," Willow added. "I'm off all weekend but work on Monday."

"I'll call Lizbeth at the library and fill her in." Rachelle leaned back to make room for Rhonda to set plates on the table.

"Maybe Lizbeth can look up about that moonstone locket. She can find anything." Willow stood, and turned sad eyes to Jancie. "Guys, I've got to get to the kitchen. Let me know what we're doing this weekend."

"Will do, and I'll mention looking up information about the locket to Lizbeth." Rachelle repositioned her plate in front of her.

"Thanks, Willow," Jancie said and bit into a fry. The salty crispness tasted good, and she reached for the ketchup. Having friends on her side eased both her nerves and stomach.

"So what does this hot male witch look like?" Rachelle forked a piece of meatloaf and dunked it in gravy.

A grin lifted the corners of Jancie's mouth. "Tall with dark brown hair in a low ponytail under his hat. Big brown eyes. Chiseled jaw with a five o'clock shadow. Wide shoulders and ripped. I ran into his chest. Solid."

Rachelle lifted a single brow. "How?"

"Being a dope. I wasn't looking when I entered the gate."

"Good move. Wish that'd happen to me." Her friend paused for a bite. "Sounds like your type. It'd be your luck to fall for a witch. Your dad would have a coronary." Rachelle chuckled.

Jancie snorted. Munching on a pickle, the grin wouldn't leave her face. She loved her friends. They always made her laugh when things went wrong. She wondered about Rachelle's comment about falling for Rowe, but his life was so different than hers. She'd learned that the opposites attract thing didn't work from dating Harley.

The two women ate in silence for a while, and the couple of witches from the bar walked hand-in-hand to the check-out counter. While the man paid their bill, the woman scanned the room, and her gaze stopped on Jancie.

Like when she first saw Rowe, Jancie couldn't look away. There was a sense of familiarity, but she'd never seen the woman before that she could remember. She studied the witch's hair. Brunette in a chin-length bob that curled into a soft roll along the ends. Round horn-rimmed glasses overshadowed her perky nose. About thirty-five, the petite woman carried a few extra pounds in her hips.

The tall, thin man who accompanied her took the woman's arm, and they left.

"That was creepy," Rachelle mumbled through a mouthful.

"You saw the way she stared at me?" Jancie leaned in. "The weird part was that I couldn't look away even when I tried."

"Get out. Really?"

Jancie nodded and finished the last of her sandwich.

Rachelle wiped her mouth and said in an urgent tone, "We have to go there now."

"Where? The carnival?" Jancie asked and took a long drink of water. Going back to hear Rowe's moonstone tale was a must, but Jancie didn't expect to go now. Her friend's impulsiveness spread over her.

"Sure. Don't you still have time before you have to be back at the bank?" Her friend waved for Rhonda.

"Thirty minutes, or a little more since I'm the manager. Let's get going."

"There you be." Rhonda laid their bills on the table. "Have yourselves a great weekend."

"Thanks, Rhonda. You too." Jancie quickly left a tip and moved to the register.

Outside, Rachelle took her arm. "With all these strange things happening, I'm too curious to stay away."

Jancie pulled her friend with her as she jaywalked toward the intersection of Maple Street. Fear tickled the back of her throat and spilled out as a stream of giggles.

The pair race-walked down the mile-long incline to the edge of town.

Chapter Five:
Opening Night Jitters

IN THE TINY BOOTH inside the carnival's entrance, Rowe checked the ticket sale records book. He thumbed back to the bookkeeping for the previous year. Only four hundred. That Friday night and most of the weekend last year had been rainy and cool. Both of the coven's seers, Keir and Sibeal, predicted the current Indian summer weather would hold up several days. *Good for the coven and good for me. Large crowds will keep Adara busy.* He secured the record book in a locked drawer, left the booth, and pushed the heavy wooden gate open a crack to leave. Vintage cars and trucks belonging to coven members lined the road.

Rowe's familiar, Busby, followed at his shoulder.

About a quarter mile up the hill toward town, two young women hurried in the direction of the carnival. Jancie and another whom he vaguely remembered. The carnival didn't open until five o'clock. He stepped out to greet them.

The wind lifted Jancie's golden-red hair. It caught the sunlight and looked like strands of gold. Even at this distance, her energy felt familiar. The other woman wore her layered brown hair to her shoulders. She walked with long strides, and the hem of her skirt whipped in the strong breeze.

Rowe gave them a wave, and Jancie's arm shot into the air returning his gesture.

She attempted to speed up her pace, but the stony roadside gave her trouble with her high-heeled shoes.

The two women hesitated before an intersection.

A Dodge Ram pick-up pulled up on the cross road about a hundred yards away from Rowe, and turned toward town and the women, slowing as it approached them. The driver rolled down his window and thrust out his gray head. He yelled at the pair, but Rowe couldn't make out the man's words. His energy reeked of hot rage.

"Busby, stay there," Rowe called over his shoulder and ran toward the women.

From the other direction, Logan's burgundy Nash Ambassador drove down the hill.

The man in the truck shot a glance at Rowe, and then sped away.

The young women talked to each other, arms moving rapidly, then turned toward town.

"Jancie!" Rowe called as he ran.

"I can't talk now," she called over her shoulder, not stopping as she and her friend climbed the hill.

Rowe wanted to know if Jancie was okay. Something about the interaction he'd witnessed was wrong. Really wrong. But he'd just met her and didn't feel he had the right to interfere in her life. He wondered who the man in the truck was and about his relationship to Jancie. Rowe stood motionless at the side of the road, confused by the scene, wondering what he should do. He watched Jancie walk up the hill.

A trace of urgency from her energy wafted to him. She gave a backward glance his way but kept her pace.

Eyes fixed on her, Rowe took a step forward.

Logan pulled up and leaned over to roll down his old sedan's passenger window. "Are you hexed?" Logan laughed, and his blond hair fell forward into his eyes. He brushed his bangs away.

Rowe moved to the open window. "There's something about her. The girl with the ginger hair. I know she needs my help." He lifted the pendant away from his chest. The moonstone gave faint flashes of blue and purple.

"Check that out!" Logan slapped his thigh. "That old gem does have some magic left in it. Get in and tell me what happened. I've been wanting to talk to you. Vika told me an earful. We'll take a drive and check the local motels for tourist capacity."

After a last glance at the two women, Rowe slid onto the passenger side of the bench seat. He took a look at his friend Logan and wondered why Adara hadn't chosen him as her conquest. He held high stature in the coven as a powerful witch even though he didn't come from a founding family of the coven. Women found Logan handsome, with his boyish golden blonde hair and blue eyes offset by a strong Roman nose and chiseled jaw. At twenty-six, Logan was only a year younger. It was well known that Logan disliked Adara, but Rowe didn't like her either, and that didn't seem to stop the woman. More likely it only would provoke her to seduce his friend.

Logan put the car in gear, and the old Nash chugged and lurched forward.

"You need to get this boat worked on. The transmission sounds off."

"Yeah, well I didn't get lucky enough to inherit those fine Studebakers like yours or the Packards a few others drive. Maybe I'll get lucky at the carnival and tell some rich guy's fortune. Better yet, advise someone how to win the lottery and cut me in." Logan chuckled and ran a hand along the curve of the steering wheel.

"Attendance should be up this year." Rowe lifted his fedora and smoothed his hair before replacing it at the proper cocked angle. "With the nice weather holding for a few days, you might make a pretty penny."

"So fill me in about that girl back there."

"Not much to tell." Rowe pulled his hat lower onto one brow, hoping to avoid his friend's piercing glance.

"Uh huh. Sure thing." Logan's voice lifted with sarcasm.

"Really. I just met her Wednesday. Her name's Jancie. She came to the carnival looking for the witch with the moonstone. She missed her mother's passing and wants to connect to say goodbye."

"Sounds sweet and simple." Logan turned past the Hideaway Inn. "Full up with cars. Yee-ha! I'll be making money tonight." He glanced at Rowe. "By the look on your face back there, it's not that simple."

"Sweet maybe. But far from simple. I began to tell her the ancient tale, and she set off the magic. My stone started flashing. I'm sure it was going to open, but Adara showed up and stopped everything."

"Ah, Adara. Vika told me about your problems with our fearless leader, but I didn't know you had this other young thing on the line."

"I don't." Rowe squirmed in his seat. "I told you, I just met her."

"The intense look on your face back there said differently." Logan's brows rose. "But what if she can open the locket? Are you ready for that?"

"I don't know." Rowe's voice cracked, and he looked out of the passenger window.

They drove in silence until Logan passed another motel. "Looking good! The Bentbone Lodge has a no vacancy sign. What I don't understand is why Adara is after you? No disrespect, but there's lots of available coven men like Keir or Shaw. Or me. I'd love to take her on and come out on top." He winked. "In both ways."

Rowe chuckled. "You've always had a love-hate relationship with her. You're two of a kind."

"Wrong on both counts. I do hate her but would love to control her any way I can. And she and I aren't the same, or you wouldn't count me as a friend."

"I'll give you that." Rowe chuckled. "You have a heart buried somewhere deep inside, albeit small and shriveled. You do more than your share of charity work." He admired his friend's tireless work with the coven's elderly.

Logan nodded. "Thank you for acknowledging my benevolent side. But my efforts aren't completely altruistic."

"Last I heard, you were getting schooled in the ancient dark arts by Skena Stoddard." Rowe glanced at the driver.

"That's been working well. In return for household magic which she can't do anymore, she's taught me how to draw darkness from shadows. It's incredible."

Rowe laughed. "If you can trust her ninety-five-year-old mind."

"Don't forget about her acclaimed skills that won her a forty-year term on the council. She's sharp as a tack. I wasn't born into a high coven position by inheriting advanced magic. I've had to scrounge for it wherever I can." Logan's face lit with a wide grin. "And I think I'm finally ready to challenge our lovely leader. She has no idea what I can do and will be caught off guard. Besides, I have a friend in need." He stopped at an intersection of county roads and faced Rowe. "According to Vika, I have to thank you for providing me such an opportune reason to go after her."

"Why don't you skip all the backbiting and just run for coven leader?" Rowe shook his head. "The Mabon equinox is only just over three weeks away. Coven leaders can be overthrown in an election after the ceremony's closing."

"And when was the last time that happened?" Logan scoffed.

"Well." Rowe ran his hands down his thighs. "I don't remember when it happened, but my parents talked about it."

"That means a long time before Adara's mother and father were coven leaders. No one would vote against a Tabard, if they value their life."

"I don't know. People aren't too pleased with Adara. We've lost a lot of coven members during her three years as high priestess."

"Seventy-three since she was appointed."

"Just my point."

"Those who left won't be voting. Coven people with lesser powers, less courage, remain and fear her. You take that for granted since you can hold your own against her. I remember Adara's mother cornering my mother. Ma had used some of our neighbor's share of blackberry foliage to do some spellwork. White magic to heal some children when we had an outbreak of chickenpox. Grizela Tabard wanted the glory of curing those children for herself and charged Ma with using more than her quota of the herb's harvest. I was there, peeking around the corner of our barn when Grizela ignored Ma's pleas and burned all her hair off."

Rowe sat straighter and gave a sharp exhale through his nose. "That's why your mother always wore a head scarf?"

Logan nodded and clamped the steering wheel. "It never did grow back. It's almost a blessing that she's lost her memory of that now, in her old age."

"I didn't know this. I'm sorry. I do remember when I was a kid, Mother whispering to Dad about something she heard at the orphan's home." Rowe rubbed a hand across his brow trying to figure out a way to stop Adara from following in her mother's footsteps. "You're right that I don't fear Adara personally. I'm confident I could take her in a duel of powers. My problem is that there are rules preventing that action against the coven leader. Unless she causes permanent damage to someone I consider a friend. Knowing Grizela hurt your mother, I suspect Adara won't hesitate to harm those in her way. That's what I fear."

"Vika said Adara tricked Lenore Whiting into taking a vow of chastity. Doesn't that count?"

"A vow of chastity to save her fertility for the gods at Mabon."

Logan sighed. "That's an honorable sacrifice to promote fertile spring crops for the coven. Hardly a disgrace or torture. Is Lenore upset?"

"Not that I can see. But I suspect she's enchanted."

"Hmm." Logan pulled the Nash up to the carnival entrance behind Rowe's Studebaker. "I'm going to be on

Adara like a hawk, looking for anything she does to harm someone. Can I count on your help?"

"You've got it."

"I'm going to pay our friend Keir a visit as well and see if he'll join with us. A seer could be useful."

Rowe opened the car door and placed a foot on the ground. "Always good to have a seer on our side, especially since Adara considers Sibeal her best friend." He stepped out and joined Busby who perched atop the wooden privacy fence next to Rowe's coupe.

***

At home, Rowe fed Busby some grain and gave him free time to chase mice before they needed to leave for the carnival. In the large farmhouse kitchen, Rowe poked his head into the refrigerator, an electric upgrade to the original icebox his mother insisted upon. His parents adhered to the coven's expected traditions of 1930s lifestyle. But they finally relented and remodeled the turn-of-the-twentieth-century, art nouveau house with electricity and indoor plumbing. Some inconveniences were just too much. They were among the first in the coven to update their home, and over the years all others followed suit as they could afford.

Rowe rubbed the stubble on his chin and pulled out a milk carton. His stomach was in knots, and he didn't feel like eating. He sat at the breakfast table with his glass and thought about the horrible experience Logan related to him about his mother. As coven council members, Rowe's parents had always supported the governing group's usefulness to insure fairness and trusted that an unfair coven leader could be removed or controlled. They must have known about Grizela. How had they dealt with the situation? He made a mental note to visit Vika to see what she might remember.

He rinsed the glass and moved to the library, combing the walls of books for any kind of journal, diary, or records of coven business his parents may have used. Nothing turned up in the shelves of spell books and animating studies. He looked around for another place to search, but the Westminster grandfather clock that housed Uncle Ernie's spirit yelled, "Get your butt to that carnival and do your job!"

The clock rang three o'clock louder than usual, and Rowe knew the noise was meant to get him moving, as if Ernie's reminder wasn't enough.

Rowe ran upstairs to shower and change into his formal witch's attire. A double-breasted suit in black pinstripes. Despite the summer weather, black was required for show. He swapped his cream-colored summer fedora for a black one with a chocolate band. As a special touch, he animated a white handkerchief for his jacket's breast pocket. It sparkled a trail of miniature silver stars and moonbeams whenever he moved and encircled the moonstone resting against his black shirt.

Outside he hurried to the pale green roadster and checked his pocket watch. Moving quickly, he heaved one of the garage doors open. "Busby, are you in there? Time to go." The bright sunshine outside hampered Rowe's vision inside the dark, repurposed barn. "Busby, are you here?"

Receiving no answer, Rowe stepped out and scanned the nearby rooftops and trees. He called out, "Busby, it's time to go." Training a familiar sure tested his patience. He turned all around, hand shielding his eyes.

"Here I am, Master," Busby replied as he sailed up from the back of the property. "Mice hide in the daytime. Better eating along the crick."

"You found some dinner?" Rowe lifted a brow.

"Yes, I did. Ready for duty."

"Good. We're going to the carnival again. You know the way?"

"Yep. By heart."

Rowe slid into the driver's seat and drove the usual route. If there was a chance the little owl could help him against Adara, Rowe wanted him along.

He parked in the adjoining empty field used as a parking lot. Colored lights of the Ferris wheel and the witch's brew spinner competed with the afternoon sun. Smells of sugary and savory fried foods made his empty stomach growl.

He and Busby entered the carnival through the unmarked back gate in the privacy fence reserved for coven folk.

As he passed inside, a dozen children surrounded Rowe, while his barn owl circled above their heads.

"Mr. McCoy, look at my carnival dress." Little Charlize O'Malley worked her small hand into Rowe's. When he faced her, she pulled the hem of the full skirt out, and her face lit with a cute grin that lacked both upper front teeth.

Rowe beamed. "Did the Tooth Fairy help you make this lovely sunshine yellow dress?"

Her smile broadened, and she gave him a shy look through her lashes. "It changes color. Watch!" She dropped his hand and twirled on the heel of her black patent shoes.

"Beautiful!" Rowe clapped. "The colors of the sunset, just like your golden hair. My compliments to the Tooth Fairy for her guidance."

The little girl faced Busby. "Do you like it?"

"Yes. It's wonderful." The owl perched on his master's shoulder. "You look very pretty."

Charlize grinned and skipped beside her older sister who hung at the outer edge of the circle with the young teens showing each other their school projects.

A hand pulled on the back hem of Rowe's jacket, and he turned with care to not step on any of the children. As one of ten rotating teachers, he taught coven children the basics of animation, a favorite subject especially among the little ones.

"Mr. McCoy, look what I brought to sell at the toy booth!" Eight-year-old Dewey Malcolm pushed a toad under Rowe's chin and commanded the critter "Come on. Make some noise." He gave it a squeeze between his dirty-nailed fingers, and it yapped like a lap dog.

"Wow! That's great, Dewey." Rowe bent to examine the toad. "You moved some dog's spirit into a toad. Good job on that difficult technique. And the dog? Does it croak now?" His brows inched up as he gazed at the boy.

Dewey kicked the ground with the toe of his shoe. "Not quite. Maybe if you listen real close. Mostly Mrs. Vottel's Fluffyboots is pretty quiet."

Rowe ruffled the boy's shaggy head of thick, brown hair. "That's okay. You're learning. And I'm sure all of Mrs. Vottel's neighbors are much happier."

Rosella, his sharpest middle-grade student, held up a doll that spoke to Rowe. "Mr. McCoy, you're looking handsome tonight." The twelve-year-old witch blushed and said, "I...I need to make some adjustments."

A pack of boys snickered, and Dewey led them in a chant. "Rosella has a crush. Rosella has a crush."

"Quiet boys," Rowe directed. "Rosella, it's outstanding." He couldn't help grinning at both her red face and her accomplishment." You've been able to animate spontaneously based on a set of programmed emotions. Fine work. You're an excellent animator."

One by one, Rowe inspected the marvelous achievements of his students, making sure to move among the older children in the outer circle. "Good job, everyone! Now go place them in the proper booths—either to sell or for display. Both are near the entrance and some mothers will be there to help you."

The children scampered away as he watched. Mothers and fathers stood nearby and escorted their young ones toward the entrance. A stab of melancholy hit Rowe's heart remembering his own stillborn child and departed wife.

Charlize took hold of his hand and pulled. "Come on. Don't look so sad, Mr. McCoy. The carnival is about to start."

Her corkscrew blonde curls bobbed, and he couldn't resist.

With a grin, he submitted and allowed her to lead him and her parents. Rowe's head pivoted in search of his familiar and found the owl chattering with the robin familiar belonging to one of the mothers. "Busby, come here and stay close by my shoulder."

"Coming, Master." The owl took wing and glided above Rowe's side.

The path wandered between easy roller coasters and flying rides for young children. They passed into the central part of the carnival where rows of games of skill and chance were sprinkled with numerous closed tents in a rainbow of jeweled hues. Larger tents housed shows with magical light, sound, or assorted effects. In smaller tents, solitary witches gave readings and predictions.

Along the main corridor, they paused among the group of children. A few ran back and forth across the wide path from the booth where they could sell their projects to the display exhibit.

After a few minutes, Rowe called out, "Make your decisions and place your projects."

Mothers who worked the booths guided the stragglers and beamed at every child as they handed over their projects. Once all were placed, one plump, middle-aged mother waved to Rowe. "Mr. McCoy, you've outdone yourself this year."

He joined Mrs. MacElroy at the sale booth. Surrounded by all the wondrous toys and sparkling lights outlining the display, she looked like a plain Puritan. Her high-necked black shirtdress and her salt and pepper hair pulled into a severe bun drew no attention. But her wide smile and cheery blue eyes held her special magic. No one could resist her warmth. "That says a lot coming from you, Matilda."

"You seemed to pour all of your extra time into these children this past year, more than ever. And just look what they can do." She beamed.

"Time with them helped me." The main lights tripped on, and the entrance arch blazed behind the still-closed gate. A crowd on the outside cheered. By the loud noise, Rowe guessed there were at least a hundred or more people waiting for the grand opening.

She patted his shoulder and grinned. "A fair trade. I can see in their eyes that they learned much more than animation. Such fine young ones. We should all be proud of both them and you."

Rowe shot her a smile. "Save some of that charm to sell these items."

"Will do." She faced Busby. "And I see you have a smart, young familiar. The son of Maiera should do fine for you."

Among witches darting in all directions, Adara sashayed past in black satin evening dress that clung to her curvy hips. She stopped to talk with Lenore and glided into the ticket booth.

Matilda set to work straightening the projects while she kept an eye on the high priestess who reappeared, clipboard in hand and nodded their way.

Rowe nodded in response, teeth clenched at the thought of Adara keeping watch on him. He disliked seeing Lenore under her influence and hoped she was okay.

Luckily, another female witch ran up and pulled the high priestess away to tend to some urgent concern.

"You may soon find use for a witch's familiar," Matilda said with a loud sigh. "Have a wonderful evening, Mr. McCoy."

Rowe inched his brows up. It appeared people already knew of his troubles with Adara. "And you as well." He checked his pocket watch. "Ten minutes. I'm going to get some of Babbett's pastries before we start." He looked at Busby. "Maybe Babbett will have a sample for you."

"Be sure to try her new fillings. I was her taster this summer. You have my word, they're good."

"Thanks." He tipped his hat and took long strides toward the food vendor area along the front fence wall.

Busby flew close by his shoulder.

Nestled between the elephant ears and snow cones stood Babbett's Magic Pastries. Several coven-produced food booths were sprinkled between those featuring the sugary, greasy foods the public demanded.

"Evening, Babbett." Rowe stepped up and scanned the pastries in the long glass case that spanned the entire length of the counter. "Matilda said to try the new ones. Which are those?"

"Cheese All, Spiceberry, and Coon Hollow Truffle." The petite, dark-haired woman grabbed a paper sack and rubbed her plastic-gloved hands together. Her brown eyes darted over his head at visitors chasing in all directions along the path. "Sounds like a good crowd outside."

"I think it'll be a packed house with this warm weather. Those new types all sound good. I skipped dinner, so I'll have one of each. A coffee too, please. And do you have a treat for my owl?" He pulled out his wallet and laid down a twenty dollar bill that would cover the order plus a generous tip.

"I sure do." She glanced over her shoulder to her high-school aged son. "Bring a raptor cake from the freezer." She wrapped each crescent shaped pastry in paper and placed them in the bag, while her son filled another bag and served the coffee. "There you be," she said with a smile and placed the order on the counter. "The cake might be a bit big for your little owl, but he should like it. Let me know how you like these new pastries. I'm hoping they sell. I'm not sure."

Rowe nodded and gathered the food. Hungry and eager to ease her concerns, he pulled out the Cheese All and took a bite. The flaky layers of crust melted in his mouth, characteristic of all of Babbett's pastries. But the cheese filling contained the real magic. The initial Swiss flavor morphed into Colby as he chewed, then into mild cheddar and finished with provolone before he swallowed. "Fantastic! You've outdone yourself with this Cheese All. I'll talk this one up for sure."

She grinned wide and nodded. Her hairnet's elastic slipped over her long earring and set it swinging. "Thanks, Rowe."

He nodded to Busby and secured the half-eaten pastry in the bag, then cut between paths, winding between backs of tents and picking his way over mazes of electric cables. With his free hand, he lifted the flap of his own tent and set his dinner on a side table. Everything lay ready from his preparations this morning.

His owl flew inside and sniffed the bag with his treat.

Rowe broke the raptor cake in half, held it out in his palm, and stepped to the tent door. "Eat this just outside, but stay near this tent."

Busby snatched it in his beak and followed outside.

Working with the children and their projects was the fun part of Rowe's job at the carnival, not the role that would occupy the rest of his evening. Storyteller of the griever's moonstone. Rowe fought to tie up the flap, the rope slipping from his sweaty hands. Finally successful, he admired the golden cords and strands of miniature blue lights outlining his tent. He exchanged waves across the path with the lady witches who stood ready. Tanya the tarot reader and Penelope the palm reader, his neighbors from last year for this affair—his first as the bearer of the moonstone.

While his familiar munched and smacked his beak, Rowe fingered the pendant resting against his chest. It felt heavier. The more he thought about the stone and its history, the more it weighed. Strange sort of magic.

His thoughts turned to the crowd. Was Jancie among them? His heart raced, and he blew out a slow exhale to calm himself. If she could open the locket, nothing would be the same.

The chain of the pendant cut into the back of his neck. The huge gates creaked open. Cheers filled the air. The crowd thronged in, and after their weeks of preparation, the carnival got underway.

Chapter Six:
The Herb Garden

JANCIE'S PHONE BEEPED when she left the bank at five o'clock Friday afternoon. Three voicemails displayed on her inbox: two from her father, and one from his wife, Heather. She drove home and listened to the first, fully expecting his anger for spotting her and Rachelle headed toward the carnival grounds at lunch hour.

"Jancie, have you lost your head, girl? You seem bent on doing exactly what I told you not to do. Your mother must not have raised you right. If I had—"

Unable to listen to him bash her mother, Jancie pressed delete and moved to the next, sent only a few minutes later.

"Jancie, I'm sorry I slammed your mother. That was wrong of me." His recorded voice broke and paused.

No doubt about that. Jancie sighed.

"Truth is, she wanted me to look after you once she passed. You've been a good daughter, and done me proud. I know you're grown, but if you need anything, I'm here for you, to help and protect you. Hanging with those witches will bring you trouble. Your mom wouldn't want that. Please, Jancie." The recording clicked off.

Her finger hovered over the delete button, then moved away. She replayed the recording, trying to decide whether his words rang true. She'd never heard Mom dead set against the coven's witches. Jancie couldn't decide. Parked in her own driveway, she went on to the third voicemail, an hour later, from Heather.

"Jancie, it's Heather. I've been wanting to go shopping in Indy for fall clothes, but your dad won't go with me. How about you and I take a girls' trip this weekend and stay at a nice motel? You've been telling me you need new clothes bad. Dwayne said he'd foot the bill and kick in some shopping cash for you. Let me know."

Jancie shook her head, tossed the phone in her purse, and walked to the back stoop of her house. She'd heard enough. Heat burned in her face. Any other time, she might've been pleased to get to know her stepmother better. And Jancie did need new clothes. But this weekend, the offer could only be a bribe to stay away from the carnival. The more she thought about the intent, her father's manipulation, the angrier she became. She knew during their marriage, Mom had trouble with him telling her what to do. Jancie's whole body shook. She wouldn't stand for it anymore.

The onslaught of calls from Dad made her miss her mother's gentle but firm guidance. Mom always understood and never manipulated.

Jancie bent low over the neglected flowerbed that filled the small angle between the steps and house. A scrawny volunteer zinnia planted by her mother years ago held up a single orange blossom. *The last rainy spell must have given it a boost.* Jancie studied the stubby plant that had managed to reseed itself and grow without care. It reminded her of how alone she felt without her mother. She stood tall, pushed her shoulders back, and took a deep breath.

The hardy zinnia prompted Jancie to survey the back yard. She paid the teenage boy down the street to mow and trim the sparse grass. Against the eastern garage wall, her mother's garden looked like it suffered from a bad hair day. Vines and stems poked in all directions smothering the few flowers. At the bed, she lifted the hem of her dress above her knees, knelt in the grass, and ran her fingers through the dirt at the base of one perennial. Her mother's silver ring on her finger felt warm against her skin. The organic smell of soil and the fragrance of the leaves her hand brushed reminded her of Mom.

Jancie sprang to her feet and ran inside to her bedroom. She changed into jeans and an old, soft t-shirt and wadded her hair into a ponytail. At the kitchen door, she considered taking her phone as usual, but chose to leave it behind. She needed to spend time alone with her mother's garden.

She rested a thermos of water under the shady maple tree and rummaged through the garage. Weighed down with armloads of tools, bucket, and watering can, she staggered to the wild patch.

Jancie set to work on the large garden that spanned the entire length of the garage, weeding and trimming out dead and overgrown stems. Her mother had called them herbs, but only some were meant to eat.

When her weed pile grew several feet wide and tall, Jancie sat back and checked her progress. Sweat stung her eyes and soaked the hair at the nape of her neck, but the sun on her back felt like the warmth of her mother's smile. Only a third done, she got back to work.

Angelica had seeded itself and grew wild between branches of the rambling rose along the garage wall. While untangling the growth, a thorn scratched the back of her hand. The line turned red, then formed an oozing trickle. As she rose to return to the house for a bandage, it seemed as though the heads of golden yarrow fought their way through the thicket. She recalled her mother's voice. *Yarrow leaves mend cuts.* Jancie pulled off a silvery leaf and applied it to her broken skin. Within moments, the bleeding stopped.

She smiled and cleared the weeds from the clump of yarrow, then moved behind to the showy purple coneflower. She ran a finger across the prickly rust-colored center, like she did as a child, and tried to remember how Mom had used this plant.

At the base, runaway runners of mint plants climbed the sturdy coneflower stems. She clipped the mint back to the confines of its pot. The spearmint's fragrance filled the air. Jancie took a deep, soothing breath remembering winter evenings spent eating fresh-baked cookies with a pot of mint tea. Mom always kept sprigs of mint with fresh flowers on the table. Lessons Mom had taught her about how to use herbs came flooding back to Jancie.

She collected her cuttings into a bucket and sat under the shade tree for a break. Like her mother often did, Jancie pinched off a couple of mint leaves, crushed, and added them to her thermos water. After a brisk shake, she took a sip. The cooling scent relaxed her, and she leaned against the tree and closed her eyes.

A bird singing a sharp note above her prompted Jancie out of the daydream.

Slanting rays of the setting sun streamed across her outstretched legs. *How did time pass so fast?* Jancie stood, found the shears cast off in the grass, and cut a few stems of whatever still bloomed into her bucket with the mint: marigolds, purple coneflowers, yarrow, and the last roses of the season. She surveyed her progress, and a pang of hunger rumbled through her stomach. Not even half done. *I'll be back for the rest of you tomorrow.* She gathered an armload of tools and stored them in the garage, then picked up her bucket and headed into the house.

With a dirt-crusted hand, she brushed hair from her face. She stepped out of her tennis shoes, padded to the china closet in the living room, and selected a well-used vase. She filled it with not only the flowers, but also sprigs of mint like her mother always did to protect the house. When asked from what, her mother would laugh and mention some made up names of goblins. Jancie's stomach sent out another complaint. *Ugh. I'm covered with dirt and am so tired. What is there to eat that's easy?* She set the vase on the table and decided to order a pizza.

After calling in the order, Jancie enjoyed a hot shower, and hurried back to the kitchen. The fragrances of the bouquet filled the entire room, just like it did when Mom was able to work the garden. Jancie inhaled the scents and smiled.

A knock on the front door sent her scrambling to collect her wallet. Her hand touched her cell phone, and she purposely left it there, out of sight and turned off. She was glad for her decision to remove the landline phone. She didn't want anyone to interrupt the healing connections she'd made working through soil warmed by her mother's hands.

Piping hot pizza box in hand, she sat at the table and ate her fill. With a full belly and happy thoughts of her mother, drowsiness made her eyelids heavy. She peaked out the back door window at the improved garden, checked the doors, and turned off the lights. At the hallway leading to her bedroom, Jancie hesitated and turned back to get the vase of flowers.

She placed it on the dresser next to Maggie's leather-bound diary. She picked up the book and snuggled into bed. Reading more about her mother's family seemed like the right way to finish her evening.

Jancie read entries about Maggie's baby Dorothy's first milestones. It dawned on Jancie that Great Aunt Starla mentioned Dorothy had been her cousin. Jancie skimmed to find how Maggie was related to her. Riffling through the book, a loose page dislodged. A yellowed birth certificate for Betty Forsbey. *My Gran! Maggie was my great grandmother.*

The document listed Maggie and Louis Forsbey as the parents of Betty, born June 30th, 1939, in Evansville, Indiana. In an earlier entry, Maggie's first husband, Marvin, died young of a heart attack. Her grief led her to visit a male witch in the coven who wore the moonstone locket. Jancie hadn't read about any man by the name of Louis.

If only she'd found this diary before Gran passed, five years ago. Jancie read the diary's last entry dated March 21, 1939. It told about Maggie moving away from Bentbone. Although, by the dates, she must have been pregnant with

Betty, there was no mention of her carrying a child or of her husband Louis. Only Dorothy. In the last line, Maggie wrote, "With heavy heart, I must make this my final entry. I'm leaving my family for the sake of my own children."

Curious about why Maggie had moved away while she was pregnant and why the diary stopped at that point, Jancie picked up reading where she left off, when Dorothy was a baby. She read for clues about Betty and Louis, and ties to her mother. Despite Jancie's determination, page after page about happy times and family outings, combined with the mint fragrance wafting through her bedroom, lulled her to sleep.

***

Early the next morning, sunshine called Jancie outside, opposing her will to solve the mystery of Maggie's diary. After a moment's thought, she promised herself to return to the diary in the evening. She skipped her usual run, avoided her cell phone, and headed straight for the garden. Intent upon seeing the end result that day, she worked quickly and efficiently.

Weeding and pruning for hours, she filled a trash can with debris. The rose trellis tested her carpentry skills. Her repairs resulted in a mashed thumb.

With the sun high in the sky, she stood back and took in her accomplishments and gave them a satisfied smile.

Jancie ran into the house and returned with paper envelopes to hold seeds for next year's marigolds, snapdragons, and angelica. She potted renegade mint runners into a few old clay pots from the garage and set them in the patch's open spaces. Stems of sage and mint were cut, tied into small bundles with twine, and hung from wall hooks in a dark kitchen corner beside the pantry, where Mom always dried her herbs.

She rummaged in the garage for any leftover bags of manure. Only two bags slumped against the potting bench. She searched for other fertilizer, without luck. Her mother had insisted on organic gardening. Jancie made a mental note to get more before cold weather.

"What the heck are you doing?" Rachelle called, head poked out of the driver's window of her car as she parked behind Jancie's Camry.

Rachelle, Willow, and Lizbeth spilled from the beat-up boat of a Chrysler New Yorker, classic early nineties.

"What does it look like?" Jancie looked up with a grin. "Haven't you ever seen someone tend a garden?"

"Don't you answer your cell anymore?" Rachelle asked, her husky tone deeper and her words pointed. "I've only texted you at least ten times."

"Yeah, well. I've been kind of avoiding the phone." Jancie dug in the bag and scooped a double handful of moist compost around a few plants.

"What now?" Rachelle threw up her hands. "Harley or your dad?"

"Dad. And Heather." Jancie sat back and squinted up at Rachelle's silhouette in the afternoon sun. "They left three voicemails Friday after he saw you and me near the carnival. He tried to lay a guilt trip on me, and then later said he was only concerned and watching out for me 'cause Mom wanted him to keep me from the witches. Fat chance of that. She never said that before."

"That's not your mom." Rachelle shifted her weight to one side.

"Nope. Sure isn't," Willow chimed in.

Jancie nodded. "Then, his new wife, Heather, called wanting me to go shopping in Indy all this weekend. Out of the blue. Just this weekend. Dad was going to foot the bill and give me spending money. Can you believe it? If they'd been sincere, I'd have jumped at the—"

"Damn." Rachelle twirled a bracelet. "What lengths will your dad go to, to keep you from being around witches?"

"I don't know, but spending time in Mom's garden has made me feel grounded. If that witch with the moonstone can help me connect more, that's what I'm doing. For me."

"That's the Jancie we know." Rachelle grinned.

"Heck, I want to go now just to find out what your dad is so worked up about." Willow knelt and took a whiff of the yarrow blossoms.

"That, too." Jancie laughed and dug into the manure bag to feed another plant.

"Ick. You're actually touching manure...with your hands?" Lizbeth shivered and fingered the end of her waist-length brown braid, something she did when out of her comfort zone. She took a step closer and wrinkled her pug nose so much that her wide brown-framed glasses slipped.

"It's sterilized, or supposed to be anyway," Jancie replied. "It doesn't smell." She held up a handful toward Lizbeth, who gave a cautious sniff.

Jancie laughed. "You need to get out of your books more often."

"Organic fertilizer, the only way." Rachelle dropped down onto the lawn, her bracelets clattering. Jewelry for Rachelle was always required, even with casual skinny jeans and t-shirts on weekends. "I can remember when we were little and your mom had us help her with this garden. You and I would dangle earthworms at each other."

Jancie tossed her head back and laughed. "Yes. We pretended to be brave."

Rachelle snorted. "Something like that. The loser was the one who screamed or flinched the most. Sometimes you're mom had to decide the winner."

Jancie shook her head and grinned. "Good times."

Willow wandered around inspecting the progress, her blue eyes bugging out. "Just look at the size of that trash pile! You've been working it, girl."

"This isn't work." Rachelle studied Jancie and leaned in to pull a bramble out of her hair. "This is therapy."

"That's what Mom always said about her garden." Jancie beamed.

"Oh, yeah." Willow tucked a strand of white-blond hair behind her ear. "Mrs. Sadler used to give us Christmas gifts of homemade tea bags. Her tea was awesome."

"And her bath sachets were divine," Lizbeth added. "Any chance you'll be making those for us this Christmas, Jancie? Hint. Hint." She fluttered her long, dark lashes toward Jancie.

Jancie laughed. "If you put in some muscle tending the garden, I'll think about it." She tossed the bag of manure at her friend's feet.

Lizbeth jumped back, and Rachelle rolled onto her knees to scoop a handful from the bag for a nearby plant and looked up at their reluctant friend. "You're allowed to get dirty when you're not in that library."

"After that jab about my books, I'm not sure I should tell you all what I found out about the moonstone."

Jancie stood. They all faced Lizbeth. She pushed her braid behind her shoulder, and her hazel eyes gleamed. "I learned that moonstones are linked to cycles of the moon. They're more powerful for witchcraft during the waxing moon, which we're in now until the harvest full moon in six days."

"So, there's a better chance of it working now?" Willow asked, eyes bright.

Lizbeth gave an assertive nod and continued. "Moonstones are prized for their abilities to work out problems between loved ones. Their energy is receptive in nature, and can transfer vibrations from one person to another as a form of communication when other pathways are blocked."

"That sure makes sense for helping folks connect to loved ones who've passed," Jancie said. "Did you learn anything about the moonstone this coven uses? Like what sort of magic they put in it? Why only one witch wears it?"

Lizbeth shook her head. "Sorry. I don't have access to coven records. I've been trying to find a link to someone who does though. There's an old witch who visits the library often. I left her a message that one of the books she'd requested has come in. She likes me a lot and might be willing to help."

"Good lead, Liz," Rachelle said.

"But what if you're not working when she comes for it?" Willow asked.

Lizbeth grinned, and lifted her chin. "Already on that. I hid it where none of the other workers will find it."

Jancie held her hand up to high five Lizbeth, who started to slap hands, then recoiled and said, "Sorry, I don't do manure."

Willow folded her long legs as she scooted next to Jancie. "Are you sure you want to do this moonstone thing? You might not want to mess with the supernatural. Strange things can happen, you know?"

Jancie leaned back and faced her friend. "I'm not worried. It's important that I talk with Mom once more."

Rachelle stood and looked at the others. "So when are we going to the carnival?"

"I'm ready." Jancie wiped her hands on her jeans.

"You are? Right now? Dressed like that?" Willow asked, blinking.

"No, silly." Jancie shot her sweet but sometimes naïve friend a smile. "I mean I'm mentally ready, regardless of what might happen, good or bad."

"Okay. So you go clean up for your time with the moonstone man. What's his name? Rowe?" Without waiting for a response, Rachelle looked around. "Let's help her get this stuff put away. We'll all meet back here at five. That's two hours to get your glamour on, ladies."

While her friends scurried around, Jancie emptied the last of the manure bag on the now tidy garden. That job completed. More yet to do tonight.

Chapter Seven:
Arcane Aviary

UNLIKE HER DELIBERATION over an outfit for Dad's dinner, Jancie wasted no time choosing what to wear to the carnival. Connecting to all of the gardening things she used to do with her mother grounded her sense of purpose. She was determined to do all she could to have their lost goodbye.

After a shower and make-up, she tugged on a pair of black denim jeggings and whipped a white lace swing tank over her head. Jewelry amounted to simple silver hoop earrings. She added the leather ballet flats and made her way to the kitchen to gather her usual black shoulder bag. Digging in the purse, she stashed a pinker shade of lip gloss than the neutral work color. With time on her hands while waiting for the others, she picked up her phone. Old texts from Rachelle and a new voicemail from Harley. She read through Rachelle's texts, sorry she'd worried her friend.

Jancie listened to the new mail. Harley's voice said, "Hey, Jancie, it didn't sound like you were gonna listen to your dad about the carnival. I'm going tonight. I'd be glad to drive you, or just meet there and hang out." She shook her head and wondered what made him think she'd want to spend time with him. Dad must've put him up to it. At least that voicemail tipped her off she'd need to be on the lookout to dodge him.

A horn tooted outside, and Jancie stowed her phone and house keys. Purse in hand, she ran out and joined Willow.

"You clean up good." Willow lifted off gigantic sunglasses that dwarfed her delicate features. The gentle breeze lifted strands of her fine hair off the ruffled collar of her pink sleeveless blouse. She rubbed her pale, bare arm. "I didn't bring a jacket."

"Me neither. I just learned that Harley will be there, so I'll keep warm running from him." Jancie leaned against the hood of Willow's Honda Civic.

The vintage Chrysler beast turned into the driveway with Rachelle and Lizbeth. There was never any discussion about who would drive when the four traveled together. The other two women slid into the cavernous backseat. A wave of perfume spilled over the split front bench seat.

Willow sniffed the air. "You two smell good. Out to catch yourself some guys?"

"Heck, with all the tourists here, why not?" Rachelle laughed. "That reminds me." She slipped a few bangles from her wrist and passed them back. "Jancie, these might help your cause tonight."

Jancie gave a nervous laugh as she accepted. "I'm not after Rowe. Just trying to get his help."

"Yeah, right," Rachelle quipped. "That glimpse I got of him yesterday—he was a hottie."

Jancie scooted forward. "I checked my phone and found a voicemail from Harley wanting to hang out together at the carnival tonight. Good of him to alert me."

Rachelle sighed. "Predator turned bodyguard. My mission for the evening." She turned onto Main Street. "Check out this traffic, even two miles away. Maybe we can give Harley the slip if it's crowded."

"Look at all those lights." Willow hung over the back of the front seat and pointed to the carnival in the distance. "More every year."

Jancie nudged next to her. The electric lights glowed, but a subtle twinkling effect came from magic. Every color of the rainbow. The Ferris wheel stood tall—the crowning jewel.

A few minutes later, Rachelle turned onto Maple Street and inched the car through the parking field. Attendants guided her to a spot.

Lizbeth glanced over her shoulder above her thick eyeglass frame. "Okay, it's crowded tonight. Keep your phones handy in case we get separated." Always the one keeping things orderly according to rules, Jancie understood why Liz did well as a librarian. Her dark hair, parted in the middle, enveloped her shoulders. Only narrow braids framed her face. The few times Liz wore her hair loose, on special occasions like this, she reminded Jancie of Morticia from the Addams' Family.

They spilled out and headed toward the main entrance. Arms of whirling rides carrying squealing riders reached above the tall gray fence. Smells of fried and sweet fair food greeted Jancie. She was eager to be a part of the fun with her friends, like years before. After all the grief and problems, she hoped that was possible.

When they reached the entry, a new illuminated arch spanned the walkway between ticket booths on either side. Before Jancie allowed herself to enjoy the lights, she checked the surroundings for Harley or Rowe. Dad never attended the coven's public gatherings, but she made a second pass just in case and reminded herself to be more watchful.

"Wow!" Willow craned her neck looking at the display. "This is new and awesome the way the colors shift."

From under a cloak of hair, Lizbeth stretched out an arm and grabbed Willow's. "Come on. The line's moving up." Jancie wasn't sure what Liz wore underneath the hair other than something white above skinny jeans and sandals.

Jancie stepped to the window and handed her money to the ticket taker, who appeared to be a high-school-aged girl. Behind her stood the sexy woman Jancie had met along with Rowe. The coven leader, Adara.

A perpetual grin seemed plastered on Adara's dark red lips. Although the woman's make-up had looked perfect the other afternoon, tonight it was theatrical. A chill shot through Jancie. Powder lightened Adara's pale complexion to a luminous white, and more liner than even Rachelle dared to wear gave a mask-like appearance to the one visible eye. The other peeked from behind a wave of iridescent hair that reminded Jancie of a raven. Adara's piercing black pupils stared through Jancie. The coven leader stepped forward and rested both hands on the counter. Each finger wore a glittering ring and finished with a long, black nail. "So good to see you here tonight, Jancie." Cleavage spilled from the plunging v-neck of her black satin dress.

A lump caught in Jancie's throat. "Thank you," she sputtered. "Looks like we'll have fun."

A chandelier earring with black gems grazed Adara's pale shoulder as she leaned closer. "I'm sure you and your friends will have a wonderful time. Enjoy."

With trembling fingers, Jancie grabbed her ticket from the girl and joined her friends.

Lizbeth gathered them together. "So let's make a plan."

"I want dinner." Willow rubbed her stomach. "I'm starved. I didn't eat much today so that I could sample everything."

"Jancie, you're the one with the agenda. What do you want to do first?" Rachelle looked her way while fluffing wrinkles from the back of her long, tiered skirt. Rather than her standard loose-fitting peasant tops, she wore a close ribbed camisole that revealed more than it covered. She'd rimmed her eyes with black liner and gel gave a bit of spikiness to her hair. Her on-the-prowl look.

Jancie raised a brow. She wasn't the only one with an agenda. "Actually, my stomach's churning. I could use a little something to eat to steady my nerves before I look for Rowe."

Willow patted her shoulder. "Don't be nervous 'bout seeing your mom as a ghost. It'll feel good. I've heard that lots of people talk with ghosts."

"I'm fine with that." Jancie glanced back inside the ticket booth to make sure that Adara was still there and no closer. "It's just—" Jancie found the coven leader missing and choked on her words. She spun around and looked down the three paths leading from the main arch.

Rachelle stepped closer. "What's wrong? You look spooked."

"The coven leader I met last Wednesday gave me an evil look." Jancie pushed her hair behind her shoulders. "I'm fine. Let's get something to eat."

Rachelle nodded and linked her arm in Jancie's.

Willow took the lead and made a beeline for the food area. She faced her friends. "I need to try their sausage rolls so I can figure out how to make them. I want Dad to add them to our menu at the Fern." She stepped to the food stand, and the others three friends spread apart.

Minutes later, they gathered in the center of the path. Jancie and Rachelle pulled wads off a huge elephant ear, while Willow studied the cornmeal-encased pork. Lizbeth walked up with a bag of magic popcorn. "Check this out!" She fingered a few kernels that turned purple with her touch, then shoved them into her mouth. "Grape," she muttered through the mouthful. "There's more." She picked up another kernel which turned yellow. "Bet this one's cheese."

"Oh! I have to try some." Willow took a break from her sausage analysis and sampled the popcorn.

The others followed suit, and Jancie ended up with a rust-colored, peppery hot handful.

Half an hour later, with sticky fingers, they wound their way out of the food path's far end into the adult rides.

"Look at that one!" Willow hopped up and down. "It's new. I have to go on that one." Individual swings hung on cables from a central point on a main column. When the ride started, the swings swept out in a wide circle. The cables, a unique color for each swing, twisted and untwisted into an ever-changing pattern of complex braids.

"Ooh. Me too." Lizbeth clapped her hands together. "It's called the Celtic Plait. Maybe I can learn some new ways to braid my hair."

"What could you learn?" Rachelle replied. "You already braid that stuff a hundred ways. And we need to help Jancie first."

"You're right. I'm sorry. I forgot." Lizbeth faced Jancie. "Lead the way."

"I'm not sure where Rowe's tent is." Disoriented by the people milling everywhere, Jancie turned in place. "I think the readers are mixed throughout the rides." She pointed past the braiding swings. "Let's try this way. I see tents." She took hold of Rachelle's hand and snaked the group through the human maze.

Tents in richly colored satiny fabric dotted the spaces between rides. A line formed outside of an emerald green one decorated with heavy silver cording. A hand-lettered wooden sign above the doorway read 'Sibeal, the Soothsayer'.

With great difficulty, Jancie wound along the line for the favorite ride—Racing Serpents. A roller coaster race between two gigantic, golden live snakes. Riders sat in cars tied to the snakes' backs and undulated up and down as the serpents coiled at full speed following a winding, elevated wooden double track. She promised herself a ride, if she got through what she came for.

Rachelle yanked on Jancie's hand. "This way. I see Harley up ahead."

Heat prickled down the back of Jancie's neck as she followed her friend to a large red tent hung with glittering glass ornaments along its horizontal support. In ornate gold script, the sign read 'Arcane Aviary.'

Inside, at least a hundred folding chairs stood facing a three-sided stage. People filled half of the seating, and a sign on a tall easel showed a clock face indicating the next show time would be at seven o'clock. Jancie checked her phone. Five minutes.

She led her friends to places along a side aisle in case Harley followed and a quick escape would be needed. She leaned forward across their row. "Have any of you seen this before? How long does it take?"

Willow shrugged. "I'm always too busy eating or riding."

"Or chasing men," Rachelle added.

Lizbeth raised a hand. "I saw this with my parents when I was about ten. It's wonderful. I think it lasted about twenty minutes."

"That long? I need to find Rowe." Jancie blew out a sharp breath through her teeth and checked the door. "Maybe we can duck out earlier."

"Don't worry." Rachelle, seated next to Jancie, patted her hand. "We'll get you to him."

The female witch with the dark bobbed hair who Jancie had seen staring at her in the Fern Café walked along the aisle where she sat. Again, she seemed familiar, but Jancie couldn't place the connection. The familiarity seemed positive. On gut instinct, Jancie spun and faced the approaching woman. Her pulse rang in her ears as she asked, "Excuse me. I need to find the tent of the man who wears the moonstone. Do you know where that is?"

A wide smile covered the woman's petite face almost to her large pearl button earrings. "Of course. You're very close." She pointed a black gloved hand in the direction opposite from the Racing Serpent ride. "Turn left when you leave here. His tent is four more down on this side." Her brown eyes sparkled beneath horn-rimmed glasses. "You look familiar. I saw you in the Fern the other day. Do I know you?"

Jancie couldn't resist returning the warm smile, not only for the helpful directions but also because the woman seemed so caring and friendly. "I don't think so. But thank you for the directions. My name is Jancie." She stared into the woman's eyes, trying to remember some previous connection.

The woman held out a tiny, gloved hand. "I'm Cerise. It's nice to meet you, Jancie. I feel certain we've met in some way. Enjoy the show. Austan and his wife Zelma are amazing." She smiled and walked backstage through a side door.

Jancie made a mental note of that door as an alternate exit and wondered how she might have met Cerise before. Jancie faced Rachelle. "Did you hear that? Rowe's tent is only four down from here."

"Yes! We'll head straight there after the show," Rachelle's husky voice rose. "Lizbeth has been telling us about the bird show. If we have to hide out, I want to see it."

Harp music played, and Jancie settled back in her seat, glad to know that Rowe's tent was close. Something about Cerise's warmth made Jancie feel like things would somehow work out.

A woman in a dress of gauzy layers in every shade of blue bounded to the center of the stage. Her legs, clad in light blue tights, spread wide into aerial splits as she sailed to a graceful landing on the soft sole of her ballerina slippers. She curtsied to the audience. "Hello. Thank you all for visiting the Arcane Aviary. My name is Zelma. Allow me to introduce my husband and partner, Austan." She held her arm to the side of the stage and nodded.

The man wore a black, double-breasted sport coat over wide-legged pale blue trousers. He tipped his black fedora and bowed to the crowd's applause. "Thank you. You are in for a real treat. Now, I present our mysterious array of avians."

Zelma waved a graceful arm, and a spotlight hit a mirrored disco ball hanging from the tent's central peak.

With a single clap of Austan's hands, a flock of ten songbirds materialized, one from each finger. The birds flitted around the tent's ceiling, their plumage in bright shades of red, turquoise, salmon, lime, yellow, cobalt. Tweets and warbles blended into a happy melody.

Lizbeth leaned across Rachelle and said, "Look carefully at the birds. They're glass."

Jancie craned her neck to watch the closest sail past. Caught in pinpricks of light, the canary yellow bird gleamed with the opalescence of fine glass. She leaned across Rachelle. "How does it flap its wings?"

Lizbeth shrugged and grinned. "Magic."

Zelma pirouetted, and a golden frame of bars appeared behind her. She extended a hand in the air, and the birds sped to the perch.

Austan stepped to the side of the stage and returned with a molten orange ball of glass at the end of a blowpipe almost as long as he was tall. He twisted the pipe as he blew into it. The soft glass slowly took shape. A beaked head became visible. Wings spread to the sides and grew to what looked like more than a six-foot wingspan. Jancie sat of the edge of her seat, wondering how there could be enough glass to create the enormous bird.

The male witch paused for a breath and looked at the audience, his face red and shiny with sweat. He stepped nearer the edge of the stage, and people cheered for him to continue. He flashed a smile and blew into the pipe, creating the bird's tail. He filled his cheeks full of air and puffed into the tube, which set the bird free and gave it life. Or magical life. With one mighty flap, it soared above the heads of the crowd, taking on the colors of an eagle. Its white glass head scattered light in all directions.

Jancie clapped and cheered but couldn't hear her own noise over that from the people around her.

While the eagle glided in circles, Zelma spun again. She continued spinning, so fast that her dress of various blues blended into one hue. She lifted her arms, and a peacock formed in her spread hands. The crowd roared. She slowed to a gentle rotation and set the bird into flight. It made one close turn around the mirrored ball, then took center stage and displayed its fine glittering, glass plumage.

The couple continued creating birds, each in turn more amazing and spectacular, as if trying to best each other. In the finale, all the birds took to the ceiling and paraded in a circle.

Jancie enjoyed the show, but the moment the birds disappeared, she sat straight in her chair, ready to leave. When the couple turned to leave the stage, she pulled Rachelle with her into the aisle. Jancie looked back for Lizbeth and Willow, but they seemed fixed on cheering for an encore along with others. "I'm not staying any longer," Jancie said under her breath to Rachelle and wound through the slow-to-leave crowd.

"Liz!" Rachelle called back and pointed in the direction Cerise had described. "Catch up to us four tents down on this side."

Lizbeth nodded as Willow stepped over her knees to join the others.

Jancie took a step out of the tent and checked both directions along the path. No sign of Harley or Dad. She glanced at Rachelle and Willow. "All clear. Let's go."

The threesome twisted in and out of the packed walkway, dodging kids with sticky cotton candy and obese women. They passed a massive gold tent advertising a juggling performance. Walking traffic stopped them in front of a small purple tent with a sign showing a glowing crystal ball The sign "The Griever's Moonstone" hung high on a blue tent ahead. Jancie focused on that sign and tried to shut out the noise and chaos around her. The purple door flap lifted beside her. From inside, a beam of white light streamed onto her and broke her concentration.

From the instant she froze in that spotlight, things happened fast. Adara stepped from between tents and laughed at Jancie. "It looks like the crystal ball is searching for you. Hope you're having a good evening."

Before Jancie could answer, Harley's voice yelled from behind. "Jancie, wait up!"

She darted forward, wanting to dive into Rowe's tent before Harley reached her, as if just by stepping inside, she'd be safe. But hearing him shout at her again, she grabbed Rachelle's hand and changed course, slipping along the far side of the next tent. Only the long entrance to the Ferris wheel stood between her and Rowe's tent. Thankful the cuing line was packed with people, she moved behind the tent and faced her friends. "I'm going to duck low and cut across this line over to Rowe's tent. Can you wait for Harley and lead him another way?"

"Would love to." Rachelle's lips curled as she twisted her bracelets faster. "Anything for my bff."

"I'll go back a ways and make sure he sees me." Willow spun and sped away.

Jancie slunk down and aimed for the densest parts of the Ferris wheel's line. Squirming between bellies and backs, she reached the other side and heard Willow's shrill drawl.

"Lizbeth, we're over here. We're all cuttin' through here to the prize games."

Jancie followed the back of Rowe's tent to remain out of sight longer, then edged along the far side to the main path. She peeked out and, finding no threats, she zipped through the open flap.

Chapter Eight:
The Crystal Ball

ADARA STOOD beside the ticket taker, welcoming guests to the opening of Friday's carnival. Sensing a unique energy in the crowd, she jerked her arm away from where it rested on the desk. *Curiosity has brought the girl back.* She looked down the line and didn't see Jancie but felt the younger woman's presence.

Elaine, the high-school aged clerk, glanced over her shoulder at Adara. "Are you all right, High Priestess?"

Adara took a step back. "Yes. I'm quite fine." She waved a hand for the girl to resume her job and leaned against shelves along the back wall of the tiny booth reflecting upon her first brief encounter with Jancie.

The moonstone's magic had sparked for Jancie that day outside the gate. The idea the locket would open for her seemed possible, enough for Adara to be on high alert. If the moonstone responded to Jancie, nothing for the girl or Rowe would ever be the same. Good or bad, that girl would influence his life. Adara gnashed her teeth at the thought.

Rowe's rebuff of her advances the other night still stung. Even though he denied wanting her, she remained resolute to prove to him how right they were for each other. No one was going to interfere.

It had been exhilarating to remove Lenore from claiming Rowe, although Lenore's simple desire possessed no element of magic. The strength of the moonstone was another matter, posing a far greater challenge for Adara to overcome. Goosebumps rose along her skin as she thought of the challenge. If she could overpower the moonstone, no one would question her supremacy or reign as high priestess. They'd honor her as her mother was revered.

Blocking the moonstone's call to Jancie would be difficult, though Adara relished the test. However, if the locket opened, she didn't know whether or not she could break the centuries-old bond. She looked down and found herself fidgeting with her snake ring. *Stop that sign of weakness,* she scolded herself. *I'll win this challenge with grace.* The corners of her mouth lifted.

"I know that devious smile." Dearg, her familiar, lifted his wings from where he perched on the top shelf. "May I play?"

"Only if you can keep up," Adara quipped, her gaze fixed on the people filing past the window.

"Sweet! I'm in." The crow sidestepped to hang over her shoulder. "What's the low down?"

Jancie came into view, and Adara stretched over the upper counter to greet her. The girl flinched at the sight of her, and Adara's smile widened. Playing upon opponents' fear was always a good strategy. She leaned closer and held Jancie captive with eye contact until the girl's fingers trembled while she paid for her ticket.

Upon releasing Jancie, Adara exited the booth and wound behind tents to a point where she could watch the girl pass. A group of three girlfriends protected her. Or at least one did: a hippie Bohemian sort wearing a long, full skirt and armfuls of bracelets, stood close enough to protect. The other two gawked at carnival lights.

Adara glanced up at her crow perched on a nearby tent support. "We'll need to separate that group of four young women. I'm interested in the one with red hair."

"Hot doll." Dearg winged onto the path, then headed in the direction of the group.

"Get back here," Adara hissed under her breath. "You're drawing attention to me. One more exclamation like that, and you'll be back on graveyard patrol for the night."

"Take it easy, dollface. No one noticed." Dearg resettled on his perch.

"They're moving. Use your high vantage to see where they're going. I'll follow at the edge of the path until you circle back and direct me."

"Will do." The crow flapped above peoples' heads as they pushed along the crowded path. A few looked up and took pictures of him with their phones. They probably thought a harassing crow was part of the special effects.

Adara shook her head and chuckled. She worked her way from tent to tent, pausing to stand beside doors. She said hello to carnival-goers and then moved to the next tent, where she met Dearg.

"Heading over to the food area." He lifted off and across the path, and Adara followed.

At the path's edge, she paused, looking for a break in the traffic. To her pleasant surprise, people stopped to let her pass. She rewarded them with her gracious smile and elegant gait as she moved past to the other side. Too bad that feeling of majesty wore off when she darted between tents and wormed her way to gain a glimpse of Jancie's group.

Adara grew bored and restless while the women stuffed their faces for nearly half an hour. *The moonstone connection must be weaker than I expected.* She folded her arms and paced the rear of a tent. *I don't know whether to be relieved or upset. Overpowering the moonstone would have been a fine feather for my bonnet.*

"Patience, your Highness." Dearg eyed her from a lamppost. As her dancing fingers shot heat at the arching metal, he lifted one foot then the other before taking wing. "I think I'll do a fly-over and see if they've finished eating."

A few minutes later, he returned and circled above Adara. "Time to move on."

She shrugged, wondering whether this escapade could achieve what she wanted. "Which way?"

"Toward the rides. Seems normal. Is that supposed to be suspicious?"

She clenched her hands into fists. "It's about time she headed for Rowe's tent. Let's go."

The crow cackled and fell a few feet below the tent rail before he spread his wings. "Someone's horn-swaggled."

"You mocking piece of dung feathers." Angered by his insightful joke, Adara stormed off along the back alley with Dearg muttering apologies at her back. When she approached another public path to cross, again the crowd parted and formed her private walkway. She slowed her pace and savored the moment.

When she reached the far side, from some distance a man called, "Jancie, wait up!" She thought of Rowe, but the voice belonged to someone else.

Adara's head spun in the direction she'd heard the plea but was unable to determine who uttered it. She waited, hoping the man would repeat his request. Without luck, she listened intently to each man passing by. Hearing acuity was not among her exceptional talents as a witch. She turned toward one group, then the next, watching lips for movement. Frustrated, heat spread across her cheeks. *I'm as helpless as a commoner.* She clenched her jaw, determined to overcome the limitation.

A middle-aged couple stopped to thank her for her work with the carnival, and an idea sprang into Adara's mind.

She strolled into the middle of the path and turned to face the traffic moving into the ride area. She smiled and greeted every group, her gaze focused on the males. Every adult responded.

After addressing at least thirty groups, her plastered smile felt like it would soon drop off her face. She approached a set of three young men, one a well-built, curly-haired blond. Attracted to his good looks, she thrust out her hand. "As high priestess, I'd like to welcome you to the carnival."

He accepted. "Thanks, ma'am."

Adara's lips parted. That voice. He was the one. She gripped his hand tighter while casting a charm on him through her focus amulet, the marcasite snake ring. "Be sure to go on Racing Serpents. We've improved the snakes this year to actually hiss and nip at each other to make the ride even more exciting." She rambled in order to buy time for the charm to transfer.

"Cool." He responded with a flat tone and looked at her with an unblinking stare.

"Come on, Harley. Let's go," one of the other guys urged. "Jancie and her friends turned left up ahead. Them girls are hot."

"Jancie. Oh, yeah. She's a babe," Harley replied.

The mention of the girl's name enacted Adara's spell. Instead of following the girl from a distance like a puppy, pleading with her to wait, he would now stalk her like a panther. His mission: keep Jancie away from other males.

Adara released his hand. "If you'd like to cut in front at Racing Serpents, I'd be glad—"

"No, thanks." Harley's glassy eyes fixed on the path ahead. "I have someone I need to find right away."

"Okay, then." Adara motioned them forward with a wide smile. "Have a wonderful rest of your evening." She moved to the side and watched Harley zip through the crowd, his friends struggling to keep pace.

In the back alley, she located her crow and shot him a satisfied grin. "Well, our job just got a lot easier. But let's enjoy watching the fun."

"Carnivals are all about fun, even for witches." He extended his wings and flew near her shoulder as they wound their way to Rowe's tent.

At the edge of the pathway, Adara found no sign of either Jancie or Harley or their energies in the immediate area. She wondered whether her spell caused Harley to corner Jancie already or if the moonstone even called to the girl. Adara's long nails dug into her palms. Her palm! That was the key.

She darted into the crystal ball reader's tent just two down from Rowe's.

Lumena sat with her bare, gnarled fingers spread over the crystal ball, conducting a reading for a young couple with a small boy. Inside the ball, white smoke swirled, indicating the process had just begun. The reader glanced up at Adara. "Welcome, high priestess. It is an honor." Lumena's shoulder-length iron gray hair stuck out like stiff straw in all directions. Yet her dress of black-flowered sheer cotton lawn fabric with a white lace collar softened her look. Her fingers and wrists, kept bare for her style of channeling, contrasted with half a dozen amulets decorating her neckline, along with swinging chandelier earrings dangling from her wrinkled earlobes. In equal contrast, her face was bare of make-up save for vivid pink lips. Lumena was all about opposites, in appearance as well as personality. Adara would need to be careful what she said to Lumena.

The crystal ball displayed an image of the couple where the woman was pregnant, the little boy playing at their feet. The woman clasped her hands together and let out a squeal. They thanked the reader, and the man handed her a bill as Lumena showed them to the door. She lowered the flap and faced Adara with a smile. "What may I help you with?"

Not wanting to whisper and draw suspicion, Adara took a determined step closer. "I need you to predict what will happen tonight to a young man I put a spell on."

"Mortal or witch?"

"Mortal."

Lumena lips formed a pink "o", and she tilted her head. "All right." She slid behind the orb and took a seat.

Adara took one of the four chairs set out for patrons and studied her right palm. "This is the hand I used to convey the charm. I assume it still has traces of his energy."

"It should, along with your own of course." The old witch extended her hand. "Let me have a look." She cradled Adara's hand from beneath, avoiding the palm. She gently placed it on the glass, framed by her own. She closed her eyes, and her orchid lips moved with an inaudible chant.

Fearful of what secrets would be exposed about her own life, Adara focused her mind on Harley. She didn't know whether that would block transmission of her personal history or not, but most readings worked on joint channeling. A bead of perspiration formed along her upper lip.

Lumena's eyes shot open, and she hunched over the sphere. As her experienced fingers caressed the glass, teasing the swirls of smoke, they changed from white to gray to steely blue. "Is the young man's name Harley?"

"Yes, it is." Adara leaned in, unsuccessful in her attempt to make out what the reader saw.

"He is strong and young, in his mid-twenties." Lumena's voice grew deep and flat. "He pursues a woman named Jancie, his ex-girlfriend. She left him, and he wants her back. But I see more." She traced a fingertip around the outline of Adara's hand.

Adara's mind drifted with the smoke's undulations. *So that's how Harley and Jancie are connected. Useful information to file away.*

The smoke changed to a midnight blue, and Lumena closed one of her hands into a fist. Her action gathered the inky darkness into a small region. She arched a shaggy gray brow and glanced at Adara. "That is your essence. I did my best to not look, but dare I say, danger surrounds you. Some by your own calling. Be careful with your wisdom."

Adara shifted in her seat. "I advise that you keep to the request I put upon you. Nothing more."

Lumena pursed her lips into a thin line. The contained darkness fell to the bottom, and white smoke filled the ball again. The wisps thinned to reveal an image of Jancie stepping inside Rowe's tent, and a moment later the door flap closed. At the sight, a gasp escaped Adara's lips.

Lumena teased a side of the image to show a second image connected by a smokeless tube.

In that vision, Harley wore the same green t-shirt as when Adara charmed him. His jaw was set, and his drawn face caused his eyes to bulge beneath lowered brows. The picture widened to reveal him running and darting, arms wide to keep his balance as he twisted and changed directions. At times, his head turned back and forth, eyes scanning.

"He's searching for her. Jancie. So wild, like a hungry animal. Is that your spell? Peculiar, since he already wants her back." The reader shot Adara a questioning glance.

"It is." Adara responded without giving explanation.

"His desire to possess her is maniacal. Dangerous," the reader's voice became shrill.

"I didn't know of their relationship, or that he wanted her back. That must have intensified the spell." Adara bit her lip for being played by the crafty old witch to reveal more than she intended.

"Indeed." Lumena dragged fingernails along the images' edges. "I assume you want to find him to remove your spell?" The old witch regarded her with piercing, narrowed eyes.

"Of course," Adara replied in a neutral tone to placate the interfering hag, but didn't plan to take action on her words. She didn't want anyone to be harmed, at least not for the present. But seeing her spell make Harley so dedicated to her purpose, power surged through her veins.

The moment the reader succeeded in expanding the views, the entire inner ball became pitch black. Lumena's body fell back, slumped against her chair.

Adara moved to the old witch. "Are you all right?" She lifted Lumena's limp hand, which the reader jerked free.

"Do not touch me with your darkness," she spat at Adara.

Adara wondered what might have happened. She considered the moonstone's magic. Jancie would reach Rowe. Could the moonstone somehow block this reading device? And why?

"Only once before has my ball dropped into total black." Lumena spoke in a whisper. "When evil happened, and your older sister Fia was sent away."

Adara laughed. "My sister's own magic gifts caused her to go insane, knowing the fate of those she loved but not soon enough to protect them from harm. No evil chased her away. She asked to leave us so she would have some peace of mind."

Lumena shook her head, her eyes set on Adara.

"Will Harley find Jancie?"

"I didn't see, but I hope for her sake that he doesn't," the reader responded with a scolding tone.

Adara cupped a hand around her father's onyx pendant to gain his strength and make her words more convincing. "In that case, will you help me find her so I can protect the girl?"

Lumena stared at Adara. "Tell me more."

"We know Jancie will reach Rowe's tent. Can your crystal ball reverse its action and be used as a signal? Like a beacon, to shine on her when she walks past your tent to reach his? That way I can physically stand between her and Harley and break my spell quicker."

The reader nodded and struggled to drape her body over the orb. "I'll do that much, and only once. After that, I wash my hands of your troubles. I will not allow your darkness to follow me home."

Chapter Nine:
The Griever's Moonstone

ROWE SAT BEHIND THE OAK PARLOR TABLE laid with fine antique linens crocheted by Charlotte Oatley, the wife of the moonstone locket's creator, Jude Oatley. The table runners, normally kept in careful storage, were handed down to successive bearers of the enchanted jewel for its public display. Despite continual wear for over two hundred years, the pendant had withstood the test of time better than the yellowed crochet pieces. While Busby dozed at the top of a brass coat stand in the corner, Rowe leaned back from the table and studied the intricate threads. He wondered how the lady's plight and the magic may have been woven into her handwork.

Only his second year serving as the bearer of the griever's moonstone, his role at these public events still seemed unfamiliar. He gazed around the tent, which had been decorated by the coven council. The walls were hung with clear and milky quartz crystals. They radiated soft light from the fringed ivory shades of vintage brass floor lamps in each corner. A Turkish wool rug laid over a protective plastic tarp covered the floor. At least those items reminded Rowe of typical décor in the more well-to-do coven homes like his own. They seemed familiar and benign compared to the questionable potential of Charlotte's linens and Jude's locket.

Not far from his tent, Rowe sensed a tangled web of intense energies. He sat straighter, watching those passing his open door flap, but those milling past seemed unaffected. He heard no shouts or warning cries in any direction.

He rose to investigate, looking outside both ways along the path. Only happy carnival-goers passed. Some meandered while examining the light displays crowning each tent and ride entrance. Others wove between slower-moving groups, intent on specific destinations.

Few folks this evening had been curious enough about Rowe's special psychic offering to peer through the doorway or step inside his tent. One middle-school aged girl had coaxed her mother to make Rowe tell the moonstone tale. When the gem failed to react, the girl seemed unimpressed, as though she expected something spectacular to happen since she'd just lost her pet cat. During his year and a half in charge of the moonstone, he'd told the story dozens of times always with the same result. Nothing. In fact, all written records of the moonstone locket opening happened before his or even his parents' lifetimes.

When the mysterious energy disturbance faded, Rowe stepped back inside. The moment he turned to retake his seat, Jancie darted inside and stood anxiously on the Turkish carpet.

Busby jerked his wings open and lifted a foot off his perch.

Jancie's chest rose with deep, rapid inhalations. Wisps of her red hair caught the lamp light and formed a golden halo around her head.

"Jancie." He smiled and extended a hand to steady her. "I'm glad you returned. Are you okay?"

"Yes. I am. I really want to talk to my mother."

"Wonderful. Please have a seat." He motioned to the chair opposite his. "I saw you yesterday around noon with a girlfriend walking toward the carnival. When a man stopped you and you turned around, I worried. Is everything all right?"

She looked away and sat down, her tone matter-of-fact. "Just my father. Nothing I can't handle."

Rowe's brows pulled together, but he didn't press her for more information. "Make yourself comfortable while I close the door so we aren't disturbed."

The previous unsettling energies and Jancie's uneasiness about her father made Rowe tie the flap closed and secure it with a spell. He returned to his seat.

Busby took a new perch, his talons clamped on the back of the chair beside Jancie, and she gave a start.

Rowe grinned. "This little barn owl is my familiar."

"Oh." She leaned away and eyed the bird with caution.

"He won't hurt you. His name is Busby." Rowe addressed his familiar. "Please speak to Jancie to reassure her."

"Hello, Miss Jancie." The owl lifted a wing tip in her direction.

Jancie gripped the seat of her chair and gave a weak smile. "Hi, Busby."

Rowe nodded to him. "Busby, if you remain there, be still and quiet during the story."

The owl resettled his perch. "I will, Master."

Rowe faced Jancie. "Let me repeat some things I said before to be sure you understand the magic of the griever's moonstone. If the stone's energy connects with you, it will cause the locket to open. At that time, you may see or hear the presence of your departed mother and be able to communicate with her."

Jancie scooted to the edge of her seat.

"Strong magic always comes with a price." The moonstone had sparked twice before in Jancie's presence, and Rowe believed there was a chance it might open for her. He felt compelled to warn her about what little he knew of the consequences. Usually he took for granted the locket wouldn't open and was lax about giving cautions, unless for theatrical effects. "If the locket opens and connects you to your mother, like I said before, there will be consequences, good or bad. This is not magic I can predict or control. I am only the appointed bearer of the gem, the teller of the tale because I too recently lost a loved one."

"Oh, I'm so sorry. Who?" Her hazel eyes found his and softened.

Rowe closed his eyes and focused on a vision of Edme, then looked at Jancie. "My wife and our unborn child."

Jancie shook her head. "How horrible to lose them both. Have you used the moonstone to speak to her?"

"I have been able to make contact, but not through the gem."

She smiled. "I'm glad you had that chance."

He nodded and removed his hat to lift the pendant from his neck. "Again, there will be an unknown price if the locket opens. Are you okay with that risk?" He restated the question as much for himself as for her. His life would also be changed by triggering the enchanted gem. According to what he'd been told, if the locket opened, the moonstone's magic would repair his heart, helping him to find another to fill the void. But, as he reminded her, strong magic comes with an equal price. The path to happiness could drag him through a lot of pain. That journey could be long, and Jancie might only be a person who would lead him to his new love. He was more than ready to replace grief with love, but doubted whether he could endure more pain.

Jancie tucked loose strands of hair behind her ears and sat straighter. "Yes, I'm ready for whatever happens. I need to say goodbye."

He swallowed hard and reached a hand across the table. "Please give me your hand." Cradling the back of her hand, he placed the moonstone into hers. The oblong milky gem, nearly an inch wide and an inch and a half long, covered most of her palm. He glanced at her, then looked at gem. "This locket was made in 1850 by Jude Oatley, a witch who lost his wife, Charlotte, to tuberculosis. While I tell his tale, keep your eyes on the stone." Rowe cleared his throat. "Jude and Charlotte had a tremendous love. Jude placed the essence of that love inside this gem. They lived in a small village outside of Albany, New York. As part of his trade as a silversmith, he often traveled great distances from home to meet the train and exchange his wares for sale in the city. Other times, he rode by horseback for days into Quebec to trade with Indian tribes for raw semi-precious gemstones. On these long trips, the enchanted moonstone allowed Jude to carry Charlotte's love with him."

As if on cue, the moonstone in Jancie's hand shined a brilliant blue. She gave a start, and her eyes widened but remained fixed on the gem.

Rowe cupped the back of her hand more tightly.

Busby's white face reflected the blue color, his huge black eyes steady on the gem.

They leaned farther over the table, and Rowe continued. "It gave him real comfort both while she lived and after she died. Her loving face appeared to him, and she offered her support."

"Eventually wanting to move past his grief, Jude put the moonstone away. Several years later, when he found it in himself to go though and give away Charlotte's things, he rediscovered the enchanted stone. When he held it, the locket opened and guided him to find the purity of her love in another woman."

Rapid-fire flashes from the moonstone reflected off Jancie's eyes.

Their joined hands grew warmer, and Rowe worked to keep his voice steady. "I feel the magic strengthening in your hand. Are you certain that you want to continue?"

Jancie nodded, met his gaze, then looked back to the gem. "Yes, go on."

A trickle of sweat ran down the nape of Rowe's neck. "Decades later, as an elderly man with a large family, Jude looked back on his life with gratitude and recast the moonstone's spell, so that it could be used by other witches burdened with grief, to help themselves as well as others."

The moonstone flashed faster until its surface shined a constant opalescent blue. And then, the rose-gold clasp which secured the locket sprang, and Jancie gasped.

Rowe took a deep breath as the locket slowly opened. A black and white photograph of who he presumed to be Charlotte Oatley came into view.

Jancie's hand shook, and he wrapped his fingers around the edges of hers to steady her.

Busby leaned so far forward, Rowe feared he'd fall.

The carnival noises outside the tent faded.

"Everything went quiet, but that's all." Jancie's voice faltered. "How will my mother appear?" She asked, without taking her eyes off the open locket.

"I don't know." He steadied their hands with his other. "It hasn't opened in generations. Keep watching."

Her shallow, irregular breathing and his own rapid pulse pounding in his ears were the only sounds he heard for what seemed like several minutes.

Finally, a faint glow formed around the edge of the portrait. It grew more pronounced, then expanded into the air above the locket. They followed the white vapor as it rose. An amorphous shape of light filled the space over their heads.

Busby's wingtips fluttered at his sides, but otherwise he remained collected, which made Rowe proud of his familiar-in-training's restraint.

"Mom?" Jancie sputtered.

The formless mass responded and twisted into the shape of a human figure, a woman with long hair at her shoulders.

"Mom! It's me. Jancie." Her hand shook so much that Rowe gripped it hard, fearing if the locket slipped out, the connection might break.

The image grew more detailed with definite facial features, high cheekbones and a pointed chin, like Jancie's.

"Is that you, Mom?" Jancie begged.

The diaphanous woman reached a white hand down. "Yes, Jancie. It's Mom. I've missed you, sweetie." Her gentle voice spread over them with the comfort of a warm quilt.

Rowe stared in awe at the woman's spirit. Sensing their intense love, his heart swelled. He'd helped them connect. He was grateful for his continued communication with Edme after her death. He wondered why he was able to see and hear Jancie's mother, but was overcome being a part of their special moment.

Jancie reached her free hand up to clasp her mother's. "Oh Mom, I love you and miss you too."

The white fingers laced between Jancie's. "I know it's hard to be apart, but you have a good life ahead. I want you to live that life and be happy."

Tears streamed down Jancie's cheeks. "I will, Mom. But I'll still miss you. I'll never forget."

"I know you won't, sweetie. And neither will I." A wide smile formed on her mother's pale face, and her voice cracked as she continued. "I saw you tending my garden. Thank you, sweetie."

"You knew I did that?" Jancie's mouth curled into a smile that matched her mother's.

"I sure did. Even saw how you transplanted the mint shoots." Her mother's smiling face radiated light in all directions. "Remember this: move the seeds with you wherever you go, and we'll always be together."

"I felt you in the garden too, Mom. And I'll always keep it for you." Jancie's voice faltered, choked on tears.

"I have to go, sweetie. But I'll be with you. Happiness will come to you, Jancie." The features on her face dimmed.

"Mom! Goodbye, Mom. I love you," Jancie cried, her grasp tightening through the disappearing hand.

"I love you too, Jancie." Her mother's voice trailed away as the image faded into the original formless vapor. "I always will." Her last words were almost inaudible.

The white light returned to swirl around the locket's inner rim, then extinguished. The lid remained open in Jancie's palm.

"Thank you so much," she said to Rowe through sniffles. "That meant everything to me." She touched his free hand with her own.

Seeing her gratitude and happiness, moisture seeped into Rowe's eyes. "I'm glad I could help you. That was incredible."

"I could see her face and everything. I felt her hold my hand." Jancie's excitement spilled out like a trickling brook. "And she knew I'd tended her garden just this weekend. She's with me!"

"It was amazing. I've never witnessed a spirit presence that clear. And never channeled a ghost myself."

"Why is the locket still open?" she asked.

He glanced down. "Don't move your hand. Its job isn't finished. It will exact the price, whatever that might be."

Upon Rowe's direction to Jancie, the owl clamped his relaxed wings back against his sides.

Jancie shot Rowe a questioning glance, then she looked deeper into his eyes, and her brows calmed.

Her gaze held Rowe, like she'd worked a spell on him. He flinched and attempted to look away, but a powerful energy, coming from the open locket, controlled his attention. After an uncomfortable minute, he stopped resisting. While he looked at Jancie's face, he saw a strong woman with an enormous ability to care for others. He saw not only her gorgeous red-gold hair and sparkling hazel eyes, but a complex, inner beauty. A fascinating young woman, with a purity as delicate and amazing as a rose.

Her lips parted, like opening petals. "What did the moonstone do for you?"

"Well," he began, unsure how to answer. "According to the legend, when the moonstone responds, I'll be freed of my grief." He studied her eyes. They glinted and crinkled at the outer corners with her smile. He returned her smile. Her joy brought a surprising sense of peace throughout his body. Until released, the stress carried by hundreds of small muscles for so long hadn't registered.

"From the look on your face, I'm guessing it worked." Her free hand cradled his.

"Yes, somehow it did." His fingers entwined with hers, the open locket resting in the bed of their joined hands.

"That's wonderful. I'm so glad something good happened for you too." She pursed her lips. "But you said there'd be a price for this magic. I don't see anything wrong or difficult."

"There is a prophecy: the person who can channel the moonstone's energy and open the locket is the one who takes away my grief. In a way we may not understand, you will help me, directly or indirectly, fill the void left by my loss."

Jancie tilted her head to one side. "Hmm. I don't feel any burden." She paused, then shrugged. "You've helped me so much, I can't even find words to thank you. Helping you in turn only seems right."

The still locket came to life pulsing with blue light that emanated from the moonstone beneath.

"What's happening?" Jancie clasped his hands tighter.

Before Rowe could respond, blue swirled around Charlotte's photo again. "No idea." He leaned forward, ready to protect her from any fierce repercussion.

Rowe's familiar mirrored his actions and crouched with wings poised to fly.

Light overflowed and spilled onto the necklace's chain, forming a circle. Once complete, the chain lifted into the air above Jancie's head and settled around her neck. The open locket touched her skin and closed.

"What does this mean?" she asked.

Crowd noises from outside the tent reached Rowe again. "I expect the locket will remain with you until you complete its price. How do you feel? Any different?"

"No. I don't feel anything. Just thrilled that I saw Mom." She lifted her purse into her lap. "I'll write down my phone number so we can keep in touch for me to help you." She scribbled onto a small pad of paper.

Rowe pulled a business card and pen from his inner jacket pocket and wrote his home number on the back. They exchanged information, and he directed, "Be sure to keep that pendant hidden from view as much as possible. If people find out what it is, they may be fearful of the unknown." He paused and watched her, uneasy about whether that knowledge might frighten her.

She tucked it inside her blouse and grinned. "Easy enough since the chain is long."

"You aren't afraid to wear it?"

She held her head high and looked him square in the eye. "No. It helped me and will help you. And Mom said I'd have a happy life. I believe in that."

Rowe marveled at her strength, her ability to trust in goodness. A pure spirit. *She's the one chosen to help me, and I vow to protect her.*

A recognizable witch's energy passing the front wall of his tent broke his thoughts. Adara.

Busby sailed around the tent's ceiling, leaving a pale golden trail of protective magic. Rowe marveled at how the familiar was learning to read his own reactions and take action.

Rowe feared for how the moonstone may have marked Jancie. Being connected to him could make her a visible target for the jealous high priestess. His jaw tensed. "Jancie, before you entered my tent did you have any interaction with the coven leader Adara, who I introduced you to earlier?"

Jancie squirmed in her seat and checked the tent's door. "On my way here, when I passed the crystal ball tent, the flap opened, and a beam of white light shined on me. Just me and no one else. Right then, Adara appeared. She passed the odd incident off, but her laugh made me nervous. I knew she was lying. That light on me was no accident."

His brow lifted. "What happened after that?" He cursed himself for being a step behind Adara. She'd seen the moonstone flash for Jancie that day outside the carnival. Adara must have assumed it would open. She, of course, trailed the girl to his tent and may have set a spell on Jancie already. He swallowed hard.

"My ex-boyfriend Harley wants me back. He spotted me, so I split from my friends. They acted as decoys to lure him away from me so I could get here."

"Does Harley have a dangerous temper?" Rowe asked. "An aggressive sort?"

Jancie let out a laugh. "No, he's more of a nuisance. Won't take no for an answer."

Rowe's shoulders relaxed a bit. "Now that you've connected to the moonstone's energy, it marks you. Stay clear of the coven leader."

Jancie lifted the chain partially off of her neck.

"That won't make any difference." He lifted a palm. "When you connect to the energy of any enchanted stone, you're marked whether or not you have it with you."

"What does the coven leader want from me?" Jancie ran a finger across the gem now resting on her chest. "The moonstone's energy?"

He shook his head. "No. She wants me and will hurt any woman I'm with." He sighed, unsure how to explain what he didn't understand himself. "Kind of like how Harley chases you, but I never dated her. In fact, I really dislike Adara."

Jancie nodded and sighed.

"The problem is, Adara may hurt people who are in her way." Rowe took Jancie's hand. "I won't allow her to hurt you. We need to get you out of the carnival." That was an urgent first step, but he knew he'd need to protect her at home and wherever she went in the days to come. Vika could help with stronger protection spells than he could do alone.

"What about later, at home or my work at the bank?" Jancie's eyes widened. "Will she look for me there? What can she do to me?"

"Her goal will be to keep you and me apart. The less she sees us together, the better. I'll explain more later. Right now, we have to get you out of here. Do you have plans to meet your friends somewhere?"

"Not really. Although we talked about going on the Racing Serpent after I met with you." She opened her purse and pulled out her phone. "We did agree to connect with texts if we got separated." She opened her messages. "They did send me one: Lost Harley in Fun House. Heading to Serpents. Meet us there."

"Good." Rowe stood and motioned to the door. "We'll find your friends there, and I'll escort you all out. Or I'll take you home, if they don't want to leave."

Outside, he worked fast to tie the flap, set a protection on it, then hurried Jancie to the back alley with his owl flying close. They wound through the close corridor, picking their way in dim light over electrical cables and tent supports. Behind the Arcane Aviary's large tent, he took her hand to help her over the dark hazards. He guided them into the backstage area of the marionette theater, quiet between shows save for the elderly couple who ran the act. The door on the tent's opposite wall offered a view of the serpent ride.

Jancie paused to check her phone. "No new texts. I got the last one fifteen minutes ago."

Rowe partially lifted the flap. "Peek out to look for them."

She crouched and looked through the slit. "They aren't in line. Maybe they're on the ride." She moved to get a different view and watched for a few minutes.

Rowe checked for traces of Adara's energy, and was relieved to find none. Either she couldn't identify Jancie's friends, or she'd cloaked her powers. He hoped for the former.

"They just came off the ride." She moved under the door canvas, but Rowe's arm caught her elbow.

"Wait here." He moved past her. "I'll bring them back here where it's safer. Point me to them."

She extended an arm. "That group of three. Rachelle has the long skirt on, Willow has white-blonde hair, and Lizbeth has the long dark hair."

"Busby, stay here and keep Jancie safe."

"You can rely on me, Master." The owl puffed his feathers, trailed a thin protective veil around her, and took a lookout spot on the outer support pole above the door.

Rowe stepped out and noticed Rachelle typing on her phone while the other two stood by. He darted around the end of a low barricade and approached them. "Rachelle, Willow, Lizbeth, I'm Rowe. Jancie is nearby. Please come with me. I'll take you to her."

"Is she safe?" Rachelle asked with a husky voice, eyes wide.

He nodded and motioned for them to join him.

The women looked at each other, then Rachelle led the way after him.

Back inside the marionette tent, she hugged Jancie. "Are you okay?"

"I'm fine, and I saw Mom." Jancie clung to her friend's forearms. "She held my hand and talked with me."

"Awesome!" Rachelle replied and hugged Jancie tighter.

Willow squealed so much that Rowe feared they'd be discovered.

He heard shuffling, as if someone moved toward their location. He put a finger to his lips and touched the bouncing blonde's shoulder.

A curtain moved aside, and Logan's head of golden wavy hair appeared. "What the heck? Rowe, what are you doing here?" He stepped out and called over his shoulder. "Miss Selma, everything's okay. It's only Rowe."

"How nice. Hello to you, Rowe," the sweet, pitchy voice of the old woman replied from the other side of the curtain.

"Hello, Miss Selma," Rowe called out.

"Logan, this is Jancie and her friends Rachelle, Willow, and Lizbeth." Rowe gestured toward each. "Logan is a good friend of mine. Jancie and I hid here to collect her friends from the serpent ride. We need to get her out of the carnival right away."

"The moonstone responded?" Logan's blue eyes flashed in the light of the bare ceiling bulb.

Rowe nodded.

"That's great!" Logan glanced from Rowe to Jancie. "I can help get them out."

"Me too, Master!" Busby flew between them to land on a packing crate. "I want to help too."

"Whoa!" Willow spun around, her gaze following him. "That owl can talk."

Lizbeth stepped closer to Busby. "That's not so strange. Witches often take familiars who they command to do magic on their behalf. The old lady from the coven who frequents the library tells me about her raccoon familiar who just had a litter of babies."

"That must be Hetta. I've been helping her with them, hoping to adopt one for my own familiar." Logan grinned at the little owl and continued to Rowe. "I take long breaks to check on the elderly readers. I can be away from my tent without being noticed." He moved closer to Rowe and lowered his voice. "What's the danger? Adara?"

"Yes. She talked Lumena into shining her crystal ball onto Jancie when she walked past."

Logan shook his head. "Can't be good."

The women glanced at Jancie, eyes wide, and Rachelle squeezed her hand.

"Isn't Adara the high priestess?" Lizbeth fiddled with the end of a small braid at the side of her face.

Jancie nodded. "The moonstone's energy marks me." She pulled the gem out from the neckline of her blouse.

"She's powerful." Lizbeth held the locket away from her friend's neck and examined it. "What does she want? That energy to make her more powerful?"

"No. She wants Rowe," Jancie replied. "The moonstone connects me to him."

Logan shook his head, and the three women shot Jancie curious looks. Rachelle wrapped an arm around her shoulder.

"You guys don't need to leave with me unless you want to." Jancie looked at each of her friends. "Rowe can take me home."

"I'm not leaving you," Rachelle replied. "Are you crazy?"

Logan eyed Rowe. "You'd be gone from your tent for close to an hour? Adara watches you like a—"

"She would get suspicious, but I won't risk keeping Jancie here." Rowe's tone grew stern. "You know the risk is too great."

"I can take you home, Jancie," Logan replied.

"Thank you, but I'm going home with Rachelle." Jancie nodded to the friend at her side.

"Good." Rowe lifted a forearm, signaling his owl to perch. "Logan or I will help if needed though."

"Willow and Lizbeth, are you leaving with us?" Jancie asked.

"I didn't get to go on the Celtic Braid." Willow shifted her weight to one hip.

Lizbeth lifted her chin. "Well, I'm going with Jancie. Sneaking out from under the nose of the high priestess sounds more exciting."

"Will that Adara woman try to hurt us too?" Willow's huge blue eyes popped out.

"We'll keep you all safe," Rowe replied.

Willow crossed her thin arms over her flat chest. "Guess I'll go too then."

"I'll get you all out via the rear gate. " Rowe took a step in the direction of the alley door. "This way."

"I'll follow the group and keep watch," Logan said to him.

"Okay, you three ladies surround Jancie best you can. Busby, stay high and look through the crowd for approaching danger." Rowe lifted the tent flap and led them out.

The group squeezed along the alley and crossed one path without trouble. Three more crossings lay between them and the coven member's gate. Rowe chose to avoid the main entrance. The darker back exit would provide more cover and be closer to the parking lot. Halfway across the second path, Rowe locked eyes with Sibeal, Adara's close friend. The psychic stopped and watched the entourage pass. Rowe's pulse quickened, and he took Jancie's hand as they walked behind the tents.

Before attempting the next path in the arcade area, he paused to secure Jancie among her friends. He waited until the traffic grew thick then wound them through the dense crowd.

Above the din of voices, Busby let out a loud squawk.

With one foot off the asphalt walk, Rowe spun and looked back. He sensed Adara's presence, forceful and determined.

A strong young man with curly blond hair pushed through the crowd toward them, toppling a few teenage boys to the ground.

Rowe unlatched his pocket watch and held it in his palm.

The man made a straight line to the four women, leading with his wide chest. He bared fang-like white teeth and called Jancie's name with a growling voice. His face was distorted into a frightening grimace with the skin pulled taut. Adara's energy cloaked him in a nefarious spell, leaving Rowe only one option.

He hurled his watch across the few yards separating him from the group of women. The timepiece zipped through the air in a blue-white bolt.

The man grabbed Willow's shoulder and pulled her away from Jancie like a tissue.

Rowe's watch hit square on the man's arm, and he let out a yelp while writhing with a hand clamped over the injury.

Rowe ran back and grabbed Jancie's shaking hand, while Logan lifted Willow to her feet. The watch came back to Rowe's pocket, and the group stumbled into the dark alleyway ahead. Rowe darted into the shadows of a large tent and stopped for the others to catch up.

Rowe's owl landed on his outstretched forearm. "Good eye, Busby." He stroked the familiar's brown neck feathers with his free hand.

"What was that about?" Jancie sucked in a deep breath. "Harley never acts like that."

"Adara must have charmed him," Rowe replied.

"He looked more like an animal than a man." Rachelle put a hand on Jancie's back.

She shivered at her friend's touch. "His teeth looked like fangs, and his pupils were yellow slits." Jancie faced Willow. "Are you all right?"

Willow nodded while straining to see her palm. "My hand is scraped up and my wrist hurts."

"Let me have a look." Lizbeth ran her fingers along the wrist. "The bones are aligned correctly. Probably a bad sprain. I'll get the first aid kit out when we get home."

"Rowe, do you have a plan?" Logan scanned the surrounding shadows.

"I do." Rowe lifted his forearm to direct the owl toward a tent post, then gathered the women. "Ladies, I need you to give me something you have with you: a scarf, item of jewelry, business card, whatever personal item you're willing to part with. I'll return the items to you in your car."

Logan shot him a knowing smile. "Make it quick."

"Jancie, are you sure about this guy?" Willow leaned in. "He isn't some kind of thief?"

Jancie touched a thumb to the backside of her mother's ring and decided against that item. She dug in her purse and handed him her lipstick.

Rachelle yanked off a bangle and handed it to Rowe. "Willow, you can stay here and dodge the Harley-Cat if you like."

Lizbeth passed her library card down the line. "I can easily replace this."

Willow shrugged and handed over her recipe notes about the sausage roll she'd scribbled on the back of her ticket.

Rowe held the four items in outstretched hands. Blue-white light filled his palms. The items floated to positions beside each woman, sparked with his energy, and transformed into clones of their owners.

The women stared at their duplicates, transfixed.

He whirled his fingers in the air, and the clones ran back the way the group had traveled. "Those clones are high frequency animations I created from your personal items. My magical specialty. When you reach your car, the clones will disappear. The items will reappear inside your car. You may now walk out of the carnival with little or no notice."

He pulled a handkerchief from his pocket and wiped the

sweat from his brow. High frequency animations were taxing, especially four at once. He took a deep breath and led them along the alley.

Jancie found his hand. "Thank you. That was amazing."

The touch of her hand made him feel rested and comforted. He glanced at her, bewildered. It normally took a night's sleep to renew from that much animation. He wondered what she possessed that restored him. He lifted their joined hands. "No. You are amazing."

They traveled through the gate to Rachelle's car without incident, although Rowe's barn owl insisted on keeping a high lookout in flight.

Rowe and Logan secured the women in their car, where they all found their personal items except Rachelle.

Rowe promised to find her bracelet and set a protective spell on the Chrysler's doors.

"Is that normal for animation items to get lost?" Logan asked him on their walk back to the carnival.

"It's possible. That was a lot of animation at once." Rowe let out a sigh. "I was spent. What was really strange was when Jancie took hold of my hand afterward, somehow she almost completely renewed me."

"That is something. Normally don't you have to sleep it off?" Logan slapped his friend's back. "She might come in handy. Not as rough an outcome as you were expecting."

"Uh huh," Rowe said absently as his gaze followed a shadow darting between cars. He pointed to the movement. "Check that out."

Busby lifted higher from where he glided at Rowe's shoulder.

"Looks like just a dog or a bobcat," Logan replied.

"That's no dog." Rowe moved to see the animal pass under a security light.

Busby darted back, trembling.

Jancie's enchanted ex-boyfriend sprang from car to car in the direction of the main road.

Chapter Ten:
The Long Way Home

JANCIE PERCHED ON THE EDGE of the Chrysler's backseat as Rachelle drove through the maze of parked cars toward the exit of the carnival's lot. The girls remained quiet, checking in all directions.

Jancie steadied herself with a hand on the back of the driver's seat. Jittery, like she'd had too much coffee, her body felt exhausted although her mind raced. So much had happened in the last few hours that she couldn't process it all. Seeing and talking with her mother brought Jancie peace and resolution, something she'd wanted the entire past six months.

New worries threaded into Jancie's thoughts. Harley now stalked her like a predator. She shivered. He'd even looked like some sort of fierce cat. The coven leader Adara was out to get her for a reason Jancie didn't fully understand. To Jancie, the moonstone simply connected her to Rowe so they could help each other. It was only fair for her to return his favor and help him get over his own grief. That didn't seem like enough to make Adara jealous. Rowe had warned her there would be a price for her connection to Mom's spirit. Were these strange troubles the price? Jancie couldn't help but think the problems with Adara and Harley were connected.

Jancie sank into the plush, velour seat and remembered her interaction with Mom: how she looked, her familiar voice, the warm touch of her hand. *How did she know that I tended her garden?* She hugged her arms around her chest. Mom watched out for her. Knowing that was worth any consequence. Jancie was glad she'd not listened to her dad's advice.

Rachelle turned the car onto the road that became Maple Street in town.

They slowed to a stop at the intersection of the next county road. A loud thud hit the rear end of the Chrysler. Jancie whirled around.

Hands clutched the antenna's base at the upper part of the trunk.

Jancie screamed.

Willow whipped around and her high-pitched squeal split Jancie's eardrums.

Harley's face plastered against the rear window. Vertical pupil slits glowed an eerie yellow-green in the dim light. His bared teeth seemed longer and more pointed. His ears protruded from thick, matted hair and pinned back like those of an angry dog.

"Oh shit!" Rachelle exclaimed and swerved the car.

Lizbeth hung over the back of her front seat, but Willow pushed her aside attempting unsuccessfully to crawl forward between the headrests.

Jancie leaned back and hit the glass near Harley's face hoping to startle him so he'd fall off. When her attempts failed, she screamed at him. "Harley, go away!"

"Never," he growled. "You're mine, Jancie."

She yelled, "Rachelle, swerve the car back and forth to throw him off."

"Geez, I don't want to kill him and go to jail." Rachelle's eyes shined in the rearview mirror. "Lizbeth, call the sheriff."

"I will but don't count on much." From the passenger side, Lizbeth punched buttons on her phone. "As a rule, they don't help with coven matters. The newspaper is always filled with sheriff visits about wild witch sightings. Always written off as a feral cat on the loose. Or a coon digging in a trash can."

Jancie rummaged for her own phone and Rowe's business card. She dialed the number he'd written on the back, hoping it was his cell. The number rang repeatedly without an answer. On the fifth ring, she bit her lip.

In the background, she heard Lizbeth talking to the sheriff's dispatcher. "A crazy man, Harley Hincks, jumped onto our trunk. He won't let go, and he's threatening to hurt us...at the carnival...four women. No, we didn't have any beers! Or flirt with any male witches. Or taunt any females. We're near the intersection of Maple and County Road 101. Please send some help right away."

Rowe's answering machine clicked on, and Jancie left a message. "Rowe, it's Jancie. Harley is attacking our car! He looks even wilder. We're freaking out. We're on Maple just past 101 going toward town. Please help."

"Everyone, fasten your seat belts," Rachelle cried. Once Jancie and Willow clicked their belts, she slammed on the brakes, sending Harley rolling over the roof, down the windshield, and onto the hood.

His fingers gripped the frame of the hood, and he snarled at Rachelle.

Jancie's pulse raced. "Hit the windshield washers."

Rachelle turned them on high speed. They scraped his knuckles leaving bloody streaks across the glass, but he clung on grimacing with bared fang-like teeth.

Willow wrapped her long arms around Jancie.

Rachelle swerved again, almost colliding with a big sycamore tree, and Harley lost one handhold. She made a sharp turn in the other direction, only to have him find his original grip with both hands. She started to crank the wheel in the opposite direction, and he slid down the curve of the trailing fender. "What the heck? I barely moved."

"Where'd he go?" Jancie cried and shoved Willow's arms and legs off of her. Twisting in circles to look through each window, Jancie expected him to come at her from any angle like some supernatural demon.

Twenty feet from their stopped car, his tall frame bent low, staggering.

"There he is, to the right by that big bush," Jancie directed." Rachelle, slow down. He looks injured. But we didn't throw him off, did we? Did any of you see what happened?"

Willow unlatched her seatbelt and jumped left into Jancie's lap.

Lizbeth plastered her face to the front passenger window." He just looks dazed, but his eyes aren't cat-like now. There's the deputy's car. This should get real interesting now."

Jancie climbed out from under Willow and edged up to the right window.

Harley's face appeared normal, although his hands were bloody, and he staggered like he was drunk. He shook himself as if trying to clear his head, a puzzled look on his face as he looked around.

Another person moved in the shadows beside the bush, a man with his arm extended toward Harley. The man's shoulders were wide, in a padded suit jacket. A dark fedora sat on his head. Jancie sensed Rowe's magic. The same sensation she'd felt dissipating from his hand after he created animated clones of her and her friends. She strained to see more of him. Headlights from the sheriff's car swept across the area and shined over the bush. Only the white face of a barn owl caught the light, and the bird winged away.

Jancie's heart pounded in her throat. "Over there. Next to that bush. Rowe was there, and his owl. Did you see them?"

"No, but Harley looks like his dopey self again. Thank God." Lizbeth rolled down her window.

The deputy, now parked and out of his car, escorted Jancie's ex to the cruiser's backseat.

Rachelle continued to white-knuckle the steering wheel. "If you're right, maybe Rowe took a spell off of Harley. But how did he get that spell on him to begin with?"

"I wish I knew." Jancie let out a slow exhale through her nose and scanned the darkness for any sign of Rowe.

The deputy approached their car where Lizbeth leaned her head through the open window.

"Evening ladies." He touched the wide brim of his hat. "Were you the ones who called about a man on your car?"

"Yes, we were. He was the man you just took away," Lizbeth replied.

"No offense, Ma'am, but I tested with a breathalyzer, and he's at 0.13. Too drunk to walk a line as wide as a sidewalk much less hang onto a moving car." He leaned in close, sniffing Lizbeth's breath. "You ladies must have been spun around by the sights at the carnival."

She pounded a hand on the door frame. "Why don't any of you deputies ever want to hear the truth about what goes on around here? Aren't there any regulations you're required to follow?"

"There are, but if we follow them, no one at the state office wants to hear about the truth from these parts." He lowered his voice. "And we'd like to keep our jobs. We have families to feed." He leaned away and spat on the ground. "And 'sides, it always turns out to be some simple witch's prank; nothing harmful. You're from around here. You know to keep your distance and not strike up a quarrel with coven folks. They're really good folk and good for Bentbone's economy. They keep us on the map. You know that well as me." He touched the brim of his hand and withdrew.

Lizbeth let out a long exhale and scooted away from the window, rolling her eyes at the others in the car.

Rachelle put the car in gear and drove away, cussing under her breath.

***

The women spilled into Jancie's kitchen, their bodies limp like dishrags.

Jancie checked the doors, clicked the backyard flood light on, and peered out at her mother's herb garden. The silvery sage leaves and white chrysanthemum buds caught the light and seemed to nod a reassurance to her. She squinted and tried to call to life the filmy ghost she'd seen of her mother. Rubbing the moonstone did no good. But Mom's image still blazed in her mind, and in her heart.

Seeing Mom was worth all that'd happened, and whatever might happen in the future. Jancie resisted the urge to run out and sit by the garden, bathe her hands in the dirt and feel her mother's spirit on her skin. That would have to wait until daytime. Not in the darkness with Adara and Harley after her, for what she didn't know. But right now, Jancie was grateful for the feeling of comfort that reached out to her from the herb patch.

"Is someone out there?" Rachelle frowned at Jancie.

Jancie turned away and smiled. "No. Mom and her herbs are keeping watch."

Rachelle shook her head and reached into the fridge. Her bracelets jangled as she helped herself to some pops. "I think that witch stuff at the carnival has gotten to your head. I'm not laying stock in protection by any herbs. Not from that Harley-cat, anyway."

"May be more reliable than that deputy." Jancie put her hand out and accepted a can from her friend.

"For sure." Rachelle gave a snort.

Lizbeth pulled Willow to the sink. "Where's your first aid kit, Jancie?"

"There's one under the sink," Jancie replied. "I have more stuff in the bathroom, too."

Willow squirmed and winced while her friend washed the scraped palm.

"Stand there and pat it dry with this paper towel." Lizbeth rummaged through the kit she'd placed on the counter. "Hmm. Since I had to get bits of gravel dust out of these scrapes, they're oozing. I need a large bandage. Do you have any?"

Jancie pinched a handful of yarrow leaves from the vase of herbs and flowers on the kitchen table. "Use these. They stop bleeding and heal cuts."

Lizbeth wrinkled her nose. "They aren't sterile."

"They're fine." Jancie squeezed next to Willow and laid the frilly leaves across the injured skin. She placed another folded paper towel over top and secured it with a length of bandage tape. "There. Keep that on for an hour, then we'll change the dressing."

Willow inspected her palm. "Y'know, it already stings less."

The women moved to the living room. Rachelle plopped onto one of the leather recliners. "What the hell just happened?"

While Lizbeth and Willow sprawled on the couch, Jancie sank into the matching chair. She wanted to kick off her shoes, but her body resisted, like it was still on high alert. Her hand trembled as she lifted her pop to take a sip. "No idea. What an evening. If the coven leader Adara charmed Harley that much, what does she have against me? I know she has a thing for Rowe, but this is intense. I left a message for Rowe. I hope he calls."

"I'd say he needs to do some explaining." Rachelle nodded.

"What would Harley have done if he'd gotten a hold of me?" Jancie shivered. "Or, to you all if you were in the way?"

They looked at each other.

Jancie's ringing phone cut their silence. She checked the display. "It's Rowe." She sat forward and answered.

"Jancie, it's Rowe." He spoke in a clipped tone, a bit out of breath. "I got your message. Are you and your friends okay?"

"Yes, we're fine. At my house."

"Good. As you drove off, I saw Harley following your car. Busby helped me track him. I was able to alter Adara's spell, transforming the energy into a harmless drunken stupor."

"Are we safe now?" She swallowed against a knot forming in the base of her throat.

"Yes. I'm outside your house and will place a protection spell around the property."

Jancie moved to the side of the front picture window and peeked around the open curtain edge. A pale green roadster gleamed under the light of a street lamp. She raised her hand to the glass. "I'm glad you're here."

"I'm glad to see you safe." His voice relaxed. "The shielding won't be permanent because it's only powered by my own direct force. It will tax me to keep the protection strong, but it will hold through the night. After I set the shield, I'll leave to find a trustworthy friend who can cast a longer-lasting spell. I'll be back in the morning with her. If you need anything, or hear or see anything, call me."

"I will. Thank you." Her fingers found the chain around her neck. "Will Harley remember what happened?" The last thing she needed was more trouble from her dad telling her he'd been right.

Rowe chuckled. "Probably not. I left him drunk as a skunk."

Jancie let out a sigh and finally let her shoulders relax. "That's good."

"Why would his memory worry you?"

"Long story. My dad." Jancie kept her answer brief. She didn't want Rowe to know her dad attempted to control her like a child. She was an adult and wanted Rowe to think of her that way, regardless of whatever Dad believed.

"Something I can help with?" Rowe's voice rose.

"No. I can handle it." The moonstone on her chest reflected in the window. "Should I take off the moonstone?"

"No. Do not take it off. It guided me to find you."

Her heart beat against the locket. "Can others, like Adara, use it to find me?"

"I don't know. The moonstone's magic is old and unknown. It makes sense that I'd be able to easily track its power. And right now, I'm relieved for that much."

"Me, too."

He stepped out of his car and rounded the hood. "Try to get some rest." He tipped his hat and disappeared into the shadows of her side yard.

"I will." She exhaled away from the phone, hoping he couldn't read her fear.

Chapter Eleven:
Bones and Stone

ROWE ROUNDED JANCIE'S HOUSE, casting a protection spell as he stepped through the dew-laden grass. In the backyard, energy from what must have been her mother's garden challenged his concentration. He glanced at the plot but worked to maintain his focus.

At his shoulder, Busby swallowed a squawk that caused Rowe to flinch. "Sorry, master," he whispered and hovered above the unusual garden.

Once Rowe completed the circular safe ward around the property, he retraced his steps and met up with the barn owl perched above a silver-leafed stem and staring nose-down in fascination.

A faint violet glow, almost imperceptible, cloaked the plot, arching across long, graceful stems and twisting up wandering vines. Rowe passed a hand over his forehead, in awe of the site, certain he beheld the love between mother and daughter. Although he could detect the certain essence of Jancie's mother, Faye Sadler, perhaps in some form of animation, there was something greater happening here. Magic of the earth was not his specialty. But his Vika would know more.

"Let's go." Not wasting another moment, he motioned to Busby and strode to his car. Rowe hoped the old woman, or more likely her temperamental Maine Coon familiar, would be willing to work late into this night.

He gave a final look toward the front picture window, where lamplight formed a woman's silhouette. The power of the moonstone made Rowe's pulse beat stronger. Jancie. He raised his palm to her and drove away.

Where the streetlights gave way to darker countryside, he pulled to the side of the road and scanned the sky for his barn owl's white face. "We're going to Vika's and need to travel fast. Come perch on the back of the front seat." He stowed his hat on the floor while waiting.

"Please, Master, I can fly faster now, and I know the way." With wings stretched wide, the owl impressed Rowe.

"Okay. If you get into trouble, let out a call." Rowe pressed on the accelerator and sped as fast as he dared around a series of turns toward the woods where Vika lived. At the last turn, the waxing crescent moon shone from behind the edge of a cloud with the intense illumination of a full moon. A definite sign that her knowledge could help. Rowe slowed to a crawl, and Busby's round, pale face grew larger in his rearview mirror. Relieved, his heart swelled with pride at the fortitude of his familiar. Together, they wound through the tall trees to Vika's rambling storybook cottage.

She met them on her front porch clutching a rustic shawl about her shoulders.

Her Maine Coon cat wove between her calves.

"I'm sorry for another late night visit." Rowe leapt across the stepping stones two at a time.

"No need to be sorry." She leaned down to stroke Siddie's thick fur. "If you're needing my help, it just means you're living a full life."

A hoot sounded from a wide branch near the porch.

Vika curtsied to the mature barn owl. "Thanks for your communication, Maeira." She faced Rowe. "Edme's owl told me you were coming."

The matron owl clapped her beak as her son took a nearby perch.

"I almost skidded off a few turns to get here fast. Busby flew hard and kept pace all the way."

The tan breast feathers of the younger owl swelled in the porch light.

Rowe waved for the owls to follow them into the house. "Busby, I need you to describe to Vika what you saw in Jancie's garden."

When the owls swooped to the porch, Siddie burst into a frenzy of hisses and snarls. Silver tabby fur on end, sharp canines bared, and green-yellow eyes glinting, she looked like a lynx protecting her den.

Busby squirmed to a mid-air hover, while his mother pinned her ears and dove for the huge cat.

Rowe lifted his forearm up to encourage Busby to land clear of the skirmish. Talons cut through his coat jacket and grazed his skin, and Rowe pulled his squawking owl next to his torso.

"Siddie, stop!" Vika screamed as the cat and owl rolled into a single grappling ball at her feet. She filled her palm with white light and extended her fingers down. Threads of light encircled her familiar's neck and formed a magical leash.

The cat pulled at the cord and croaked a series of dry coughs at Maeira, who somersaulted backward to land awkwardly on her feet before waddling behind Rowe.

"I'm sorry to have to do this to you, sweet one. I expect you to treat these owls as our guests. They're familiars too, just like you, and are allowed inside. They've been here a few times before without this ruckus." She looked up to Rowe. "She's so used to our house being for just us two. I just don't know what this is about. Something's upset her tonight."

Rowe stooped to pat the Maine Coon. "Siddie, I'm glad to see how well you protect my dear Vika."

"Welcome." Siddie choked out the single word, lifted her long tail, and pranced across the threshold ahead of everyone shooting a backward glance at the owls.

Rowe and Vika exchanged a questioning look and filed after her with the two owls.

They gathered in the large country kitchen used for potion making. Vika tied the end of the leash around her wrist and sat on one of the long benches. Holding the table edge to bend low, she treated Siddie's wounds with her white light. Tucking the Maine Coon's wide head and as much of the body as possible under the hem of her nightgown proved harder.

The fast-thumping tail that stuck out and whacked the planked floor indicated Siddie's displeasure with her mistress's disciplinary measures.

Rowe moved Busby to the back of a primitive wooden chair where his talons couldn't harm much. He found Maeira teetering along the floor as far from Siddie as possible and encouraged her to a matching chair. After a few attempts, she hopped to the seat. A handful of Rowe's blue light soothed her injuries. She leaned against the seatback, beak open, tongue panting.

"Now tell me what in tar-nation has brought on this uproar tonight?" Vika set her gaze on Rowe as he took a place opposite her at the long trestle table. "The wind blew from the carnival tonight, and I smelled Adara's black power." She raised a single brow. "And I see you don't have your locket. I hope at least that part is good."

"I think it is." His hand moved automatically to his chest. "The moonstone connected to the young woman, Jancie. I helped her say goodbye to her deceased mother whom she cared for during a long illness with cancer."

"Poor girl. I'm glad you could help her." Vika's eyes moved beyond Rowe as if lost in thought. "And now she's obligated to return the favor of lifting your grief. She's either your new love or will lead you to that lady. And that set off Adara's torrent, which I felt.'

"I'm afraid so." Rowe leaned his elbows onto the table and explained the incidents involving Harley. "I've set a simple protection ward around Jancie's house, but it won't last."

Vika shook her head. "Lots of strong magic in the air tonight. No wonder these familiars are acting up. Siddie was off her feed earlier tonight."

"I need your help to keep Jancie safe until Adara gets tired of her game."

The elderly friend focused on him. "That could be a good long time." Her hooked nose twitched. "Then again, there's a full moon in seven nights, and powers will run high. And the Mabon equinox comes in just over two weeks, a good time for Adara to be helped down a new path. Hmm." She touched a finger to the wriggling nose as if thoughts were stuck there. "This being a holiday weekend, Jancie should be home from work until Tuesday, right?"

"Yes, I think so. She works at a bank."

"Your basic ward will only last about a day. I'll prepare some preliminary potions tonight but will need to finish and apply them at her house in the morning."

"I'll take you there whenever you're ready."

"On what to do to actually stop Adara, I've got a hunch, but I need to spend time thinkin' on it." A slow hissing sounded from underneath her, and she peered to the floor. "Siddie, be a good girl." Vika continued to Rowe. "Before she acts up again, what did your owl see that might help me?"

"When Jancie connected to her mother's ghost, they discussed a garden on the home-place where Jancie still lives. It belonged to her mother, and they'd worked the plot together when she lived. The ghost seemed aware that Jancie had recently tended the patch." Rowe rubbed a hand along his forehead. "The odd part was when I was at the house setting my ward, there was an energy around the garden plants. Some sort of loving bond between mother and daughter, so strong it was transfixing. But there seemed to be something more there than I could read."

"Interesting. Anything visible?" Vika leaned forward.

"A faint purple glow loosely followed the stems. Almost imperceptible." He looked to Busby. "You took more time studying those plants. What did you see?"

The smaller owl fluttered his wingtips, which drew a hiss from the cat.

"It's all right. Go on." Vika dropped a hand to her side.

"There were tiny voices, but I couldn't make out what they said. I heard their tone, in quick bursts like they were scared of me, so I drew back a little bit. After a while, I saw things climbing the plant stems, and I hovered closer. I saw pinpricks of purple light darting behind leaves."

Rowe placed a hand on the tabletop and stared at Vika. "Fae?"

She nodded, her white brows pulling together.

"Those faeries can be directed to help Jancie, right?" Without waiting for a reply, Rowe moved to his familiar and ruffled the bird's neck feathers. "I'm grateful for your keen eyes and ears, Busby." He gazed at Vika who now gripped the table edge, a frown deepening the wrinkles around her mouth. His jaw tightened, and he asked in a flat measured tone, "How did those fae get in Jancie's garden?"

"That's what worries me. Fae have died out in most home gardens and only live in the wild along forest steams. I have a healthy community of them around my herbs but know how to keep them. Most don't. Not even here in the coven. It takes a good Earth witch. Like Adara." Saying the coven leader's name made Vika grimace as if in pain. "If she set them there, they can cause serious danger that I'll be hard pressed to fight." She exhaled between clenched teeth. "We don't want that battle." She pushed herself away from the table. "Time to get to work."

"Can I help you?" he offered.

She shook her head. "No, thank you, dear. Siddie and I work as a well-oiled team. More hands would only slow me down."

"When should I come back for you?" Rowe held his forearm out for Busby.

Paying no notice to the departing owls, Siddie jumped onto the bench and peered at the stained page of the well-worn family grimoire alongside her mistress.

Vika didn't look up to see them out. "I want to arrive at Jancie's an hour before dawn. No later."

***

Rowe sped home almost overtaking his headlights, although he didn't know why he hurried. Vika was the one under pressure of time. But the biting fall night air stung his face with dark magic.

He pulled open the front door against the strong north wind and held an arm out to prevent the owls from entering before him. Over his shoulder he whispered, "Let me check for any foreign energy first." In the foyer, crystals of the grand entry chandelier reflected the security light shining through the open door. He addressed the massive hall tree. "Uncle Bertrand, did anyone enter the house while I was away?"

The oak boards creaked. "No one. I assure you we've kept the house secure." He swung an umbrella hanging from one of his hooks in front of his mirror.

Rowe returned his deceased uncle's salute.

Maeira sailed past to a familiar brass perch that had been hers when she served as Edme's familiar. The owl slumped down onto her feet, and Busby took a place on the opposite rung.

Rowe paused. Maeira had roosted on that perch during his happy marriage to Edme. He sighed and flicked on a Tiffany table lamp in order to examine the matron owl. He passed a palm of blue healing light over her body but found no residual injury. Before he finished, she gave soft snerts of slumber. He was glad to be able to offer her the comfort of the home where she'd lived with Edme.

A knock on the door startled Rowe. He spun on one heel and swept both arms up. Waves of his power alerted the animations of his departed family.

"Rowe, it's me, Logan," the familiar voice of his friend called from outside.

"And Keir," added a second male voice, Rowe's hiking buddy.

Surprised they were there at that late hour, Rowe dropped his arms and cracked the door. Seeing it was in fact them, he opened it wide. "Sorry to be so cautious." Rowe glanced at Keir, fully adorned in his ceremonial necklaces, and wondered if the seer had foreseen something he needed to know.

"No problem," Logan said as he and Keir hung their fedoras on Bertrand's outstretched hooks that lifted to secure the hats. "There's some strange shit in the air tonight. Is Jancie safe?" Logan ran a hand through his unruly golden curls. The muscles along his chiseled jaw spasmed.

Rowe nodded. "I set a protection ward, and Vika will help tomorrow."

"That'll do." Logan unbuttoned his suit coat and loosened his tie. "No one's better than Vika." He waved off Bertrand's offer to hold the jacket.

Keir lowered a leather satchel to the floor, while his familiar, a dark-haired coyote named Waapake, streamed in beside his master, quick eyes scanning every corner.

Rowe glanced over his shoulder at the owls.

Maeira slept on, and Busby only fluttered the ruffled ends of his wing feathers. No surprise, since, unlike Siddie, Waapake was a calm and calculated sort, a gift presented to Keir upon his remarkable achievement in studies with a Shawnee Indian wise man. The coyote's name meant 'to see,' and the canine made shrewd use of his master's magic. Waapake's kept his huge ears pricked high and wet nose lifted.

"It's really true." Keir's usually pale blue eyes turned a steely gray as he lifted a palm to Rowe's chest. "Look into my eyes."

Standing close and inch for inch all of Rowe's height, the seer commanded his complete attention.

"Logan told me about the moonstone, but I had to see for myself. How strange." His hand jerked, then he relaxed it to his side. "The gem's energy is still there. But it's laced with that of a lovely ginger-haired young lady." He raised a bushy, black brow as a grin cut across the stubble shadowing his face. "She must be why I haven't had the company of my hiking partner the past week. Just me and Waapake. Up in the hills, we did have a curious talk with Cyril that I'm still digesting. You remember the raccoon king of Coon Hollow?"

Rowe nodded. "Big old silver-haired fellow who can bite a sapling in half."

"That's the one."

"You two hang out with some wild dudes in those hills." Logan shrugged and led them through the hall into the library. He gestured to a wide coffee table and sank his sinewy frame into a soft leather club chair.

"Sometimes." Keir nodded with a grin. "I couldn't make out what he was jabbering about other than two secret charms."

Rowe lit several lamps which had moved nearer to the assemblage, the spirits of his ancestors obviously curious to the goings-on. One sat precariously at the edge of his father's oak desk. He put an unanimated dictionary in front of it.

Keir perched on the edge of an ottoman with the coyote curled at his feet. The seer dug in his satchel and withdrew a beaded pouch. In the amber lamplight, his near white skin took on the ruddiness of an American Indian. His cropped coal-black hair blended with the shadows of his charcoal suit jacket lapels. Rowe watched his friend transforming into the essence of his mentor. "Hold this bag in your hands." The contents clattered as Keir held it out to Rowe.

Rowe accepted, and Keir removed two of the many necklaces he wore. He waved a Wiccan quartz amulet and a string of Indian beads around the outside of Rowe's hands while chanting in a Shawnee Algonquin tongue. The chant completed, he took the bag, opened its drawstring, and spilled an assortment of small bones and stones across the table.

The stones Rowe recognized as local river rocks worn into various shapes by currents, but he puzzled over the other pieces. "What are we looking at?"

Logan blew a breath out from between his teeth. "Some scary native American witchcraft only he knows."

"River pebbles and coon bones all from this hollow." Keir leaned over the arrangement for at least a minute before sitting back.

Logan draped himself over his knees, fidgeting as if he wanted to say something.

Rowe knelt at the table wanting to urge their friend to speak but knew better than to hurry a seer.

Keir swallowed hard and gave a slow exhale. "After the harvest moon, the weather will grow stormy, more and more leading up to Mabon." He pointed to an intersection of two of the largest bones. "Winds from north and south will fight a grueling battle where life will be lost and neither will win."

Rowe shivered, and the lamps flickered.

Silence hung between the men as they looked from one to the other, broken only by the wind rattling the tall windows.

"So, what does this mean?" Logan looked up, his blue eyes gleaming with an edge of steel.

"The winds might represent people, but who?" Rowe moved to sit beside Logan on the couch. "Adara is an expected force. Who will be her opposition?"

Logan lifted his head higher.

Rowe placed a hand on Logan's shoulder. "I know your ambitions. Be careful, my friend. Death is foretold."

Waapake threw back his head and howled as a sudden gust shook both the doors and windows.

Keir stroked the coyote's long ears. "He reminds us that the north wind is known as the wind of death."

Logan buried his head in his hands, and Waapake moved to nuzzle the crown of his head.

Keir gathered the scattered objects. "I will take this riddle to my shaman. He may be able to help with the meaning. Logan, will you go with me?"

Logan sat up. "I sure will. We all need some good advice about now." The invitation seemed to spark life back into him. "And I need to visit Skena Stoddard and her old friends. Maybe they can find some records of covered-up wrongdoing by the Tabard family while serving as coven leaders."

Rowe glanced at his father's desk. "I started to search the house for my parents' council records. I'll get back to that." He rubbed his chest out of nervous habit, feeling for the locket. "I need to conjure a fake moonstone so the entire coven isn't up in arms about what happened tonight. Before dawn, I'll work with Vika at Jancie's house to protect her and learn more about the unusual garden her deceased mother left behind. Filled with fae."

Keir flinched and stared at Rowe. "The north wind is gathering force." The seer stood. "Rest in what's left of this short night. In the days ahead, there is much to do."

Chapter Twelve:
Garden Fae

THE SHORT NIGHT BROUGHT ROWE only fitful sleep, and he rose early. While his coffee percolated, he roused Busby and intended to let Maeira sleep, but she stretched her wings and legs and seemed intent on joining them.

Checking his phone, Rowe found no reply to the text he'd left Jancie after Keir and Logan left last night. He hoped working with Vika in the pre-dawn outside Jancie's windows wouldn't frighten the young woman or her friends.

Rowe washed down a slice of toast with coffee and poured a second cup into a travel mug, one of the small but essential modern conveniences he allowed himself beyond what the council permitted. He stared at the unapproved items, mug and cell phone, and a ray of clarity hit.

Accepting Adara's offer to sit on the coven council now seemed like a good idea, but for no reason she would welcome. Until Jancie had awakened the moonstone, he'd been mired in self-pity after losing his beloved Edme. Coven matters hadn't affected his hermit-like existence. Keir's reading the previous night expanded Rowe's view. The coven was in for turbulent times. Lives would be lost. With his family's good standing, he could protect innocent people from being harmed.

Rowe accepted the fact that adherence to the traditions and lifestyle that existed at their coven's conception kept the magical practices pure. But dictating practices as small as how to consume coffee was suffocating the spirits of individuals. Personal growth needed to be part of coven life for the community to thrive. A principle his parents strongly adhered to and defended. Newly married and too busy making a family of his own, Rowe had failed to uphold their values after their deaths.

The Tabard family, including Adara, had long been strict about maintaining status quo. It served their interests to remain as leaders. And in recent years, drove members out of the coven.

His parents must have kept records. Rowe strode into the library, sat at his father's desk, and yanked open file drawers. Folder after folder contained coven bookkeeping which had been his father's primary council responsibility. Rowe dug to the back of a deep drawer, and his hand met a leather book. He pulled out a green notebook and thumbed through pages of hand-written entries. Meeting agendas were annotated with his father's personal observations and opinions. Some entries were written in his mother's hand.

Rowe was eager to spend more time studying this. He placed it in a safe he kept secured with not only his own ward, but a couple other protections supplied by his departed uncle Ernie and aunt Tanita. Rowe looked forward to the time when his parents' spirits would rest in a favorite household object. He expected his father's essence to return sooner. Since Mom had relations throughout the southern part of the state, as well as Kentucky, she might wish to visit them for awhile first.

Coffee in hand, Rowe called up the stairs. "Any barn owls going with me to pick up Vika?" Quicker than he expected, they winged down the staircase, and he ducked to avoid being hit. "Whoa! I admire your enthusiasm."

The pair flew overhead as he drove to Vika's. Still in the darkness of the same night, it felt like Rowe's visit with Keir and Logan had been a dream. If only that ominous prediction had been one.

When they arrived, Vika's face appeared in the window beside her front door. She turned on the porch light which illuminated leather suitcases and wicker market-baskets with bottles and branches poking out of the tops.

Rowe met her on the steps with a chuckle. "Are you moving out?"

"Something's gotten you in a high mood." The old woman eyed him as she slipped her arm through the handles of two baskets. "With all this danger, it'd do me good to hear what you're about."

"Like you said last night, I'm living a full life." He grinned and hoisted the two suitcases into his car's trunk. "A few days ago, Adara offered me a seat on the council, intending to keep me close to her. I've decided to accept for a different reason. I think the council needs my help."

Vika clucked her tongue and shook her head. "You are your father's son, turning a gathering storm into a time to build windmills." She chuckled. "You'll do us all some good, but see to it you keep yourself safe."

He steadied her shoulder and helped her stiff body into the passenger seat. "You can be sure of that."

Paying no attention to the owls, Siddie slid into the narrow space behind her mistress's seat and curled into a tired-looking ball of fur. Lack of sleep must have dampened her jitters over the evil in last night's air.

On the drive, Rowe shared Keir's reading with Vika. She didn't comment or show surprise, but her fists clenched in her lap.

An hour before dawn, Rowe parked at the curb in front of Jancie's house. Busby and Maeira waited on the neighbor's TV tower.

As soon as Vika cracked her door open, Siddie coiled out and stood guard, her tail flicking in all directions as if sensing for danger. "These old bones aren't as fast as yours, sweet one," the old woman said as she wedged herself from the leather seat and arched into a standing posture. Hands bracing her low back, she peered from under the shawl drawn around her head to examine Jancie's house. "Your ward is still plenty strong, Rowe. You're too modest about your powers. This house has old native limestone walls that I'm sure hold centuries' worth of secrets."

Rowe unloaded the trunk. "Where do you want these?"

"Leave them here until I've had a look at that garden." She waved at Busby who flew closer. "I need to first determine the orientation of plants and fae. Busby, will you lead the way?"

In a few strides, Rowe caught up to the rest. Even though well-protected by three familiars, he didn't want her to trip in the dark backyard and break a bone. He took hold of her elbow, and she let out a small yelp of delight.

"Look at that garden, teeming with fae." She veered off the driveway. "Everyone stay clear, even from overhead." She hunched low and paced around the bed's perimeter. "Drat. Footprint energies are too numerous and overlapping. I can't rule out that Adara might've been here." She drew a step nearer and peered across the bed. "It's so dark, the faeries' glow blots out what I can see of the plants." She folded herself down onto the grass, legs sprawled out from her long, full skirt. "I need to join the energies that are here in order to identify their natures." She patted the ground beside her. "Siddie, help me girl."

The Maine Coon obeyed and spread her body, all except the fluffy tail, flat to the earth between Vika and the bed.

Rowe signaled the owls to perch on lookout branches of the yard's large shade tree. He dove a hand, fueled with blue light, into his pants pocket, fingers touching his pocket watch.

Vika took a deep inhale and settled herself. "Mother Earth. Feel my bones, my skeleton, my flesh. Pull me to you. Make me part of you." Her voice grew stronger and louder. "A mountain of your creation. I am grass, trees, grains, fruits, flowers, beasts, metal, and precious stones. At your will, I will return to dust, to compost, to mud. To my mother." The old witch sat in silence, her breathing deep and steady.

Siddie's body flattened closer to the ground, but her tail remained alert. Always on watch, a quality of an exceptional familiar.

The quiet around them unsettled Rowe. His skin prickled. Vika seemed peaceful with her connection to the earth, but his magical tendencies, aside from his gift of animation, were more aligned with air magic. Even the gentle breeze in town, carried a tinge of dark energy.

Unaware, or tuning it out, the old witch sat in silent meditation. The tails of her wiry, white hair floated out from where they were gathered in a black ribbon.

The back door to the house creaked open, and Jancie poked her head out. Slim, bare legs stepped onto the stoop. Her hair hung loose around her shoulders. A close-fitting nightshirt skimmed the curves of her slender body. Rowe felt the tightness in his chest relax. Somehow, Jancie's purity obliterated the evil in the air.

He moved toward her and offered his hand, fingertips still glowing a faint blue.

Barefoot, she descended to meet him and gave him a wide smile that lifted his heart.

A few moments later, a tremor shook through Vika's spine.

Jancie flinched, and Rowe gripped her hand tighter. He whispered, "She's fine."

Siddie sprang to attention and bounded to Jancie's feet, as if to pounce on an invader, then became still and purred between her legs.

"It seems my big kitty has taken to you, young lady." Broken from her meditation, the elderly lady faced them, blinking. "I'm Vika."

"Hello. I'm Jancie. Thank you for coming." The younger woman knelt beside the older. "May I help? I know a fair amount about this garden. Mom had me help her, even as a child."

"Can you answer how such a thriving colony of faeries came to live here?" Vika rubbed her cat's long ears.

"Faeries? Really?" Jancie gasped and leaned closer. "I see a glow around the yarrow heads and chrysanthemums. And along the sage leaves."

"That's it!" Vika leaned in, and Rowe drew nearer.

"That is so cool!" Jancie exclaimed, then sat back. "Is it safe?"

Vika said over her shoulder to Rowe and Jancie, "Not to worry. The energy is all good. Adara didn't put these wee folk here. Or guide them with her evil either."

The owls sailed down and perched on the garage gutter at the back of the garden.

Jancie gave Rowe a questioning glance. "They've looked like that as long as I can remember."

"Look closer." Vika pointed to a leaf. "See those purple pinpricks?"

Busby hovered low, fanning the cavalcade of light spots with his tail feathers until they moved faster.

"Yes!" Jancie squealed. "That helps, Busby." She picked a leaf with a single fae.

"Well, those fae are there to do good, not only for the plants, but also for this property." Vika allowed a few to crawl onto her thumbnail, then passed one to Jancie and another to Rowe. "The question is how they got here. Fae are rare in home gardens anymore. An old practice. Now they exist almost entirely along forest streambeds. I have a colony at my house, not even half of this one, but I work like the dickens to keep them happy there."

Jancie stared from the fae in her hand to Vika and shook her head.

"Well, no need to find that answer now. We can set to that problem later since there's no evil afoot." She looked up at Rowe. "Will you please bring my supplies?"

"Will do. Busby, come help me." Rowe walked away as Vika talked a blue streak about her favorite topic—Earth magic. With the help of the two owls each carrying a basket in their beaks, he completed the task in one trip.

From one of the suitcases, Vika withdrew a large flat river stone. "This is a guardian stone that will keep evil from your garden and property. I'll show it to the four winds to gain their blessings." She lifted the stone to the east, south, west, and north before holding it to her breast and closing her eyes. She placed it at a front and central position in the bed and rummaged in one of the baskets for a small flask. "I sprinkle the stone with my potion to empower it with life." She replaced the flask and sat back. "Now, Jancie, it's your turn." Vika handed over a short branch devoid of bark.

"Is this a wand?" Her young assistant eyed the stick.

Rowe leaned over her. "I wondered the same, but I've not seen you use a wand, Vika."

The old woman chuckled. "It is a wand charged with Earth energy. The only use I ever make of such a thing."

Jancie ran her fingers along the smooth wood. "So cool!"

"With the end of the wand, draw three symbols all in one row in the garden dirt. A plus sign, a heart, and another plus."

Jancie drew the indicated marks and handed back the wand.

"Excellent." Vika beamed, her eyes glinting in the pink light of dawn. "You should retrace this pattern at least once a week to keep the protection strong. Use your finger since it's contacted my wand. These two protections will keep you, your fae, garden, and home safe. Now we need to find a way to protect you when you leave home."

"I could possibly animate an object with your protections, something that Jancie could carry," Rowe said to Vika.

"Hmm." She ran a bony finger along one temple. "Now that it's getting light, I can see many plantings here give off both love and protection. Fine qualities for a home to have. That lilac bush overtaking the far side of your house offers great protection, especially now that I've boosted its energy. These garden herbs—angelica, yarrow, mint, and chrysanthemum—are all protective in nature. As are those peonies lining the drive. Amazing."

"Mom loved them all. Flowers were everywhere in the yard when she was alive."

"They will be again with just a little of your care." Vika patted Jancie's bare knee, then gazed beyond the girl. "Look at that mighty maple in the center of this back yard. All about love." Vika slapped the ground. "Double drat. I almost forgot." She rummaged in the other suitcase and pulled out three old horseshoes. "Siddie, my dearest, will you please bury one under that maple, another under the lilac, and the third between the peonies?"

"Gladly, m'lady." The Maine coon clutched one in her jaw and trotted off, tail tasting the air. Claws extended, dirt flew fast from between her hind legs. Positioning and burying the bespelled horseshoe required more time and effort.

While the cat worked, Vika faced Jancie. "You seem to have been close to your mother. Do you have anything of hers you can keep with you at all times? A piece of jewelry maybe?"

Jancie sat straighter and raised her right hand. "This ring is my mother's. I've worn it for years. She gave it to me when she found out she wasn't going to..." Her words trailed off.

Rowe knew what she'd not said and also sensed her pain. A lump formed in his throat. He knelt and lay an arm around her shoulders.

She leaned into him, until a round of dry sobs quieted.

Vika stroked Jancie's hair. "For this next protection, you'll need to have some faith. We'll charge the ring with the protections we just put in place. Let me examine your ring." She accepted the silver band from Jancie and closed her hand around it. The old witch's face drained of color, and she returned the ring. "I was going to have you place the ring in the garden, but it's much too precious. Can we get into your garage? With this common wall, that space will work for what we need."

Jancie hopped up, and with the house keys on a stretch bracelet at her wrist, she opened the wide door.

"Rowe, help me gather a dozen or so small rocks from across the garden." Vika placed her findings in the apron over her skirt. Her joints crackled as she stood, and Rowe transferred most of the load to his arms. Inside the garage, she located a rickety shelf under a small window overlooking the garden. "Perfect." She accepted the rocks and arranged thirteen into a circle. "Jancie, hold your mother's ring in your dominant hand. Magic travels best through the power hand. Concentrate fully on a mental image of your mother. Hold that tight in your mind while you place the ring dead center in the circle." With the ring in position, she continued. "At dawn tomorrow, the ring will hold the same protection we placed on your home. It will keep you safe whenever you leave."

"Thank you so much." Jancie took Vika's hand in hers.

The older woman stepped back and leaned her weight onto Jancie's car.

"You're tired." Jancie looked to Rowe.

"That much casting will drain strength." He rubbed the shoulder of his dear friend. "Not to mention she stayed up all night preparing the supplies."

Jancie pulled Vika into her arms. "Thank you. Would you like to come in and have some breakfast or tea?"

"Thank you, child." The witch returned the embrace. "I think I need to get myself home to bed. This old body isn't used to such late hours. Maybe we can share breakfast another time. I do need to learn how those fae came to your garden. It's not in me to do that today."

"Yes, of course." Jancie pulled away. "I'm a good cook and would be glad to have you back any morning I don't work."

"Oh, I'd like that, dear." A wide smile cut through the wrinkles on the elderly witch's face.

Jancie's eyes twinkled. "I'm so curious to learn about my mother's past. I'll be eager for your help."

Rowe smiled inside, watching the two interact. There was a kinship he marveled at, connecting souls that gave each other's life new purpose. He felt that way about Jancie himself. Witnessing his friend's similar feelings, validated his own.

Laughing together, Jancie guided Vika arm in arm back to Rowe's car. He and the owls carried the supplies, and Siddie circled them all with her tail held high.

Rowe gave Jancie a quick hug. "I need to get her home. I'll call you tomorrow. I think we all need some rest today. If you see anything frightening or strange, call me right away."

"I will. Thank you for everything." Her gaze met his. "You look tired too. Stay safe and get some sleep."

As he drove away, Rowe watched in the rearview mirror until Jancie disappeared from view. He glanced at his own image. His eyes did look tired, but instead of dragging from lack of sleep, he now felt rested and restored. Realizing it was her touch, he smiled. It would be nice to be able to spend more time with her.

His thoughts drifted to her ring that Vika empowered. Jancie hadn't given him that ring in the carnival to create animated clones. In hindsight, he was grateful for that stroke of fate since her friend's bracelet remained missing. He hadn't seen it appear in his house, like most misplaced animations. He made a mental note to look again. A pain shot through his jaw. Could the bracelet have been intercepted? Could Adara do that? He clenched the steering wheel and glanced at Vika, slumped into the seat. "Thank you for your help."

She rolled her head to face him. "Oh, you don't have to thank me. I'm just glad I could."

"I saw you turn pale when you held Jancie's ring. You must be exhausted."

"I am, but that wasn't the problem with the ring." She worked a feeble hand up to grasp his. "That ring has strong magic, like I've never seen."

Chapter Thirteen:
Horseshoes and Pancakes

JANCIE WALKED BACK INSIDE HER HOUSE, her arms wrapped around herself trying to keep the warmth of Rowe's embrace from escaping. She checked the kitchen wall clock. He'd only been there an hour, but she missed him like he'd been gone for days.

The house was quiet. Rachelle snored softly from the living room couch and no noise came from Lizbeth and Willow in the guest room.

Jancie yawned. Her body was tired, but her mind jumped with thoughts. She'd never be able to sleep after all she saw and learned from Vika.

That old woman was such a kind soul, full of knowledge and purpose. Jancie sometimes worried about inheriting her mother's cancer. Mom had been cheated. Jancie wanted a better chance. For years, it'd seemed like her life was put on hold. During the past few days, her pulse raced with every exciting hope and new direction.

Faeries in her garden. Jancie rubbed a hand across her forehead. She hadn't even thought they existed outside of fantasy books. Their presence kind of explained how the plants had survived her neglect for almost two years. And she couldn't deny seeing the specks of moving light. She wondered whether Mom had known they were there when she was alive. Previous owners could've put the faeries there. County records might have a list of who owned the house before her parents.

Loneliness washed over Jancie. She found her terry robe and looked out of her bedroom window over the backyard. Limbs of the lilac brushed the pane, and she thought of the huge Maine Coon familiar working like all the others to protect her from danger. She shook her head. It was surreal. She didn't know if her friends would believe what had happened while they slept. She'd find a way to tell Rachelle. Best friends since grade school, they told each other everything. The others, Jancie wasn't as sure about. It'd been hard keeping up with what girls her age did while seeing her mother through cancer. She didn't need another reason to feel like an outcast.

But after all Rowe and Vika and their helpers did, Jancie couldn't deny she felt safer, more protected. She lay on her bed and thought about the way Rowe held her by the garden when a wave of crying welled up. It was like the pain drifted out of her body into his. She wondered how he did that and why. She snuggled a pillow and imagined his face, her fingers cupped around the moonstone.

***

Pans clattering in the kitchen woke Jancie, and she stumbled to the kitchen. She rubbed sleep from her eyes to see Willow commanding her kitchen, ordering Lizbeth and Rachelle around.

"Mornin'," Willow said with a sunny smile.

"We thought you could use a good breakfast after last night." Rachelle finished laying silverware at places on the table and gave her a bear hug.

Jancie buried her face in Rachelle's shaggy hair, burning to spill to her all that'd happened at dawn.

"Did you get any calls from anyone?" Lizbeth glanced her way while making a pot of coffee. "Rowe was supposed to bring some witch friend to bolster the protection on your house."

"They came around dawn," Jancie said through a yawn. She wormed her way to the sink and filled a kettle for tea.

"I'm sure glad he did." Rachelle poked her head out from the fridge, hands filled with butter, maple syrup, and juice.

"Darn." Using a fake red nail, Lizbeth pressed the brew button with flourish. "I intended to watch what they did. Why didn't you wake me up?"

Jancie pretended to ignore her question and rummaged in the pantry for tea bags.

Willow paused in her pancake flipping and shivered. "Did they do anything gross? Like with dried toads or bat wings?"

"Eye of newt?" Rachelle asked with a laugh.

Jancie grinned. "No. Nothing creepy. Buried some old horseshoes around the yard. Placed an enchanted stone in the garden."

"That's all?" Lizbeth rolled her eyes. "I stayed up last night googling witchcraft protection spells. Seems like they'd call upon the powers of the winds and such. Channel energy from the plants. Nothing like that?" Her dark brows crept up her forehead.

"The important thing is that you're safer now." Rachelle said between gulps of orange juice. "How's Rowe going to protect you when you leave your house?"

"They're adding protection to my mother's ring I always wear. It'll be ready tomorrow morning."

"So you're grounded today. That sucks." Willow flopped golden cakes onto a serving plate.

Jancie shrugged. "It's Sunday. I don't mind."

Rachelle faced Willow. "Why? Did you want to go back to the carnival?"

Willow screwed up her mouth. "Well, sort of. It's the last night. They're only open during the daytime Monday, and that's not as fun."

Rachelle scowled and took a seat at the table. "Go ahead. You don't need us to go. Have fun with Harley-cat."

Willow placed the mountain of pancakes on the middle of the table. "I just might. I don't get many days off work like you all." Her fluty voice squeaked with a hint of pain.

Lizbeth pulled a plate of bacon from the microwave and added it to the table. "Dig in."

"Looks delicious. Thanks guys." Jancie filled her plate, thankful for the meal to silence the strained conversation.

After a mouthful, Rachelle said, "These pancakes are awesome. Great job, Willow."

Everyone appreciated the food, and the atmosphere lightened with laughter and giggles.

Once the dishes were cleared, Willow offered Lizbeth a ride home. During goodbye hugs all around, Jancie whispered to Rachelle and asked her to stay a while.

After the other two left, she wrapped an arm around Jancie's shoulder. "What's up? Is everything okay?"

Tears rolled down Jancie's cheeks, some happy, some frightened, as she spilled all that had happened at dawn.

Rachelle stroked Jancie's hair and led her to sit on the steps of the back stoop. "I'm weirded out by all of this witchy stuff too. But it's all right. We've never heard of anyone being hurt from dealings with the coven folk. You heard that deputy. Nothing to worry about. I think your dad's fears are getting to you."

Jancie shook her head. "It's not Dad. Getting to talk with Mom outweighs all those fears. It's Rowe. Everything with him is all so different and familiar at the same time." Jancie struggled to find words to describe the new feelings. "I'm not used to things happening this fast in my life."

Her friend faced her and snatched up her hands. "Has he done something to hurt you? He may be a witch, but he's still just a man. And they can be real bastards at times."

Jancie gave an odd laugh through a nose stuffy from crying. "No. He's fine. The problem is he makes me feel good, in ways I haven't felt before. It's like my feelings are whirling around. I'm so used to life being slow, weeks passing into months with nothing much or nothing good happening. Now, I feel like I can't even catch my breath."

Rachelle laughed and pulled her into a hug. "Girl, you're just living life. And maybe falling in love. God, I hope so. If any of us deserve to find love, it sure is you."

Jancie flinched, then a smile crept over her face. "Love?"

"Relax and see what happens. And whatever you do, don't let your dad find out."

"Oh, no. He'd have a coronary." Jancie's hands flew to her mouth imagining how her dad would react.

Rachelle patted Jancie's knee. "Are you going to be okay now? I need to get going."

"Yes. Fine. Thanks for listening."

"No problem. That's what I'm here for. You've sure been there enough for me lots of times." Her friend made her way to the long Chrysler. "Call me if you need anything." She waved from her open driver's window and backed out of the drive.

***

Jancie spent the lazy afternoon inventing chores around her garden and lawn. She'd done most of the hard work already, but with the enchantments and the news that faeries lived there, she couldn't resist poking around. She trimmed, tied up wayward limbs, and took cuttings for another vase. While creating the arrangement, she wondered if there were faeries on the cut stems, or if they'd dropped off and stayed in the garden. Could they live inside the house? Were they good to have there?

Having more questions than answers, she was eager to spend more time with Vika.

Evening set in with a cold breeze from the north. After a light dinner, Jancie made a pot of tea and settled in with Maggie's diary. She hoped there'd be some clues that tied to garden faeries.

Betty's birth certificate stuck in the diary jarred Jancie's mind. The names on the document listed Maggie Forsbey and Louis Forsbey as the parents. The date was June 30th,

1939, in Evansville, Indiana. Louis remained a mystery to Jancie.

She thumbed back to where Maggie had met a male witch in the coven who wore the moonstone locket. Like Jancie, the woman needed to see her departed loved one again. Jancie read for clues about Louis, the pregnancy with Betty, and ties to her own mother.

Page after page was filled with excited notes about the growth of baby Dorothy. It warmed Jancie's heart to realize how Maggie was able to go on with her life and find happiness after the opportunity to see her deceased husband again. Jancie related to the emotions behind the faded cursive writing. The sentences were choppy, as if one happy thought fought with the next to be recorded. Jancie's mind swarmed in just the same way. At times, joyful tears flooded Jancie's eyes, like she'd met someone who shared her exact feelings. A weight lifted from Jancie through finding this woman who shared her own experiences and thoughts.

Near the end of the diary, Jancie came upon an entry with a different tone, hushed and cryptic like Maggie had a secret that she badly wanted to tell.

> The love of my life is now a true part of me. The news makes me happier than I ever believed possible, and also in the darkest despair. It seems unfair the past should be allowed to shape the future. Bloodlines dictate too much. Although I cannot risk telling anyone, Louis and I now share two bonds that no one can cast asunder no matter what be known.

Jancie understood the secret had to be Maggie's pregnancy with the baby who would be Betty. That was one bond, but Jancie puzzled over the second. She read on to learn more.

A few pages later, she paused at another entry where Maggie wrote:

Wonderful news! I am bursting to tell someone, although I mustn't for fear of defiant interception. Through a cousin who strictly holds my confidence, I have just learned I have distant relations in New Wish on the Kentucky border around Evansville way. They are willing and happy to take in my little family. The three of us, and our blessing, will leave soon.

The final entry in May, 1939 told how Maggie moved away from Bentbone with one daughter, Dorothy, and one on the way—Jancie's Grandmother Betty. Maggie wrote, "With heavy heart, I must make this my final entry. I'm leaving my family for the sake of my own children."

Jancie closed the diary still pondering the clues. What bloodlines could make Maggie need to leave to protect her children?

Jancie stored the diary in her dresser and sunk into bed with the quilt Mom had made for her. Wind whipped at her window, and lilac branches scratching the panes woke her several times. She clutched the quilt to her chest, remembering dreams filled with images of a pregnant woman fighting to walk against a sharp wind.

***

Those visions still haunted Jancie in the morning. The woman's desperation and confused fears squeezed at her own throat. She raced to the garage not bothering to cover her nightshirt with a robe. She threw the door open and let out a loud sigh when she found her mother's ring still there. She slipped it on her finger and sank against the side of her car, heart pounding. She wanted to see Rowe and needed to feel his warmth to relax the thoughts whipping in her mind.

Jancie trudged back inside and fingered her phone. He promised to call today. She expected that would be in the evening after the carnival ended in the late afternoon. But she needed him now, and a phone call wouldn't be enough. Now with freedom to leave the house, she considered going to the carnival to find him. Instead, she plunked down at her kitchen table. *Not with Adara out to get me.*

Jancie convinced herself to wait for his call and went about her day, doing laundry and cleaning. No amount of busywork calmed her unrest. By afternoon, her nerves still on edge, she could take no more. *Maybe I've been at home too long. A drive might help.*

Fall weather had forced out the Indian summer weekend, and she changed into jeans and threw a light jacket over her white t-shirt. Her mother's ring felt empowering against the steering wheel of her Camry.

Jancie turned onto Maple Street. *Surely driving past won't hurt.* Only a third of the cars in the lot compared to Saturday night. The carnival appeared to be winding down. She longed to stop and see Rowe. She let out a sigh, knowing the thinning crowd would only make her a more visible target for Adara.

Jancie drove on, past the carnival into the country. The recent warm sunny days had brought out bright fall colors. Broad-leaved sugar maples looked like candy apples, their topmost leaves dipped in red while their lower parts stayed yellow and green.

The quiet of the countryside made Jancie feel alone. Unable to see Rowe, loneliness set in and added to her stress. The hollowness inside her widened the further she drove. At the next intersection, she made a U-turn and sought out something familiar.

She parked at the Bentbone cemetery, and her feet followed the sidewalk she knew too well. Every chip and crack. Every slab lifted by welling tree roots. She knelt by her mother's grave and steadied herself with a hand on the headstone. To her surprise, no tears came. Her grief had changed. She leaned into the stone and rested her forehead on the back of her hand. "Mom, I need some guidance. Things are happening so fast."

"Jancie." Rowe's familiar deep voice washed over her.

At the sound of her name, she flinched. "Rowe?" She took hold of his outstretched hand.

Chapter Fourteen:
Welcome

HOLDING ROWE'S OUTSTRETCHED HAND, Jancie stood, and he guided her close to him, his other hand at the side of her waist. Her breathing slowed and deepened, tension leaving her body.

He wore no hat. Strands of dark hair near his temples worked loose from his ponytail, framing his kind face.

He let go of her hand and wrapped both arms around her.

She rested her cheek against the front of his dark wool suit jacket.

"Better?" he asked, his breath warm against her crown.

She nodded and worked her hands to rest behind his neck.

Tumbling leaves blew around them in the crisp breeze. Cold cut through the thin sleeves of her khaki jacket, but in his arms she stayed toasty.

"Indian summer lasted only long enough for the carnival." He pulled away slightly. "After working all day, I'm starved. Would you like to visit my house? I might be able to find us some dinner."

"Yes. I'd like that very much." She wondered what amazing new things she'd see there.

"I'd be glad to drive and then bring you back here to your car later." He took her hand, and they strolled to the parking lot. "It'd be safer to not have your car seen in the coven."

"That's fine." His caution reminded her of her dad's warnings. Despite a bit of apprehension, she was eager to learn about Rowe and his lifestyle.

Rowe's barn owl let out a hoot and swooped to perch on the hood ornament. Chest out, he seemed to contest that the chrome lady with her flowing hair and gown could be the true protector of his master's car, rather than himself, a masterful bird of prey.

"Busby, Jancie and I are going to my house. Check with your mother. If she's still overtired, bring her along." Rowe opened the passenger door of his pale green 1930s model convertible.

"Will do, Master. Meet you along the route home." The owl extended his brown wings wide and lifted away.

Jancie slid onto the passenger side of the bench seat, and Rowe made his way around the car checking latches of the tan cloth top. "I just put the top up today on my way into the carnival but didn't have time to double check the fastenings," he said through the open driver's window. "Summer's over. Almost time for me to get out the sedan." He found his seat and pulled away, changing gears with a shifter and clutch. The tan leather of Jancie's seat was worn buttery soft as her mother's kidskin gloves.

"My dad owns a mechanic shop and just started working on the old coven cars." She ran her hand across real wood trim that decorated the dash. "I've always wondered why coven folks live like they're in the thirties."

Rowe chuckled. "Sometimes I wonder that myself." He pulled a new cell phone from his pants pocket. "Not everything we use is vintage."

"How do you know what new things are allowed?"

"The coven is governed by a high priestess or priest, like Adara Tabard, and also a high council. Together, they regularly update a list of changes made to the list of approved modern conveniences. Regular members of the coven can petition to have changes made. The allowances are few and made after strict consideration. It's common thought that adherence to the coven lifestyle that existed when the group was officially formed will help maintain strong, original magic traditions. The transmission of the witchcraft needs to remain as pure as possible."

Jancie twisted in her seat. "I can understand the importance of cell phones, but I see a travel mug. How is that allowed?"

"Shh." He grinned. "Actually, cell phones aren't either. Something I intend to change soon since I've just been appointed to the council by the high priestess."

Jancie's brows jumped several inches. "Cell phones are forbidden? Get out of here. No way." She eyed him. "And doesn't Adara want you on that council just to keep you near her?"

He nodded. "Yes, that's right. There's danger in dealing with her, but I should have enough magic to take care of myself. I want to bring about some much needed changes. My parents served on the council for decades. I need to continue their efforts, now that they're gone."

"What a wonderful thing to do, carry on their dreams." She tucked a strand of hair behind her ear and smiled at him. "But be careful."

He returned her smile. "I'm glad for your concern. Somehow I don't think that part has anything to do with the moonstone's power, but it feels good to have someone care."

The corners of her cheeks lifted higher. "It does."

"It sure does." He pointed to a group of three knotty oaks still clinging to withered, brown leaves like old ladies huddling together in thin, winter coats. "Those trees mark the coven boundary on this road. Have you ever been here?"

Jancie studied the first farmhouse they passed. "Hmm, let me see." A vintage pick-up with faded red paint and a wooden bed sat on the gravel drive. Electric wires swooped to one eave, and an oblong propane tank squatted behind a big lilac. Nothing odd-looking there. She'd hoped to see more differences. She faced him. "A couple of times. Mostly on dares in high school, when we tried to sneak into the coven's cemetery."

Rowe chuckled. "That's pretty far into the center of the coven. Did you ever get there?"

"Yeah. Two or three times. Once it was so dark, I don't remember seeing anything. We heard noises, dogs barking from nearby log cabins, and ran. One time I did see the statues. Some were so beautiful. I heard a rumor that they talk. Do they?"

"Yes, they do." He nodded and glanced her way. "But only to witches."

"That one time, I thought I heard a boy call my name. Rachelle didn't believe me, so I guessed it was only the wind, but now I'm not so sure. Do you think fate brought me to connect to the moonstone?"

"Fate, or inheritance, or both. That moonstone connection may have triggered an entombed soul to speak to you." He rubbed a hand along the dark stubble of his jaw. "Interesting."

"Maybe we can go there some time?" she asked.

"Umm." He hesitated, eyes scanning the horizon. "Yes, some time." He pointed into the distance to the left. "There, in that big woodlot. That's where Vika lives. We'll definitely add that to your list of places to visit. She'd love to show you her potion kitchen."

"Oh, yes! A potion kitchen. How cool is that. I want to go. "Jancie squinted but couldn't see any part of a house. She noticed that Rowe avoided promising to take her to the cemetery. Some of the pain of losing his wife must've still hurt him a lot. That was why Jancie needed to keep helping him find a way to ease that burden—her responsibility in their moonstone connection.

Against the dark eastern sky, white faces of two barn owls drew nearer. Jancie pointed. "Look! There's Busby."

"And his mother, Maeira, who used to be my wife's familiar. She usually watches over Edme's statue in the cemetery, but lately she's been involved with Vika's work.

Maeira took a tumble with that big Maine Coon, and I've kept an eye on her health."

The owl pair sailed overhead as Rowe turned onto the twisty river road that wound through the entire valley.

The rising moon lit up a gorgeous display of yellow-leaved maples and cottonwoods along the creek. Cozy cabins were tucked in among the trees. Jancie leaned forward. "How pretty it is along here."

"My house is just ahead around the next bend."

Jancie strained to catch a glimpse of it. Light bricks along the top edge of a chimney stood taller than surrounding trees.

Rowe turned onto the circular driveway of a sprawling mansion. The house had a shabby chic look, still grand even though some of the white bricks were stained or chipped.

Jancie stepped onto the drive where he'd parked in front of wooden front doors. Two turrets stood sentry. Looking at the house, she imagined lively parties from years ago where flappers sat gracefully in the wide, arched windows or lounged in the garden rooms. "This reminds me of the 1920s."

"It was built just after the turn of the twentieth century. Art Nouveau style."

"The windows with the leaded glass are so fancy." She moved closer to admire a front window.

"By moonlight, they look amazing. He waved her to the door. "Come inside."

Jancie crossed the threshold, breath held, eyes scanning every direction. She expected to find the unknown in a witch's house, especially one with this much old wealth and history. She turned to come face to face with her own startled reflection a foot from a hall stand's mirror. Hadn't it been more than three feet away moments ago? She jerked to the center of the entry, pushing into Rowe's side.

Busby and Maeira sailed through the open door. She perched on the banister, while he sat on top of the menacing furniture beside Jancie. She looked to him for help, but the little owl only gave a round of hoots and clacked his beak. This seemed to do nothing to slow her attacker.

"Uncle Bertrand, please be less helpful." Rowe took her hand and motioned toward the looming piece of furniture. "This is Jancie, who is not a witch and isn't accustomed to animated souls."

"Forgive me, my dear." The wide stand straightened his hunch. "Pleased to meet you."

"Hello," Jancie squeaked.

"In human form, I was Rowe's great, great, uncle Bertrand. I made it with my grandpappy. I knew straight away when I honed my magic skills as an animator along with learning carpentry, that this was would be where I'd leave some of my spirit after I passed. And I'm proud to serve and help young Rowe now." He bowed, hinging below his central mirror.

Unsure what to do, Jancie nodded but couldn't decide what to say.

Rowe patted his free hand along one of Bertrand's shelves. "No need to be afraid, Jancie."

Before she could bring herself to touch the animated piece of furniture, dozens of what appeared to be Rowe's deceased relations congregated around her.

Rowe laughed and held her hand tighter. "The candleholder is Uncle Petrus, the silver handled pistol is Maxwell, and there's Tanita, the fireplace poker." The numbers soon overwhelmed his attempts to keep pace with introductions. "Wona and the rest of you all, introduce yourselves to our guest, Jancie." He held up a palm. "Not you, Tilly. Please wait where you are, and I'll be sure we come visit you."

Jancie did her best to touch a hand and smile to each animated object. The way some jumped and vied to greet her warmed her heart.

Rowe took hold of her elbow and whispered, "Come this way or we might have a fight break out over who gets to meet you." He led her to the living room where the open French doors were blocked by an oversized, upholstered wing chair. "Jancie, meet my great aunt Tilly."

Seeing how the huge chair seemed to relax back into the room with their attention, a chuckle escaped Jancie's lips. She looked at Rowe. "You certainly have some very loving and caring relatives. How wonderful to be able to stay in contact with them all." Since Mom passed, Jancie longed for family. Dad couldn't seem to accept her as an adult, but Mom's aunt Starla had been great.

He smiled, leaned against the door frame out of the way of the cavalcade approaching her, and folded his arms across his chest. "It's a great comfort. I just wish my parents would decide to return and settle their spirits here. I miss them."

"Oh. Is anything wrong?" She straightened.

"No. Nothing that I know of." He brushed a hand along his facial stubble, a gesture Jancie knew revealed concern. "I expect them to come back soon though."

Tilly cleared her throat and spoke in a gravelly voice. "Miss Jancie, I seem to recollect meeting you before, but I don't see how that can rightly be possible."

"I know I've never been here, and I sure would've remembered you, dear Aunt Tilly." Jancie touched her hand to one of Tilly's flared wings.

Maxwell's pistol jumped to the chair's upper edge. His point waving at Jancie made her flinch even though Busby sailed up beside him. "I was just thinkin' the very same, Tilly, as if this young woman do seem remarkably like a lass I've known afore," Maxwell said with a thick Scottish accent.

"That's funny." Jancie ran a hand along her temple. "A coven lady noticed me in town and then said the same thing when she saw me at the carnival this past weekend."

"Oh really?" Rowe drew nearer. "Who?"

"Cerise. A pretty woman in her thirties. She came up to me in the Arcane Aviary."

"That's interesting. Nothing to worry about that I know. She's a nice and upstanding coven member. I teach her three boys in grade school. Cute little fellows." He tapped a finger against his pursed lips. "Some of her relations live outside the coven. I wonder if there's a connection."

"You teach school?" Jancie smiled. "And want to serve on the council. You have a big heart."

"Thanks. I teach animation to all school levels."

Jancie's eyes lit. "I remember seeing a booth of magical projects at the carnival before, and at some of the other holiday events. Those are amazing." The more she learned about Rowe, the more she admired him. It made her proud to be able to help him through their moonstone bond.

When all of the animated relations had greeted Jancie, she and Rowe made their way to the kitchen.

The two owls settled on a brass perch at one side of the spacious room.

Jancie looked around. "There's no one here to meet me?"

Rowe laughed so hard that he struggled to lower his voice to a whisper. "My relatives are too pompous to take up in lowly kitchen gadgets. So you're safe in here."

"That's a relief." She grinned. "Do you use magic to cook, or do things the old fashioned way?"

"Some witches can cook with magic, like Babbett at the carnival who sold the pastries that change flavors in your mouth."

"And the popcorn that changes. That was delicious. How do they do that?"

He shrugged with a grin. "No idea. Not my kind of magic."

She located the sink and washed her hands. "Let's see what sort of kitchen witch I can be with the food you have on hand. Don't hold back on helping with whatever powers you have," she added with a grin. She located some chicken breasts and enough ingredients to make a marinade. Along with frozen veggies, she created a simple meal.

While they sat and ate, Jancie made quick glances his way.

"This is so good," Rowe said and dug in. She smiled with relief, happy she'd pleased him.

Afterward, the lack of a dishwasher surprised her, but she set to work at the sink.

Rowe rolled up his shirtsleeves and helped her at the sink. "One of the modern conveniences that probably won't happen in the near future."

"That's okay." She lifted a handful of suds and blew them at him. "At least it's fun to do together."

He flipped water from his fingertips at her.

Jancie squealed and laughed.

"Washing dishes is definitely more fun with you here." He chuckled and picked up a pan to dry.

When they finished cleaning up and the owls were fed grain and turned out to hunt the property for the evening, Jancie looked at her watch. "I need to be getting home. I have to work in the morning."

Rowe located his keys on the kitchen counter and motioned to the side door. "Let's leave this way so my relatives won't have to take your time saying goodbye."

"They're so nice. I really like them." Jancie stepped outside, the chilly air cooling her cheeks flushed from their laughter. She couldn't remember the last time she'd laughed so much. It felt nice. Mom was right; she would have good times ahead and this was one.

When they headed back to her car, Rowe turned on the heater. "Vintage cars have vintage heaters. They require patience."

She shivered, and he held her hand between shifting.

They drove in silence, but Jancie sensed a thousand thoughts springing into her mind from the feeling of their fingers interlacing. His touch was so warm and comforting, and it seemed to travel up her arm and make the rest of her body melt. When they left the tree cover of the river road, she glanced up at the sky. "The moon is bright out here in the country."

"The moon is waxing." He leaned forward over the wheel to peer upward. "It won't be long until the full harvest moon, an important time in the coven."

"What happens then?"

"Witches' powers are stronger at the time of a full moon." He rubbed his thumb over hers, sending a chorus of delicious shivers along her skin. "And this one leads us into the Mabon equinox festival. At that time we honor the earth to keep the seeds that will bring us new and abundant life come spring."

He pulled into the Bentbone cemetery's parking lot. He stopped next to her car and paused to look at her. "Jancie, I had a wonderful time tonight."

"Me too." Her words came out as a whisper.

He cupped her hand in both of his and looked into her eyes. "I can't remember the last time I had this much fun. Thank you."

She smiled, surprised and happy to not feel the expected awkward struggle to look away. "Me neither. It was great."

He leaned in, and his arm slid along her upper arm, turning her toward him. His touch left a trail of tingles, and she moved closer. His warm palm rounded the curve of her shoulder and caressed the skin on the side of her neck.

She shivered at the delicious sensation, and he brushed his lips against hers. She sighed and touched a hand to his shoulder.

His butterfly kisses covered her mouth, and she leaned closer, tasting his lips. For a moment, she wondered if the tingles and heat she felt were from the moonstone. After a few more kisses, she decided it wasn't important to determine the source of this magic. It was wonderful.

Chapter Fifteen:
The Phonograph

JANCIE WATCHED THE CLOCK during the last hour of her work day at the bank. She arranged and rearranged her desk, closed out one of the clerks registers early, and assigned the teller some busywork. Any way to speed the end-of-day routine.

At precisely five o'clock, Jancie stepped out of her office, purse in hand. No stops for errands tonight, she drove straight home. On her way from the garage, two bright yellow mums newly opened since lunchtime caught her attention. She kneeled in the grass to marvel at the blooms and to redefine Vika's protection symbols in the soil. Jancie filled her nose with the mums' autumn scent and headed inside to the kitchen. After a simple dinner of leftovers, she proceeded to the bedroom and hurriedly stripped off her plain business dress. While waiting for the shower to heat, she glanced at the outfit she'd deliberated over last night before bed. The dark green pencil jeans and flowing cream-colored peasant top would do well.

Thirty minutes later, Jancie perched on a living room chair and twisted her mother's ring on her finger, her usual nervous habit. Touching the ring jolted her. Her thoughts filled with Rowe, she'd forgotten to worry about attacks from Adara. Either the ring protected Jancie or the coven leader hadn't bothered.

Unable to sit still, Jancie jumped up and checked her hair in a wall mirror, fluffing curls set by the curling iron. The doorbell rang, and she spun around. The moonstone resting against her chest flashed a brilliant blue, and she opened the door with a smile.

Rowe returned her smile and scanned her body. "You look pretty." Pleasant tingles followed the path of his gaze.

"Thanks. You too." More casual than usual, he wore gray pleated and cuffed trousers and a black dress shirt open at the neck. His hair hung loose in layers that kissed his jawline and dropped just past his shoulders. "Let me get my purse," she murmured and disappeared inside.

A moment later, she appeared on the front porch beside him, and they walked to his roadster. "I can't put this car away for the season yet. I'm not ready for winter's long, lonely days."

"I understand. I had lots of hard days last winter." She slid onto the bench seat.

Once they were out of town and Rowe didn't need to shift, he inched his hand over to take hold of hers. "How was work? Did you see Adara or did anything odd happening?"

"No. Nothing. The typical boring day at work."

"You're a manager, aren't you?" He shot her a grin. "That doesn't sound boring." He asked her more about her job, which she gladly answered.

His exotic work with magic intrigued Jancie, and she inquired about his council work. In order to learn details of his parents' projects while on the council, Rowe had contacted a couple members and done some research.

"I also visited Mom today." Excited, she squeezed his hand.

"At the cemetery?" He gave her a quizzical look.

"No. I went home at lunch and talked to her at our garden. I know she can feel me there, and it just feels closer in a happy way. She and I can move on together there. At her grave, I only feel hollow and empty." She turned more towards him. "I told Mom that you and I were going to spend time together tonight. The cool thing is that when I came home two yellow mums were newly open."

He glanced and her and smiled. "A sign."

She nodded. "Yes. I'm sure it is. Or I hope anyway. One flower for each of us."

"What does your dad think of us being together?"

She gazed across the horizon in front of them. "I haven't told him. He never wants me to be around witches. Really paranoid something bad will happen to me and very controlling. I'm old enough to decide what's best for me."

"It's too bad he feels that way." Lines formed across Rowe's brow. "I don't know of anyone really hurt by coven folk. Maybe a prank or two if some teens poke into where we don't want them. Has he always been this way?"

"Yes. But more as I got older, high school and after." Jancie fidgeted with the hem of her blouse, not wanting to talk more about her father.

"I'll be careful what I say if I happen to run into him then."

She nodded but added nothing, hoping the topic would die.

Silence settled in the car. Jancie regretted having to reveal her dad's disapproval so soon, fearing it might turn this wonderful man away. Budding relationships were fragile, and she hoped to hold onto this one. Compared to Harley, Rowe was mature, intelligent, responsible, and deeply caring. It was hard to believe he was only three years older than Harley. But at least dating Harley helped her discover what she didn't want. And Rowe was nothing like Harley.

"Jancie, are you afraid of being around witches?" Rowe's voice held a deeper tone.

"No. Not with you." She squirmed in her seat. "I don't know if I can answer for every witch. But Cerise seemed very nice. My great aunt Starla isn't afraid of witches. She's the one who encouraged me to find you, to help me connect with Mom."

"Really?" He tilted his head and glanced at Jancie. "How did she learn about the legend? It's not talked about much, even in the coven."

"She read about it in an old diary written by my great grandmother. She wanted her deceased husband to see their new baby, and she asked the moonstone witch to tell the tale."

Rowe's eyes widened.

"It opened for her, and she saw her husband."

"Really?" Rowe pulled onto his driveway and faced Jancie with a wide smile. "Then what I said about inheritance is right. You do have a connection to the moonstone through your family. I'll have to share this with Vika."

"I wonder if this information will help her answer how faeries ended up in Mom's garden."

"Oh, I expect so." He leapt out of the car and led Jancie inside.

After saying hello to what seemed like a hundred animated relations welcoming her, Jancie slipped into the parlor to see the sunset shine through the ornate leaded glass windows. Angled sunshine streamed through a clearing in the trees in front of the house onto the thick glass. Amber, pink, and purple light swirled across the walls like a giant kaleidoscope.

Rowe came up behind her and wrapped his arms around her waist. "My mother loved these windows. She'd sit in here after dinner with her tea."

"Look at the shapes the light makes. Some look like animals." Jancie pointed above where the wingchair occupied by Tilly's spirit sat. "There's a horse. And a hawk."

"And you have my mother's eye." He leaned over her shoulder, his cheek next to hers. "She found those animals too, as well as many other Coon Hollow critters."

Jancie sniffed the air. "I smell jasmine."

"You do?" Rowe stood taller and inhaled deeply. "I don't smell it. Only your sweet perfume, like honeysuckle. Jasmine was my mother's favorite scent. You seem very in tune to my mother. It's no wonder I like you so much."

Jancie lifted her face higher. "It's gone now. Do you think that's a sign her spirit is trying to return?"

"I was thinking that exact thing. I sure hope so." He released her and stepped to a side table where he opened a large wooden box about twenty inches square and half as high. Inlay decorated the lid that he unlatched from the lower portion.

Jancie drew nearer. The bottom half of the box housed a record player. She'd seen similar vintage devices in antique stores.

Rowe turned a hand crank on the side several times and placed the needle arm on the outside edge of the vinyl record as wide as a Frisbee. As music peppered with static began to play, he turned to her and extended a hand. "Would you like to dance?"

"Umm." She took his hand but hesitated. "I don't know how to dance to this."

"A slow, easy foxtrot." He placed his other hand at the back of her waist. "Follow me and move your feet from side to side."

She glanced down hoping not to step on his toes. But with one look into his eyes, she gave up worrying about her feet since her whole body seemed to glide on air.

A male crooner's voice sang, "How much do I love you?"

With Rowe's hand firm at her back, he swept her with him in a smooth circle.

"How deep is the ocean? How high is the sun? That's how much I love you, now and forever." The fluid voice and orchestra music swirled around them.

"Some of these old tunes are the best for dancing close," Rowe pulled her to him and whispered in her ear.

"Mmm. Very romantic." She leaned in and extended her forearm higher onto his shoulder.

He danced them around the parlor's perimeter, in and out of the twirling sunset reflections.

Feeling like a fairytale princess, Jancie relaxed into his arms and hoped the music would never end.

After a few more times circling the grand room, the music faded, and their feet shuffled in smaller steps. Their bodies barely moving, Rowe held her closer.

Pressed tight against his chest, Jancie felt delirious. Her head rested on his shoulder. No pleasant feeling she could remember compared to this.

The phonograph needle proclaimed the end of the record with a loud cyclic hiss of static. Their cheeks brushed, and Rowe's mouth covered hers in a deep, passionate kiss. Heat rushed into Jancie's head, and her whole body floated.

They clung together. Jancie imagined if she let go, the amazing dream would end. Life had never been about happiness like this. When she paused to take a breath, he tasted her lips with soft kisses. She held tighter to his shoulders with both arms. If she could be just a little closer, maybe the dream wouldn't end.

In response, Rowe ravaged her mouth with a probing kiss until he gasped for air, his cheek pressed against hers. "You're the one the moonstone meant for me. I feel so alive with you."

"I've never felt this happy." She beamed a smile over his shoulder. The sunset had given way to hazy purple shades of dusk. Stillness fell over the room, making Jancie feel like she and Rowe were the only two people for miles. Eyes closed, she inhaled the woodsy scent of his cologne and ran her fingers along the firm edges of his shoulder muscles.

Moving her hand around the back of his neck, a jolt of pain shot through her chest. "Something's wrong." She stepped back and clamped her hand to the moonstone that flashed wildly. Her hand jerked free. "It's burning me."

"What==" Rowe filled his hand with blue light and reached for the locket.

Not waiting, Jancie tried to lift if off by the chain, but the locket clung to her chest.

His magic encased the reactive stone, but he also failed to remove it. "I don't understand."

Jancie leaned against the massive wing chair, which reached out and cupped her waist. "It's not burning me now with your magic around it." She ran a hand across her forehead to wipe away sweat forming along her brow. "I'm so hot, and my hands are clammy."

Rowe took her arm and led her to a loveseat. "This isn't supposed to happen. You should be able to take it off now. Once both people have their grief eased through the moonstone, the gem goes dormant. It's then removed and stored for the next coven member who faces a loss."

A knock sounded at the front door, and he gestured for Jancie to remain where she was in a dark corner of the room. He lifted the arm of the record player and hurried to the door after a second and louder rap.

From where she sat, Jancie heard a woman's voice, shrill and patronizing. "Too busy to open the door tonight?"

"Working on ideas I have for the council." Rowe gave an immediate and calm response. "I've decided to accept your offer of a position. Thank you."

Jancie scooted to the loveseat's other end to be better hidden in the corner in case the leader stepped farther into the house.

"Oh, how wonderful," Adara cooed. "I'm so glad you reconsidered. It will be my pleasure to have your company at my beck and call."

A reflection of red shined at Jancie from one of the parlor's angled French doors. She swallowed hard and hoped the corner shadows kept the woman from seeing her in turn.

"And what, may I ask, made you change your mind?" The red glow enlarged, and Jancie held her breath.

"I was impressed by how well you orchestrated the carnival." Rowe's voice grew louder. "I have new admiration for your talents and wanted to work with you."

"Indeed," the leader replied with an assertive tone. "I do agree that we will work fabulously together."

"Then I'll look forward to the meeting tomorrow evening." Rowe's speech was matter-of-fact and clipped.

"Yes." Adara trailed her affirmative response as if she wasn't ready to leave. "I sense a change in the energy of your house. I'm not a great animator like you. Have the spirits of your parents returned?"

"Not yet." Rowe hesitated. "But I expect them any day."

The red reflection filled the entire door. Jancie trembled and held her mother's ring out in front of her like a shield.

"Still something is decidedly different and adversarial."

"You must be sensing Maeira, the barn owl familiar." Rowe spoke loud and fast. "I've been nursing her the past few days after an injury."

"You're always the tender heart, Rowe. See that you extend some of that care to your leader." Adara laughed. "Oh, and the clean-up crew found this bracelet in your carnival tent. Perhaps you know who the owner is and can return it?"

Jancie clamped a hand over her mouth. *Oh no! She has Rachelle's bracelet. Can she use it to work evil?*

"Umm. No," Rowe stammered. "But I'll be glad to keep it in case the owner tries to find me to retrieve it."

"That's why we have a lost and found at the main gate," Adara said with a silky smooth voice. "It's open once a week. She can find it there. I'll look forward to seeing you in council tomorrow night."

Footsteps clicked on the hardwood. "See you then," Rowe replied. The door closed, and the house fell quiet.

Rowe entered the parlor with a solemn face.

Jancie let out a loud sigh. "She's gone?"

He nodded and sank down beside her. "She wanted me to know she has your friend Rachelle's bracelet. And I'm sure she has no intention of placing it in the lost and found."

"Can she use it to hurt Rachelle?" Jancie clutched his thigh.

He rubbed a hand over hers. "Yes, she can."

"Will you be okay in that council with her?" She searched his eyes.

"Yes." He moved his hand away and forced a grin. "I can take care of myself. I'm more worried about you and Rachelle. I need to get you out of here. You're safer at home."

"Did Adara know I was here?"

"Something was here that she didn't like, but how much she knew I couldn't tell." Rowe clenched a fist. "She makes an art of deception."

Jancie held up her mother's ring. "I saw Adara's red reflection in the glass door coming closer. I used this as a shield."

"Vika does good work." Rowe took hold of her ringed hand. "That might have confused her sensing abilities."

"Let's hope." She rubbed his finger with her thumb.

"I wonder why she's so interested in when my parents' spirits will return. I'll ask my friend Logan who works with the elderly or Keir who's a seer. They both know more about the spirit world."

Jancie glanced down at the moonstone. Rowe's blue magic had reduced to a slight halo, and she touched a fingertip to the gem. "It's cool again and white." She tried to lift the chain, but it clung to her neck.

He ran a finger over its surface. "Hmm. You still can't take the moonstone off. It connected you to your mother, and you've eased my grief. The enchantment should release you now. I'll ask Vika about it. That hot flaring event. It's almost like—"

"Adara triggered it." Jancie finished his sentence. "How is she connected to the moonstone?"

A shiver shot through Rowe. "There's too much happening I don't understand. And it's not good." He stood and offered her a hand. "Let's get you home. Do you feel okay?"

"Yes, fine." She stood, trying to catch his gaze to learn more about his thoughts.

Rowe backed the black sedan out of the garage and put the sportier roadster away. "No one will be looking for me in this car tonight."

They drove in silence. Jancie touched the moonstone wondering what it still wanted from her and why Adara was able to trigger it.

In Jancie's driveway, Rowe sat rigid, hands clamped on the wheel, and faced Jancie. His jaw clenched, he wore a determined expression, but sadness spilled from his eyes. "Jancie, I've involved you in too much danger. Your bargain with me through the moonstone is fulfilled."

Jancie's lower lip quivered anticipating what he was about to say. "It doesn't need to be."

He didn't move a muscle. "I cannot in good conscience continue to put you at risk for my selfish pleasure to have you in my life. Adara is too dangerous for you to face."

"No. There'll be a way." She couldn't believe her dream was shifting into a nightmare this fast. It didn't seem real.

"I promised to keep you safe, and I will honor that with my life. Call me at any time you are in danger. Don't worry. I'll work to get the moonstone off of you. I'll get Vika's help." He took a deep breath. "Part of my pledge means I can't have any connection romantically to you in the future."

"No. Please. No," she begged. A painful twist formed in her stomach.

"I'm sorry." A tear leaked from his eye. "It has to be this way."

Her eyes brimming with moisture, Jancie fumbled to find the door handle and stumble into her house. At the front window, she clutched the knot in her stomach and watched his headlights back out and fade away.

Chapter Sixteen:
Devil's Shoestring

ADARA COILED HER POINTED RED fingernails around the Packard's steering wheel and drove away from Rowe's house smiling to herself. *Once in a while things do go my way, and I have Rowe right where I want him.*

She drove home watching the waxing moon peek above trees, always a confidante eager to learn about her recent successes. With that crow of hers nowhere in sight, her old friend would have to do.

She exhaled a slow breath, savoring the fact that Rowe would now spend time with her serving on the council. A clear victory.

Also, she'd given that simple girl Jancie, who by some accident managed to open the moonstone locket, the scare of her life through an enchantment on her ex-boyfriend. Adara smirked. He was delicious to look at but dumber than her mother's familiar, a deranged buzzard who now excreted his foul waste on the back porch steps. It'd been almost too easy to pull off the charm that kept watch on Jancie. Adara wished she could've seen the looks on Jancie and her friends' faces with that crazed were-creature after them.

Too bad the fun ended with the ex taken in by a sheriff's deputy. Adara learned about the incident from Sheriff Todd himself during their daily carnival security updates.

The drunken charges left her to assume someone from the coven had transformed her spell on the young man. She twisted her lips to one side considering who would have done it. Rowe seemed likely, along with his friends. She turned a corner and slapped the wheel. "Logan." He would've helped Rowe get the girls out of the carnival. The thought of that man prickled her skin as if she'd had a run-in with a patch of thistles. An angry pit-bull, always eager to challenge her. His parents had been poor farmers with the barest of skills, little more than hedge witches, without magic enough for their departed spirits to inhabit cemetery statues. He couldn't lay claim to any standing in the coven. Licking her lips, she relished finding a way to retaliate against Rowe and Logan.

She might find a way using the bracelet belonging to Jancie or her friends. While Adara had chased through the carnival keeping an eye on the bespelled boyfriend, a stream of orange copper particles swept past her. Rowe's energy surrounding the transmission piqued her curiosity. After a huge expenditure of her own energy, she wrestled it back to its material form, the bangle now on her wrist.

Well worth the price, considering how the mere sight of the bracelet in her possession caused Rowe's face to blanch like an Indian pipe wildflower in sunless forest depths. That alone gave it value, but Adara felt sure she'd find even more use for the treasure.

When she opened her car door outside of her garage, a sharp coldness slunk up her spine and wormed its way into her head. An uncomfortable niggling sensation that something important wasn't under her control. What was it? She wracked her brain. She was so distracted that the stiletto heel of her pump slid off of a paver on her way to the back porch. "Damn." She found her balance, but the unsettling chill persisted.

An idea hit her as she turned the key in the lock. Rowe hadn't given off familiar energy from the moonstone he wore. She shoved the old, stuck door with her shoulder. *Does he really think he can fool me with a fake?*

She tossed her clutch and keys on a kitchen counter. Stymied, she grabbed a bottle of claret from the fridge, poured a glass, and took both to a chaise in the parlor. Under the soft glow of a prized Tiffany lamp, she gulped the first glass and settled into the cushions to let the alcohol permeate her mind. For clarity from the confusing question about Rowe or for relief from the persistent icy sensation at the back of her head, she didn't care.

The fuzzy warmth of the wine made her smile with confidence. Whatever Rowe was hiding made for a fun game. He wanted to be with her on the council; that much seemed certain. Perhaps a cat and mouse relationship turned him on, and he must think he held a few cards unturned. If he wanted to play, she could do that. She licked her lips. "With pleasure." Her words purred from her curled lips, and she poured a second glass. She settled back savoring the idea that she and Rowe were even better suited than she'd thought.

A waft of pungent geranium assaulted Adara's nose. She flinched, sloshing wine onto her red dress. "Damn!" She sniffed the air and shivered, knowing full well what she was up against. Her mother's favorite scent. Adara took a long gulp of wine pretending to ignore the growing cloud around her.

She jumped up and out of the haze, moving across the room to the scroll-top writing desk and flicked on a lamp. From the locked chamber, she withdrew the family grimoire and thumbed through its pages. Not finding the needed spell, she started from the beginning again. Another time through with no luck, a thin line of perspiration formed along her upper lip. *Keep it together. Don't let her get to you.* Her fingers trembled. She coughed in the murk of geranium. Her eyes wept.

On the desk, a fountain pen rose above a tablet of paper. Words scrawled in front of Adara. "You're still a foolish, drunken girl. Under your nose, Rowe is falling for the one who channeled the moonstone. He is protecting his new love. Fight for what is truly yours. If you can."

Adara shoved the pen and pad off the desk and grabbed up the grimoire. Waving the heavy, black book, she screamed, "I have this now, even though you didn't want me to have it. Didn't think I deserved it." She lifted her father's onyx pendant from her chest. "And I have Daddy's focus amulet. I don't need your advice. Or your precious Sight that your darling daughter Fia inherited. And I don't need your approval. Leave me alone."

Adara panted. Her heart thumped, but she sat stiff and straight.

The air slowly cleared of the stench.

Adara replaced the magic book inside the desk, making sure to reset the locking spell. Chin in the air, she collected her glass and wine bottle. Checking her posture, she took small, ladylike steps up the stairs.

Portraits along the walls of the stairwell and upper hall emitted noxious odors of trillium flower, camphor, and stink bell. Denunciations from deceased Tabards. One oversized painting of an elderly matron in a wide blue gown let out such a prodigious puff of skunk cabbage, the frame scratched across the wall and hung crooked.

Once in her bedroom, Adara downed the contents of the glass and collapsed on the bed, hoping her mother couldn't see her there. Adara rolled onto her stomach and sobbed into the pillow. A loop of blame and inferiority ripped through her thoughts.

When no more tears would come, she turned over and clenched a fist around her father's onyx pendant. Her eyes burned away residual moisture. "He will be mine or no one's." What her mother wrote was true, Adara couldn't deny. The bouquet of love she'd smelled in Rowe's house wasn't meant for her. She'd avoided the truth. No more. He hid a new love but there was something else other than that fragrance. Rowe's goal for serving on the council likely was to continue his parents' dangerous coven reforms. Changes that would undermine traditional powers as well as her family's leadership. When his parents' spirits returned, he'd be even more influential.

Adara shuddered. It was well known his mother had relations near the Ohio River. Her spirit could be eavesdropping on Adara's sister Fia who lived nearby. An icy stab shot through the base of Adara's skull and made her wince. Fia's Sight could be Adara's undoing.

Adara vowed to learn everything there was to know about Jancie. But now, she needed sleep. Another glass of wine helped diminish her pain.

***

Awake at dawn, Adara threw away the stained red dress she'd slept in and changed into a fuzzy gray bathrobe. She stumbled to the kitchen, the only safe zone in the house where she could be totally free from her prying relations. She peered out at the drizzly morning that matched how her body felt. Her head ached from the wine, but at least it had dulled the chill, stabbing sensation. Staring at the perking coffee pot on the stove, she pondered what Jancie's last name might be. Rowe hadn't supplied a surname when he introduced them.

Through remnants of Adara's spell, a connection to the girl's ex might remain. After what she'd already done to him, the young man would most likely panic if she got near him. She could dampen his hysteria, but since he didn't have much mental power to work with, numbing him probably would create a useless zombie. She sighed, poured a cup, and sat on a barstool at her tiled counter.

She considered consulting Sibeal. That might turn up some useful information, but also meant spilling more of her cards than she wanted to right now. The seer was a good friend. Perhaps useful as a second choice. Intuition told Adara to work through more possibilities.

Her gaze wandered to the fog rising in the woods at the edge of the lawn. It mirrored the rich steam wafting up from her coffee cup and soothed her senses. Her body coming back to life, she rubbed her hands along her upper arms and noticed the curious bracelet prize she'd claimed. *That might contain what I need to know.*

From what she knew about releasing energies in metals, she'd need to heat the copper with herbs that unlocked its secrets. She set about researching it and brought the grimoire back to the counter along with her four-inch thick herbal tome.

The grimoire indicated that copper collected energy. A plus as far as Adara was concerned. Governed by the goddesses of Venus, the metal should be particularly receptive to feminine energies. Another plus. She ran her finger down the page and read that copper aligned with the water element. *Okay, I'll use a water bath.*

Always most comfortable relying on herbal magic, she wanted to use her strongest gifts to coax as much information as possible from the bracelet. At least one of each alignment: feminine, Venus planetary, and water elemental. She consulted the ponderous tome to decide upon the correct alignments. Pleased her stores held the correct supplies, she got to work.

With her bathrobe sleeves rolled up, Adara hoisted a cauldron onto her stock-pot-size stove burner and filled it with water and a pinch of sage to promote transfer of wisdom. As soon as the first bubble broke, she added a handful of dried foxglove blossoms, a feminine herb which tinged the water pink. This she followed with a crushed stalk of goldenrod for Venus, which she pulled down from the rafters of her back entry, hoping its fall harvest would be dry enough. The pungent, bitter scent of powdered birch bark made her grimace. A dash of bark strengthened the water element. Fizzy spray erupted, and she slipped the bracelet into the brew.

Without waiting, Adara added a tablespoon each of dried Devil's Shoestring and Club Moss to encourage transfer of power.

Once bubbles formed, Adara reduced the heat to still the surface, held her breath, and waited. Two minutes passed. Nothing. Another minute without results. With no patience left, she leaned down eye level with the cauldron and took a deep breath that tickled her throat. She muffled a cough and blew across the surface. In the path of her breath, letters formed spelling the names Jancie and Ann. "I need surnames!" she shouted and blew at varied angles which revealed Rachelle Ann Dorset. "Damn!" She blew more until dizzy from hyperventilating. Head spinning, she gripped the edge of the counter and read: Willow Fernsworth; Lizbeth Johnson; Jancie Sadler.

"Sadler! Holy crap!" Adara wiped steam from her forehead. "Can that be the same family?" Dumbstruck, she stood motionless staring at the letters as they faded.

The bracelet scraped across the bottom of the cauldron and startled Adara. "Wait, don't sink yet. I need to know where to find her. Where does she work?" She leaned over the water and blew again. She groaned. Reflex made her hand reach to the stove's knob and increase the flame, even though reason told her the stored energy had already fully released. If she'd acted right away, there may have been a chance. Not now.

She leaned against her porcelain sink and stared through the window, hoping to find guidance from the rain pattering on the panes. The answer of the girl's last name gave her new questions.

***

Under cover of heavy mist, Adara slipped onto the whitewashed front porch of Sibeal's red brick Victorian. Before she rapped the brass knocker, the shutters banged as if in anticipation. Such was the clairvoyant nature of generations of seers whose spirits took residence in the house itself. Her mid-heeled Mary Jane's didn't offer enough height, so Adara bounced on her toes to peer through the door's frosted sidelight pane for any hint of movement.

A loud squawk sounded behind her, and she jumped back from the window.

Her crow Dearg waddled along the porch rail in her direction. "There's my sweet patootie."

Adara glared at her good-for-nothing familiar. "Where were you last night? I could've used your help last night when Grizela decided to pay me a visit."

The bird let out a series of squawks. "Can't handle your own mama yet? Well, rather than taking the fall for her harsh judgment, this bird caught some good buzz at the cemetery."

Adara tilted her head toward the crow. "It better be good."

"Sure thing." He hopped closer. "The word at the circle is that someone wants you to kiss off and will turn the south wind on you."

She laughed. "No one's strong enough to remove me from power. That's all you came up with?"

Before the door opened more than a crack, Sibeal's smiling voice called, "Adara, I expected you." Dressed in an everyday black bias skirt stretched tight over her protruding stomach, a matching peter-pan-collared blouse left untucked colluded to hide the seer's higher midriff rolls. A grin curled across her narrow ferret face, and she stepped aside for Adara to enter. "Apprehension and anxiety are drippin' from your pores, my dear. Let's hope I can help you."

Adara straightened and shot an authoritative nod to her crow. Shaking off her friend's desperate description of herself, she peeled out of her wet trench coat as if her problems clung to it. "You're slipping. Just raindrops falling off of me." She hung the coat on a hook and managed to lift the corners of her mouth.

"For your sake, you best hope I'm a better seer than that." Sibeal chuckled, and a strand of peppered hair floated from bun to collar. She settled at her mahogany dining table and reached for a tea pot shaped like a toad. "Tea?"

Adara lifted a palm. "No thank you. I've had more than my share of coffee this morning."

Sibeal's beady eyes met hers. "Working on a new potion, eh?"

Adara shrugged and folded her arms across her chest. Not enjoying her friend's intrusive stare, she changed the topic. "I don't remember that pot. I'm not going to have to turn you in for possession of inappropriate new house wares am I?"

"Good goddess, no. Things like this are scarce as hen's teeth." The seer poured a dainty cup from the toad's mouth, added three sugar cubes, gave it a stir, and took a loud slurp. "I dragged this one out from the basement in a box left by my grandma. Pretty keen, huh?"

Adara lifted a single brow. "Interesting."

"I can tell somethin's not settin' right with you. Try to keep your shirt on." She turned the teapot's handle toward Adara. "By the looks of you, this is what I need to try. Go ahead. Pour yourself a cup. Drink it down and hand me the empty cup."

After a whole pot of coffee, the first sip of tea disagreed with Adara. With lips pinched, she managed to finish. "There." She held out the delicate china cup.

The seer examined the white porcelain inside, turning it in several directions. Her narrow eyes squinted to pinpricks while she hummed and hawed. "Looks like your big effort to get Rowe is coming out the wrong end of the horn."

Adara looked down at her hands and shook her head. "I've got that issue in hand, thank you. What I need is for you to discover where to find a young woman from Bentbone named Jancie." She pursed her lips and glared at the seer. "And I'm not wasting time drinking another cup."

Sibeal chuckled. "If you and I hadn't been friends since way back in grade school, I'd surely think you were mean enough to steal acorns from a blind hog. The man's in love with Jancie. Leave them be. I know you're heart still aches, but he isn't the one."

Adara blinked back moisture seeping into her eyes. "Doesn't that cup tell you her last name?"

Her friend took a closer look. "No. It doesn't."

"It's Sadler," Adara declared, her voice flat, but her stomach churned with emotion.

Sibeal's jaw went slack, and she put down the cup. "Are you sure?"

Adara nodded and picked at her nails. "The words formed in my cauldron when I released energy from her friend's bracelet."

"Oh, sweet goddess. Let it not be the same Sadler." Sibeal stepped to a tulip lamp on the buffet and stuck her long, thin nose close to the cup. After a moment, she closed her eyes and took a deep inhale. A moment later, she looked to her friend. "I'm so sorry, hon. It is the same Sadler. Their only child. She works at the Federal Bank. "

Adara balled her hands into fists and gritted her teeth, but still a tear slipped from the corner of one eye. "She will pay. Whether or not I get Rowe, she will pay."

Chapter Seventeen:
The Terrazzo Floor

THE NEXT AFTERNOON, outside the ascetic limestone front of the Federal Bank, Adara rechecked both her suit jacket's peplum and her posture. With head high, she glided through the glass doors. From under the jaunty tilt of her wide-brimmed hat, she worked to exude elegance, superiority, and power. Both her carriage and the trail of magic she emanated defined those qualities. The jealous fire within her escaped only through the heat of her exhalations, flaring her nostrils wider than she would have liked. Curbing that last detail, a slow grin spread across her lips as she approached the manager's door displaying Jancie Sadler's nameplate. Adara stood outside the closed door and studied the girl through the office window.

Jancie poured over a stack of papers on her desk. Her simple surplice dress in plain forest green gave the perfect accent to her ginger hair. A single barrette held the glowing strands from her creamy complexion. Adara bit her lip and considered how that simpleton attained such effortless grace and beauty. She corrected that display of weakness only to have her nostrils spread with fiery breath. She took a slow, deep inhale and knocked on the door.

The manager looked up, and her eyes widened. She moved around the desk and opened the door. "Come in, Ms. Tabard." Jancie motioned Adara to a cheap vinyl upholstered chair. Once she moved past, the girl hesitated at the door and finally closed it. The corners of Adara's lips curled a bit at the thought of Jancie being frightened to be alone with her. "How may I help you?" Jancie asked as she worked into her seat behind the desk in the cramped office.

Adara placed a manicured hand on the edge of the desk, the marcasite eyes of her snake ring glinting with her intentions. "You may help me by removing yourself from my life."

Jancie blinked. "Excuse me?"

Adara gave a dry laugh. "That would save me the bother."

The girl touched a silver band on her right ring finger but said nothing. A curious gesture.

A hard lump formed in Adara's throat which she swallowed with minimal discomfort.

Jancie met her gaze. "What am I doing to cause you trouble?"

Adara pursed her lips, not prepared for that naïve question. She hissed her response. "It should be obvious you've had a hand in breaking my heart."

The girl pulled the moonstone locket from under the neckline of her dress and displayed it with her neat but unpainted, short nails. "Rowe and I are only connected through this gem's magic. We are helping each other through grief from losing a loved one." Her lowered eyes showed she hid something, but what? Why did she possess the locket? And Rowe wear a fake one?

"I have heard otherwise, and my sources do not lie."

Jancie bristled and looked at her. "I am not a liar."

"And I say that you are."

The moonstone flashed a vivid blue that reflected on the desk's polished glass top. Adara flinched but covered the aberrant reaction with a subtle move to adjust her hat.

Jancie let the locket fall and took hold of the ring again. *Did the moonstone surprise Jancie too?* Adara studied the girl, looking for answers but found none.

"Rowe and I are not romantically involved." Jancie's voice was resolute, although her fingers trembled across the ring. "If I cannot help you with a banking matter, you should leave."

Adara leaned over the desk and shook her head. "Not yet." A web of shadowy magic wound round her fingertips.

Jancie pushed back from the desk. "I've done nothing to hurt you. Leave me alone." She held the ring out in front of her as if she could possibly defend herself from a powerful witch.

Adara smirked. "Rowe isn't the only man I'm referring to," Adara spat and hurled black magic at the girl's hands, enough to severely burn all exposed skin.

The threads enveloped Jancie except for her ring which cast a silver glow. Adara's darkness dissipated leaving the girl almost unharmed. Only her cheeks suffered with what looked like a sunburn. What just happened? Her flesh should be singed. The knot reformed in Adara's throat, and she coughed until water leaked from her eyes.

"I'll get some water." Jancie raced out of the office, probably looking for a reason to escape. At least Adara managed to scare the girl, even if the effects of her magic went array.

Adara clamored to her feet. Her plan backfired, and she wasn't about to diminish her stature by accepting aid from her foe. Outside the office, her stiletto heels clicked across the wide terrazzo floor.

"Adara, here!" Jancie darted toward her carrying a paper cup. "Here's some water." Adara couldn't believe the girl actually followed through. Was she that brave to face a strong witch, or too naïve to realize the danger, or a sickeningly compassionate do-gooder? Whatever the reason, Adara didn't have use for her or her offer.

Bent to conceal her coughing predicament, she covered her mouth with one hand. The elbow of the other arm pinned her clutch pocketbook to her waist, while the forearm flapped, waving Jancie away. Caught in this unsteady posture, her only recourse was to skitter as fast as possible to the door.

Jancie rushed after her and pushed the heavy door open. While somewhat glad for the favor, Adara would rather have dealt with the obstacle herself than be made a helpless spectacle.

Twisting to gain distance from the despised girl as Adara passed through the door, she bumped into a person in front of her. Strong hands grasped her shoulders, and her head spun to see who else witnessed her vulnerability.

"Adara." The smile of the familiar voice warmed her like the finest liquor and eased her coughing.

She tilted her neck back to see out from under her hat's wide brim. "Dwayne," she rasped, still clutching her throat to guard against more spasms.

His hands held steady, supporting her, and he glanced behind her at Jancie. "What's happening here, young lady?" His voice turned harsh and pointed, as if from a man Adara didn't know. "I told you to not get involved with witches."

Adara backed off from Dwayne and regained her composure. "Is your darling daughter too good for your ex-girlfriend?" She eyed him, wanting to reach inside his brain, burn through the membranes, and learn the truth. The temptation tortured her. Adara reached a hand to her father's onyx focus amulet. Her heart ached to know more, to understand what had happened years ago. A moment, frozen in time that she still replayed over and over from memory, when her life had ended. But she couldn't treat him like the others. He was better than that. She dropped her hand. He was better than her. Self-doubt crept into her thoughts. "She's the reason you left me, isn't she?"

Adara slunk past him, while he held up a hand to contradict. Shadowy vengeance, a familiar emotion, twisted and gyrated in her mind. Her lips curled. Her breath on fire, she yanked off her hat and strode with fresh confidence to her sedan, its chrome gleaming in the sharp afternoon sun.

Chapter Eighteen:
Pizza Night

JANCIE LEANED AGAINST THE OPEN bank door, letting its weight keep her balance while her thoughts collided. "Dad, you dated her?" The words leaving her mouth tasted bitter and sounded worse.

His gaze swept back and forth, avoiding her eyes. He hesitated, looking down and rubbing his brow with agitated fingers before speaking in a stern and gravelly tone. "I'll explain later. Come by tonight. I need to have a talk with you."

"Did you?" she probed, unable to move past that one looming, life-size question.

He took a step closer, his voice hushed. "Jancie, this isn't the place."

"Answer me. Did you date her?"

"Yes, but..." His words trailed off as he reached for her arm.

Jancie jerked away, unable to process what hit her ears. She turned and made her way through the tellers gathered inside the door.

"Jancie," Dad bellowed after her. "I'll be expecting you at the house tonight."

She dove into her office, shut and locked the door. Her breath shallow, she strummed her fingertips on the desk. She dialed Rowe's number, desperate for him to answer.

"Jancie, hello." His voice rose. "Has something happened? Are you all right?"

"I'm not sure." She pushed any residual awkward feelings aside about their break-up and told him the whole story about Adara's visit to the bank. She took a gulp of air.

"Did she hurt you? What did her magic do to you?"

"No, I think I'm all right. My cheeks feel hot like I got too much sun." She touched a hand to the scorched skin. "That's all."

"Thank goodness. You're lucky, and Vika did a good job on that ring of your mother's. It protected you better than I expected. Thank goodness. I'm betting Adara intended a lot worse." His words spilled out so fast, Jancie envisioned him pacing.

She stroked a thumb against the palm side of her ring. "Yeah, Adara didn't seem to expect me to have any defenses. I was just as surprised as she was. She started choking and ran out. After talking to my dad she seemed even angrier. I'm frightened she'll find a way to hurt me or possibly him. What should I do?"

He gave a long sigh. "This keeps getting more and more complex. How do Adara and your dad know each other?"

"I guess they dated before he married Mom. This is the first I've heard of it." She blew out a slow breath between her teeth. "It must've happened before I was born. Adara asked him if I was the reason he broke up with her. I'll see what my great aunt knows. She's my mom's aunt."

"Good. I'll arrange for Vika to come over to your place to help with more ways to protect you. Maybe tomorrow to give her some time to prepare? Can you take off work? We need to understand what's going on."

"Yes. I'll make arrangements. I'll try to see Aunt Starla tonight. How did your council meeting go last night?"

"No problems. Adara treated me like I didn't exist. That was fine with me." He gave a short laugh, but Jancie could feel his tension. "I'll ask around to a few council members and friends I trust to see if I can piece this together."

Silence hung on the phone connection. Dreading the awkward ending of their conversation, Jancie hoped that signal had been lost.

A moment later, he said, "Well, I'm glad you called me. I do want to help."

Jancie shut her eyes and scrunched her face to hold back tears. "I miss you." Two days had passed since they'd talked. It seemed like forever.

"I need to keep you safe." Rowe stumbled over the words. "I'll head over to Vika's right away. I'll call you when I know more. Call me if you have any problems."

"Thanks. I will," Jancie muttered, disappointed with his response.

After their goodbyes, she called Aunt Starla and Rachelle to set up a girls' pizza night. Whatever Dad wanted to lecture her about could wait until he cooled down. She thought Adara would go after her, not him. Jancie couldn't believe Dad had hidden his connection with a witch while expecting her to stay away from them. "Do as I say, not as I do," she mouthed to her office wall. She definitely had questions for Dad, but first, she had her own problems to solve, and hopefully some of his too.

***

Not bothering to go home to change clothes, Jancie called in the pizza order, then drove straight to the print shop and picked up Rachelle.

"What's up?" Her friend settled into the passenger seat wearing burgundy capris and a purple tunic with her usual dozen bracelets. "Why is your face red? Did you go to a tanning salon during lunch?"

"I wish." Jancie turned the car in the direction of the eldercare apartments. "It's a long story, and I'll wait until we're with Aunt Starla, but I had a run-in with Adara today."

"Really?" Rachelle faced her. "During lunch?"

Jancie shook her head. "Nope. She came into the bank about an hour ago."

"No! Are you all right? Did you call Rowe?"

"Yes and yes. I'm just shook up. Rowe is getting Vika's help now. He'll bring her to my house tomorrow."

"That's good. And you'll get to see Rowe again that way." She made a thumbs up sign. "Be sure to wear some sexy perfume and tight pants."

Jancie rolled her eyes. "I don't think that's gonna help. I told him on the phone I missed him. He just ignored me and went on about keeping me safe."

Rachelle blew a pink gum bubble that popped onto her nose, then laughed. "What on earth did you expect him to say? That is more important. You were just attacked by the evil coven leader. If he wasn't more interested in keeping you safe, I'd kick his cute butt."

"Thanks for making me feel like the most super-sensitive, foolish girl on the planet." Jancie turned onto the street of Starla's apartment complex.

Rachelle patted Jancie's shoulder and grinned. "No. Just a woman in love, that's all."

Jancie returned her grin and parked in a visitor spot.

Aunt Starla opened a window and hollered, "Hello, girls. Come on in."

Once they entered the inner hallway of the complex, Jancie smiled when she saw Starla's head poked around the half-open door. Jancie slipped off her dress shoes and jogged down the long hall.

"Lord sakes, don't tackle a poor old lady." Her aunt gave a belly laugh as she folded Jancie into her fleshy bosom. With an open arm, she pulled Rachelle into the hug too. Starla's familiar scent of rosewater and liniment made Jancie's clenched shoulder muscles soften. "Come in and sit a spell." She waved an arm toward the couch.

Jancie didn't have to be asked twice. She sank into the soft cushions and pulled the granny square afghan around her shoulders. "I'm glad you were home tonight, Aunt Starla."

"Where in tarnation did you think I'd be if you needed me?" Starla lowered her wide hips backward into an easy chair. Her long legs shot out so fast that she lost a pink bunny slipper.

"I never know your schedule of bingo and bridge and crochet nights," Jancie replied.

Rachelle headed for the kitchen. "May I get a pop, Aunt Starla?"

"You sure can, hon." The eighty-five year-old lady turned her head to follow the young woman. "Grab me one, too, please. Jancie? Want one?"

"Yes, please. Diet, if there is any." Jancie snuggled into the soft throw, sensing the love her great aunt had put into her handiwork. "I called in the pizza about twenty minutes ago. Thursday nights are slow, so they should be here soon."

Rachelle handed pops to each and took a seat at the other end of the couch. She kicked off her high top sneakers and tucked her feet under her as she took a sip.

"So what's this all about?" Starla faced Jancie. "You've got me worried."

Jancie took a deep breath and started the story from the beginning. "Well, I took your advice, or Maggie's advice, and found the moonstone teller." She explained all that had happened at the carnival. Her eyes gleamed to tell about the moonstone. "Aunt Starla, it worked! It really worked. I got to see Mom and talk with her."

"Lord! Lord!" Starla clapped her hands together. "That brings joy to my old heart."

"And Mom can feel my presence when I work in her garden. It's like we're connected there. I can feel her, too." Jancie leaned forward. "Did you know there are faeries in Mom's garden?"

Starla slapped her hand against the chair's armrest. "I can't say that surprises me none. Your mother Faye was a fine person. But she never seemed to fit in when her mother, my cousin Betty, moved them to Bentbone." The old woman tapped a finger to her chin. "She must've been about thirteen then, an awkward age for any girl with all the female changes. A pretty thing, but painfully shy. Which seemed right odd 'cause as a child she laughed and played games outside, chasing through the woods past dusk till her mama grew hoarse from calling her home."

"Were you close with Mom when she was little?" Jancie asked.

Starla nodded. "My folks and me would take trips in the summers down south near the Ohio river where they lived. I remember one fourth of July there when I met a few handsome fellas at the park festival. Both Betty and my ma made me take little Faye, no more than four-years-old, with me to see fireworks with the local young adults." Starla shook her head. "Betty said Faye would keep me safe. Well, I didn't get in any trouble with a little one hanging round, that's for sure." Grinning, she stared across the room.

"Why did Gran Betty move here with Mom?" Jancie leaned forward.

"Betty's pa, Louis, died after a long illness. I'm not sure what with, but when I met him he was plumb out of his head. After Louis passed, his wife Maggie died a few months later, like her heart broke and her body followed. Betty's direct relations were here, her sister Dorothy who'd moved back years before, as well as my family." Starla tilted her head. "I took Ma and Betty to New Wish at least twenty or so years ago for a visit. That's the last I've been there."

The doorbell rang, and Rachelle jumped up. "I'll get it."

Jancie dug in her purse, and handed her friend a twenty-dollar bill as she passed.

After the pizza boy left, Starla motioned them to the kitchen table and asked, "Why is all this talk about people long gone important?"

"What does all this have to do with the coven leader attacking you today?" Rachelle blurted.

Starla choked on her pop and reached for a napkin to dry her eyes. "Jancie, you've got some explaining to do."

Jancie recounted the afternoon's events while the others filled their plates and munched. "I'm trying to understand why Adara thinks I was the reason Dad broke up with her. There's got to be some clues from the past."

"Oh hon, all I know is that when your dad started dating Faye, he was real serious, almost pushy. Me and Betty weren't too sure of him 'cause he came on so strong. But then your ma got pregnant with you and..." She lifted her hands, palms up, and dropped them to the table. "We couldn't say much after that."

Jancie laced her fingers together. "I don't know how to connect what you've told me and what was written in Maggie's diary to what Adara meant today. Hopefully, Vika will know how to find the missing links when I see her tomorrow."

"What did you find in the diary?" Rachelle picked the pepperoni off her pizza and ate them first. One of her many strange habits that Jancie had come to love.

"Not much. That Maggie got pregnant with Gran Betty while she was here by a man named Louis. Maggie was really happy about that but also sad because she had to leave Bentbone. The reason didn't make sense to me, something about it being for the sake of her children. The entries ended there." Jancie looked at Starla. "Do you know why Maggie and Louis had to leave town?"

Her great aunt nodded. "Louis was a witch from the coven here, while Maggie wasn't. I always figured that intermarriage back then was forbidden. That wasn't long after the coven originated, and rules might've been stricter."

Rachelle set her pizza down and stared wide-eyed at Jancie. "Whoa. Jancie, you have witch blood."

"My great grandfather was a witch," Jancie said the words aloud hoping they would sink in. Instead, questions raced through her mind, and her fingers trembled as she picked at a pepperoni on the pizza. "How did they meet?"

"I don't know for sure. Back then, townies and witches never mixed like today." Starla pulled a slice to her plate. "You know, I'll reckon he might have been the moonstone storyteller." She reached across the table and took Jancie's hand. "Let's hope that Vika can teach you more about the moonstone you're wearing. More than Maggie knew."

***

Jancie watched through her front window as Rowe's black Studebaker pulled into the driveway. The round headlights cut through light mist settling with the sunrise. The soft, yellow glow reminded her of lanterns on autumn Girl Scout camping trips to Turkey Run and Brown County State Parks. Ten years ago felt like another life. So much had happened since then. Decisions made and paths followed without choices or experience to know what she wanted for herself.

Rowe stepped out of the car and dashed to the passenger side to help Vika.

Jancie swallowed hard. Even if Rowe didn't turn out to be 'the one,' she was grateful for knowing him. She admired his responsibility and ability to care for others, and his sense of purpose. She wanted people like him in her life, and wanted those qualities for herself. Finding her own purpose might take a little more work.

Jancie headed outside and called, "Hi!"

Vika looked her way and opened her arms wide. "It's so good to see you."

Her grin melted Jancie's heart, and she hurried to accept the hug.

The old witch pulled her close. "I'm glad you took today off so we have time to sort through things."

"I never mind having a long weekend." Jancie forced a nervous laugh.

Vika's Maine Coon cat rubbed among their legs, purring.

Busby hovered overhead, as if he wanted to join them.

Jancie pulled away and flashed the owl a smile, then asked Vika, "Can I help carry supplies inside?"

Vika pointed to the backseat, and Jancie moved around to where Rowe unloaded the car.

"It's good to see you, too," Jancie said to him, trying to sound pleasant and not desperate to get back with him. She picked up two totes.

He leaned close to get a large basket, and his woodsy cologne sent tingles along Jancie's skin. "You look nice," he said, then stood and peered at her for an awkward moment without saying anything. "Umm. I mean it looks like you're not stressing over Adara's attack. I'm glad. I was worried."

Jancie grinned at his roundabout way of covering the compliment that slipped out. Rachelle's advice to look sexy worked. Black leggings, a close-fitting ivory tunic, and a splash of jasmine perfume did the trick.

"Are we going inside, or just standing around gawking the whole time?" Vika laughed and tottered to the front door. "Some of us have work to be done."

Heat flushed Jancie's already burned cheeks. Beneath lowered lashes, she glanced at Rowe, then headed after the old witch.

"Coming, Vika," he called ahead.

Vika scanned the house. "Ah, yes. I need to give a listen to this wall." Over her shoulder, she said to Rowe, "If you'd told me Jancie's last name was Sadler earlier, I would've done this the first time I was here. Might've saved Jancie a bit of that surprise she had at work yesterday." She clucked her tongue and stepped onto the porch. Arms spread wide and fingers splayed, she clung to the blocks like a giant spider. "This limestone has secrets to tell, if I can hear them." With her ear pressed against a wide, flat stone, she closed her eyes.

Siddie dusted her fluffy tail along the porch wall.

Jancie and Rowe stood behind in silence for at least a minute.

The old woman's straw-like white hair stood straight out as if charged with static. Her flared black skirt and white apron billowed like sails.

The cat let out a wild yowl like a tomcat on the prowl, and her eyes glowed vivid green.

Jancie glanced at Rowe, but he only shrugged.

"Shoo!" Vika stepped back and dropped her arms to her sides. Her hair and skirt went limp as well. "This house can sure talk. Like it wants a friend."

Jancie and Rowe gathered around her. "What did you learn?" he asked.

"Good ole Salem limestone from the local Bedford quarry in around the late 1930s. This house was built in post-war boom time. Fewer families than I expected have come and gone from this home." She rubbed her temples and lifted onto her toes. "But so much detail, it's hard to sort through. Jancie's grandmother bought it from the original owners. The stones say she looked at only one house, this one, and decided to buy on the spot. It's stayed in Jancie's family ever since."

Siddie whipped her tail against her mistress's leg.

Vika bent low and talked in what sounded like gibberish with the cat, then said, "Good girl. Thank you for reminding me." The witch stood and continued. "An odd fact is that this stone came from the very vein that was first used to make at least a hundred coven houses and shops. Some built entirely of it or just the front face and chimneys of log homes. When I was a girl, that vein caved in and was sealed off, too dangerous to quarry. Hasn't been used since, 'cause workers say it was hexed by us witches."

"That is so cool you can hear all that from the walls of the house." Jancie touched a hand to Vika's shoulder and flinched from a slight shock.

"This stone's a talker. It has a kick, if you can understand the language." The old witch laughed. "Jancie, you seem to get a kick from the signal. I'll have to see if I can teach you how to do this someday."

"I remember Mom telling me that story about how Gran bought this house. I wonder if that ties in with the garden having faeries?" Jancie asked.

"Could very well be." Vika stepped toward the door. "Let's get on that now."

Inside, they spread out books and supplies across the kitchen table, and Vika settled onto a chair. "Siddie, my dearest, take a seat here beside me. But no table walking. Jancie might not like that in her home."

The cat eyed Jancie, unblinking.

"Can I get you all something to drink?" She hoped to tempt Rowe to stay, rather than just drop Vika off and leave. Jancie faced him where he leaned against a counter. "I have tea, hot or cold, pop, juice."

The old lady's eyes crinkled at the corners with her wide grin. "Hot tea with lemon would be ever so nice, Jancie. Thank you."

Jancie set water on to boil and assembled a bowl of various teabags on the table.

"I think it's best if I leave." Rowe pushed his hands into his trouser pockets. The soft wool of his slacks draped over the hard muscles of his thighs. "Vika is the expert."

Jancie nodded. He looked so good, she wanted to push further but didn't want to seem overbearing. It was obvious the decision was difficult for him. That he still had feelings for her would have to be enough for now.

"Call me when you've finished, and I'll pick her up." He made his way to the door.

She trailed after him and stood on the porch until he drove away. Only then, could she get herself to go back inside and shut the door.

Vika patted the arm of the empty chair on her other side. "Come have a seat, dear. Rowe's sweet on you. Don't you worry. He told me about his decision to not date you. He's been a bundle of nerves since."

Jancie poured the hot water, transferred the mugs to the table, and slid onto the chair. "I guess I'm glad for that. Adara said my involvement with Rowe didn't mean much to her, or at least that's what she said. I doubt that a lot. But me being my father's daughter was definitely a real issue for her. So now she has two big reasons to hate me."

"Let's get one thing straight." Vika ripped open a bag of Earl Grey. "Adara doesn't hate you. She doesn't even know you. It's just how she is. She's 'fraid of people. Thinks no one will like her. What she's after with you and everyone she meets is power. Plain and simple."

Jancie blew across the top of her tea. "I don't understand being like that."

Vika patted Jancie's hand. "That's because you get friends by helping people. They like you because you care about them. Adara started out a better person, but she's had problems."

"That's hard to believe." Jancie's brows rose.

"It's true. As a teen, her heart was open, and she often did kind acts for other folk. Too bad her mother Grizela, the high priestess, didn't recognize Adara's efforts." Vika took a loud slurp from her mug. "When Adara met your dad, she fell hard. Grizela didn't approve of her dating a townie. That made the gap between mother and daughter widen into a chasm. In her will, Grizela promised the family grimoire to her oldest daughter Evelyn, then to the middle girl Fia, and lastly to Adara, the young one. But after the two older daughters died, Grizela went so far as to hide the grimoire from Adara."

"So why does Adara think I caused Dad to break up with her? Wasn't I born after they separated?" Jancie asked.

"I know some of that answer, and maybe you know the rest."

Siddie gave a scolding meow.

"And your information will help us too, my dearest." Vika rubbed her cat's pointed ears. "About twenty-four years ago, when Adara was eighteen, she and Dwayne had a summer romance. One evening, they were out drinking and joy-riding in his hot rod. He swerved into an old model T driven by Adara's brother Clement. Her sister Evelyn was in the passenger seat. Both were killed."

"Oh my gosh." Jancie clasped her hands together.

"Adara and Dwayne were cut up bad. Had a few broken bones. That's how she got that wicked scar across her cheekbone." Vika sighed. "Word was that she never saw Dwayne again. Perhaps he feared comeuppance from Grizela Tabard. Most would, since she was so cruel. Or maybe he was afraid of the law, being charged with manslaughter. The sheriff back then didn't take kindly to townies who mingled with witches. Either way, right soon we heard he was getting married to your mother Faye, and that she turned out pregnant with you."

"So by having to marry Mom, Dad couldn't go back with Adara? That's just life, the way the cards fall." Jancie set down her mug. "Why is she still harboring a grudge? And at me?"

"I'm with you. There's got to be another side to this coin. What do you know?" Vika squeezed a second lemon slice into her tea and filled her beaked nose with the steam.

Jancie stood. "I need to get something." She dashed to her bedroom and returned with Maggie's diary. "This is a diary written by my great grandmother on Mom's side. My great aunt Starla gave me this to let me know about the moonstone locket, so I could say goodbye to Mom. In addition to that, there are some odd entries." She locked onto Vika's eyes. "Do you know of a Louis Forsbey, a coven member from the mid-thirties?"

The witch nodded. "Sure do. Quite a mysterious tale around him. He left the coven in the middle of winter with a townie woman. Seemed he had to leave to be with her. It was all kept hush-hush, but then I was only eight or nine then and wasn't told much about love."

Jancie rubbed a hand over the leather cover. "The woman he left with and married was my great grandma Maggie."

Vika's eyes popped out. "Sakes alive! Then you have witch blood in you from our coven." Jancie stared back. What had seemed almost unreal while talking with Aunt Starla, now sunk in.

"Maggie got pregnant with my gran Betty while here in Bentbone. Maggie was really happy about that but also sad because she had to leave Bentbone. The reason didn't make sense, why her children were in jeopardy."

"Hmm." Vika passed a finger around the rim of her mug. "Intermarriages were frowned upon for sure, but nobody would've harmed those children. I grew up knowing kids from mixed marriages. What does the diary say on that?"

Jancie opened near the end of the book and read, "The love of my life is now a true part of me. The news makes me happier than I ever believed possible, and also in the darkest despair. It seems unfair the past should be allowed to shape the future. Bloodlines dictate too much. Although I cannot risk telling anyone, Louis and I now share two bonds that no one can cast asunder no matter what be known." She looked up. "The pregnancy is one bond, but what is the other?"

Vika shook her head.

Siddie jumped onto the table, pranced out of her mistress's reach, and grazed Jancie.

"Dear one, please be a good girl." Vika's grasping hand met air. "We're guests here. I know we don't get out much, but manners are good to have."

The cat's long tail whipped across Jancie's chest.

After a sneeze from fur in her nose, she took hold of the moonstone locket. "This! Was Louis the moonstone teller?"

"I was too young then." The witch leaned close and reached toward the diary. "May I see that entry?"

Jancie passed the book.

"Come closer. Watch over my shoulder." Vika plucked a silver leaf of wormwood from the vase on the table and crushed it between thumb and forefinger, then touched the entry.

Jancie held her breath as she leaned in. Green words and sentences appeared between lines and in margins: Bittersweet. My pregnancy is our joy, but our moonstone bond is our curse. Sweet sorrow.

"Are those Maggie's thoughts?" Jancie wished she could do that magic. She'd be up all night rereading every page.

"Yes. What she was afraid to write." Vika glanced over her shoulder. "That answers your question. He was the moonstone storyteller. You are walking in your great grandmother's footsteps."

Jancie shivered. "I'm not sure that turned out so well. Aunt Starla said once the family moved, he went mad with some illness. Maggie nursed him, then died just after he passed."

"That still doesn't answer why Adara is out for your skin." Vika passed the diary back. "Anything else in here that struck you odd?"

Jancie turned to the last few pages and read Maggie's entry, "Wonderful news! I am bursting to tell someone, although I mustn't for fear of defiant interception. Through a cousin who strictly holds my confidence, I have just learned I have distant relations in New Wish on the Kentucky border around Evansville way. They are willing and happy to take in my little family. The three of us, and our blessing, will leave soon."

"There's the answer." Vika clapped her hands together, while Jancie stared at her, bewildered.

"New Wish is another coven, much smaller than ours, kept very secret, and using very different magic. Maggie must have had New Wish witch blood. And so do you. That is why Adara's magic wouldn't work as she intended. And why the moonstone won't come off because you have more to do to serve the gemstone. There's more to the moonstone bond we need to find out about. I felt New Wish magic in your mother's ring when I first held it but wasn't totally sure. Faye Sadler was a strong witch. And so are you. Adara had no chance against the two of you to get back with Dwayne."

"I'm a witch?" Jancie murmured, the words shaking off her tongue.

Chapter Nineteen:
The North Wind

SITTING AT HER KITCHEN TABLE, Jancie twisted her mother's ring around her finger. New concerns worried her. Did all of this about witch blood in her family have to do with why Dad didn't want her around witches? But Mom had been a witch. Did he know that and love her anyway? Maybe her being a witch brought about their divorce. Jancie faced Vika and asked, ""If I'm a witch, am I able to stop Adara? How do I use my powers?"

"Excellent question." The old lady stroked a hand along her Maine Coon's arched back. "Any ideas, Siddie dearest?"

"Open her heritage to her," the familiar purred while she rubbed against her mistress's hand.

"Yes, of course." Vika faced Jancie. "That might help you utilize subconscious knowledge about New Wish magic, which would work well against Adara." She leaned closer. "I'd like a look at that moonstone. I'm curious whether New Wish witchcraft is in it. Since you can't take it off, it's guided by some spell other than the original enchantment."

Jancie lifted the locket toward the old witch.

Vika pushed her wire-framed eyeglasses up her hooked nose. "Moonstone is a receiver. It's love-drawing in nature."

"Is that why it works to lessen grief?"

"Right you are." She twisted her wrinkled lips to one side. "Hmm. But there's another purpose related to love going on here. All I can tell is that it's to do with romantic love and not over a loved one. It's got New Wish hallmarks."

"What tells you that?" Jancie asked.

"There's a mysterious softness about their craft. Kind of disguised. Maybe not to a New Wish witch, but it is to me." Vika waved her bent fingers in the air. "The milky haze of the moonstone swirls across its face. The luster on your mother's silver ring does the same thing. And their magic just plain feels different. I don't know how to describe. Like the vibrations ebb and flow with that twisty pattern."

Jancie held the ring before her face. "I can't see that. What I feel is strong and reassuring. When I touch it, it reminds me of my mother."

"As it well should, dear." Vika replaced the locket gently at Jancie's chest and patted her shoulder. "To figure out exactly what this locket intends for you and how Rowe might be involved, we're going to need a New Wish witch."

Jancie's eyes widened. "How? Can I just go to New Wish and ask for help?

The old witch nodded. "Wearing this locket, someone will want to talk to you. But before that, just to be able to step into the coven..." She tapped her index finger against her chin.

Jancie sat straighter. "My aunt Starla has been to the town many times. She's not a witch, but she knows folks there."

"That might—" Vika's words were interrupted by Siddie's thick tail whacking her face.

"Mistress, remember Cerise," the cat said and curved her tail around her side.

"Why, yes. Thank you, sweet one."

"I know Cerise," Jancie said.

"You do?" Vika's gaze fixed on her.

"I met her in town and then at the carnival we talked. She said I seem familiar to her, like she's met me before."

"Interesting." Vika placed a hand on Jancie's forearm. "We might be onto something. Cerise has cousins that are witches at New Wish, in-laws, not by blood. She goes there often enough to know some about their magic."

"Do you think she'll take me there?"

"I wouldn't doubt. She's a nice woman, always glad to help out. And she already knows you. Maybe your aunt can go along."

Jancie nodded. "I'd like that."

"Before you go, we need to unlock your deep memories. Hopefully, we can stir up some basic knowledge of New Wish witchcraft from your mother, either things she taught you or abilities you inherited. Since her spirit is strong in her garden, I'll help you form a plant ally."

Jancie pushed back from the table. "I'm ready."

Vika's smile grew, and her cheeks pushed up wrinkles that nearly swallowed her eyes. She rummaged in one of her baskets at the far end of the table and pulled out a pint amber bottle. "You're going to be a right good witch, no matter what magic you use. Let's head out to the garden."

Outside, Vika motioned Jancie to sit beside the herb garden.

Siddie curled into the folds of her mistress's full skirt.

Vika waved across the garden and faced Jancie. "Is there a particular plant here that's your favorite or one you seem to check whenever you come here?"

Jancie surveyed the bed. "The peppermint. It's always sending runners to take over new areas which I find interesting. Also, Mom used it in so many ways in our home, which makes it special."

The old witch nodded. "Good. It sounds like that plant would be very willing to become your magical ally. It may even help you remember some of your mother's New Wish practices. I'll lead you through the ritual. New Wish magic is based on elements of nature. We'll test how you react to different wind energies from the four compass directions. If we read nothing, then we'll try other element connections. Remember, you are safe here with your mother's spirit watching over you. That will help you keep your mind clear and focused."

Jancie tugged at the knees of her leggings and to be more comfortable.

"Ground yourself and come into your senses. Sit with the peppermint plant for a while. Use your senses to observe it. All of your senses—to look, listen, smell, touch, and even taste a leaf." Vika un-stoppered the amber bottle and held it out to Jancie. "Sprinkle a few drops of these waters of the world at the plant's base as an offering."

The dirt around the plant seemed to soak up the dribble of water like parched desert soil, even though it had recently rained.

"Now sit still, breathe deep, and close your eyes." After a moment, Vika's warm voice continued. "Picture the mint in your mind's eye, and ask permission to enter it and make alliance with it."

Jancie envisioned the peppermint and murmured, "May I enter your roots, stems, and leaves to make alliance with you?"

A waft of the plant's crisp scent answered her request, and she grinned.

"If you sense the answer is yes," Vika's voice lifted with a smile Jancie easily imagined, "then imagine the mint growing larger and larger. When it's larger than you are, imagine a magic door opens to you. Step inside the plant."

Jancie felt like she swam in a fragrant bath of minted water.

"Take a deep breath. Turn to the east inside your plant and notice what you see, hear, feel, touch, and taste."

"The air is fresh and clean and makes me feel strong and renewed," Jancie observed, eyes still closed.

"Now take another breath. Turn to the south inside your plant. Observe what you sense." Vika's voice was calm and supportive.

Jancie touched a hand to her cheek. "My face feels warm and alive, like when sunshine kisses your skin." A gentle current of warm air passed over her arms and shoulders, and she recognized her mother's spirit. Jancie swayed into the energy. Wispy remembrances of carefree summer days playing with the south wind appeared, how she used to alter its path with moments of her fingers. The vision from her childhood disappeared, but how she altered the wind's course remained. It was her power and had always been.

"Again, take another deep breath before you turn to the west inside your plant. Observe all there is to know."

Reluctant to move away from the touch of her mother's spirit, Jancie took her time turning. A light mist cooled the previous warmth. Her eyes dampened with more than the collecting dew. Words would not come to describe the growing feeling of loss. Yet traces of her mother's warmth clung to her shoulders, and Jancie held onto that.

"Now take another breath." Vika's spoke slow and clear. "Turn to the north and experience from your position inside the mint what you sense."

Jancie shivered. "I feel empty." Her voice broke, and her teeth chattered. "Icy cold. My stomach is knotting with anger, jealousy, and envy." Tormented, she trembled from head to toe, unable to feel her mother's warmth at all. A scream rose from the base of her throat.

"Stay with the feeling. Keep your eyes closed," Vika said.

Jancie hunched, the darkness threatening to consume her. Her mother's ring was the only detectible warmth. She clutched her opposite hand over it, and in one motion threw her chest and shoulders back. As her neck and head lifted, her mouth opened. A scream spewed from so deep, it felt like she'd retched her lungs. The moment her outpouring ended, her mother's blanket wrapped her entire torso in a secure hug. Jancie sank back, exhausted.

Vika stirred beside her. "Now take one more deep breath and turn to the center inside your plant. Notice what is there. Explore the world inside your plant."

Jancie wanted to open her eyes and break from the trance, but Vika's calming suggestion helped to push her forward. A minty smell again tickled Jancie's nose, and she took a deep, revitalizing inhale. She sensed both the peppermint and her mother supporting her. The world inside the plant glowed green behind her eyelids.

"Ask the plant to make itself known and to speak to you," Vika directed.

Jancie flashed a happy smile. "It already has."

"Ask if it has information for you. Take the time you need to listen and learn."

Peppermint, what can you teach me? A moment later, a tiny female voice answered inside Jancie's mind.

"You're a strong south wind witch like your mother, but do not fear using powers of other winds for more strength. Keep my leaves with you always. This is my and your mother's wish alike. Then, both of us can help you, like we did today."

How do I contact you? Jancie asked.

"Touch the leaves or think of me, and I'll be with you," the small voice replied.

Jancie nodded. "I've heard its lesson," she said to Vika.

"Ask if there is an offering you can make or some way you can give back to the plant spirit," Vika continued.

How can I repay you? Jancie asked the mint.

The voice giggled, like the tinkle of sleigh bells. Jancie imagined a faery. "Keep me healthy and strong like you already have," the mint faery said.

I will. Thank you so much. And thank my mother too, if you can.

"She heard and smiles with me."

Jancie squirmed, too excited to sit still, a huge smile crossing her face.

Vika let out a laugh. "Let's get finished. Turn to the center and say goodbye and thanks. Turn to the north and say goodbye and thanks. Turn to the west and do the same. And to the south. And east. Remembering your anchor, say goodbye to the mint plant, and find your way out through the magic door. Close it behind you. See and feel the plant becoming smaller and smaller, until it is back to its normal size." Vika sucked in a deep breath. "Open your eyes. Breathe. Stretch. Say your name out loud, clap your hands three times, and thank all you've invoked."

"Jancie Sadler, my name is Jancie Sadler, witch of the south wind." After three claps, Jancie stood and spun in circles, arms out, laughing.

"Well, well." Vika worked to stand and opened her arms to Jancie. "What did you learn?"

Jancie recounted the lesson, including feelings which had been too intense to describe earlier. "Was that a faery talking to me?"

Vika shook her head with a grin. "Land sakes, talking with a plant's faery. My plant allies only send me images. You tasted the winds and how they affect your base power. And you know how to call upon your allies, the mint fae and your mother's spirit." The old witch patted Jancie's shoulder. "You did good."

Jancie kissed the old lady's fuzzy cheek. "Thank you, Vika. You knew just how to help me. Can I fix you some lunch?" She bent and picked a sprig of mint and placed it in her jeans pocket.

"That sounds lovely, my dear." The old witch glanced at her cat brushing against her calves encased in support hose. "And something for Siddie, too?"

"Of course." Jancie smiled and took Vika by the arm. They made their way into the house with the Maine Coon purring underfoot.

***

Jancie wiped her wet hands on her leggings and opened to door to greet Rowe. "Come on in. We're just finishing washing up."

"How'd it go?" He looked at her, brows lifted.

"Great! Can you believe I have both Coon Hollow and New Wish witch lineage? I was blown away to find out. Vika found the moonstone contains New Wish magic. She helped me form a plant ally, and with that we learned what type of New Wish magic I have." Her hands flew around as she talked and led him to the kitchen. Jancie hoped the amazing details she and Vika had discovered would warm him up to being involved with her again.

"Wow! That is incredible." He worked to hide a smile and moved to the sink counter where Vika dried a pan. He hugged his old friend from behind and kissed her white head. "You're amazing. How did you do that much in just a few hours?"

She looked over her shoulder at him, a twinkle in her eye. "It's all about picking the right path for the right job. That's all."

"And knowing lots of magic, so you can pick that correct path," he added. "It smells great in here. You had time for a nice lunch. I'm jealous."

"Jancie sure knows how to cook. If you'd stayed around like she asked, you could have had her tasty lunch too," Vika snapped back.

Jancie smiled, glad the old lady took up her cause to get Rowe to change his mind, or at least feel guilty about his bad choice.

"I know." He shook his head. "So what did you learn?"

"More than just having witch blood, Jancie's connected to the south wind. That makes her a witch and a strong one at that. She learned a bit about how to use powers from that wind and also the others."

He looked at Jancie who sudsed a pan. "That is difficult. Nothing I can do."

"You're a Coon Hollow animator, and she's a New Wish witch using wind magic. Apples and oranges. Both good." Vika accepted the wet pan to dry. "I did learn that the moonstone has a lot of New Wish magic attached to it."

"Is that why it won't come off?" He asked Jancie.

"Perhaps. I need to visit a New Wish witch to learn more. We're hoping Cerise will take me into the coven down south. Aunt Starla would be a big help too, since she went there many times when Mom and Gran lived there."

Lines formed across Rowe's forehead. "I hope they welcome you there."

Vika hung the dishtowel out to dry. "Jancie, I'll contact Cerise, and you discuss the idea with your aunt. I'd like to tag along. If they don't mind, I'm a good bit curious."

Rowe sighed. "More reason for me to worry."

"Let me add to that load." Vika gave a dry chuckle. "While the Coon Hollow enchantment on the moonstone is about love to ease loss of a loved one, the New Wish spell is directly related to romantic love. You may still be tied to that gem, even though you're doing your best to hide your feelings for Jancie."

Jancie held her breath and watched Rowe, hoping the confrontation would break his resolve to stay apart from her.

"And hidden they will remain for everyone's safety." He picked up two of Vika's baskets and took a step toward the kitchen doorway. "Vika, are you ready to leave?"

"Soon enough." The old lady packed the empty amber water bottle into a third basket. "While your reasons are just, the moonstone may call your hand." She turned to Jancie. "Thank you for a wonderful day. Watching you blossom into a fine and good witch is a blessing for me." She touched both hands to her heart. "It warms me here. Thank you."

Jancie stepped close and pulled Vika into an embrace. "Thank you for everything, helping me learn about myself. I'll be in touch about our trip. I want you to be with me at New Wish." She pulled away and gave an awkward wave to Rowe.

A grin lifted the corners of his mouth, then he looked down at the baskets and the grin was gone.

Jancie hugged her arms over her chest to ward off the emptiness she felt.

Vika patted her shoulder as she stepped onto the front porch after Rowe. "It'll all work out. Don't worry."

Jancie watched them leave. Again, a knot formed in her stomach. Every time his black sedan pulled out of her driveway, it felt like she'd never see him again.

***

Outside of her father's house, dusk had settled. A chill breeze made Jancie shake. The cold slithered inside her jacket collar, sending icy fingers of anger, dread, and blame down her spine. The calling cards of Adara's north wind. Jancie worked a finger into her jeans pocket to touch the peppermint leaves. At once, her resolve strengthened, and she fought off the darkness. With an open mind, she stepped to the front door, prepared to hear whatever Dad had to say.

Her step-mother Heather opened the door. "Jancie! Come on in where it's warmer. Winter's a comin'. Have a seat." She motioned to the couch. "Did you eat already? If not, I can whip up something for you."

"No, I'm fine. Thanks." Jancie perched on the edge of a seat cushion.

"Maybe some coffee or pop?"

Jancie wondered when the woman would remember that she never drank coffee. "I'll have a diet."

Heather called back from the kitchen. "Dwayne was so happy to get your text about coming over. He had to run out to check on something at the shop. He should be back any minute."

Jancie placed a hand over the pocket holding the mint leaves. She needed all the help she could get to remain level-headed.

"Here you go." Heather placed the pop on a side table next to Jancie as the front door opened. "Hi, hon. I made a fresh pot of coffee if you're wanting some."

"Yeah, thanks." Dad gave Jancie a cautious glance. Dark circles rimmed his eyes, and his face looked pale. When he peeled off his jacket, she caught a wave of energy she now recognized as Adara's north wind. Had he been to see the high priestess this evening? Had he rekindled a relationship with her?

Jancie shivered and pushed those thoughts aside.

"I'm glad you decided to come after all." He accepted a steaming mug from his wife and took a seat in the nearby reclining chair.

Jancie nodded and took a sip of her pop, trying to hold her tongue and wait for him to talk.

Heather perched half of her wide butt on the arm of his recliner.

He placed the mug on the table and leaned toward Jancie. "Honey, it's not what you think. I did date Adara back before I met your mother. Adara and I were out cruising one summer night and, well, we'd had a few too many. I was driving. We hit her brother's car, and he and Adara's oldest sister died in that accident." He ran a hand through his gray hair. "I'd killed two of the high priestess's kids. I panicked. Either Grizela Tabard or the sheriff was gonna ruin my life." He looked at Jancie.

She swallowed, aware he waited on her response. "That was a bad situation."

"One of my buddies told me about a girl in our math class who was a different sort of witch. He'd been out with her a few times, but it didn't work out. He thought she might be able to help me. I was desperate. Grizela had made threats."

"Did Grizela do anything to you?" Jancie asked.

He shook his head. "But the rumors were flying. I thought about dropping out of school and leaving town." He leaned forward, elbows against his knees. "The girl from math class was your mother. She and I dated on and off, and the threats from Grizela stopped. Faye and I never talked about what had happened or her own witchcraft. We didn't share that much. But I sure was relieved that knowing her protected me. Before Faye, I thought my life was gonna to end." He looked down at his clasped hands. Usually clean, his nails were ringed with stains of motor grease. "Seemed like no time and she was pregnant with you. I thanked my lucky stars."

"You got Mom pregnant to keep Grizela from hurting you?" The words slipped out of Jancie's mouth before she could catch them.

Dad reached a hand out to Jancie, but she folded her arms across her chest. "It wasn't like that. I loved your mother," he pleaded.

Heat flooded Jancie's face, and she snapped, "Why'd you leave her then?"

He sat up and hurled words at her. "'Cause she started trying to teach you to be a witch. You were mine. Even though I loved Faye and she was a good witch, I couldn't stand for that. Not after what I'd been through. And she knew it." He stared through Jancie, his pupils beady, nostrils flaring. "That's why I keep you from them witches. You're my daughter."

"I can understand how scared you must've been after that accident." Jancie took a deep breath and stood to leave. "But you don't own me. If you're really worried about me having the same problems you did, don't." Her voice shook as the words formed in her mind. "I have blood from both our coven here and the one in New Wish. Dad, I'm a witch." Hot tears welled in her eyes, from anger at his attempt to control her, and from shame that being a witch didn't please him.

He jumped up, grabbed her upper arms hard, and shook her. He glared into her face. "You aren't no witch, you hear." His face turned beet red and tears rolled down his cheeks. His words slurred. "You aren't. Not my little girl. They can't have my little Jancie, too."

Jancie felt his pain, searing with a fresh wound. They both hurt.

It was hard enough for Jancie to find her path as an adult, but as a witch with powers she didn't understand, it was overwhelming. She needed her dad's support but wasn't sure she'd get it after all he'd been through.

She reached her arms around his waist, and he pulled her close.

Chapter Twenty:
Before the Full Moon

"I TELL YOU, I'M NOT seeing Jancie." Rowe's voice rose as he repeated the declaration for the third time to Adara. With mounting frustration, a prickling sensation bothered his right fingers. He wanted to retaliate against her for attacking Jancie at the bank yesterday. He thrust the hand deep into his trouser pocket to keep the inevitable telltale blue magic from revealing his anger.

Adara lifted her single brow left uncovered by the over-dramatic wave of raven hair across her face. "Think carefully. I have no room for deception on my council."

He nodded and looked through the open council office door to the entry hall.

"And what about that fake moonstone you're wearing?" Her words curled around his face and forced him to turn back to her. "What are you hiding?"

"Nothing. I don't want to draw attention to Jancie. A simple courtesy to her for a few weeks until she's accepted the connection she made with her mother," he snapped out his prepared answer. "Do we have any other matters to discuss?" Rowe huffed, removed his fedora, and stepped toward the doorway.

She commanded his gaze for a moment more, then released him.

He breathed a sigh of relief and strode into the council room. At the previous meeting, he'd been too worried about his reception by other members to look around. Originally built as a school, the floor planks showed a patina that often whispered with children's laughter. The sturdy oak chairs arranged in two rows looked to be a variety of teachers' desk chairs. Ornate carving decorated the leader's chair at the front. Not a part of the school's furnishings. The walls held black and white photographs of early progress made in the coven. In no hurry to talk to the two members present, he sauntered around the perimeter noticing the predominance of limestone—Salem limestone according to Vika. He took a seat behind an old biddy and straightened his tie and suit coat.

Gladys spun around, pursed her lips, and peered at him above the rim of her bent, wire-framed eyeglasses which teetered near the end of her pointy nose. Her gray bun pulled at her hairline. Rowe suspected the tautness strained her brain. "I see you're still with us for a second meeting," she said with a sneer. "Grizela Tabard's spirit must be fighting to get out of her cement likeness. Another McCoy to deal with."

Rowe nodded his head with a grin. "I intend to do my best to uphold my family's tradition."

"Hmpf." She turned around and whispered to the other older lady beside her who looked just as upright in a starched shirtwaist dress. Rowe didn't count either as an ally.

When Clarence Douglas and Art Kerry and his son Kyle stepped through the door, Rowe waved them to him.

The faces of the three men lit up. Between them, they owned one-quarter of the coven's property and half of its wealth. Progressive men, the older two had been contemporaries of Rowe's parents. They pushed the limits of adherence to archaic methods, upholding tradition when needed to maintain witchcraft, not livelihood.

Clarence's dark eyes gleamed from under a thick shock of gray hair. "Glad to see we didn't scare you off." He slapped Rowe's knee as he took a seat.

Art folded his tall but still trim frame into the chair on Rowe's other side, while Kyle stood behind. Art leaned in and said, "Clarence and I are game for what we discussed after the last meeting. Sound ideas about modernizing the workplace, son."

Rowe shook hands with them and twisted to extend a hand to Kyle, a tall, strong young man in his early twenties. He was a valuable influence on the council, since most positions were for life, being handed down. Without heirs, coven members could run for the vacant seat. Which was how Kyle gained his early position upon the death of Rowe's mother.

When another member passed, Nathan Wells had gained a spot. He was a studious and determined man of about the same age as Kyle. Nathan seemed focused on upholding the truth at all cost.

Rowe's council seat, although inherited, required approval of the high priestess. More than a year had passed since the vacancy was left by his father. Rowe regretted his neglect, but grief had taken the forefront during that time.

Oscar Burnhard, a portly middle-aged man, squeezed through the doorway and lumbered to the opposite end of the room. The floorboards creaked under his heft, crying for mercy. With a groan, he lowered himself onto the widest of the motley chairs. He wiped his jowls with a handkerchief, then nodded to the others. A staunch fundamentalist, he uniformly supported Adara and the Tabards before her. Clarence and Art had joked with some degree of hope that another new member might be coming soon, the way Oscar courted a heart attack.

The members stood while Adara made her expected grand entrance, sashaying into the meeting room.

Kyle waved at Nathan, who entered after Adara. The two stood at chairs beside Clarence.

Art whispered to Rowe, "Kyle tries to get Nathan to swing our votes. Works sometimes."

Adara's midnight satin dress emphasized every wiggle as she stepped onto the raised dais at the front of the room. Once seated, she arranged her dress so the side slit showed a long line of thigh. "Thank you all for coming. Please, be seated." She nodded to Viola, the woman next to Gladys. "Will you be recording notes?"

"Yes." Viola readjusted her seat and opened a notebook.

"Then, I'll call this meeting of the Coon Hollow Coven Council to order." With a monotonous tone, Adara rolled through a list of recent rule violations. Routine discussions among the council followed, and restitutions were established.

Adara peered up from the page she held. "It seems now that we have a new council member, we've also had an influx of appeals to change the approved list. Mr. MacElroy wants permission to upgrade his automatic milking machines. Mrs. Gaddie, who runs the school cafeteria has requested microwave ovens. Mr. Candish would like the use of battery-operated drills for use in his cabinetry shop."

Art stood. His height alone was imposing, and he spoke in a firm voice. "I believe wholeheartedly the use of modern conveniences in the workplace, the source of one's income, should be permitted."

Gladys spun her head around as well as Rowe's owl Busby. "And how exactly do you intend to regulate that? Mrs. Gaddie would likely take one of those new ovens home, and we'd not be the wiser."

Nathan dug in a scuffed briefcase and withdrew a bound document.

"After adjustment to the rule is made known, there needs to be some trust." Kyle replied.

"It is stated in our doctrine that coven members are assumed to be good." Nathan held up the well-thumbed covenant. "Those who fail to follow the rule will face consequences and serve as role models for others to do better."

After other council members shared opinions, Adara called for a vote through show of hands. "Those in favor." She clenched her teeth as Nathan's hand went up. "Those in opposition." She uncrossed her legs and planted her feet on the floor. Gripping both armrests of her throne chair, Rowe thought she looked like an angry sphinx. "The amendment has passed with a vote of five in favor and three opposed." The words hissed from her lips as though unpleasant to her sensitive palate. "Viola, please see to it that this change is made known as well as limitations for use of such modernization outside the workplace."

Rowe enjoyed watching her tortured facial expressions, like a caged animal trying to hide its distress. Change threatened her power. He caught her gaze, and she squirmed in her seat.

Then, without looking away, a change came across her face, a slight curling of the corners of her crimson lips. "Now that we've reached the end of the planned business, I have a new matter to bring before council." She worked to dampen her grin. "There has been a misuse of magic that needs to be dealt with."

Rowe's face grew hot, and he worried about what maliciousness she was up to.

"One of our own council, Rowe McCoy, has made inappropriate use of witchcraft."

The others faced him with varying expressions. His allies appeared annoyed with Adara's apparent pettiness, while her supporters wore smug grins.

Adara rose and stood tall on the elevated platform, looking down at them. "Following his wife's death, Rowe McCoy was made official bearer of the griever's moonstone. He was appointed to wear the enchanted moonstone until he connected with another soul under the same duress who could command the locket to open. His own burden would then be lightened by the encounter with that person. This much has happened to Rowe McCoy. The enchanted gem should now be dormant and placed in safekeeping here in our vaults until another coven member faces such a loss and becomes the new bearer." She stepped off the dais and slipped between Gladys and an empty chair to where Rowe sat.

Nathan pulled a thick volume from his briefcase and flipped through pages.

Adara waved a hand toward Rowe's chest. "Yet he still wears the moonstone. Except this is not the moonstone of binding magic. It is a fake. He's hiding the fact that the original is worn by the woman who was able to open the locket. It must be returned to the coven's vaults."

"Who is this woman in possession of the moonstone?" Oscar asked.

"Her name is Jancie," Adara spat.

Rowe stood. "Jancie Sadler, daughter of Dwayne Sadler."

The older members gasped and looked from Rowe to Adara but said nothing.

Children's laughter from the old school encircled the room, invading the silence.

Clarence leaned over to Kyle and Nathan, his whispers audible above the fading giggles. "Dwayne was Adara's lover who, with her along, accidentally drove into and killed Adara's brother and oldest sister. The tragedy caused the middle daughter to go mad and created a rift between Grizela and Adara."

Adara returned to the platform and scanned each face. "The moonstone must be returned. It belongs to the coven."

"Regardless of any personal connection in this, she's right." Oscar looked across the room. "The task of the enchantment is complete. The gem belongs here."

"Absolutely." Gladys nodded her head like a bobble-head doll.

"Yes, I agree," Viola added with a mousy voice.

Clarence and Art looked at Rowe, who shook his head but remained silent.

Nathan planted a fingertip in the middle of a page. "Here it lists the griever's moonstone directives. The magical interaction proceeds just like Adara described. 'Once the recipient has been in contact with the deceased loved one, the moonstone bearer will, in time, have his or her burden likewise lifted. While that period is variable, the gem shall remain in possession of the witch bearer for the duration. When the witch's needs are satisfied, the gem will be stored in a coven stronghold until the next griever from our population is identified." He faced Rowe.

"Is that all it says?" Rowe asked. "Anything in the amendments?"

Nathan scanned the page with his finger and turned to the newer section. "Yes, that's all." He looked back to Rowe. "Adara is speaking the truth. It must be returned."

Sweat trickled down the nape of Rowe's neck. Jancie was a witch with both New Wish and Coon Hollow blood. The moonstone wouldn't come off of Jancie's neck because it had more work for her to do, tasks not listed in the covenant or its amendments. Perhaps not written for a reason. His gut knotted and told him to keep quiet.

"Let's put this to a vote." Adara glided to the edge of the dais. "All in favor of Rowe returning the moonstone, raise your hand." All council members except Rowe held up hands. "By unanimous vote, Rowe McCoy, you must return the griever's moonstone to this coven office before the next full moon or be subject to consequences of losing your position on this council and your community job in the schools."

Rowe clenched a fist, blue light dripping from his fingertips.

Adara smirked. "Expect to pay the costs, and Jancie will be brought to this council and forced to give up the gem."

Rowe stood. "I am prepared to leave the coven with Jancie to protect her."

"Leave if you wish. But know that, in such an event, there will be a greater price to be paid." Adara's haughty laugh trailed after him, even through the closed door of the building, as if the bespelled trees carried her cryptic warning into the evening darkness.

***

Rowe dropped into his car frustrated and confused. More than anything, he worried about how best to protect Jancie. Adara's words of warning rang in his ears. He started the car and drove with no destination, turning down one road then the next while his mind wandered.

After a few miles, recognition of Keir's red brick Victorian house broke his delirium. The lights were on, and he turned into the drive. At the door, Rowe struck the knocker and leaned against a porch post, his balance affected by his confusion.

The door opened, and the seer's coyote nosed through the crack before his master appeared. "Waapake, calm down. It's just Rowe." Keir bent and steadied his familiar while glancing up at Rowe. "I expected you. I heard the trees singing a threatening song. That's why Waapake is upset. Come in." Keir stepped aside.

Rowe made his way past the small parlor where Keir received customers seeking his sage advice. In the large, front parlor, Rowe sank into the soft leather couch. He glanced at the windows hung with dream catchers. "I think you'll need to close the drapes. We have things to discuss that must remain secret from any wandering familiars or transformed witches."

"Waapake, bring bones," Keir said to his coyote as he pulled the dark green drapes shut.

He turned away from the last window and met his familiar sitting with the large leather pouch in his mouth. "Thank you." Keir accepted and rubbed the coyote's tan ear and sat in a carved ladder-back chair near Rowe. "You've come from the second council meeting. By your energy, I sense it didn't go as well as the first." He leaned close, looking Rowe in the eye.

"Much worse." Rowe rested his head back and looked up at the ceiling. "There's no end to Adara's evil. She's made it nearly impossible for me to protect Jancie. She worked my council allies against me to demand retrieving the moonstone from Jancie and returning it to safe keeping in the gathering hall's safe."

Keir gave a wry grin and shook his head. "Let me guess. Nathan provided supporting verbiage in the original covenant."

"Right you are." Rowe rubbed his eyes. "Did you use your awe-inspiring talents as a Shawnee wise man or just plain-inherited-Coon-Hollow-seer abilities to see that?"

His friend chuckled. "Neither. I grew up babysitting Nathan."

"Can't say I count him among my friends after tonight." Rowe tipped his head forward and met Keir's gaze. "Adara was all too eager to use his findings. Art and his son Kyle and Clarence couldn't refute the written rules. I have three days to return the moonstone locket."

"By the day of the full moon." Keir patted his coyote's raised head. "Why can't Jancie take it off? You said Vika was with Jancie today. Did they learn something?"

Rowe nodded. "A lot. So much I don't know where to begin to protect Jancie now. Vika found a New Wish spell on the moonstone overlaying our magic. It seems there's more Jancie needs to accomplish before it will let go. In addition, Jancie is a New Wish witch strongly aligned with the south wind."

Keir's thick, black brows shot up. "We now know the players from my vision—the north and south winds."

Rowe nodded and rubbed a hand across his jaw.

"What's your penalty if you don't return the moonstone?"

"I lose my council position and my teaching job. Worse yet, Jancie will be brought in and dealt with."

Keir groaned.

Rowe leaned forward, elbows balanced on his knees. "It gets worse. When I threatened I'd leave Coon Hollow with Jancie to protect her, Adara countered there'd be a higher price for that action. She set the words of her threat with a spell that echoed through the woods."

"I heard it and read their language. That's why I expected you."

Rowe locked his gaze on his friend. "What's the price? Did you hear? Or was the spell just some evil trick of hers?"

"I heard fragments, but Waapake is better at nature's language." Keir shook the pouch, and the bones and stones inside rattled.

The coyote sat up, long ears pricked forward, golden eyes following the shaking pouch.

Keir smoothed the rising fur along his familiar's back. "Use these to show us what you heard." The seer bent low and emptied the bag's contents onto the hand-loomed tribal rug.

For the next few minutes, Waapake's silver muzzle pushed pieces in different directions, while Rowe and Keir leaned close, watching in silence.

The coyote nudged two long bones until they lay parallel, then barked at Rowe.

Rowe moved closer and knelt beside Waapake.

"All right," Keir joined them. "Waapake, let me know if my interpretation is incorrect." He pointed to two parallel bones that lay inside a small circle of round bones and smooth stones. "These must represent Rowe and Jancie." He passed an open palm over the pile and then over another of more angular pieces. "These represent the two covens. New Wish being smaller, but the magic is time-worn and older. Coon Hollow is newer with sharper edges, not yet honed smooth." He glanced at the coyote, who remained calm, and continued. "Rowe and Jancie, while together within New Wish, are separated."

Waapake sat quiet on his haunches.

Keir looked at Rowe. "Adara's threat, enforceable or not, intends to keep you from Jancie if you go to New Wish."

"Her magic can't work there, can it?" Rowe asked.

"I don't know. But it follows from what Cyril told me the other day during my run out on Dead Tree Trail."

"The coon king?"

His friend nodded. "I didn't understand his meaning then. Now it makes more sense. He said, 'Tell who you call friends that sparks will soon fly, when two secret charms reach the moonstone's eye.' You and Jancie may be stumbling into spells hidden in that gem she's wearing. At any rate, there are rough times ahead. Be careful, my friend."

Chapter Twenty-one:
Dance With Me

JANCIE'S MIND WHIRLED as she drove away from Dad's house.

She was a witch. What did that mean? How would her life be different now? Everything she thought she knew has suddenly shifted. Sweat beaded along her upper lip. She gripped the steering wheel to pull her back to the reality of the traffic around her.

She knew Dad loved her and wanted what he thought was best for her, but that wasn't possible. He'd been hurt bad, and that made him overprotective. Even though he was grateful Mom had been a good witch and protected him from Grizela Tabard, he just couldn't accept Jancie being a witch. She understood his concern, but that didn't make it right. She had to be her own person. She hoped, in time, he'd love her as a witch. She bit her lip and wondered how long before that day would come, if at all. He was so dead set against witches.

What dreams did Dad have before he was lucky to have just one good path to follow? She thought back to all the plans she'd made before Mom got sick with cancer. *A good life isn't about having lots of paths to choose from. It's about making the one path you do have the best it can be.*

She pulled to a stop at a light and smacked a hand against the wheel. "Damn. I need to listen to myself." *I have one good path in front of me, and I'm not following it.*

She changed her turn signal to make a right turn rather than a left onto Maple Street toward the coven.

Her headlights caught the three bent old lady oak trees still huddled in their thin coats of withered brown leaves. She drove past the farmhouse where the pickup with a wooden bed sat sentry. The sights of the coven seemed different now. Whether they were or not, she couldn't tell, but knowing her great grandfather Louis was a Coon Hollow witch changed everything. She was part of this place. Not an outsider.

Jancie turned onto the river road and wound her way past log cabins billowing chimney smoke to the big white brick house with the lovely art glass windows. She glanced at the dark property as she turned onto the drive. Was he home? Her pulse quickened. She hadn't expected him to be gone. She parked, ran to the front door, and rapped the knocker. Scuffling noises sounded inside, and she smiled, ready for the door to open. But it didn't. She knocked again. Still no answer. She trudged back to her car, thinking back to whether he mentioned where he'd be this evening. *No, he's trying not to be friends with me, remember.* She leaned against her car door and scanned the yard. Loneliness passed over her.

Something rustled in the bushes at one corner of the house.

Jancie took a tentative step toward the noise. She took a deep breath, afraid it might be Adara in some altered form.

In the flood lights from the garage shed, orange eyes glinted through a black mask.

Jancie gasped and backed away until she caught sight of a striped tan and black furry tail. Just a raccoon.

"Lassie, I feel the south wind about you." The coon stepped away from the bush. "I'm Cyril, coon king of this here hollow."

"Umm, hello, Cyril." Jancie cautiously leaned forward. "I've heard the playground song kids sing about the coon king, but didn't think you were real."

"Very." He swished his tail from side to side and chattered. "I felt your breeze a blowin' through the hollow and been lookin' for you since. I've a warning for you that sparks will soon fly, when two secret charms reach the moonstone's eye."

Jancie clasped a hand around the locket resting on her chest. "How do you know this?"

"Heard it in a gully trickle when I washed a juicy berry."

Was this strange critter telling the truth? Jancie guessed the one secret charm must be the trace of New Wish magic Vika found on the moonstone. She didn't have a clue about the other one. "What are the two charms?"

"I only know they carry scents of the two strongest winds. North and south. The rest is up to you, lass."

"Thank you for your information, Cyril." Jancie knelt and reached a hand out to the raccoon, but headlights along the road scared him away. Blinded, she could only make out the round shape of the old style lamps. She wished she could have slipped into the darkness with the raccoon but she was caught like a wild animal, the advantage with the unknown driver.

"Jancie!" Rowe's voice called out as the car turned onto the drive.

She let out a loud sigh. Spots in her eyes, she stood with effort as he wrapped an arm around her shoulder.

"Are you okay?" He led her onto the porch and through the door.

"Yes, just blinded from your car's headlights." Inside, the lamps helped her eyes adjust.

He let his arm fall from her shoulder to her hand.

As he put distance between them, a knot formed in the base of her throat. She needed him but couldn't find the words to convince him that she or Vika hadn't already said. The ache dropped into her heart, and she grabbed for his fingers slipping away.

"It's not safe for you to be here. Why are you here?" His gaze met hers and he flinched, then threaded his fingers through hers.

A tremble shook through her throat as if the disorganized words were jumbled and stuck. "I...I'm a witch. I belong—"

He pulled her into a close embrace. "With me. We belong together." His arms held her tight. "Whatever lies ahead, I'll be with you."

Her cheek against his chest, happy tears slipped from Jancie's eyes as their corners crinkled with a wide smile.

She hoped her dad would eventually accept her as a witch, but there was no guarantee considering how dealing with witches had changed his dreams. She belonged with her mother, but Mom was gone except for traces of her spirit. Jancie's friends weren't witches. Just another reason she couldn't fit in. Except with Rachelle, who loved her no matter what.

Like Dad found only one path in his life, Jancie's one wonderful direction was with Rowe and finding her own purpose as a witch. And that felt just right.

Rowe looked down at her and smiled as if he understood her thoughts. He kissed the trail of tears along one cheek.

"I need to go to New Wish," she murmured.

"Not tonight. Dance with me." His warm hands moved along her back, holding her close as he led her in a slow foxtrot. His mouth found hers for a passionate kiss.

Heat rushed into Jancie's face. The song they'd danced to before began to play in her memory. Their feet shuffled back and forth. Their bodies swayed as one in arcs through the foyer. When they swept past the parlor's French doors, she noticed the phonograph turning, the needle set on a record, Tilly the large wing chair nearby. She couldn't help but smile in the middle of a kiss. And felt his lips curl, too.

Rowe's hands followed the curve of her waist and moved lower, cupping her bottom.

A moan escaped her lips, and she gasped for breath, holding to his strong shoulders to keep her balance.

He danced them to the stairwell and let the music play on while he led her up the stairs to his bedroom.

The burgundy velvet bedspread and drapes were warm and inviting, like his touch on her bare skin. She melted into him.

Clothing came off in a hurry, tossed aside with no care other than to be as close together as possible.

Rowe's touch made her coo and squirm against him in complete ecstasy. At one moment, the back of her hand brushed the moonstone lying between her breasts. The gem flashed blue, and a vision of her great grandparents, Maggie and Louis, passed through her mind. She sensed their intense love for each other. The same feeling that swelled in her heart for Rowe.

Chapter Twenty-two:
Herbal Tea

JANCIE TOOK HER TIME driving back into Bentbone, choosing the more scenic twists and turns of Owls Tail Creek Road. Sleepy log cabins peeked from under heavy yellow and orange maple limbs. The sun shined on a lazy Saturday morning as it reached toward its highest point in the sky. Her Camry kicked up puddles of colored leaves. She could see why vacationers chose their little valley for weekend getaways this time of year. The hollow was dressed in its finest colors, the best she could remember in years. Or maybe she just hadn't looked with the right eyes. She smiled to herself. Now that she was in love with Rowe, it seemed hard to believe that problems could touch her.

Her cell phone rang and broke her happy delirium.

"Hey, Rachelle. What's up?" Jancie answered.

"The print shop owner has to leave and close the store at noon today. Let's celebrate! How about lunch? Maybe some shopping too?"

Jancie glanced at herself in the rearview mirror. "I'm a wreck. Can you give me an hour?"

"An hour? Did a train hit you?"

"Not quite. But I'm not home. I'll be there in fifteen minutes."

"You don't sound out of breath, so you're not out running." Rachelle squealed so loud, Jancie held the phone away from her ear. "You stayed at Rowe's last night, didn't you?"

"I did."

"Tell me everything. What's it like doing it with a witch?"

Jancie laughed. "Well, he's amazing. How about we save details for lunch."

"Damn, girl. Hurry up." Rachelle said something to someone in the background and then spoke do Jancie again. "How about I meet you at your house? We can talk while you clean up."

"Great. Come on over any time." Jancie hung up and shook her head, wondering where to begin telling her best friend all that had happened in the past twenty-four hours.

After she turned onto Main Street and entered Bentbone's tiny business district, the phone rang again, this time with Lizbeth's ringtone. "Hi Lizbeth."

"I'm at work but had to call. I just got some references I'd ordered after we talked about that moonstone last weekend. You've got to hear this."

"Do I want to hear it?" Jancie checked traffic and braced herself for bad news.

"After all the old-fashioned research I had to do, you're going to hear it."

Jancie laughed. "Thanks. I owe you. Tell me."

"It turns out that the creator of the moonstone, Jude Oatley, who enchanted it back in 1850, wanted it to gather positive energy from those it healed. That way, the magic was strengthened for future use. I got a copy of his journal when he made the stone. The strange thing was he worried about the gem's receptiveness being too great. Getting it just receptive enough caused him trouble."

"That doesn't sound good, but I think Vika is aware of that. We're trying to find someone who might know more about this exact idea. I'm glad to know what you learned."

"Jancie, be careful. I'm worried."

"Thank, Lizbeth. It's good to have friends who worry about me. Are you working all day?"

"Yeppers. And tomorrow. Why?"

"Rachelle got off early, and we're spending the afternoon together. Though you might join us."

"Thanks, but sorry. Hey, my break's over. Catch you later."

Jancie turned onto her street, and Rachelle's boat of an old Chrysler already sat in her driveway.

Rachelle leaned against the back bumper, the hem of her Bohemian green print skirt hanging on the gravel. "Yep, you've got that new lover glow," she called out when Jancie stepped from her car.

"That bad?" Jancie fluffed the short front sections of her hair. The back she'd gathered in a ponytail at Rowe's.

"Nah. You look perfect. In love." Rachelle draped an arm around Jancie as they made their way inside.

Jancie plopped her purse on the kitchen counter. "I took a shower at Rowe's but need clean clothes and some makeup. That won't take me too long." She motioned for her friend to follow her into the bedroom.

Rachelle flopped onto the bed. "Spill."

Jancie opened her closet and dug for a pair of jeans and a long-sleeved top. She tossed them beside Rachelle with a grin. "Well, he's a good dancer."

Rachelle lifted a single brow. "You danced at his house?"

"Mmm. Yes. He does a sexy foxtrot."

"A romantic."

"Very." Jancie wriggled out of the jeans she'd worn yesterday and imagined the cloth against her skin to be his hands caressing her.

"Romantic men make good lovers. They're not in a rush. Am I right?"

Jancie's grin grew wider.

Rachelle leaned on one elbow. "Did he use magic when you did it?"

The word 'magic' made Jancie fumble with the blouse she wrestled with. Her head poked out with the garment backwards. She sighed and hoped her friend would accept her as a witch with real powers, not just having witch blood.

Rachelle laughed so hard she snorted. "That good, huh?" When Jancie's head appeared again, her friend pressed more. "So was his touch magic or what?"

Jancie's phone rang on the dresser with a special ringer she'd assigned to Rowe and Vika. She dove for it.

"Must be loverboy," Rachelle sang.

Jancie looked at the phone. She shook her head and answered. "Hello, Vika."

"Jancie, I'm hurt bad and need your powers to help me." Her voice was a hoarse whisper. "Adara was here. Siddie chased her away. I don't know where my sweet cat is. Rowe needs to find her. Call him. Bring your mother's peppermint and come fast."

"I'll be there right away. I'll call Rowe. Is anyone with you?"

"No. I called the neighbors down the road," Vika's voice grew weak, "but they didn't answer."

"Okay, stay calm. I'm on the way." Jancie shot Rachelle a concerned look, and her friend scooted off the bed. Jancie hung up and pressed Rowe's number. "Answer. Please, answer." As soon as he said hello, she blurted out, "Vika called me. She's been injured by Adara."

"Oh, no! Did she say how bad?"

"No, just that she needs our help right away. Siddie didn't come home after chasing Adara. Vika wants you to look for the cat. I have to gather an herb Vika wanted, then I'll be right there."

He gave directions and mentioned a dense woods, which made Jancie anxious. His lowered his voice. "Jancie, if you get there first, be careful. Adara may have laid a trap."

"I will." Jancie rushed to the pad of paper on her nightstand and scribbled his directions while repeating them. She hung up and wrangled her shirt into place and worked on some easy slip-on loafers.

"Vika's hurt?" Rachelle asked.

"Yes, by Adara, and I need to help at her house. Are you coming with me?"

"Of course. Let's go."

Jancie raced through the kitchen and grabbed a plastic bag and shears on the way to the garden. There, she crouched and cut several stems of peppermint and shoved two leaves into her jeans pocket. She tried to stand, but something made her pause. Her hand moved to the rosemary, and she collected two woody branches, then several short marjoram cuttings. She took a deep breath. "Thank you, Mom. Please, please be with me and help me heal Vika."

They jumped into Jancie's car, and tore through town with Rachelle on the lookout for cops. On Maple Street, Jancie depressed the accelerator down the hill, the car doing nearly seventy on the county road.

She executed sharp turns, throwing Rachelle side to side while the poor girl blurted out directions from the creased paper.

Jancie glanced at her friend. "You okay?"

"Yes. Go!" Rachelle pressed herself away from the passenger door.

Jancie sped up. Without taking her eyes off the road, she blurted out, "I have something you need to know right now. I found out I'm a real witch, with both Coon Hollow and New Wish blood. I've got to use my powers to help heal Vika. I didn't want you to be weirded out."

"Damn, girl! And you used to think your life was boring."

Once in the woods, Jancie slowed, unable to see houses for the thick growth of yellow-leaved maples and bushy pines. The second mailbox came into view and she turned onto the gravel lane. A rambling fairytale cottage with tall gables sprang up in a clearing ahead. Rowe's black sedan was parked in the circular drive. She pulled in behind, and Rachelle dashed with her to the front door.

Jancie knocked and called, "Vika? It's Jancie."

"Have you been here before?" Rachelle whispered.

Jancie shook her head, listening for any response.

"Jancie, come on in," Rowe called.

She turned the tarnished brass knob and pushed the heavy door open. The home smelled earthy with the aromas of dried herbs that Jancie recognized. She took a few steps along the wide plank flooring in the narrow hall until she saw Busby winging toward her. She picked up her pace to meet and follow him into a sitting room. Rambling roses on the wallpaper had crowded to the corner of the room where Vika lay on a Victorian chaise lounge.

Rowe glanced up, his face drawn and pale, when Jancie entered, but he continued passing his palms across Vika's body. "She has evil inside her. I heal injuries, but more spring up. The evil is spreading and working faster. I can't keep up. I need your magic."

Jancie took the old witch's hand. "Vika, I'm here. I brought the peppermint you asked for and other herbs that Mom guided me to collect."

Vika's weak eyelids fluttered, and she attempted to raise her head. Her face shined with sweat. She gasped for air.

"Lie back." Jancie leaned closer to Vika and massaged her hand.

"Jancie, I'm glad you're here," Vika labored to speak, wheezing the words out. "Adara's evil's going to kill me. I don't fear death, but this isn't how I wanted to go. Your mother's magic might counter what she's done."

"I'll do my very best." Jancie squeezed the old witch's weak hand, then set to work. "My best friend Rachelle is here to help me." Jancie eyed her friend. "Come hold her hand. Rowe, keep mending injuries."

Rachelle moved to Jancie's side and took Vika's hand. "Vika, I'm Rachelle. I've known Jancie since middle school. Heck, we were maybe twelve then." The raspy tone of her voice was hypnotic. She brushed Vika's wiry, white hair from where it stuck in a film of sweat covering the old lady's face. "We used to chase frogs in the crick behind the principal's house." Running fingers through the bushy hair, Rachelle continued telling a rambling story about her friendship with Jancie.

Vika's breathing slowed and became more regular. Jancie was thankful for her friend's good judgment.

"Where's the kitchen?" Jancie asked Rowe. "I need to boil water."

Busby lifted off his perch on a chair back before his master voiced a request. The owl flapped through the narrow hall, past a small galley kitchen to a huge country kitchen.

Jancie's eyes popped out at the sight of Vika's potion room. Walls of shelves with bottled herbs and rafters hanging with drying bunches. She turned her focus on the simple task of filling a tea kettle with water and setting it to boil.

To steady her nerves, she pulled the peppermint leaves from her pocket and closed her hand around them. Eyes closed, she inhaled and exhaled deeply, then replaced the leaves and set to work, mind clear.

Jancie found mortars and pestles on a shelf above the sink. She reached up to select one set, then withdrew, sensing traces of an energy unlike what she knew from her own garden. "Better to shred my herbs by hand." She looked around for a drinking mug without success.

She found Busby clinging to the back of a wooden chair. "Is all the cookware, like drinking mugs, back in the little kitchen?"

"Probably." He flapped his wings and followed her.

There, she found a mug, cup-size strainer, and teaspoon. Working there, she tore the peppermint into the strainer along with a few crushed leaves of marjoram and rosemary. When the kettle whistled in the potion room, she retrieved it and poured steaming water into the mug. She placed the strainer on top and let the herbs steep. Her hands moved to form a tent covering the mug, like her mom used to do. Jancie didn't know then what her mother did was witchcraft, but the practices stuck in her mind. Jancie blew on her cupped hands until the mint's vapors tingled her skin and made her ring glow. "It's ready, Busby. You fly into the sitting room and have Rachelle help Vika sit up so she can drink."

Without a word, he winged away.

Jancie removed her hands and lifted off the strainer, surprised to see no steam rising from the water. The concoction smelled amazing. And familiar. She remembered the smell, although not as strong, from the tea Mom served her when she had strep throat with a horrible fever. *This better be strong enough to kill more than bacteria.*

Balancing the cup as she walked, she reached Vika's side and Rachelle braced the frail woman's shoulders. "Healing tea to drive out the evil."

Rowe glanced at Jancie. "Her lungs are filling with fluid. Give her only small swallows."

Vika managed a weak grin. "Smells good." She took a sip while Jancie held the mug. Vika gasped for breath. "Mmm. Like I'm dancing in the garden." She took another sip before her strength gave out. She sputtered, rested her head back, and closed her eyes.

Rowe continued passing his healing touch around her torso but kept his gaze on Vika's face.

Jancie held the mug ready in case more was needed.

Vika extended a shaking hand to Jancie.

Guided by what she remembered her mother doing, Jancie accepted with the hand wearing her mother's ring. She clasped the frail skin as tight as she dared. She sensed Vika's breathing, her heartbeat, the air filling her lungs, the blood flowing through her veins. Jancie closed her eyes and willed the herbal tea throughout Vika's body. Jancie's eyes flew open. "It's working, but you need to drink more."

Rachelle lifted Vika's upper torso, and Jancie brought the mug to her lips.

Vika swilled the rest down and collapsed.

Again, Jancie worked to push the elixir throughout Vika's system. Jancie leaned down and blew on their joined hands.

Vika's eyes opened and color returned to her face. She smiled but clung to Jancie's hand with both of hers.

"It's working!" Rowe cried, still applying healing. "The damage I fixed is staying healthy."

Vika took a deep, full breath with only a slight sputter on the exhale. "My lungs are clearing. You did it, girl. I knew you could. Thank you. You're a mighty fine witch."

Jancie handed the empty mug to Rachelle and wrapped her free hand around Vika with great tenderness. "You and Mom believed in me. That had to help."

Rowe dropped his hands to his sides and knelt on the floor, his face wet with sweat. "I'll check again in a few minutes to be sure you're okay. Can you tell us what happened?"

"It wasn't anything sneaky. Adara came to my door, didn't say a word other than hello, and when I went to ask her in, she hurled a spell at me." Vika gave a slight cough. "I fell to the floor, and Siddie took off after her. I managed to crawl to my phone and called Jancie. That's the last I remember until you got here and used your touch."

Rowe looked at Jancie. "Adara must've attacked Vika for helping you."

"Lucky you," Rachelle sunk to her knees on the floor and looked at Jancie. "Having been the one to break the evil witch's heart twice."

Jancie sighed and slumped beside her best friend.

Rachelle rubbed Jancie's shoulder. "It was kind of cool watching you do magic. My best friend's a real witch." She grinned. "That might have some good perks, you know?"

Jancie returned the grin, glad for some cheering up.

Vika strained to get up, but Rowe stopped her. "Did my Siddie come home?"

Not answering her question, Rowe stood and stepped toward the hall. "Busby, will you go have a look around for Siddie or Adara? Be extra careful in case Adara might still be in the area. You know she can transform into a badger."

"Yes. And I'll watch for her foul crow Dearg, too." Busby sailed after his master.

Jancie and Rachelle kept watch on Vika.

Moments later, Rowe knelt and rechecked her internal body. "Still fine." He smiled at Jancie and pulled her into an embrace. "You're incredible. Thank you." He released her and gave Vika a comforting hug. "I can't lose you. You're like family to me."

"I won't go by the hand of evil, if I can help it." Vika wrapped a gnarled hand around his shoulder. "But enough of this, we need to get on with putting that woman out of power as high priestess. Jancie, you need to make a trip to New Wish and really learn about your mother's magic. That's what can overthrow Adara."

Jancie nodded. "And about other spells that are on the moonstone. My librarian friend, Lizbeth, got a copy of Jude Oatley's journal. He made the stone receptive to gather positive energy from those it healed. That way the magic would be strengthened for future use. But he worried he'd made the stone too receptive to outside energies."

"So, when are we going to New Wish?" Vika's dark eyes gleamed.

"Are you okay to travel?" Rowe stared at her.

The old witch laughed. "You both fixed me up fit as a fiddle. Just try and stop me."

Rowe nodded. "Nothing I want to take on. I'll be going along, too."

Vika's bushy white brow lifted, and she shot him a grin, "Oh, you've seen the light of day and now want to be around this fine young witch."

"I gave up trying to keep away. Too much work." He laced his fingers through Jancie's.

The old woman pursed her lips. "Well, we need to ask Cerise since she needs to get us into the New Wish coven. I called her last evening. She's happy to help Jancie at New Wish, but we didn't set a date."

Rowe nodded. "I'll talk to her right away and also with Keir, Logan, and some of the council members who support me. Folks here need to know what happened today. "

"And I'd like Rachelle to come along." Vika glanced over her shoulder at Jancie's best friend. "She might not be a witch, but her voice and manner kept breath in my body. She's not Jancie's best friend for no good reason."

Rachelle beamed. "When are we going? I'll be ready."

"Let's shoot for tomorrow noon," Rowe replied in a take-charge tone.

Jancie grinned. "I'll call Aunt Starla. She's been in the town of New Wish lots and knows people."

"While making all of these arrangements, let's try to use the buddy system as much as possible," Rowe said. "I need to—"

Busby whipped into the room with something in his mouth. "I found this collar but didn't see Siddie or any witch or familiar."

Vika wrung her hands. "That belongs to my Siddie. Rowe, please find her before we leave."

Rowe stood and pulled out his phone. "I'll contact Cerise, first. Jancie, I'll give you a call to let you know if it's certain we're going tomorrow. I think you should stay here with Vika until I get back with a group to search for Siddie. I'll be quick." He motioned to Busby and headed out of the room. "We've got work to do."

Chapter Twenty-three:
The Secret Meeting

ROWE PULLED INTO VIKA'S DRIVE after a quick trip home to get supplies. He'd hurried knowing Jancie needed time to arrange to be gone from work, contact her aunt, and pack. He also wanted to be near Vika in case Adara made a return visit.

Jancie met him on the porch, and Busby and Maeira landed on a railing. "That was quick. Glad you're back," she said and looked beyond Rowe. "Looks like we have company."

He followed her gaze to the end of the driveway where Logan's burgundy Nash Ambassador approached. "That's Logan and Keir. More are coming."

"I made good use of time and called to get off work for a while. My manager wasn't too happy, but I haven't taken a vacation in ages. Aunt Starla's already packing." Jancie let out a laugh. "She's called me at least half a dozen times asking about what to wear."

"I beat her." Rowe chuckled. "I'm already packed. I'll stay the night here. It would be a good idea for you, Rachelle, and Starla to do the same for safety."

"We'll do that. I already asked Vika if she had room. She laughed and showed me all around the bedrooms in this old family home. What about Cerise?"

Tension Rowe had been holding in his shoulders eased a bit knowing Jancie, Rachelle, and Starla would stay at Vika's for the night. "She and I both thought she'd be safe at her house since she really hasn't had any noticeable connection to you or me. I'm sure my two buddies here will be happy to keep tabs on her family while she's gone."

Logan and Keir and his coyote Waapake made their way to the porch, and a dark green Packard pulled in the drive.

"What are your two buddies going to do?" Logan asked with a wry laugh.

"Cerise is taking Jancie and me, along with Vika, Jancie's friend Rachelle, and her aunt Starla, to New Wish in southern Indiana. I need you two to keep an eye out for Cerise's family."

Logan's brow crinkled. "Okay, but why?"

Keir pulled him aside for a private talk while Rowe greeted Art and Kyle Kerry and introduced them to Jancie.

A tall, trim man, Art stood his full height and took quick initiative to shake hands with her. His son Kyle followed his father's lead and used a solid grip to show his acceptance. Glad to see their support, Rowe felt assured about the success of his intended plea for their assistance.

Vika poked her head out. "Come on in. I've made pots of tea and Jancie's friend Rachelle whipped up some tasty cookies for you all."

Clarence Douglas hobbled up the porch steps, the last to arrive. "My arthritic leg's acting up today. Must be some change in the air. That's the only time it bothers me."

"More changes than you might think, Clarence." Rowe offered a hand to support his fellow councilman. "I'd like you to meet Jancie Sadler." Rowe motioned to her.

Clarence extended a hand to Jancie, and she accepted. "Glad to meet you," he said looking her in the eye. "I've heard a curious mention about you in the coven's gossip. You've got some witch powers about you, but you're Dwayne's daughter. Isn't that right?"

"Yes to both." She gave him a polite smile.

Rowe guided them to follow the others inside. "Clarence, it will all make more sense in our discussion."

Rachelle greeted everyone at the doorway to the potion kitchen. "There are pots of Earl Grey and Oolong tea on the counter. Help yourself." She waved a hand at one of the two rows of trestle tables. "Be sure to get some cookies there on that table as you find a seat."

Rowe smiled at her as he passed, understanding why both Jancie and Vika wanted Rachelle to join them. She held up well in the company of witches, only getting a little skittish around Keir's coyote.

Busby sailed in a circle around the ceiling, nearly colliding with Vika's drying herb bunches, until he calmed down and took his usual perch on an odd chair back beside Maeira.

When everyone seemed settled, Rowe presented the facts detailing Adara's attacks on Jancie and Vika.

The men's faces fell, except for Keir's who understood the attack incident intuitively. "What reason could she possibly have to do such vile acts?" Art asked and ran a hand through one of his graying temples.

"She's got to be stopped." Logan tipped onto the back legs of his chair. Rowe sensed his friend's pent up anger.

"We can all agree on that," Clarence added. "It's past time the Tabard evil was cut down like a diseased tree."

Chatter buzzed around the room, and both owls hovered above their perches.

Rowe raised his palm for silence. "For some reason known only to Adara, she set her sights on me as her intended love interest. Most likely some ploy for more power through alliance with me and the good name of my family. The moonstone enchantment complicated her plans when Jancie became bonded to me to ease both her grief and mine." Rowe nodded at Clarence. "You rightly sensed Jancie's witchcraft, quite obvious since she just performed a difficult spell to save Vika today."

Logan turned to face Jancie and gave her a thumbs up. "Kudos to you, Jancie."

"Yes, great job countering a Tabard," Clarence added, followed by a chorus of appreciation.

When the floor quieted, Rowe continued. "What Jancie used was New Wish magic. Her mother, Faye Sadler, was a witch of the New Wish coven. Something that was kept quiet in the community, especially after she married Dwayne."

Art nodded his head. "I remember rumors about her when I was a teen, but we didn't interact often with townies, so I never sorted those out."

"This is making real sense now," Clarence added.

"Why was Vika targeted?" Kyle asked.

The old woman sat straighter. "Because I helped Jancie learn about her powers and how to begin using them."

"Good for you." Keir applauded her, setting off another round of positive remarks. He stood. "I'd like to relate a reading I did shortly after the moonstone brought Jancie to Rowe and sparked the first antagonism from Adara." He brought his hands together in prayer position, then spread them apart. "The winds from north and south will fight a grueling battle where life will be lost and neither will win."

Keir's coyote howled until his master pressed his hands together and took his seat.

"Adara is the north wind, and Jancie is the south," Logan said in a loud voice. "We need to work to keep loss to a minimum. And to support Jancie in every way possible."

Jancie set down her cup and massaged a temple. Rowe suspected she'd guessed at an upcoming conflict between herself and Adara, but the outcomes must've taken Jancie by surprise.

He stepped behind her and placed a hand on her shoulder.

Vika caught Jancie's gaze and shot her a knowing smile.

"Logan and Rowe, what can we do to help?" Kyle asked.

Logan rose. "In my work with the coven's elderly, I've been recording information from them about any instances of wrong use of magic by the Tabards. And I've accumulated a surprising list."

"They'd be the ones brave enough to speak up," Art added. "Their dreams now are for better lives for their grandchildren. Others would likely fear Adara's wrath, like they did with her parents before her. We all can do what Logan's doing, as well as searching through old records."

"Won't that just stir up the community and put Adara more on the aggressive?" Clarence asked.

"Keep your investigations as secret as possible," Kyle said, sparking a wave of individual discussions.

Logan waved his arm. "There shouldn't be any problems. Mabon is one of the two calendar times specified by our covenant where the priest or priestess can be challenged by a successor."

"But that's after the Mabon ceremony by popular vote, not by force, No one would dare vote against a Tabard for fear of reprisal," Keir added. "We need to keep my prophecy secret to this group."

Rowe raised his hand. "A show of hands to vow secrecy of Keir's prophesy and our interpretation of those representing the winds." All in the room raised their hands, or owl wings, and a paw in Waapake's case.

"Good." Rowe clasped his hands together. "In preparation for Mabon, some of us—Jancie, her aunt Starla, Vika, Rachelle, and myself—are leaving tomorrow noon for the New Wish coven in southern Indiana with Cerise as our guide. There, Jancie hopes to learn more about how to use her mother's powers she inherited."

Logan spoke up. "The rest of us here need to watch out for Cerise's family, that they don't end up Adara's newest targets. And keep an eye on Rowe's and Vika's places for the same reasons."

"We sure will." Art glanced at his son, who nodded.

Keir and Clarence pledged their support as well.

Rowe raised his hands. "Before we leave, I have one more request. Vika's familiar Siddie, the Maine Coon cat most of you know, has gone missing. She chased Adara after the attack. If you can, please spend time with me now to search for her. Clarence, would you please remain here to watch over Vika while Jancie and Rachelle go home to prepare for the trip?"

"Will do." Clarence laid a hand on his knee. "Best thing with this leg acting up."

Keir had Waapake sniff Siddie's cat bed. The coyote let out a yelp and raced through the doorway.

Cups were laid down, and the others filed out of the warm kitchen into the blustery, overcast afternoon.

***

As dusk turned to darkness, Rowe and the men returned to Vika's where she met them on the porch.

Her face fell when Siddie wasn't with them.

Rowe avoided her gaze, unable to find the words he'd have to say.

Art and Kyle embraced Rowe, then took to their car.

Jancie drove up as they were leaving.

When Rowe hugged Jancie's aunt, he realized his shoulders were knotted and stiff with stress. Ignoring his pain, he, Keir, and Logan helped unload Jancie's car and get everyone situated into sleeping places. Rowe was glad for the company of others at the end of this hard day.

They gathered in the potion kitchen where Vika and Clarence were working to prepare a meal. A savory smell of sage dressed chicken greeted the tired crew.

Waapake nuzzled Rowe, and he knew it was time. "Vika, we found Siddie. Just outside of the woods near the turn onto Road 210."

Vika came closer and took his hand. "I know what you have to tell me." Her eyes clouded over.

"Her body lay dead in the ditch, burned with Adara's dark magic." Rowe looked to Keir.

Jancie and Rachelle hugged each other.

"I was there when her spirit set free from her body. Waapake and I communicated with her in that form. It was her wish to take on a new body to continue as your familiar, rather than wait for you in the cemetery. We buried her empty body there, and it will remain until her spirit is ready to rest." A tear slipped down his cheek. "She left us with words for you. 'I will find you and serve you always.'"

Vika collapsed into Rowe's shoulder, sobbing.

Waapake rubbed his side against her bare legs and filled the room with a mournful howl.

Rowe held Vika's shaking body tight. His heart swelled with determination to right these wrongs.

He was sure Jancie's feelings of pain, anger, and purpose met his. One by one, he sensed the same from each friend. He said a silent gratitude and looked around the room, meeting their gazes.

Chapter Twenty-four:
The Elder

ON ONE OF THE TWIN BEDS in a small bedroom of Vika's house, Jancie packed the last few items into her suitcase.

Her best friend, who shared the space, stumbled back from the bathroom with a groan.

"What took you so long?" Jancie asked.

"I didn't know this old house wasn't wired for hair dryers." She tossed the offending appliance into her bag, her layered hair more frizzed than styled. "I spent the last fifteen minutes dodging cobwebs in the basement to reach the fuse box and trip the breaker."

Jancie's hair hadn't looked much better, but she controlled it with the two sides secured on top of her head with a barrette. She'd opted for comfort with jeans and a knit top for the drive.

"Fun. And New Wish is even older." Jancie zipped her luggage closed and yanked it off the bed onto the floor. "Don't expect more conveniences there. On your way through the house, did you notice whether Siddie, in a new form, had found Vika yet?"

"I only heard Vika and Starla laughing like old friends in the kitchen."

Jancie let out a sigh. "My aunt's a dear, cheering Vika up. I'm sure glad to have you and Aunt Starla along."

"No problem." Rachelle shoved last night's pajamas into her bag. "Hey, I was wondering...how do you feel about being a witch? Are you okay with it?"

"Yeah. I don't really feel any different. I guess Mom taught me more about being a witch than I knew. I thought all mothers did strange stuff with herbs."

Rachelle chuckled. "Hardly, but your mom was great."

"Controlling my powers does feel odd, like I don't exactly know what I'm doing." Jancie grinned. "Kind of like everything else in my life."

Rachelle shot her a smile. "I hear you on that one."

Jancie hoisted the bag into the hallway, and Logan plucked it from her hand.

In the other, he picked up Aunt Starla's from outside of her door and headed downstairs.

The delicious smell of bacon wafted up in his wake and made Jancie's mouth water.

Her aunt and Vika talked in the galley kitchen. Jancie wondered how the two could fit into that narrow space, but when she reached the door, the two women operated with consideration and efficiency. They even wore matching red bib aprons.

"Can I help?" Jancie asked.

"Only with your appetite." Aunt Starla's eyes twinkled. "Grab a plate and dig in."

Jancie couldn't help but smile at her great aunt, clearly happy to be useful.

Vika motioned to the counter. "We have a hearty breakfast all ready, complete with fried potatoes and onions, bacon, sausage, scrambled egg casserole, and Starla's famous cornbread."

Jancie and Rachelle each took one of the mismatched plates and sampled everything, including a large piece of cornbread.

Logan and Rowe blew in, rain-soaked, and joined the women. Rowe dressed casually in a dress shirt and trousers, with a trench coat rather than a sport jacket over top. "I'm sure glad you offered your car, Rachelle," Rowe said between bites. "No one else drives anything big enough to hold six people and their suitcases."

She grinned while she munched a strip of bacon. "The boat comes in handy more than you know."

"The boat?" Vika's brow creased.

"Slang for an oversized, old car," Logan replied.

"Really? Is Rowe's Studebaker sedan a boat?"

Logan chuckled and shook his head. "That's older than old."

Over his glass of juice, Rowe glared at his friend with mock annoyance. "Just vintage. I happen to like my dad's cars." He lifted a forearm and motioned for his owl to land.

Busby settled and accepted a bite of cornbread.

"While I'm away to New Wish, Busby, you and Maeira will remain here."

The little owl hung his head and hunched his shoulders.

"I'd like for you to come along, but I really need your help here. As my familiar, you alone share my powers. Someone needs to keep watch over our house and property. While I'm away, I entrust you to use my powers to keep the homestead safe."

Busby rolled an eye up at Rowe.

Maeira flapped her wings from her perch on a side chair. "My son, that's a huge responsibility for a familiar. Be proud your master trusts you that much with his powers."

Busby's cream-colored chest feathers puffed, and he lifted his head. "Thank you, Master. I'll keep the home place safe."

Rowe rubbed a hand across the owl's head. "I'm relieved to be able to count on you. If you have any trouble, report to Keir since he's good with familiars. He'll have some grains for you and Maeira daily."

Busby cocked his head and winged out of the room. A minute later a knock sounded at the front door. He called back, "It's Cerise. Someone, please come open the door for her."

Rachelle darted out to help, laughing. "You mean you haven't learned how to open doors yet? I'm going to have a word with your master about that."

Jancie giggled at her friend's humor and easy manner. It was wonderful that she seemed at ease with these coven folk and hoped her reception in New Wish would be the same.

With Rachelle and Busby leading the way, Cerise stepped into the potion kitchen. "It smells so good in here." She blessed each face with her warm smile. Her perky bobbed brown hair curled neatly under at chin-length, and her horn-rimmed glasses highlighted her friendly dark eyes. Petite and dressed in a powder blue trench coat, she fit Jancie's mental image of her mother's garden faeries rather than a witch.

"Have you eaten, dear?" Vika jumped up and walked to the witch, half her age, and took her coat.

"I had a quick bowl of cereal between getting my three boys and husband up and fed."

"Help yourself to food in the small kitchen." Vika nodded to her new pal. "Starla, Jancie's great aunt, made the best cornbread I've ever had."

"Starla!" Cerise zipped around the table, and the two women hugged. When Cerise pulled back, she fixed her grin on Jancie. "I'm beginning to figure out how I know you. I remember your aunt and grandmother when we all happened to be visiting New Wish. I was just a girl then. You look so much like them. I'm glad to be able to help you out."

Rowe pushed back from the table. "Let's plan to leave in twenty minutes."

"I left my bag on the porch," Cerise said to him as she made her way into the food kitchen.

***

A few minutes before noon, Jancie and the others huddled on the porch. Big raindrops came down with force enough to smart. She folded her arms across her chest, staring at what seemed like one more in a string of deterrents to reaching her goal. One by one, they darted through the hard rain to Rachelle's car, parked close to the porch.

Rachelle insisted on driving since the weather was so bad. She spread her wet skirt out while the others peeled off rain jackets.

Logan waved them off from Vika's front porch.

"Damn, this car is loaded." On the main county road, Rachelle pressed the accelerator to the floor to get the car going.

Jancie sat on the narrow center part of the divided front bench seat, snuggled against Rowe's shoulder.

He squeezed her hand and pointed to the right-hand ditch.

She nodded, sensing the lingering traces of burnt evil held down by the rain.

From the backseat, Vika sobbed softly. "I really don't like leaving home while Siddie's spirit is missing. At least I have dear Logan to stop by every day in case she returns."

The car filled with conversation to cheer Vika, but everyone quieted when Rachelle turned onto State Route 46 and headed west out of Bentbone.

After an hour, Jancie stretched and turned.

Vika leaned against Starla, both asleep with mouths open, while Cerise worked on her cell phone.

Jancie nudged Rowe and rolled her eyes toward the backseat. "You're not the only one."

He glanced behind. "Nor should I be. We need cell phones. I'm working toward that with Clarence, Art, and Kyle." He rubbed his forehead and massaged his temples.

"Are you okay?" she asked.

"Just a bit of a headache." He leaned his head back, and she threaded her arm through his and held his hand.

As they drove the last leg of the windy route south, Jancie bent low and craned her neck to see the tops of the taller Appalachian foothills. The rain had stopped. Mist rolled above the colorful trees, taking on hues of red, orange, and yellow, like the balls of cotton candy sold at last week's carnival.

"Heads up, everyone," Rachelle called out. "Only ten miles to New Wish."

Those in the backseat roused and groaned.

It was mid afternoon, when the Chrysler chugged up a huge hill. At the crest, the highway followed a high ridge to the right while Rachelle made a left turn and descended a steep grade into a valley. "And we thought our Coon Hollow was isolated."

The road wound through brigades of fifty-foot oak and hickory soldiers protecting various outcroppings of log cabins.

"This looks creepy." Jancie scanned both sides of the road and looked into the backseat. "Cerise and Aunt Starla, is this the coven or the town?"

Starla chuckled. "It's both, dear. Coven homes are marked on the front with five-pointed pentangles."

"Only the ceremonial grounds and meeting house are kept protected and separate." Cerise sat up and placed a hand on Jancie's shoulder. "It looks a lot different than the Hollow, doesn't it?"

"It sure does," Jancie replied. "Like we've entered a secret place with the nearby hills so steep they're like walls." From her early years of college down south along the Ohio River, she expected deeper valleys than the rolling hills at home. But the remote stillness here surprised her. Almost frozen in the time period of early settlement. Barns, larger than most homes, stabled horses. Split-rail fences marked off grazing areas. On drives and lawns, horse-drawn buggies were parked, not the black Amish sort, but fiery red, emerald green, and cobalt blue. Cars were scarce, and then only old pickups with rust that defied recognition of their ages.

"I do see log cabins with partial walls of limestone like the style in our coven, but not any Victorian houses at all," Rowe added.

"And no open areas with livestock or small farms like home," Vika said.

Jancie looked out of Rowe's window. "In Bentbone, cabins are mostly used for tourist shops and motels or artist galleries and homes. Here, those are all I see."

Rachelle sighed and glanced at a group of three houses tucked into a pine grove. "Look at the smoke curling from their chimneys. I want to live in a cabin. My dream."

"You've wanted a cabin forever," Jancie said.

"Still saving for one."

"Bet they're plenty cheap down here, Rachelle," Starla called from the backseat.

"Umm, no thanks. Too isolated." She pulled to a stop and looked both ways before crossing in front of an oncoming one-horse red buggy. "No cars? Are there any stores?"

"I saw a gas station and a farm market," Jancie replied.

"You won't see no Wal-Mart here or any motels neither," Starla added. "It's not the place for tourists."

"The main part of town is just ahead," Cerise directed. "Drive through that, and I'll show you where to turn."

The business district made Bentbone's five blocks seem like a thriving city. A long square-logged cabin spanned a whole block. A wooden sign declared it to be the town hall of New Wish. Across the street stood the only brick buildings Jancie had seen. A grocery, a hardware store, and a pharmacy occupied the block. Both sides of the street had angled parking to accommodate the extra length of horses and buggies. Close to a dozen rigs were parked. On adjacent corners stood a feed store and a blacksmith. That was the extent of buildings created as businesses. Scattered cabins ahead were marked with signs for a seamstress, a doctor, and a lawyer.

Folks walking the sidewalks or sitting on benches stared at their car as they passed. Residents of New Wish looked normal, most wearing jeans, plaid shirts, and hiking boots. Some women wore full-skirted dresses that reminded Jancie of pioneer clothing she'd seen at historical reenactments near home.

"Something tells me there's no internet access here." Rachelle glanced at Jancie. "Check your her phone."

Jancie shook her head. "Nope. No service."

"Turn left at the next street," Cerise directed. "Then on the right, you'll see a house with a huge pentangle at the door. Turn in there."

A tidy two-story log home sat closer to the road than cabins they'd seen farther out of town. Fading perennial beds flanked the wide front porch.

They spilled out of the car, and Cerise sprang up the brick walk.

A prominent circle of wood painted with a colorful pentangle hung above the porch steps.

"Hold up a bit," Vika protested. "Us old timers need to stretch our legs." She and Aunt Starla lumbered up the walk after the others, holding onto each other up the steps.

It wasn't until Jancie reached the porch that she noticed her own legs were stiff. Her right arm where she'd leaned against Rowe was pricking as blood rushed back into it.

Rowe missed a step, and she caught his hand. Apparently, he was overeager too.

Purple coneflowers missing a few petals turned their heads from the afternoon sunlight to face the dark porch. Yellow-eyed blue periwinkle asters did the same and partially closed their centers as if squinting at the visitors.

Vika took Jancie by the elbow and nodded toward the flowers. "See those plants? They're checking you out."

Jancie flinched. "Me?"

The old lady nodded. "They smell your New Wish blood."

"Or the peppermint in my pocket from Mom's garden that likely came from this area." Jancie chuckled and patted her jeans pocket.

Cerise grinned at Jancie and knocked on the door.

A tall, robust older woman in her fifties poked a head out, then pushed the door wide and stepped out. "Cerise!" She held her arms open, and the two exchanged a quick hug. "You've brought us some company, both old and new in so many ways that I'm getting dizzy." The woman nodded to Rachelle and Vika. "New faces." She grinned at Jancie and Rowe. "And new faces and old spirits." Her gaze locked on Starla. "And one face I could never forget. Starla!" She stepped across the porch and embraced her old friend.

Starla lit up. "Neala, it's sure good to see you, after what is it, more than two decades?"

Neala matched Starla in height, tall with a sturdier frame like a tree trunk compared to Starla's soft rolls of flesh. While Starla's hair hung in thin white curls around her head, Neala wore her stick straight salt and pepper hair cropped close. She dressed simply in jeans and a chambray work shirt, a silver pentangle at her throat.

"Neala is the chieftainness or high priestess of New Wish," Cerise said to the others while the two women were occupied with each other.

"Cheiftainess? My lands." Aunt Starla stroked Jancie's arm. "Neala's ma helped our Maggie care for her husband Louis when he fell ill. That'd be Jancie's great grandparents."

"Do tell." Neala extended a hand to Jancie. "You must be Faye's daughter then."

Jancie smiled and accepted her hand, which felt warm and certain like her mother's always had.

"I can tell a lot about you by your touch." Neala grinned. "I'm sorry to feel Faye's early passing and how hard it was for you. I also feel new beginnings in your life now, love and purpose. And I'm sure you can read my touch. Right? It's something all New Wish coven kin can do."

Jancie nodded with a grin. "Your touch makes me feel relaxed, but I can't pick up any details."

Neala shot a knowing smile. "You're new to witchcraft?"

"I just found out that my mother was from here and a New Wish witch. I never knew about all this when she lived. It was kept from me. My dad's decision." She nodded to Vika. "With Vika's help, I've learned I have powers like Mom's, from the south wind. I want to learn more."

Neala's smile faded, and she shook her head. "No, you're here because you need to learn more. There's evil chasing you from the north wind." She clasped her hand together. "Well, you've come to the right place. Don't you worry." She looked at Rowe and Vika. "You two give off strong Coon Hollow energies. Prominent coven members with remarkable talents." She bowed her head. "I'm honored to meet you both."

Vika held Rowe's shoulder as she attempted to curtsy, while he extended a hand to the chieftainess.

Cerise introduced the leader to Rowe, Vika, and Rachelle.

With his touch, Neala gave a start and stared at him. "Can this be? Your mother was Hazel, am I right?"

He gave her a curious look, forehead crinkled. "Yes, she was. I miss her a lot. I've been expecting her spirit to come home soon."

"I'm sorry for your losses. Your mother's spirit's been in and around the past month floating without form."

"I knew she had family along the Ohio River, but didn't know she had blood ties to New Wish."

The leader gave him a warm smile. "Like Cerise, to some of the town folk, not the coven. But I've been friends with them both for decades. I'm sure your mother will feel your presence and come by, or we'll chase her down."

"Great. I want to see her." He beamed.

"Will do." Her smile flattened. "I sense you have a complex love relationship with Jancie, one with multiple spells woven around and between the both of you." She glanced from him to Jancie, who pulled the moonstone locket from underneath her blouse.

"This was Rowe's griever's moonstone. It helped me see and say goodbye to Mom, but now it won't come off."

Neala clucked her tongue. "Another thing for us here to help you with. That might take a bit more work. It seems something of a mystery since there're several types of magic involved. Vika, I may need some of your knowledge added to the cauldron."

Vika straightened. "I'll be glad to help out."

"Come on in and let me get you some refreshments while I make a few calls." Neala held the door until Rachelle passed, then pulled her aside with a long arm around the girl's slender shoulder. "You might not be a witch, but you're welcome here just the same."

While enjoying Neala's own herbal tea and crackers with homemade herbal spreads, Jancie eased into the curving back of a bentwood rocker. The cozy sitting room was decorated with handmade furniture, loomed throws, and beeswax taper candles. Cheery, crazy quilt pillows and cushions gave a homey look. The comfy place and Neala's easy manner made Jancie relax more than she had in a long while. Her concerns about the initial creepiness of New Wish fell away. The enclosed sensation gave way to security.

Neala joined them, bringing a comb-back kitchen chair with her to sit upon since all other seats were taken. "Judging by what I know of your reasons for visiting New Wish, you'll be staying a little while. My home has enough beds, if you don't mind sharing rooms and lending a hand in the kitchen for meals."

"Fine by me," Starla said in a loud voice. "Vika and I have found a real knack for cooking together."

The others chimed in with agreement.

"Jancie, it's easy enough to teach you how to use your skills of our order, but that moonstone bothers me. Let's start with that concern. I got the word out to our elder, Eartha, who knows more about ancient and peculiar magic. She's well past one hundred years old and lives alone to concentrate on her studies. We treasure her spirit and knowledge and pay frequent visits to help her with chores. She'll receive you this afternoon. I've sent for a buggy driver to take you there." Neala faced Starla and Rachelle. "I'm sorry but Eartha won't accept non-magicals in her presence while she works. I'll be staying here with you, and we can see some sights of the town together."

Jancie looked at her friend and great aunt, not wanting to leave them out. She couldn't decide.

A distinctive clop clop clop of horse hooves sounded on the street outside. "That's Georgie. He'll take you to visit Eartha and bring you back."

Jancie, Rowe, Vika, and Cerise filed out after Neala. "Hey, Georgie." She waved to the man driving the bright blue rig. "These folks need to go to Eartha's and be returned here afterward."

Georgie was a beanpole of an older man with unshaven silver whiskers and a shock of stiff, gray hair that poked out from under a navy and white striped train engineer's cap. Limber for his age, he hopped from the driver's seat and offered a hand to each as they climbed into the open-air buggy.

The last to step up, Rowe hesitated, lost his footing and fell backward holding on by the outside handle. He quickly gathered himself, and, with Georgie gripping his waist, hoisted himself up and took a seat beside Jancie. Rowe's face was wet with sweat.

"What happened?" Jancie touched his knee.

"I had a dizzy spell. I've had a headache since we left." He ran a hand across his jaw. "Probably just lack of sleep. I tossed and turned all night, worrying."

Vika leaned forward from the opposite bench. "When we get back, I'll talk with Neala about getting you some herbs to help you rest tonight."

"Eartha will do you some good that way, sir." Georgie scampered up into his high seat. "Even better than Neala, but don't tell the chieftainess I said so." He gave the sleek Standardbred filly a gentle flap with the reins, and they drove round the circular drive onto the street.

The four exchanged waves with their friends left behind on the porch.

The drive took them away from town on lanes only wide enough for the horse and buggy. The air smelled dense and woodsy with forest leaf mold accumulated in the bottom of the low valley. A few cabin windows peeked at them from their seclusion deep in the woods. The rustic way of life and slow pace calmed Jancie's agitated nerves. Adara's wrath seemed a world away.

The little horse turned down a gravel path, and Jancie strained to see a house. The thicket on either side threatened to overtake their buggy. "Just ahead," Georgie said. He kissed to his horse to prompt her onward.

Jancie smelled pine smoke before she caught sight of the tiny log cabin, its back set against a rocky cliff face in the rising hillside.

The horse drew up and their group made their way to the dwelling, the driver leading them. He knocked and called out. "It's me, Georgie. I brought you four guests from Neala's."

There was no response for at least a minute, but he didn't turn away.

Finally, the planked door creaked open on rusty iron hinges, and a hunched elderly woman appeared. Her simple charcoal shift dress hung to sensible brown lace shoes and tied at her bird-like waist with an intricately knotted cord. "Thank you, Georgie." She rolled her eyes up and peered at the visitors through cloudy cataracts. "Come in. I was expecting you all. I'm Eartha." She let go of the door and shuffled into a dark sitting area lit only by a glowing fire.

The limestone fireplace covered an entire side wall of the home. The back wall extended into the cliff, a cave of sorts excavated from the rock. Aside from a front window next to the door, all other wall space was covered with shelves. Thick dust obscured book titles and the contents of glass jars. A long roughhewn table occupied the middle of the room, and Eartha waved toward it. "Have a seat."

Rowe and Vika sat on either side of Jancie on a handmade bench, Cerise beside Vika.

Jancie introduced them, while the elder lit a taper candle on the table and covered it with a glass hurricane. Her frail hands shook, and her motions were slow and deliberate. Fine strands of her shoulder-length, white hair rose with her trembling. She sat opposite of them and said, "Neala related some of your concerns. Please lend me your hand, Jancie."

Jancie extended her hand across the table to the aged witch. After the initial cold fish feeling of the woman's loose, thin skin, Jancie felt warmth that compelled her to shut her eyes. Her mother's spirit draped across Jancie's shoulders, and the south wind blew hot in her face. She opened her eyes, surprised to feel strands of her hair blowing back.

"A young and strong south wind witch. Rare indeed. And a good thing since an evil north wind chases you." Eartha's voice sputtered in breathy bursts. She let go of Jancie's hand. "Neala told me about a moonstone layered with spell upon spell. Please let me see the stone."

Jancie pulled it from her neckline. "It won't come off."

"Come closer, child. My blind old eyes cannot see that far."

Reseated beside the elder, Jancie held the locket up.

Eartha pressed a palm to its smooth surface and stared into the fire across the table. "This is enchanted, the same exact griever's stone I've seen once before." She cocked her head to Rowe. "Young man, please tell me about your family and your magic."

"My full name is Rowe Alan McCoy, son of Hazel and Walter McCoy, both deceased and former long-standing members of Coon Hollow Coven's council. The family magic is animation. I teach that skill in our community schools."

A toothy grin interrupted the deep lines of her face. "Ah, Hazel. I visited with her last week, appeared from the fire in my fireplace one morning." The elder's glassy eyes stared off into the flames. "You were fortunate to have such fine parents, Rowe McCoy. But you've known death of a wife and bore this moonstone after your loss. And you are also fortunate to hold the heart of this south wind witch seated beside me."

She faced Jancie. "And you set off the stone's enchantment to face the loss of Faye, one of our own."

Jancie nodded. "Yes."

"Help an old mind with names. Faye was Betty's child. Betty's mother came to New Wish pregnant. That woman was..."

"Maggie, Margaret," Jancie added.

"Maggie, of course. I should've remembered. She and Louis, a Coon Hollow witch, came in the worst winter. They couldn't marry according to that coven's customs. She feared her unborn child would be ostracized, and probably so." Eartha gazed into the fire and caressed the moonstone. "She wore this very moonstone and came to me with the same problem as you. It wouldn't come off. I was still a girl then, in my twenties and living with my parents. The mystery of this stone drew me to my calling, part historian of magic, part seer, part diviner of plain old common sense." She chuckled.

"Through wild ways of my own magic and a heap of research, I learned the moonstone was overlaid with a spell set against New Wish blood. A Coon Hollow female witch by the name of Mabbina Tabard fell in love with a male witch from her coven, a widower wearing this very locket. But he loved a New Wish witch and wanted nothing to do with Mabbina. Enraged and owning a black heart, she laced the moonstone with evil to keep the lovers apart. They weren't accepted as a mixed couple in Coon Hollow, and when here in New Wish, a mental illness drove him mad. Within a year's time, he had no knowledge of his new bride." Eartha looked away from the fire and let go of the moonstone. "And bits of records told me this had happened once before, between the Tabard family and a New Wish witch who stole the heart of a Coon Hollow male witch." She squinted her eyes. "The lovers' names were Victoria and John, and the Tabard girl...Judith or was it Priscilla? Anyhow, a pattern stood out to me when—"

"That's what happened to my grandparents, Maggie and Louis." Jancie twisted in her seat. "Is that going to happen to Rowe and me?" Her jaw went slack. She looked at him, suddenly aware that his headaches and dizziness were signs. The familiar knot formed in her stomach, and she reached across the table for his hand. "Can you stop this from happening to us?" she asked Eartha.

"No. I cannot. I could not help Maggie."

Jancie's throat constricted. "There must be something. Please help us," she choked out the words. Her gaze met Rowe's, his face ashen, already showing weakness. Angry heat flooded her face. She'd come here expecting help, but none was to be had.

The elder coughed. "I could not help Maggie." She gulped air, inflating her sunken chest. "That was because although she possessed New Wish blood, she was not a witch with active powers. Only a carrier. I presumed the locket came free after the man Mabbina loved died, and later it found its way to Maggie. At that time, seeing history repeating in desperate young love, I laid a spell of my own on this gem. I never thought I'd live to see it help any of our own, but here you are. Jancie, I hope you're the one destined to break this curse."

Jancie's breath grew shallow as she hung onto every word Eartha spoke, every movement she made.

The elder removed the hurricane from the candle in front of her. She cupped her hand around the flame with fire licking between her fingers, but didn't jerk or cry out.

Vika and Cerise leaned closer, and Rowe squeezed Jancie's hand.

Eartha's hands glowed orange, she turned to Jancie. "Keep hold of Rowe and give me your other hand. Do not be afraid." The elderly witch pressed her flaming skin to Jancie's.

Jancie braced to resist the reflex to pull away, but none came. The fire's energy spread throughout her body. A supercharged dose of New Wish magic. The orange color changed from yellow to green to blue.

The elder withdrew. "The color blue is important. It has chosen you, Jancie. It tells what element of nature here in New Wish will teach you to use your powers. I perform this ritual with our strong witches whose powers are blocked, much as yours have been suppressed. The term 'new wish' holds meaning for many here today and for those who chose this location more than a century ago. You have the spark within you from your grandmother's blood and fanned by your grandfather's powers. You are the witch Maggie never could be. Find your element and ask of it your one new wish, and it will be granted. May you break this curse."

Chapter Twenty-five:
A Mother's Love

DARKNESS BLANKETED the isolated valley as their horse's feet clopped with a steady rhythm back to Neala's.

Jancie wrapped an arm around Rowe as he leaned into her, complaining of a blinding headache.

Her thoughts wandered into the spaces of still blue dusk, searching for where she might find the blue element that would open her powers and grant her one wish. Blue indicated water, or was it sky? How would she know her element? The one wish seemed easy enough. But maybe not. To break the Tabard curse on the moonstone so she could share love with Rowe seemed the obvious wish. That meant she'd have to rely on her own power to overthrow Adara. She sighed inside herself.

She worried about Rowe. Other than getting him back to Coon Hollow, Eartha hadn't given a way to stop the illness that the evil spell brought on him. But, being back home in his coven might not even work. The curse seemed to activate when they left, but there was no guarantee of reversibility. She wondered if any of Neala's herbs would hold off Rowe's symptoms to buy Jancie time to find her element.

The horse trotted through the tiny downtown and pulled up on the circular drive where the chieftainess met them on her porch. The yellow glow of lamp light inside her cabin was inviting. If only Rowe felt well, and they could enjoy the time away in New Wish.

Neala and Georgie steadied each passenger as they stepped down from the buggy, giving special attention to Vika and Rowe.

"Does anyone know any herbs that can help at least slow the effects of the curse on Rowe?" Jancie asked. "I know breaking the evil is up to me, but I can't do that tonight. I'm worried."

"Won't hurt to try. I know grape leaves strengthen mental powers," Vika offered.

"Along with rosemary, spearmint, and savory." Neala added. "Those are still growing strong in my potion garden. We can make a tea. I spoke to Eartha after you left, and she told me about the curse."

"And mustard greens." Jancie took hold of Rowe's hand in case he faltered while climbing the porch steps. "Mom always made mustard green and rosemary tea for headaches."

"I'd appreciate a tea to ease this throbbing." He massaged a temple.

"Dinner's ready and waiting. After our walk, Rachelle, Starla, and I whipped up a meal." Neala called back to the buggy driver. "Georgie, I've got some dinner for you to take home and a pumpkin pie as well. Something for your efforts today."

He scurried after them. "Thank you, Miss Neala. A thoughtful treat for me and my missus."

Jancie admired how Neala conducted herself with kindness. She leaned into Rowe. "She's so nice to everyone."

"A sharp contrast to how Adara leads by power and fear," he replied and eased into a three-legged primitive chair at the kitchen table.

"You look tuckered out, Rowe." Starla set a basket of biscuits on the table. "Are you all right?"

He took a sip of ice water. "Terrible headache."

Neala and Jancie, with Vika hovering at their elbows, worked to prepare herbs for a medicinal tea.

Rachelle placed dinner plates on the table filled with fried chicken, mashed potatoes, and gravy, which seemed to get the others to come to the table.

"Smells and looks right good." Vika sampled a forkful. "Mmm. Your chicken melts in my mouth. My compliments to the cooks."

"That would mostly be Starla." Rachelle added the last table items and sat down. "We just assisted."

"Mighty fine work on the gravy, Rachelle." Neala winked at her. "Rowe, try this." She set a cup of amber liquid beside him. "It's a tea that helps relieve headaches and strengthen mental clarity."

"Thank you." He took a sip and wrinkled his nose. "As bad as that tastes, it has to work." He ate a few bites of food and laid his fork down. "I'm going to lie down for a while. Save my dinner, please." He stood and moved to the sitting room where Jancie arranged pillows to make him comfortable on the couch.

She leaned over a side table. "I set your tea here. Try to get that down." Back at the dining table, Jancie stared at her plate. "I know once I'm able to make my wish, this will be over. But what if I can't easily find my element to grant that wish? I feel like I should go out tonight to look for it. Can anyone guide me to blue natural elements here to speed things up?"

Neala shook her head. "I'm sorry, Jancie. I understand both your pain and Rowe's. No one can help you find your element. That's part of why it works. This is about you connecting to your powers. You must seek that element. When you find it, you will also discover your powers."

Jancie poked at her food, slowly managing to eat her chicken thigh. She gulped water, her frustration burning hot in her face. A lively conversation went on around her, but she was in her own world. She feared going out on her own, but her love for Rowe was stronger than her fears. With resolve, she looked up with a new idea. "Neala, is there a map of the valley that might help me get prepared to search come dawn? May I use a map in this ritual?"

"I don't see why not. I have a simple copy of a hand drawn one I'll get for you after dinner."

Rachelle tilted her head and looked at Jancie. "Since I'm not a witch, would it be okay for me to go with her on her search? Just for moral support?"

Neala twisted her mouth to one side. "That's a request I've not run into before. Let me think on it and maybe get in touch with Eartha."

Jancie sat straighter and grinned at her friend. It would be great if Rachelle could go with her, just to keep her calm. A little more hopeful with that idea and the use of a map, Jancie ate the rest of her meal, then joined Rowe while the others had dessert.

His tea cup was empty, and he slept fitfully. By the tightness around his eyes, she knew he still suffered.

She covered him with a crocheted afghan. Rubbing her hands along her upper arms, she stepped to the fireplace constructed of the familiar limestone but far less impressive than Eartha's. She noticed wood already laid and called over her shoulder into the kitchen, "Neala, may I light a fire?"

"Yes, please do. The evenings are chilly now." The chieftainess poked her head around the corner. "Be sure to open the flue. Matches are on the mantel."

Jancie bent low and yanked the metal lever to open the chimney.

As soon as she did, a whoosh sounded with air rushing down and into the room.

Jancie stepped back, staring at a loosely formed vaporous ball of blue light hanging in the air in front of her. "Neala, come quick! Something came down the chimney."

The light moved around Jancie while she stood stone still, arms clutched across her chest.

Everyone rushed into the sitting room. "Hazel! I'm glad you're here," the chieftainess cried out. "Your son is in a bad way." She motioned to Rowe. "Can you do anything to help him?"

Rowe's eyes opened, and he sat up, disoriented and rubbing his head as he looked at the light. "Mother?"

Jancie found her voice. "It's an old Tabard curse, punishing any griever's moonstone bearer from Coon Hollow for loving a New Wish witch. It makes the bearer go mad. He's in extreme pain. Please help."

The blue light zipped to Rowe and moved along him from head to toe, clinging to his body until it encased his entire form.

Shaking, Jancie grabbed Vika's arm. "What's happening?"

The blue light dissipated, not into the air, but inside Rowe, through his nose, mouth, eyes, and exposed skin.

He lay back, motionless, but the muscles of his face relaxed.

"She's doing what any mother would, trying to save her son." Vika patted Jancie's hand and whispered. "As his mother, she can enter his body. I'm no seer, but I'm thinkin' her spirit might be able to heal injuries like Rowe did for me. That was one of her talents when she lived."

"Fascinating magic." Neala joined them as they stared at the sight. "Nothing we do here."

A thin film of pale blue covered his body, while Rowe exhaled puffs of light that were reabsorbed by his skin.

Jancie took a step toward him. "Vika, can I touch him? I need to know he's okay." Her whole body trembled.

"Hold up." Vika moved behind her. "I want to be with you in case Hazel rejects you. She don't know your touch. Better yet, let's do it together. She knows me well." The old woman placed her hand over Jancie's and guided it to Rowe's resting on his chest.

Jancie gasped and read every small sensation. Hazel's spirit surrounded their joined hands, coursing along Jancie's skin. Every hair and fold was touched. After at least a minute, Jancie was able to sense Rowe's body, calm and at ease. No pain tormented him, but his emotions were still and unchanging, as if suspended. His chest rose and sank slower than in sleep. "It's like she slowed down his body functions."

"Yes, that's right. Hazel spoke directly to me. It was all she knew to do to keep the damage at bay." Vika wrapped her free arm around Jancie. "She's bought you the time you needed."

Happy tears ran down Jancie's face as they moved away from Rowe's sleeping form.

Chapter Twenty-six:
The Wish

JANCIE AWOKE THE NEXT MORNING before her phone alarm sounded and rolled out of the trundle bed onto the rug careful not to wake Starla in the connected bed. She and Rachelle, being younger, chose to sleep in the drawer beds pulled out from where Vika and Starla slept in the two twins. The floorboards of the old cabin creaked as Jancie padded through the hallway, with clothes and toiletries in hand she'd laid out the night before.

She brushed her teeth, washed her face in the vintage pedestal sink, and fixed her hair in a quick ponytail. In the mirror, her hazel eyes were dull, with dark circles around them.

Like she'd told Rachelle, shouldering both the new responsibilities of being an adult and a witch was daunting. The weight was hers alone to bear. Before bed, Neala had determined Rachelle couldn't accompany Jancie on the quest to find her element. Although not surprised, she was disappointed and slept fitfully in anticipation.

With a sigh, she changed from her nightgown into jeans and a long-sleeved t-shirt.

Downstairs, Jancie tiptoed to where Rowe slept on the couch. The soft blue light his mother still surrounded him with her loving protection. Jancie bent close, careful not to touch him and disturb Hazel's magic. "Rowe, if you can hear me, know that I love you. I'll find a way to break the moonstone's curse." She glanced at the blue vapors swirling between his fingers. "And Hazel, I don't know if you can hear, but thank you so much for keeping him safe."

A creak sounded on the stairwell landing as Neala descended, wrapped in a red terry robe. "I thought I heard someone up." She grinned at Jancie. "Do you need anything?"

"Thanks, but I prepared my lunch last night." Jancie moved through the kitchen toward the back door.

"You have my phone number in case of an emergency, right?" Neala asked.

Jancie nodded and wedged the lunch, her wallet, and local map to the backpack she'd left on a half log bench inside the back door. She peered out into the darkness. No hint of light was visible but songs of twittering birds meant dawn would come soon. Thankful Cerise had told them to bring hiking boots, Jancie tugged hers on and zipped into a cozy fleece hoodie that matched the light amber color of her hair.

She set off into the dark morning toward the lights of the main street. She hoped by the time she left the electric lights, the sun would help her see, but that was not the case, even past seven o'clock. She made good use of the flashlight since the steep hills with the dense tree cover delayed sunrise.

She followed the main road out of town, its smooth macadam riddled with cracks from last winter's freezes and top-dressed with loose gravel. Broken stone crunched under her boot's thick soles. The still morning air held smells of wood fires close to the ground. Jancie passed a cluster of cabins, partially draped in flood lighting from nearby sheds. Her nose twitched with the distinct fragrances of the various fires. A tangy, sweet smell of pine hissed and sparked out of one chimney top. Mellow, rich odor of oak logs smoldered from another. The pleasant baked ham smell of a hickory fire made her mouth water. And the sweet syrupy smell of sugar maple logs made her empty stomach rumble. She smiled, remembering how her mother had taught her to how to smell the differences.

Warm, yellow lights shined in a few cabin windows. Residents of New Wish were up and starting their days.

Animals also stirred. Songbirds darted from limb to limb, their colors hidden in shadows. A raucous medley of cawing gave away the identities of blue jays among a stand of pines.

When daylight peeked over the hillside, Jancie turned off the main road, following her instinct as she searched for her blue element. She examined the softening midnight sky, wondering whether that was the blue she sought. Nothing caught her attention, so she followed a twisting lane, expecting to see a blue river or at least a creek. She consulted her map, and it confirmed her guess. But brush grew so dense that she couldn't find a way to cut through. At the loud bray of a horse, she walked on.

In a clearing, stood a red barn where a huge chestnut horse whinnied at its open stall door. A man in overalls and a red flannel shirt scurried from around a corner. Harness in hand, he led the anxious animal to the front of an old-fashioned plow.

Jancie surveyed the small truck farm with rows of market produce. An undulating row of trees marked the field's far border. Certain the line bordered moving water, she followed the dirt driveway to barn.

The farmer tipped his cap, and his bushy gray brows wiggled. "Hello. Name's Samuel. What can I do for you this morning?"

"I'm Jancie." She pointed behind the barn, unsure how to explain her purpose for being on his property. "I'm looking to find my witch element. May I cross your property to reach that stream?"

His head bobbed up and down. "Be welcome here, Jancie. You're right on track." He secured the horse and motioned for Jancie to follow him toward the back of the clearing. He pointed to a weeping willow whose limbs swayed in the breeze like a Hawaiian dancer's grass skirt. "To the left of that trunk is a path to Nutter's Creek." With a smile, he lifted his cap again. "May you reach your destiny."

She thanked him and continued as he'd directed. Pushing the curtain of willow limbs aside, the rushing stream came into view. The current twisted over and around rocky outcroppings. The swift water, more white than blue, didn't trigger Jancie's intuition.

She consulted her map, looking for wider streams that might have deep, blue pools. *If I follow Nutter's Creek south, it flows into a larger stream.* A narrow but passable trail followed along the bank where she stood. *Seems like a plan.*

Weaving in and out with the meandering creek, Jancie picked her way across roots and washed out sections. She made slow progress through tangled forest broken by an occasional cabin in a small clearing or wider open areas of truck farms like Samuel's.

Before she reached the intersecting stream, hunger got the best of her. She took a seat on a wide sycamore root that had thrust itself into the water. The exposed root was covered by a tough, papery bark that mimicked mottled, peeling layers of the three-foot wide trunk. Her phone searched for service without any luck, but thankfully she'd worn a watch. *Noon! How can it be that late?* She finished half of the sandwich, saving the rest for later, and washed it down with a quick swallow of tea.

Keeping her eyes on the ground, Jancie stepped up her pace. She paused to look around and had the junction in sight. She sprinted for it. Where Nutter's Stream widened to join the other, she tripped on an exposed root. She caught herself from falling into the water by a tenuous handhold on a thin branch. Less than a pencil's diameter, it threatened to break. Although the creek wasn't deep, the water was cold. Unable to grab anything else or jump across to the opposite bank, she inched her fingers up the thin branch while working one foot back up the bank.

The limb bent lower under the stress.

What witchcraft might help me? Surely something. Jancie reached her free hand across her body toward the jeans pocket containing the peppermint leaves. Her twisting motion strained the branch. It creaked with the sound of plant fibers tearing. One foot slipped off of the muddy bank. Before she could touch the mint, an unseen force yanked on her extended wrist and pulled her onto the bank.

Jancie turned to see a woman who looked to be in her late thirties beat her hands on her thighs, guffawing.

Jancie moved closer, her hands shaking, breath shallow. "Thank you for saving me from falling in."

The woman eyed her but didn't speak. A streak of white cut through her coal black hair that straggled uneven below her shoulders. She dressed in homespun olive green fabric, not so much a dress as a frayed shroud cinched at her waist with a leather thong. Her black eyes flashed sparks of blue.

Jancie's pulse quickened, and she took a few steps nearer, eager to study the woman's eyes. "Thank you for your help," Jancie repeated in case the woman hadn't heard before.

The woman backed away, her eyes wild with piercing blue glints. She held up her palms. "Stay there, South Wind. I know you. My visions tell me." The woman side-stepped, as if preparing to run away.

"It's okay. I mean no harm. I'm Jancie. Thank you for helping me at the stream. What's your name?" Jancie needed to see the blue of those eyes. She searched for questions to keep the frightened woman from running away.

"My given name's Fia, but call me Death Teller because that's what I do." Her gaze darted in all directions. "No one wants what I can see. Too late to stop the reaper's hand from reaching their loved ones but enough to torture their own souls for eternity. Like mine is." She hugged herself, while looking up in all directions and dodging things Jancie couldn't see. "Hundreds of deaths, people screaming behind my eyes. Until my eyes bleed. Blue with the blood of their dying veins." Her eyes focused on Jancie. "Go back. Do not invite me to see death around you."

Realization shot through Jancie like electricity. *This is Fia Tabard—Adara's mad sister. Deserted and cast away Can this be? What force has brought me to her?* Jancie stared at the desperate, lonely creature before her, and her heart ached at the thought of the woman's fate. "I still want to thank you. You did something nice for me. You didn't hurt me." She stepped closer, determined to view those flashing blue streaks in the woman's eyes.

When Jancie reached Fia, the woman crouched and curled into a ball, head tucked against her knees. "Don't come any closer."

Jancie extended a hand and smoothed Fia's tangled hair. She was drawn to this woman.

Long shadows of trees fell over them, and the air grew cooler. Jancie panicked. *How can it be evening already?* She flinched. Dread, suspicion, and fear shot through her. Was this a trap of Adara's, using her sister? Jancie sensed the strength of Fia's powers. *She could kill me if she wanted.* Heat poured into her face, and sweat trickled from her hairline.

She let out a slow breath, trusting her instincts.

Fia slowly raised her head, still clutching her knees with white-knuckled hands.

Jancie's gaze lingered in the witch's blue eyes. She placed a hand over Fia's, feeling the roughness of her skin.

A single blue tear rolled down the woman's cheek, and she let go of her knee. Her fingers trembled as they embraced Jancie's. "You know death already." Fia's raspy voice choked out the words, and she stared, unblinking, into Jancie's eyes. "Your mother. You do not fear death. Your heart's brave and true. But are you brave enough to be the Death Teller's friend, I hope?" Her body shook with her hoarse speech. She cast her gaze down. "I have no friends. Not one. Ever. No family now. All have left me. Jancie, will you be my friend to share tonight's full moon?"

Jancie clasped Fia's hand into both of her own. "I will be your friend during this moon and many more."

Fia's body relaxed. She grinned and laughed in fits and starts.

Jancie's spirit soared witnessing Fia's transformation.

"Look there!" Fia sprang to her feet. "The moon, she rises above my trees and finds us."

Without thinking, Jancie embraced the ragged, lonely witch.

First with one hand, then the other, Fia returned the hug while the pair watched the full moon rise higher.

"A super moon, bigger and stronger than others. Big enough to bring me a friend." Fia hugged tighter and bounced on her toes, her smiling face lifted to the sky. She glanced at Jancie. "And for you, you know your destiny as a witch is to break a curse that plagues your people, yet the road to get there eludes you. May our friendship under this moon help you as well."

In the tiny clearing, the moon's brilliant glow shone like a spotlight on them.

"This is the time of fullness, the flood tide of power, when the Lady in full circle of brightness, she rides across the sky above us." Fia's eyes were bright and smiling. "This is the time of the bearing of fruits, of change realized. The Great Mother is pouring out her love and her gifts upon us in abundance."

Then Jancie knew. It was time for her to make her one wish. She remembered the wording she wanted to use. *I wish to break the Tabard curse on the enchanted griever's moonstone I wear, setting Rowe McCoy free of its debilitating ailment.*

Jancie looked up at the moon and surrendered her fear. Fia had cast aside decades of deep fear and pain and opened to her. The blue of Fia's eyes had taught the element's lesson Jancie needed to follow. Her powers as a witch were now unlocked and surged through her body. She wrapped her arms tighter around Fia and embraced her with the pure love of true friends.

Jancie lifted her face to the moon, and her voice rang out with her wish. When the reverberation quieted in her throat, animals of the forest and farms carried the sounds of her wish in all directions. The valley came to life around them.

Chapter Twenty-seven:
The Storm

JANCIE RAN ALONG THE DARK dirt roads, panting. Fia had begged Jancie to stay for dinner, but she needed to see Rowe more than anything else.

Before she'd left the hermit witch, they exchanged locks of their hair. Holding the jet black and ginger strands together in clasped hands, they vowed to keep their friendship alive. If not together for future full moons, they promised to hold the other's hair and remember their special meeting.

The locks were stored in tiny wooden boxes which Fia had whittled. Neighbor women sold her handicrafts in fairs to help provide a meager income.

Jancie promised to visit her new friend during the coming days. Words tumbling from her mouth, she explained her love for Rowe, how the curse affected him, and how she hoped her wish ended his suffering.

With a teary hug, Fia gave Jancie directions and sent her on her way.

Thankful for her experience as a runner but not so happy with the weight of hiking boots, Jancie tried to pace herself. Since she'd traveled a long way along a winding stream, her ability to gauge distance was unreliable. Darkness didn't help. Three times she thought she approached Samuel's farm, and three times she was wrong.

Songbirds and squirrels followed her from tree to tree along the roadsides. Their twittering and chattering brought more followers: hoot owls, raccoons, and even a few skunks. Although cautious about the skunks, the company cheered Jancie forward.

About half a mile later, the heavy boots strained her legs and forced her to slow to a jog. Hot tears trickled down her cheeks. She must save Rowe.

Around the next bend, Samuel's hefty horse brayed to her from his stall door.

She waved at the horse and found a burst of energy. Now retracing her previous route, she knew only about two miles remained. Reduced again to a jog on the main road, she considered calling Neala but pushed the thought away. This was her quest to complete alone.

The town lights came into view. Jancie pushed into a run, and a stabbing knot of pain shot through one thigh. She crumbled, moaning between gasps for air while massaging the cramped quadriceps muscle. *Not now. Damn, I can't even walk.* The moonstone locket swung into her face. Thinking it could be part of her problem, Jancie reached up and tried to yank it off. The chain wouldn't budge from her neck, and she realized the gem enchanted with Eartha's spell wouldn't release until Jancie fulfilled her destiny of breaking the Tabard curse.

Nearby critters sounded alarming cries. Sharp hoots, raucous tweets, and a chorus of howls filled the air.

Jancie shook her head and bit her lip. When her hands brushed the front of her jeans as she tried to stand, the fragrance of peppermint filled the air. She dug her hand into the pocket and clutched a limp leaf to her damp cheek. *Get me to him. Please.*

Moments later, the invigorating sensation of mint coursed through her injured leg. The exhausted muscles cooled and relaxed. Jancie took a tentative step, then another. The pain was manageable. Not chancing her luck, she kept to a walk and reached town. Heartened, she picked up the pace and race-walked the last three blocks to Neala's.

The wide log cabin porch was crowded with happy people calling to her, but she only saw one face.

Rowe ran down the steps toward her, arms wide.

Jancie tried to run, and pain surged through the quad again. With a groan, she stumbled.

"I've got you." Rowe's arms enfolded her. "It's my turn to heal you now." He swept her into his arms, carried her onto porch, and set her on a rope hammock chair.

Her friends and family crowded around, along with new faces who may have been extended family for all she knew.

Rowe's warm hands, dripping with blue light, followed bands of her thigh muscles. Healing heat penetrated the fibers, repairing tears and bringing oxygen to relieve cramps.

After he made several passes, she flexed and extended her leg. "Ah, better. Only stiff. No pain." She stood and sank into his arms.

Neala patted Jancie's shoulder. "You did well, Jancie. I'm so proud of you. And Faye would be, too."

Jancie spun in Rowe's arms and smiled at the chieftainess. "She knows. She and her peppermint faery helped me get back with this injury."

Neala beamed. "Now that you've connected to your powers, you and I will have lots to do in these two weeks before Mabon. You need to learn how to harness your source, the south wind."

"Will that be hard?" Jancie asked.

"No. Easy compared to learning to trust your life on your instincts—what you did today, as I just read through touching your shoulder."

"Welcome back, Jancie." Vika smiled and hugged the couple. "Like I've been saying, you're a darned good witch. What did your blue element turn out to be?"

The New Wish witches present hushed.

"Oh!" Vika scanned their wide-eyed faces. "Did I say something wrong? So sorry if I did." Her voice faded.

Neala patted Vika's arm. "Just a different custom. You didn't step on any toes. It's up to Jancie whether she wants to share or not. Many witches here don't, since connecting to their powers is personal."

Vika nodded and withdrew.

"Actually, I'd like to share." Jancie addressed the group of about twenty on the porch. "I think there's something for everyone to learn. It was the blue streaks in Fia Tabard's black eyes that taught me to trust my powers completely."

"Fia Tabard?" Vika clamped a hand over her mouth.

Rowe leaned around Jancie's shoulder. "Did her threats to kill you force you to depend on your powers?"

"No. In fact, it was her request for me to be her friend that made me trust my instincts rather than being afraid of her. She believed the full moon brought me to her. And I think she's right." Jancie pulled the handmade wooden box from her zipped jacket pocket and revealed Fia's hair. "We exchanged locks of hair in her little boxes, promising at each full moon to remember tonight."

Vika shook her head. "I'd have never thought it."

Rowe rubbed his chin stubble. "Me neither, but then after her brother and older sister were killed, Fia left her family."

"The accident with my dad and Adara?" Jancie asked.

Vika nodded. "Grizela said Fia went mad from being able to predict her siblings' deaths but not soon enough to save them."

Jancie blinked at the disbelieving faces staring at her. "I know Fia's sort of a wilding, but she claimed her family had left her."

Vika stroked a gnarled finger along one temple. "Now that I'm thinkin', I wonder if Fia wasn't cast out for not being able to give adequate warning."

"Now that sounds like Grizela." Rowe rubbed Jancie's shoulders. "Trusting Fia must've challenged your sense of right and wrong—the truth of a witch and source of his or her powers."

Vika clucked her tongue and shrugged. "Still, it's hard for me to believe any good came from a Tabard."

Neala tilted her head. "From the start, Fia always chose to keep to herself on the edge of our coven. No doubt her powers are strong. Just going past her house, I can feel them." She lifted a brow. "Maybe it took an offer of genuine friendship to break the dark magic of the Tabard curse."

"That could well be." Rowe hugged Jancie tighter. "At any rate, I'm so happy you found your element and broke the curse."

***

The next morning, Jancie began Neala's practice lessons to be able to use the south wind's energy. After days of routine drills, Jancie's control advanced. She made trees bend to her requests and streams flow more slowly or swiftly. She visited Fia and came back with new skills for using the south wind to draw down the moon's waxing and waning powers. Neala helped Jancie harness clouds until they surrendered themselves as her servants. She summoned their rain showers and torrents, their breezes and gales, but their lightning interested Jancie the most.

With a ball of golden lightning in her hand, she studied its properties. The crackling electricity sent her hair streaming back, and her skin prickled. The rush of energy into her brain was exhilarating.

"You should see yourself!" Rowe exclaimed as he approached her in Neala's backyard. "Your hair looks like spun gold, and your face is glowing."

"She looks like a goddess, doesn't she?" Neala smiled from where she watched on a rough split log bench.

Rowe chuckled and shook his head. "Amazing. I'm a lucky guy."

Jancie's giggles broke her concentration. She lowered the orb to the ground, detonating it as Neala had taught her. "If you hadn't made me laugh, I was going to try to throw it." She nestled under his arm against the trunk of a yellow-leaved sugar maple. The soft flannel of a new casual shirt he'd purchased to fit in with the locals brushed against her cheek.

Neala stood and stretched. "It'll come soon. You still have two more days to practice before Mabon. And practice you must. Adara will be an expert at hurling power fueled by her north wind. She will challenge your command of the clouds."

"That doesn't seem like nearly enough time," Jancie said as she and Rowe followed the chieftainess into her house.

"If you stress over time, your practice will be to waste." Neala washed her hands in the kitchen sink. "Why don't you take time off after lunch? Be mindless and mindful."

Jancie struggled with the sage advice of her mentor. Since the onset of her mother's cancer, Jancie had forgotten how to enjoy doing nothing. She and Rowe took a small buggy out by themselves to explore New Wish. They pulled up at an art fair among a cluster of cabins and strolled through the wares. Jancie couldn't help but imagine the future when she and Rowe would gather fall apples from his family's place and take turns stirring a pot of simmering apple butter. Or when she'd make crazy quilts for each of their children like her mother had made for her. Or the herbal sachets she'd make for all of her new friends. Her mind raced with so many things to fit into her future. And then zipped back to all the lessons she'd learned in the past few days. Her head ached with all the details and plans.

Rowe squeezed her hand and kissed the side of her head. "Relax. Be mindless and mindful."

***

On Sunday morning, the day marking the autumn equinox and the pagan holiday of Mabon, Jancie packed her bag and carried it down the creaky stairs. The smell of pancakes and the happy faces of Starla, Vika, and Neala cooking greeted her. "Mmm. I'm hungry." Jancie dropped her bag by the front door and nosed into the small kitchen.

Aunt Starla shot her a grin. "It's a good sign you have an appetite. Shows you're not full of nerves," I sure would be." She handed Jancie a plate with a tall stack from the hot skillet. "Will four flapjacks do you?"

"Mmm. Yes." Jancie took a seat at the table, smothered them with maple syrup made locally, and dug in.

Cerise poked her head around the edge of the front door. "Hello. I see I'm in time for breakfast."

"Look at you. So comfortable and relaxed," Vika said, smiling.

Cerise spun around to model her casual look of jeans and a hand-knit sweater, her hair pulled back in a stubby ponytail. "My boys won't recognize me." She grinned at Vika. "It's been fun to take a break from the polished Thirties look we wear in the Hollow."

"Don't bother me none." Vika chuckled and stepped beside the younger witch, displaying her own handmade Fair Isle cardigan over a full skirt. "I wear what's comfortable, but I'm old and no one gives a care."

A whooshing sounded in the fireplace. Neala and Jancie found Rowe opening the chimney flue.

Hazel's blue light filled the center of the sitting room, whipping around a thin object.

Rowe touched the light. "Mother, we're going home today. Will I see you there?"

The light encircled him for a moment and moved on to Jancie. Hazel deposited the object she carried into Jancie's hand and retreated. It was a tapered length of wood, about twelve inches long and satiny smooth against Jancie's fingers.

Jancie's powers crept out along the polished wood. She glanced up with a smile.

Neala clasped her hands together. "A wand of hazel wood, the best kind to channel south wind fire. Thank you, Hazel dear."

"Thank you so much!" Jancie said, not sure whether the spirit could hear her. To be certain, she extended the wand tip into the blue vapor, balancing it in her open palm to not transmit too much energy.

Hazel surrounded Jancie and with a faint voice said, "No, I am thanking you for saving my son."

Cerise put a shopping bag on a chair beside Jancie. "This seems to be an appropriate time for gifts." She pulled out a large item wrapped in tissue paper. "While you've been busy with Neala's lessons, the four of us Bentbone gals made you a special mask for tonight's Mabon ceremony. We used colors of the south wind. Most coven members will wear masks, except for hedge witches who may choose to attend just as spectators. The masks are to honor the Harvest Man and Harvest Queen at the equinox." She pulled off the wrapping and handed it to Jancie.

Jancie gaped. "This is amazing. Thank you all." Three-point deer antlers extended from the mask's upper edge. Red, orange, and gold leaves radiated from the two eyeholes, continuing onto the cheeks, forehead, and ears. Thick leather formed the foundation of the mask and soft felt lined the inside. "Can I try it on now?"

"Yes. Let me help you." Cerise moved behind Jancie and helped tie two leather throngs at the back of her head.

Looking through the mask, Jancie sensed her own power spark. The mask also reminded her that the standoff against Adara would become a reality tonight. No longer in the distant future, a pang of self-doubt crept over her.

Neala drew a hand to her mouth. "Jancie, you are so beautiful in that mask. I wish we used masks here. They are lovely. And a good thing to keep your identity a secret tonight."

"I guessed right!" Rachelle called as she ran down the stairs. "The outer leaves match your hair."

Jancie laughed. "Well, if my new magic skills don't work for me, I can just stand there and overwhelm Adara with my mask."

"That'd be enough to stop me cold." Rowe gave her a wink and moved toward the kitchen. "I hate to spoil this fashion show, but we need to leave within the hour."

Jancie stored the mask and hugged each of the four women, saving a special hug for Neala.

The chieftainess rubbed Jancie's back. "Be careful tonight. Mabon's a time when the veil between seen and unseen is thinnest. Rely on your intuition."

"I will," Jancie replied. "I don't know how to thank you."

"You don't need to. Your mother was a dear friend." Neala blinked back tears. "It was my gift to both her and you. Just be sure you come back and visit."

"Yes, I sure will." Jancie finished her breakfast and found her way outside, giving her wand a few tests. While staring at it and clenching her teeth, she forced her power into the tip and sent an arc of light to the ground. Successful but not smooth and sure as she'd like. With a sigh, she took a final look around Neala's yard, inhaling the smells of the plants, the same Mom had kept in her garden.

***

The last sliver of a crescent moon had long since set on Coon Hollow. Her mask tied securely and wand in hand, Jancie sat still and stiff in Rowe's passenger seat as he drove. Since her own clothing would stand out, she wore one of Cerise's long gowns. The gold satin bias cut dress clung to her like a second skin. A matching length of the fabric used as a wrap did little to keep her warm in the sleeveless and backless dress. At least the draped neckline partly covered the moonstone. She borrowed a pair of flat gold sandals from Rachelle. Although not in line with Thirties styles, they were better to run in than Jancie's pumps she wore to work.

Rowe dressed in a fine black pinstriped suit with a double-breasted jacket, a boutonniere of gold leaves tucked in one lapel. Gold cuff links decorated his white starched shirt. A black fedora sat above his sleek, low ponytail. His half mask of the same leaves sat on the seat beside him. He looked handsome enough she'd normally be distracted with thoughts of how to get closer to him. Tonight, those emotions were buried.

She checked her watch. Nine-thirty, an hour until the autumn equinox. She remembered Neala's words: *When the veil between the seen and unseen is the thinnest. Jancie loosened her grip on her wand to cool her sweaty palm.*

Cerise sat in the backseat, prepared to serve as Jancie's escort into the ceremony. She wore a tea-length dress of olive green and a mask in shades of greens and watery blues.

Rowe parked in the lot of the Coon Hollow school building. The old limestone structure, no larger than Jancie's neighborhood elementary, had a small gymnasium on one end. The windows stared at Jancie as if they knew her secret identity. Rowe faced her. "If we enter together, someone might determine who you are. You two go in first, and I'll follow later. Jancie, look for Adara to wear black and dark blue, the north wind's colors." At least thirty cars were already parked, including Adara's Packard. A dozen more turned in as Jancie and Cerise made their way through wide double doors into the gym, while Rowe remained in his car.

Jancie checked the dark sky, made even darker with gray clouds that blocked out the stars as far as she could see. She harnessed several of the largest and heaviest. The tip of her wand gave a faint glow as those clouds crashed into others, and she tucked the hazel branch into the folds of her wrap. Gusts whipped against her back, pushing her toward the building.

A covered dish of roast potatoes in her hands, Cerise leaned in. "Follow my lead during the opening, but when things loosen up, you may find your moment. The meal follows the ceremony."

Jancie nodded and filed inside, at once scanning the crowd for Adara. No woman with her figure and poise appeared in the colors Rowe indicated. Most people wore masks with varying degrees of decoration. She spotted Vika in a group of matrons, her simple green leafy mask unable to hide her wiry bush of white hair. Jancie thought she recognized Logan. But one look into the man's eyes made her frightened that she'd gotten too close to someone who might recognize her as an imposter. Her heart thumped in her chest as she kept an eye on the stranger for suspicious behavior. The gathering reminded Jancie of movies where masquerade balls hid the identity of an intruder intending to do harm. Tonight, she was the intruder.

Smells of myrrh and sage mingled with savory aromas of harvest recipes in the large, open room. Cerise placed her dish on a buffet alongside baskets of home baked bread, bowls of steaming carrots and potatoes, and tempting apple and pomegranate deserts. Long dinner tables were laid with table settings for a meal.

Cerise guided them from the tables to an open area in front of an altar where a large circle covered much of the floor. They stood on the circle at one sidewall beside the few already present. An ornate chair sat empty next to the altar table. The massive wooden buffet held a large dish covered with a cloth. An array of nature's autumn abundance decorated either side including pine cones, asters, chrysanthemums, gourds, and small pumpkins.

Masked members continued to take their places, forming a circle. Rowe stood across from Jancie and Cerise along the opposite wall.

Thunder rumbled outside the doors. Cold air crawled across Jancie's cheek nearest the entrance, and the crowd grew quiet. She faced that direction, her suspicions sending waves of tension through her body.

The high priestess wore a clinging long sleeved gown of black satin, the plunging neckline trimmed in midnight blue.

She trailed a train of blue from the dress's dramatic flared hem, and a matching cape fluttered in layers down her back. From dark, curved horns atop her head, an intricate tangle of black vines and blue feathers covered her face and draped down her shoulders.

Adara glided, head high and a crimson smile plastered on her lips, to the decorative chair. Once seated, she nodded to a young woman. "Lenore, please come forward. I present our maiden of Mabon."

The pale, slim woman wore no mask. Her simple, white gown whipped around her thin limbs as she took the wide, covered bowl from the altar and placed it in the center of the circle. After receiving a nod from the leader, Lenore returned to her place.

Adara rose and, with a flourish of her cape, moved before the altar's center. "We are joined this evening to celebrate the aging goddess as she passes from mother to crone, and her consort as he prepares for death and re-birth. Now is the time of balance, when day and night face each other as equals. Night is waxing and day is waning, for nothing ever remains without change, in the tides of earth and sky."

The words she just said! Jancie fidgeted with the end of her wand inside her wrap. *Does she know my intentions? Can she feel my power?*

Adara continued in a loud, clear voice, a wry grin lifting the corners of her lips, but her eyes never fell on Jancie. "Know and remember, that which rises must also set, and that which sets must also rise. To honor this change, let us dance the Dance of Going and Returning."

The members joined hands, and as discreetly as possible Jancie shifted her wand to the hand joined with Cerise's. The group moved counterclockwise but kept the ring open with Adara forming the leading end.

She led the line inwards from the marked circle in a spiral, tightening them around the covered dish. "Please sit."

Once all were settled, she walked to the dish and removed the cloth revealing a single ear of corn. "Be in awe of the mystery: through silence the seed of wisdom is gained."

All heads turned toward the corn, despite thunder rolling in all directions around the building and lightning flashing in the front window.

After nearly a minute, Adara raised her arms to the sky. Thunder crashed. A chill entered the room, and people huddled together. "Our hidden God now departs to the Land of Youth, through the Gates of Death to stand enthroned as horned leader of the hosts of air. Yet, as he seems unseen to our circle, he actually lies within the secret seed, the seed of newly reaped grain, the seed of flesh, hidden in earth. In him is life, and life is the light of man, that which was never born and never dies. The wise ones tell us: weep not, but rejoice."

At Adara's signal, the group rose, and she led them in a slow dance, moving clockwise and spiraling outward toward the perimeter of the circle. She took the hand of the last witch in the chain's other end to close the ring and, and with a guttural whoop, speeded up the pace till the coven was circling fast. The high priestess undulated as though possessed by some demon. Her body slithered and snaked, arms waving in the air, black power dripping from her long nails onto her breasts.

Members hooted and yelled, some making odd animal noises. Thunder boomed outside, and Jancie sensed the yank of her servant clouds growing inpatient on her tethers.

The storm gathered force, and the dancers moved faster as though fed by its energy. Thunder shook the building. The electric lights flicked out. Lit by the dozens of candle flames, the ring broke apart. Dancers moved in a surreal frenzy. The outside doors flew open.

A bobcat bounded into the room heading straight for the middle of the circle, its teeth bared in a vicious snarl.

Two owls, Maeira and Busby, along with Waapake the coyote, sailed after the fierce cat.

The dancers continued as if entranced, paying no attention to the angry beast or the three familiars.

Jancie suspected Adara held the members in an enchantment, and shot a look at Rowe and at Cerise beside her.

He danced but not with the fervor of the crowd, while Cerise spun like a drunken ballerina.

Startled from her focus, Jancie lost her grip on one of her harnessed storm clouds. She wrestled to gain more secure holds on the others. Her practice in New Wish had never involved fighting another witch to keep possession of her clouds. Adara's north wind fought against her both inside and outside of the building. The veil between seen and unseen was indeed thin.

Adara hurled a black ball covered in a vaporous gray mist at Vika who twirled arm in arm with another old woman at the edge of the circle.

At the same time, the bobcat lunged through the air for Vika's torso, knocking the old witch off her feet. The death ball of the north wind smacked into the cement block, harming no one, but a clap of thunder shook the wall and rattled pictures down.

Vika exclaimed, "My Siddie! You've come back to me."

Jancie wrestled lightning from one thunder cloud into her hand. She swept her wand out from her wrap as her power in the form of golden light channeled into it.

The moment Adara's first fire discharged, the priestess looked for Rowe and took a second aim.

Before she could fire, a torrent of knives from the dining area sped toward her and speared her cape and dress. The blades dragged her backward until they lodged into the back and arms of her altar chair. Rowe's eye gleamed at his successful animation.

Three male forms Jancie recognized as Rowe's council allies stepped forward and surrounded the captive priestess.

Teeth gnashing, she struggled against her restraints. "Rowe, as high priestess, I order you to withdraw your magic!"

When he only stood and watched her with arms folded across his chest, she wrenched a hand free and hurled a small but tight ball at Cerise.

Jancie shot back with a golden bolt from her wand that shattered Adara's magic. The sky lit, and the floor shook with the collision of the two winds. Shards of black glass projected like missiles radiating from the center of the circle.

Members of the crowd ceased their dancing and took places along the circle, watching and gasping. Many cried out and clung to one another, bleeding from cuts to their skin. All stared at Jancie glowing gold from head to toe.

Adara's mouth fell open, and she clenched the arms of her chair, her muscles stiffening. "You! You've already interfered with my life by just being born. How dare you come here and interfere with the coven, and with my magic. You're nothing but a silly little town-girl, who didn't inherit much of her mother's powers." With a groan, Adara lurched forward, tearing her cape from her shoulders, the sleeves of her dress in shreds. She glared at Jancie, a grimace contorting her painted face.

A massive ball of darkness formed in the leader's hand as she paced toward Jancie. "Death of the north wind is always stronger than your south wind's fire."

Twisting to gain compliance from her clouds, Jancie reloaded her wand.

Adara smirked at Jancie struggling to prepare and took aim.

Jancie's wand surged, like a magnificent sparkler, with light that lit the room. She sensed the moonstone warming against her chest. Its blue light shot out of the tip of her wand, mixing with the south wind's fire.

The priestess flung her arm forward, but her magic dropped only a short distance from her feet in a mass of dissipating smoke. "I cannot strike at you." She tilted her head. "You possess something personal from my sister Fia. A gift from her. She will not let me harm you." Adara shook her head, and a sly grin lifted the corners of her mouth. "Faye's daughter as my nemesis. How did I not foresee that?"

Jancie drew nearer, her wand still charged. "I ask you to step down from your position as high priestess." She and Adara locked gazes.

Adara snarled. "Who are you to make that request of me?"

Logan whipped off a mask of tree bark and stepped into the middle of the circle. He thrust a fist into the air and declared in loud voice, "It is Mabon, a time when our covenant allows our leadership to be challenged."

Rowe lunged for the high priestess, a moment too late.

Adara whipped a black ball dripping with red sparks directly at Logan's chest. She fell backward after firing, and the blue light of Rowe's hand left a gash in the wooden floor at her feet.

Logan dove, sliding on his chest, and the evil mass changed its trajectory to follow.

Jancie shot the remaining power in her wand at the red and black venomous ball.

The larger barn owl sailed into the line of fire. She spread her tremendous wings over Logan's body. Golden-white south wind light smacked into the north wind's dark energy. A formidable crash sounded. Black dagger-like shards pelted the room. One thrust into the owl's breast. A trickle of red stained her white feathers, but she remained steadfast.

The priestess waved her arm in a wide circle above her head. The glass projectiles whirled in a tornado about the room.

Jancie forced more energy from the one remaining cloud she controlled into her wand until the hazel wood vibrated in her hand. She gritted her teeth and gripped it with both hands. She lost her focus-hold on the cloud. It broke free.

Adara's blood-red lips drew into a hideous grin, and she set shards in motion, targeting Rowe. "The lovers who dare to break the Tabard curse will meet their fate!"

Feet planted, Jancie dispersed power from her glowing wand in a sweeping arc around the ceiling. Her light surrounded the missiles like a net, the glass pieces glinting with a blinding glare.

Adara cowered, shielding her eyes.

Coven members gathered around Logan and Rowe, helping them to their feet. Logan stood and spread his arms wide, "This equinox brings us a chance for change. Let your voices cry out with your support!"

The room filled with a deafening roar of cheers.

Adara slowly strode to meet him.

Jancie lowered her golden net until it circled above Adara's head. Silence spread from the center of the circle outward.

The leader scanned their faces, lingering on the council members who stood against her, as well as Keir, Logan, and Jancie. Adara's own face transformed from a flawless pale complexion to ashen gray. With a stricken look in her dark eyes, she knelt and laid her mask of plumage and finery onto the floor beside the bowl of corn.

Head down, she uttered in a soft voice, "What rises must also set, and that which sets must also rise." She uncoiled from her hunch and snapped her fingers wide. Honed obsidian arrowheads shot from her black nails.

With a flick of her wand's tip, Jancie redirected the arsenal at Adara. Several sliced long cuts in the leader's exposed flesh.

Adara let out piercing scream and ran through the open double doors into the downpour.

Jancie took direct aim at a thundercloud whirling in the south wind. She discharged the power remaining in her wand. Blue energy from the moonstone spilled into the hazel stick. A jag of lightning slashed the sky just outside the gymnasium. Its blinding light filled the entire room.

When the glare subsided, Adara's body lay crumpled on the sidewalk.

Jancie, Rowe, and Logan ran to the doors.

With the other two poised to strike, Logan checked Adara's body for a pulse. Shaking his head, he stepped back.

Rolls of thunder retreated into the distance.

Rowe returned to where Maeira lay motionless on the floor, the shard of black glass cutting from her breast. Tears rolled down his cheeks.

His own familiar nestled against his mother's wing.

Rowe spread his healing palms over her form. "There is no life to mend. She has passed." He caressed Busby's head and neck.

Jancie knelt and comforted them. She lifted the moonstone locket from her neck. "The Tabard curse is now broken. This can now serve as intended, to mend grieving hearts."

Keir removed his brown leafy mask and touched Maeira's head. "Her spirit, pure and good, has also made a new beginning, standing permanent watch over her departed mistress Edme in our cemetery."

Logan stood near and stretched his arms out to members as he turned in place. "Through silence the seed of wisdom is gained."

Quiet spread over the room. Rumbles from the fading storm receded from the hollow. Cerise and her family drew near, as did Vika and her friends. One by one, coven members drifted to the majestic owl to pay their respects and express appreciation for a chance at new leadership and goals, hopes, and dreams for a better future.

The End

A Note from the Author

If you enjoyed reading **Witch's Moonstone Locket**, please look for more upcoming books in my Coon Hollow Coven Tales series. Also, I'd very much appreciate if you'd help spread the word and post a review on Amazon, Goodreads, LibraryThing, blogs, or wherever you like to talk about books.

I welcome contact from readers. At my website MarshaAMoore.com you can contact me, sign up for my newsletter, read my blog, and find my social media connections.

If you'd like an email when I release a new book, sign up for my newsletter on the Contacts page of my website MarshaAMoore.com.

—Marsha

Other novels and stories by Marsha A. Moore
For details and excerpts please visit MarshaAMoore.com

Enchanted Bookstore Legends:
Genre: Epic Fantasy Romance
Series description:
The **Enchanted Bookstore Legends** are about Lyra McCauley, a woman destined to become one of five strong women in her family who possess unique magical abilities and serve as Scribes in Dragonspeir. The Scribes span a long history, dating from 1,200 to

present day. Each Scribe is expected to journey through Dragonspeir, both the good and evil factions, then draft a written account. Each book contains magic with vast implications.

Lyra was first introduced to Dragonspeir as a young girl, when she met the high sorcerer, Cullen Drake, through a gift of one of those enchanted books. Using its magic, he escorted her into the parallel world of Dragonspeir. Years later, she lost that volume and forgot the world and Cullen. These legends begin where he finds her again—she is thirty-five, standing in his enchanted bookstore, and Dragonspeir needs her.

When Lyra reopens that enchanted book, she confronts a series of quests where she is expected to save the good Alliance from destruction by the evil Black Dragon. While learning about her role, Lyra and Cullen fall in love. He is 220 years old and kept alive by Dragonspeir magic. Cullen will die if Dragonspeir is taken over by the evil faction...Lyra becomes the Scribe.

- Seeking a Scribe: Enchanted Bookstore Legend One
- Heritage Avenged: Enchanted Bookstore Legend Two
- Lost Volumes: Enchanted Bookstore Legend Three
- Staurolite: Enchanted Bookstore Legend Four
- Quintessence: Enchanted Bookstore Legend Five

Shadows of Serenity

Genre: Women's fiction mystery/Magical realism

Joyce Runsey spends her life savings to open a yoga studio in an historic Victorian St Augustine house, only to discover the property is haunted. A female ghost's abusive and very much alive husband still tortures her by using dark witchcraft. The disruptive energy thwarts Joyce's ambition to create a special environment to train students to become yoga teachers.

Joyce engages in a deadly battle with not only the tormented spirit, but also the dangerous husband. To protect her students from harm, she must overcome mounting obstacles. An unknown swami pays an unexpected visit to give advice on how to free the anguished ghost. Can Joyce comprehend and follow the wise man's guidance in time to save everyone who depends on her?

Short Stories:

- Le Cirque De Magie
- Sea Glass and Sand Memories

Made in the USA
Las Vegas, NV
08 September 2024

94949051R00177